BISMARCK CROSS

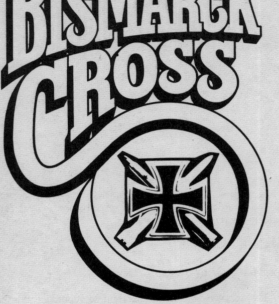

Steven L. Thompson

TOR

A TOM DOHERTY ASSOCIATES BOOK

BISMARCK CROSS

Copyright © 1985 by Steven L. Thompson

First printing: August 1985

A TOR Book

Published by Tom Doherty Associates
8-10 West 36 Street
New York, N.Y. 10018

ISBN: 0-812-50944-7
CAN. ED.: 0-812-50945-5

Printed in the United States of America

TO: COMMANDERS OF AMERICAN, BRITISH, FRENCH, AND SOVIET FORCES NOW OCCUPYING GERMANY

FROM: FRIEDRICH VON GRABOW, BRIGADE-GENERAL, DEUTSCHE LUFTWAFFE

SUBJECT: DEMAND FOR WITHDRAWAL OF ALL AMERICAN, BRITISH, FRENCH, AND SOVIET FORCES FROM GERMAN TERRITORY

1. YOU ARE DIRECTED TO WITHDRAW ALL YOUR FORCES FROM "EAST" AND "WEST" GERMAN TERRITORY.

2. WITHDRAWAL WILL BEGIN AT 0830 TOMORROW. YOU WILL HAVE NOT MORE THAN 24 HOURS TO COMPLETE WITHDRAWAL.

3. ALL MILITARY EQUIPMENT NOT HAND-TRANSPORTABLE WILL BE LEFT IN SITU.

4. UNTIL WITHDRAWAL OF ALL OCCUPYING FORCES IS COMPLETE, NUCLEAR MISSILES APPROPRIATED FROM U.S. AND SOVIET FORCES WILL REMAIN AT READY-LAUNCH STATUS, TARGETED ON NATO AND WARSAW PACT CITIES.

5. AT THE CONCLUSION OF TOTAL FORCE WITHDRAWAL, THE MISSILES WILL DOWNGRADE TO READY STATUS.

BISMARCK CROSS

For Abby and Andrew; the Future

AUTHOR'S NOTE

Like its predecessors in the Max Moss series, BIS-MARCK CROSS is a work of fiction, in which the characters and events come entirely from the author's imagination. However, like its predecessors, this book builds on today's facts. For instance, although "Bismarck" is a purely fictional airborne warning and control systems aircraft built to a similarly fictional requirement by the Deutsche Luftwaffe, the "E3G" as depicted here is merely an extrapolation of the currently produced Boeing "Sentry," known as the E3C. In the same way, both the fictional "A" model Pershing II missiles and the "X" model of the Soviet SS23 rockets are projected follow-on versions of equipment now in the field.

BERLIN
Army Appropriation Hearings
The Reichstag
23 September 1862

It is not by speechifying and majorities that the great questions of the time will be decided ... but by Blood and Iron.

> —Prince Otto Eduard Leopold von
> Bismarck-Schoenhausen

POTSDAM
The Tripartite Conference of Berlin
Cecilienhof Palace
18 July 1945

I want to raise only one question. I note that the word "Germany" is being used here. What is now the meaning of "Germany"?

> —Winston S. Churchill,
> Prime Minister of Great Britain

Germany is what she has become after the war. There is no other Germany.

> —Josef V. Stalin,
> Generalissimo of the U.S.S.R.

She lost everything in 1945; actually, Germany no longer exists.

> —Harry S Truman
> President of the United States

ONE

Willi tapped the pencil against his teeth and stared at the screen. The soft green numbers had not changed. Willi scratched his cheek with the pencil, then touched the keyboard for a moment. The numbers rearranged themselves.

"Ummph." He rocked back in the swivel chair and slumped. He drummed his fingers along the edge of the computer console. He shifted uncomfortably and focused his gaze somewhere beyond the dark screen, in the guts of the computer. He scratched an ear. He rubbed his neck.

Nothing changed the numbers. And they were not correct. They had not been correct all morning, right from when he booted up the system-check program in the first ten minutes of his shift. He had relieved Guenter, who said nothing about the master control program. He had complained—as usual—about the target-tracking software, about Lieutenant Sautter's inability to use the new patches to the communications program, and about the British wing commander's irritating habit of spilling tea on the CO's console. But nothing about the master. Surely even Guenter would have noticed.

Or maybe not. Since he had been at the SOC Willi had

1

become the computer wizard to whom the others looked for guidance. Naturally it made him feel proud. He'd never thought his two years of Luftwaffe duty would be so rewarding; for a young man who lived, ate, and slept computers, his tour so far had been unexpectedly satisfying.

After he'd made his Abitur, he'd naturally expected to go right to Technical University in Bonn to keep up his studies. But as usual, the bureaucracy had trapped him— there were too many kids like him. He would have to wait at least two years; everybody, it seemed, wanted a diploma in computer engineering. So here he was in Luftwaffe blue, doing his mandatory eighteen months service on the Dutch border, in the Goch NATO Sector Operations Center. And to his own surprise, loving it. And learning too. Even though these 9160s were older than he might have expected, they had taught him a lot about the practical realities of mainframe computer work. They had personalities. They made mistakes. Sometimes they even concocted false alarms.

But they didn't screw up their own master control programs. They didn't rearrange these numbers. Willi leaned forward and squinted at the screen.

Still wrong. Someone had hacked the program.

Willi sighed and made up his mind. He selected the PRINT option and cleared the screen. As the nearby dot-matrix printer spat out the lines, he wheeled himself back from the console and looked around for Colonel Schoener.

As usual, he sat near the CO, watching the big boards. Schoener was a smallish man, with thinning brown hair closely cropped, and dark, intense eyes. When they focused on you, you got the chills. Willi didn't like Schoener— nobody did, not even the other officers—but he respected his knowledge of computers. Even though Schoener was twenty years older than Willi, he was almost as current as Willi. To Willi, that was more amazing than the fact that Schoener had risen so high in the Luftwaffe after crossing from East Germany, where he had been raised. Willi didn't know much about politics. But he knew computers, and knew how hard it was for an older man to grasp the new stuff. And Colonel Schoener had grasped almost all of it.

Willi tore off the printout and made his way along the pit of the SOC to the CO's console. Even though it was early in the day, there was a lot of activity. All of the CRTs at the watch stations reflected the business of the center; all NATO and friendly aircraft within the sector were tagged or at least contacted, and their flights followed. No exercises were on today—as shown by the big boards—but the usual local low-level fighter work was being done by the Dutch F16s and the USAFE types. Later in the day the Brits were scheduled to stage a mock strike against the center itself, homing on the radar farm a kilometer from the center, their Tornados flying at treetop height. Apparently the object was to test the new Marconi equipment's ability to penetrate jamming. Schoener had told Willi it would begin at 1750 that evening. Since the weather outside was nice—a typical summer day on the Dutch-German border: warm, humid, sunny—every commander who could get his people in the air to practice was doing so. The pit buzzed with the chatter of the center controllers and the strolling watch chiefs.

Willi eased through the softly lit gloom, nodding to those who caught his eye. He arrived near the commander's station and waited for Schoener and the British wing commander—who was vice commander, actually, the deputy to Luftwaffe Brigadegeneral von Grabow—to motion him closer. They were watching their screens intently, speaking softly to each other. At last Schoener looked up.

"Yes, Willi?" he said in his nasal tenor. Willi caught the slightest traces of the Leipzig accent; after years in the Luftwaffe the colonel was losing it.

"Herr Oberst, uh, I'd like to speak with you about the computers."

Schoener's sharp eyes flicked to the printout. "Of course. Can it wait?"

"Certainly, Herr Oberst. Whenever you have the time."

The British officer looked up. Unlike the stereotypical British flying officer, he was short, nearly bald, and spoke perfect German.

"Hello, Willi. Something wrong?"

"No, sir. Or, maybe. I don't know. I'd like to check it with the Oberst."

The CO smiled. "Righto. Helmut, do you want to check it now?"

Schoener shook his head. "I think not." He looked again at Willi. His face was unreadable, as usual. "See me in my office in an hour, Willi. Say, ten hundred."

"Of course, Herr Oberst. Thank you."

Willi folded the printout and went back to the 9160 master panel. When he called up the control program again, the numbers still were incorrect. He sighed and got on with debugging the tracking software.

Oberst Helmut Schoener's office was spartan, a stark contrast to the offices of General von Grabow and Wing Commander Stiles. Their offices were full of service memorabilia—photos of airplanes, models of airplanes, beer steins, plaques from old squadrons, scraps from lives spent flying. Schoener's office was equipped with the standard Luftwaffe gray and green furniture. A chair, a desk, a large safe, two filing cabinets, a visitor's chair, and a side table. The only thing on his walls was a single calendar, also Luftwaffe issue. The only unusual item on his desk was the latest, most advanced portable briefcase-size computer.

The office fitted the austere intelligence officer's personality perfectly. So far as Willi and his friends knew,

Schoener had no real social life at all. No wife, not even, they said, a girlfriend. As someone who suffered the same kind of whispers because of his fascination for computers, Willi felt a strange kinship with Schoener. He sat now across from the officer while he studied the printout. Because the administrative offices were above ground, sunlight poured in through the window, now open to catch the soft summer breeze. A bee buzzed outside, near the rosebushes.

Schoener laid the sheet down and looked at Willi. He smoothed it out on his immaculate desk and pursed his lips.

"So," he said. The word carried an air of finality about it. Unconsciously Willi shivered. "So. The numbers are not correct, are they, Willi?"

"No, Herr Oberst."

"Why not, do you think?"

"I'm not certain. It looks—that is. I think perhaps someone has tampered with the master program."

"A reasonable conclusion. Else why would these be wrong?"

"Exactly. But . . ."

Schoener looked hard at him. "But what?"

Willi squirmed in his seat. "But I can't understand why, Herr Oberst. After I found this I went through the whole series, and I couldn't find any other signs of hacking."

"You checked everything?"

"Yes. Well, except for the Q programs. And I can't get to those."

"No. Of course not. But everything else is in order?"

"It seems to be."

Schoener frowned. "Seems to be? Aren't you sure?"

"As sure as I can be, Herr Oberst."

Schoener looked through him for a moment. "I hope you're right, Willi, because the Tac Eval Team plans a visit next week. As you know."

Willi grimaced, recalling the hours spent preparing for the Tactical Evaluation Team's annual sweep, hours of mental and physical work as he and the other enlisted men worked full duty days and then got their quarters into inspection-ready condition. "Yes, sir. I know."

"What will I tell him?"

Willi hesitated. "I don't know. Yet. The system is supposed to be almost impossible to enter, and the master program is supposed to be even harder to change. According to the manuals, if someone has done so, the built-in safeguards are supposed to allow tracking of everything—time of entry, records of the changes, everything. And yet when I checked the security files there was nothing. One part of the program says that it has been tampered with, but the security says it has not. I've never seen anything like it."

Schoener again smoothed the printout. "The Tac Eval man for computers is Rausch. You know him?"

"Yes, Hauptmann Rausch is a very good engineer."

"But not the best, I think. You agree?"

Willi hesitated. Criticizing officers was never wise. "Well—"

"Never mind, Willi. I tell you what. Until we have more evidence of what went on here, let's let Rausch snoop all he wants. I wager that he'll not find the discrepancy. What do you think?"

Willi bit his lip. "Probably not," he said slowly. "But shouldn't we—"

"Bring it to his attention? No. Not yet. We have nothing to report yet. If we filed reports every time this complicated software got bugs, we'd flood the Eval Team's office, wouldn't we? So what we'll do is this. I'll keep this printout and you stay alert for any other problems. Okay?"

Willi was a citizen-soldier, a conscript with no interest or understanding of the military before his induction. Once he left at the end of his tour, he would never think about the Luftwaffe again. But he knew when he was being given an order. And he knew when the order was a cover-up. In the split-second he had to respond to the colonel's camouflaged order, he weighed taking further action to bring the tampering to somebody else's attention—the Tac Eval CO, his own CO, the deputy CO—against simply shutting up, letting it drop, and getting on with his life. The Luftwaffe hadn't been bad to him; he lived reasonably well, shot at nobody, studied at night, and felt no real connection with the endless war games that his computers and the SOC played with the heavily armed fighters and bombers that flew in their sector. He knew the rules well enough to know that his real duty—led by the postwar German military doctrine of "Innere Fuehrung," or inner leadership, as opposed to blind obedience to superiors' orders—was to report the matter higher. But he also knew the other rules, the ones that said if you rock the boat, you get wet. Sometimes you drown. He had a little less than a year left, and then he'd be in Bonn, pursuing his diploma. He knew which rules he'd obey.

"Okay," he said.

Schoener managed a thin smile. "Good. I'll expect to hear if you find more. Is that all?"

"Yes, Herr Oberst. Thank you."

"Not at all. See you later."

Willi stood, saluted, and left.

Helmut Schoener returned the salute and watched the lanky young enlisted man leave. Once the door had closed, the little office was nearly silent. Outside, a bee buzzed against the window screen, which was there for protection, not against insects, but against probing microwaves. The SOC was set in a rural area, atop a small hill, surrounded by farms, its main antenna area two kilometers away.

On a warm summer day it was hard to imagine any kind of combat there, let alone electronic spying. Yet only four decades before, these flatlands had seen bitter fighting as the British and Canadians had smashed through the Wehrmacht defenses. Huge tank battles had torn the fields. Endless bombing had reduced Goch and Uedem to rubble. Many of the local people, who would merrily drink all night with the boys from the SOC in the railway tavern, had themselves been in the fighting—if not here, then in France, or Africa or Russia. It was hard today to imagine such combat. Yet here was the SOC, and above were the armed aircraft.

Schoener listened to the bee while he considered Willi and the meaning of his reporting the incorrect system status readings. To Willi the wrongness was obvious. But to most military computer techs it would not be so. Willi was a brilliant young man, obviously destined for a rewarding career in computer science. Brilliant and zealous.

Too zealous.

Schoener thought for a moment more, then punched an outside number on his phone. As it dialed he watched the tiny red light in the handset. It was dark. Nobody was tapping this time.

The phone on the other end rang eight times. When it was answered, Schoener said, "Griffon. Tonight. The usual place." Then he hung up.

The bee buzzed once more, futilely, against the silver mesh on the window. Schoener folded the printout twice and put it inside his blue Luftwaffe tunic. He stood up, his face still impassive. But he was furious. Not with Willi. With himself. There was no excuse for such carelessness. He had never done it before. As he thought about his session, carefully recalling each step of the programming, he could not remember at which point he'd forgotten the sequence. It must have been at the close. He was tired, he recalled. And he was in a hurry. Dinner with von Grabow. But that didn't excuse him.

He straightened his tie and opened his door, thinking about Willi. In his own way, Schoener liked the boy. A

brilliant career in his future. If only he had not been so
zealous or quite so brilliant. He closed the door and reset
the lock.

The concrete of the admin building shook suddenly as
one of the American fighters roared low overhead. Schoener
grimaced and strode toward the pit.

Even in the darkness and confusion the first rescue people
to reach the scene knew it was hopeless. The north end of
the barrack had collapsed and was still burning, while the
south end was a heap of smoldering rubble. As they leaped
off the Luftwaffe fire truck and ran into the hot, stinking
pile, a gout of flame gushed skyward, a spurt from the
shattered gas main. It illuminated the ruined barrack enough
that the rescue chief knew what he would find when they
began digging. Still, as his men poured foam and water
into the burning north end, he and five others frantically
pulled at the broken concrete.

As the support vehicles screamed to a halt nearby,
power was restored to the street lighting, and intense
quartz emergency lights soon bathed the smoking ruin in
an eerie blue-white glare. Lights came on quickly throughout the living area as others realized that the tremendous
explosion had been on the SOC living compound. Although it was still only 0340, the area was soon filled with
half-naked men, digging like the rescue chief, trying to
reach the men who had been asleep in the barrack.

Acrid smoke burned their lungs and ashes cloaked their
bodies, but they worked feverishly. The chief barked directions to hasten the removal of rubble. Of the twenty
men in the barrack, his bitter experience with terrorist
attacks convinced him they'd be lucky to find five still
breathing. And the lives of those few would depend on the
speed with which his people cleared the weight of the
barrack from them.

As the minutes dragged on they were joined by the civil

fire and rescue section from Uedem. Grimly they joined the struggle.

The first body was found within a half hour. The second, third, fourth, and fifth came within moments. The rest took another hour. By the time they found the only two alive—both at the north end, in what had been the upper room—dawn was breaking. It was another clear, cloudless morning, a perfect summer sunrise.

Brigadegeneral Friedrich von Grabow watched as they lined up the bodies of his men. He wore only his flight suit, the piece of clothing he could don most quickly. He stood tall and erect, a handsome man in his early fifties, slender and well-muscled, impassive in the glorious morning. Someone shoved a huge mug of coffee into his hand. He took it without looking and swallowed mechanically. Rum burned his throat. He gulped more, still watching the agonizing body count.

Finally the exhausted rescue chief stumbled over from the smoking wreckage of the building. He pulled off his helmet and wiped his face, leaving the ashes smeared and mixed with sweat. He saluted wearily. Von Grabow returned a salute gravely, and handed the mug to the officer.

"We've got them all," he said simply.

Von Grabow waited.

"Eighteen dead. We lost Mueller as we pulled him out. Only Baum and Schmidt made it." He gulped coffee and rum.

Von Grabow nodded. "Any ideas who did it?"

The captain shook his head. "Security says could have been anybody. Anti-nuclear people, Greens, Red Army Faction, anybody."

"But it was definitely a bomb?"

"No question. Planted on the south side, near a window. Right next to Willi Vogel. Poor kid was ripped apart." He nodded toward the line of bodies.

"Vogel—"

"Died instantly. He was lucky. Beckmann and Wilhelm were crushed. It's a slow way to go."

Von Grabow nodded again. The rescue operation continued, swirling around them as the morning blossomed. The rescue captain drained the mug and handed it back to the general.

"Orders, Herr General?" he said.

"Clean it up. And send Major Lindner to me."

"Of course, Herr General." The captain saluted, donned his helmet again, and trudged back to the blasted building.

Helmut Schoener appeared silently next to von Grabow. He saluted. Von Grabow waved wearily.

"Terrorists," said Schoener simply as he surveyed the wreckage. He looked carefully from body to body in the pathetic little lineup only ten meters away. His gaze stopped as he recognized Willi's mangled features.

"Yes," said von Grabow. "Terrorists. Of course." He looked hard, suddenly, at Schoener, his wide-set blue eyes piercing.

"It was necessary? Absolutely necessary?"

Schoener looked back, his face unreadable.

"Yes. Absolutely necessary."

Von Grabow held his eyes for a moment, then looked back at the bodies.

"It had better work," he said softly.

Schoener said nothing, watching as they zipped Willi Vogel into a body bag.

"It will," he said.

TWO

February mists wrapped the hills near the Klostergut Jakobsberg in a shroud of invisibility. At times the mists turned to cold, piercing rain. None of Group A complained. To a man, they had lived through much worse.

In the small clearing in one of the thick stands of pine and fir that cloaked the extensive lands of the Sport-und-Kurhotel, the ten leaders of Group A sat silently on their haunches. For some, the Southeast Asian rest position came easily, a habit ingrained from years in the jungle. For others, it was recently learned, picked up from many maneuvers with the Americans who were themselves veterans of Vietnam, Cambodia, and Laos. In this posture, a kind of fetal crouch, the body's weight balances over and spreads evenly along both feet, and the body heat is trapped in the thorax. So the rain washed over them virtually unnoticed. *Feldgrau* ponchos shed water in sheets to the soaked grass, kept cropped by the various forms of wildlife that roamed the thousands of private acres surrounding the Sporthotel. This stretch of forest, although only a half hour from the town of Boppard on the Rhine, might as well have been in the wilds of Canada or Siberia.

That was why the ten Group A leaders waited here in the rain. It replicated the terrain of their goal nearly perfectly, yet was private land, so isolated that no one would bother them. The Klostergut Jakobsberg was an ancient cloister turned first into a school in the seventeenth century, then into a huge estate, and finally into a famous "wildpark" hotel, whose current owner was a world-class hunter. The walls of the vast hotel were covered with trophies—boar's heads from East Prussia, antlers from Hungary, fierce birds and a vampire bat from South America. In such a setting, men such as those from Group A were common.

They had not arrived as a group, of course, although the staff was given to understand that they were considering a hunting expedition and were meeting to see how they all "worked" together. Most of them had the look of the sleek professional; the trained eye of the receptionist ticked them off approvingly as they registered, their expensive BMW sedans and Mercedes and the lone BMW motorcycle providing background proof, much like their leather and aluminum and hunting-canvas luggage, that these were the sort of guests the Klostergut liked to have. As they emerged from the bleak February weather she eyed them critically and satisfied herself as to their stations in life; there was a banker, certainly, by his gold-rimmed glasses and expensive shoes; there, a journalist, by his direct, inquisitive but open stare; and that one, surely, was a lawyer, his button-down look and precise handwriting confirming the guess. The motorcyclist—who arrived on the most expensive touring motorcycle the Muenchen firm built, one costing well over DM20,000—had the rugged look of an adventurer—tanned, with blond, close-cropped hair burned almost white by some fierce sun, eyebrows likewise white, lips still slightly cracked from the same exposure. He spoke to her softly in the strange tones of the Kiel area, but was obviously very well educated, and very wealthy—like the rest of the group. In a hotel that often catered to groups of bourgeois foreigners—Americans, mostly—having Germans like these pleased the staff very much. From the moment they arrived, each was treated with extra deference, extra courtesy, despite the fact that no special instructions had been issued.

One in particular was treated thus. He signed his room card "Franz Helling," but for some reason the receptionist was convinced that was not his real name. He had about him an air of mystery and command; he stood only about average height, was slight in build, but had the calm gray eyes of an aristocrat; eyes that knew the world, knew their place in it, and knew that place to be on top, without ever demanding it. His features were regular, not handsome really, his thinning brown hair trimmed short at the ear and in back, his jawline his most pronounced feature. He smiled briefly and not often. He dressed plainly but expensively, and, thought the thirty-five-year-old receptionist, suitably for a man in his mid-forties, which is what she judged him to be. He arrived in a silver Mercedes 500SLC, and his luggage was found to be exactly fitted to the car's trunk. She tried surreptitiously to examine his small gold signet ring while he signed it, but she could not identify the crest or the tiny words under it. When he spoke, his baritone was pleasant, his diction precise, no trace of an accent audible. He was High German personified.

He was also the man for whom the other men waited in the cold little clearing. With senses honed by years in such surroundings, each probed the dark forest to be the first to hear him. It was a small competition, but it was typical of them, and it was one reason among many why they, and not others, were there.

He was suddenly among them, stepping out of the dripping branches and gray-green bracken unseen and unheard. He nodded as they rose, almost as one.

Like them, he wore a poncho and a wide-brimmed hat

of camouflage material. Under his poncho could be seen jungle combat boots and perfectly creased and bloused camo trousers. He let the group stand a moment, then motioned them back down.

"So," he said at last, "we are finally ready to begin. Our friends at the hotel have been most discreet, but effective. I have examined the exercise area, and I can assure you, gentlemen, that it is most realistic. Even down to the weather." He smiled slightly, and was rewarded with answering smiles from the ten men in the clearing.

"You have all been given plans of the assault itself, if not of the subsequent action. You have been requested to give your own teams training in specifics, and our last status report showed that this was progressing well. Today will be the first—and probably only—time we are able to bring you all together until Z-Day, so we must make good use of our time. Questions?"

A man near the back stood up. "Grossman. Team Four. My question, Herr Oberst, entails a basic concern I have never had adequately addressed. That is, how can we expect troops who have never worked together to be successful in such an assault? I cannot speak for the others, but in the paratroops it is a given that such ad lib attacks are doomed from the outset."

"And so they are, if they are ad lib. Such is not the case here. You will be going over a full-scale mockup of the target today, and videotapes of the area, made from all possible angles, will enhance the troops' familiarity. Further, we actually expect little real resistance; it is therefore an assault unlike those you had to make, say, in Chad."

The big paratroop officer nodded. "I understand about the terrain familiarization, Herr Oberst. What concerns me is that no matter how well we train our sections, we still will not have worked *all* together. Even in the smoothest of operations undertaken by the most integrated troops, there is always some stumbling over items like communications and responsibilities in unforeseen circumstances. It is one thing to plan for perfect performance, and another to expect it.''

"We do not expect it. None of us here is unaware of what our eloquent American colleagues call the 'fuck-up factor.' Indeed, our plan is based on the most generous allowances for it. You will recall, Herr Major, that you are not going up against seasoned combat troops, but conscripts and green officers.''

The major stood for a second more, thinking, then nodded. The rain sloshed forward off his wide campaign hat as he said, "Yes. I know, Herr Oberst. I suppose there is no other way.''

"No. There is not. This entire enterprise is a gamble, gentlemen, of the most audacious sort. Let there be no misunderstanding about the consequences should we fail. Surely each of you knows that he is from this moment an outlaw. No one can protect us in the event of failure. Our only protection is success. We have a simple, direct part in a complex plan, and any two failures together can destroy the whole attempt. Our best-computed odds are one in seventeen for success of the whole mission, and one in three for success of our part of that mission. I personally find such odds acceptable for the gains we may make for our people on both sides. I have assumed over these last two years that the same was true for each of you. Is it?''

In answer, the other men stood up silently, joining the standing paratroop officer. Their leader surveyed them for a moment, then said, smiling faintly, "Good. I see we are still in agreement. Let us begin, shall we? Hauptmann Krasny, as operations officer, perhaps you will be good enough to start things off.''

Krasny, whom the receptionist would have recognized as the bronzed motorcyclist, pulled a waterproof map case from under his poncho. He extracted a thin packet of waterproof typed pages, which he handed out, one sheet to a man. "These are the latest operation sequence and coordination orders. You'll note a slight alteration under number twelve. This involves Grossman's section and my own. The text is self-explanatory. We should encounter little difficulty with the changes. Questions?"

There were none. Most of the Group A leaders had already tucked the page inside their ponchos. Krasny waited a moment more, then did likewise, putting his back into the map case.

"Excellent," he said. "Then, gentlemen, let us begin. As noted on the orders, we should assume our jump-off positions, then wait for the colonel's signal. Herr Oberst?"

The colonel swept the ten men with his cold clear eyes. "Yes. It is time. Let's go."

In a moment the clearing was empty again. The chill rain slowly filled the muddy footprints of the section leaders of Group A, soon erasing the signs of their presence as completely as the winds and earth and water of Germany had erased the signs of all the other warriors who had crossed that same place on their way to or from the nearby Rhine during the previous three thousand years.

In the NATO sector operations center 237 kilometers north-northwest of the target zone the leaders of Group A were slowly approaching through the gloomy Klosterwald. Luftwaffe Colonel Helmut Schoener glanced at his watch. Although he sat expressionlessly in the briefing room listening to the morning "stand-up" situation analysis, he felt an almost physical shock as he realized that if everything was proceeding according to plan, Helling and his men were now turning the years of patient, exhaustive planning into reality.

Schoener shifted uncomfortably in his metal chair, unable to avoid a dryness in his mouth. Things were now out of his control; events would soon occur one on top of another, faster and faster, until the plan would triumph or fail utterly. There would be no intermediate result.

Around Schoener the bored officers of the multinational SOC doodled on pads or stared dully at the briefer, a dried-up Dutch Air Force intelligence specialist whom they called The Professor and whose obsession with numbers numbed everyone in each briefing he produced. For the dozen men in the room, this Tuesday was just another duty day, another day of radar targets and transponder codes and hours spent with headphones through which tinny voices asked for clearances or provided visual ID of unknown targets. It had all been going on so long that not even the few combat veterans took any of it seriously.

Not a man normally given to philosophic introspection, Helmut Schoener looked around him with new eyes, and wondered about his NATO colleagues here today. Would they one day look back and say about this day what other officers had said about the day before Pearl Harbor or D-Day or Barbarossa? Unused to such open-loop thinking, Schoener abandoned the strange notion and tried to focus on The Professor.

But his mouth was still desert-dry, and his heart beat irregularly. Back in Karl-Marx Stadt, and in the special GRU school in Omsk, he had learned the tricks of body control, so vital to a spy's longevity. But in the face of the suddenly real countdown to Z-Day, the tricks that had served him so well for so many years in espionage failed. He felt the beginnings of sweat on his clammy palms.

His body knew what his mind could not suppress. Operation BLOOD AND IRON was suddenly real.

THREE

"Well, what are your plans?"

Typical, thought Max. They'd been seated at the table in the dining room of the Bolling Air Force Base officer's club less than two minutes, and his father was already through with the feeling-out period. Age and his stroke had wrinkled and disabled parts of him, but not his mind. Major General Eric Moss, USA-Ret., president and chief executive officer of Moss Electronics, Inc., was not a man who wasted time.

"Whatever they tell me my plans are," Max answered. He cracked a thin smile.

His father studied him a moment before he continued. Max had changed since they'd last met in Potsdam. Then, even at age twenty-eight, he still had acted the truculent adolescent, his lanky frame ill suited to the uniform he wore as a noncom in the Air Force, his jet-black hair unkempt, and the look in his green eyes one of a troublemaker.

But that was more than three years ago. The Max Moss who sat across from his father now wore a well-tailored Air Force first lieutenant's uniform, and if the hair wasn't much tidier, the face below it was calmer, less pinched, generally less intense. Eric Moss decided that as much as the events that had led to his son's wearing of the uniform had changed Max, age itself had been at work.

The walk from the foyer, under portraits of the great captains of the Air Force—some of whom Eric Moss had known, and with whom he'd crossed swords—had gladdened the elder Moss's heart because of the way Max had moved. Accustomed to reading men's inner selves through their body language, Eric Moss's sharp eyes had seen the confidence in Max's stride, the straightness of his back, the smoothness with which he greeted acquaintances, and Moss Sr. had relaxed inwardly. His boy, it seemed, had finally grown up.

"Obviously. But I mean your long-range plans," Eric said, matching Max's smile with his own.

Max stretched his smile into a grin. It made the little slanting scar on his chin—the result of a racing accident—disappear. "These days I don't make too many long-range plans. I seem to be in a business that doesn't work that way."

"You haven't worked out some career goals?"

"Not yet, Dad." Max sipped his coffee while he thought about the question.

It was one he'd asked himself a lot, ever since he'd recovered from the Army bullet that had put him in the hospital in Wiesbaden. Colonel Martin at the Mission had been the first one to let him know he was freed of the damning charges, and that the military had decided the only way it could handle him was to promote him—to get him out of the way for a while. The next few months should have been easy, but they hadn't been. Aside from the infection that had complicated his convalescence, there remained the nagging question his father had just so typically and so bluntly put to him: *now what?* The string-pullers at DIA knew what they wanted in return for Max's lieutenant's bars: He was expected to slip into a technical intelligence training stream. They presumed that he would be so grateful not to be up on treason charges that he would accept the assignment without question.

But Max wasn't so sure. He had warily signed up for another four years of service on the guarantee that he would stay with the United States Military Liaison Group in Potsdam, driving the exotic cars that Nubs Pierce prepared for the Recovery teams. At the time it had seemed like the right thing to do, since he wasn't keen on any of the other prospects that loomed before him as he contemplated the last few days before his Air Force hitch came to an end.

The Recovery teams were vital. The American pilots and aircrew they'd saved would testify to that—if only in secret. When the Mission had been established in 1947 by the Huebner-Malinin Agreement, it had been simply a military liaison operation, coordinating refugee and Allied matters with the Soviet zone, as well as with the Brits and French, who also maintained missions in Berlin. But then the Reds started luring American aircraft over the buffer zone with the object of shooting them down. A cheap form of technology transfer, one of his briefers had noted wryly. The American countermove was to turn the Mission, in Baron Karlfried Hasso Ludwig von Lustow's mansion, into a combination garage/safe house. It housed the cars and drivers who would attempt to reach the downed aircrew before the Vopos, and it allowed them time on extraterritorial ground to regroup, then be escorted across the zone lines, safe from molestation.

It was a crazy operation, produced by a crazy time, and the silent war waged between the Americans and Soviets for more than four decades. Trapped by the agreement they had signed, the Soviets could put their power to use only in trying to halt successful recoveries. The Americans matched the Soviets escalation for escalation. When they applied pressure to the U.S. Mission, the Americans did the same to the Soviet Mission near Frankfurt in the West. The game got deadlier, and the players got more specialized.

Into his silence his father spoke again. "Okay, so you're not sure about specifics. How about generalities? Are you in for a career here?" He swept his good arm around the roomful of Air Force officers. Max understood his reference to "in" to mean "in the service."

"Maybe. Hard to tell. A lot depends on assignments."

Eric Moss frowned slightly. "Max, listen. If you're going to play this game, you have to stop thinking like that. You no longer have the luxury of being passive about your career; if you're to make a success of yourself in the military, you have to actively pursue posts that will help you reach your goal. All these guys"—he again indicated the room—"are your enemies. In fact, you're actually behind before you start. You're at least four years older than your zone. That's going to play hell with advancement."

Max looked expressionlessly at his father. He was right, naturally. Max had known that the first time he'd walked into an O-Club with his shiny new butterbars on and realized that the kids who wore his rank were not yet in college when he'd been out of college, out of racing, and in the Air Force as an engine mechanic. It had been a distinctly odd, even unpleasant sensation to realize that he was behind. It was even more unpleasant to discover that he cared about it, because it meant that he was thinking in career terms despite what he told his friends—and himself. So far, throughout the year and more that he'd been in training, he'd been so busy he had been able to avoid it; but now there was no escape.

"I know," he said.

Eric Moss nodded, satisfied. So he did care; he was in for the long haul. Even though Moss Sr. had little use for the USAF, he was glad to hear that Max had finally worked through his kiddy-car rebellions. It mattered little that he was now an officer in the "wrong" service. What mattered was that he was an officer—and that he carry on the Moss tradition by excelling at it.

"Good. We've got that settled. Now, do you know anybody?"

Max had to smile. More jargon. For Major General Eric Moss "know" meant "is there anyone upstairs who is working on your behalf?"

"Maybe," he said. "There's Blackie Lundberg, and Colonel Martin at the Mission. And Joe Pope here. He handles all my administrative stuff: pay, quarters, that sort of thing. At DIA, besides Lundberg, not really. I have a controller—Bob Jackson—but he's only a major and a Marine at that."

"Blackie's a good man. How well does he know you?"

"Hardly at all. In fact, I've never even met him. But this whole deal came through him, and I've picked up hints here and there that he's the one who's rammed things along every time some personnel type got riled because I came in out of channels."

"No OTS?"

"Nope. Martin said it wasn't necessary. I got my commission at Ramstein, and reported directly to Lowry after a short and sweet introduction to life as an officer and a gentleman. Took about ten minutes."

"Blackie must like you. Even battlefield commissions take longer." Eric regarded his son with new respect. For an old West Pointer like Lundberg to bend the system so thoroughly must mean he saw real potential in Max. Even though he knew Max to be smart as a whip and fully capable of a sound career, such treatment surprised him.

The sudden appearance of the waiter broke into his stream of thought.

"Gentlemen?" the young black man asked, standing by with his notepad.

"Smoked salmon for the general," said Max quickly, "and I'll have the crepe du jour, which I believe is *poulet et champignons,* is it not?"

"Yes, sir," said the waiter. "And to drink?"

"A bottle of Moselle white, I think. Schloss Petrisberg, eighty-one."

"A good choice, sir. Thank you."

Eric Moss watched the waiter nod in deference and slip back through the tables. The son he had known thought no more of good food than he did of the military.

"Where did you acquire taste?" he asked.

Max grinned again, more the boy racer than the accomplished gentleman. "I hung out with the right woman in England," he said.

"She must have been something."

"She was. She is," said Max, and with one of his old lightning-swift mood changes, his face darkened slightly.

His father recognized it at once; something about Max had not changed, and probably never would. In a way, the general found it comforting. He dropped the subject of the woman, which was obviously painful.

"Anyway, you expect an assignment soon?"

The cloud passed from Max. "Yes. Maybe within the week. Jackson told me not to go too far from a phone. Secret agent X-7 will soon be in action." He grinned again.

"It's serious business, Max. And not just because you can get into some physically dangerous situations. Hell, that's your job. The serious part is that so far as I know, nobody has ever turned intelligence—especially technical intelligence—into a four-star career."

"You got to two."

"Yeah. But only because of the infantry, the War College, the Defense Electronics Agency, and sundry other feathers in the cap. If I'd stayed in the intel loop, I'd have retired a bird colonel—no more. So watch for chances to do some laterals. Get into something more visible. Where you are now you'll have to rely on good works to get your shots below the zone. And since nobody on promotion boards ever knows what the hell good works are in intel, you can guess what kind of promotion chances you've got.''

''Sounds pretty bad. Guess I'll just have to resign now,'' Max said, a wicked twinkle in his eye.

His father acknowledged the new mood and Max's obvious reluctance to discuss his career seriously. He'd made progress; that would have to be enough. Eric Moss could empathize, finally, with his son's predicament. Just coming up from the ranks imposed its own kind of stress and dislocation. Add to that the limbo in which intelligence people worked, and you had to see that scheming for promotion couldn't possibly be highest on Max's list of priorities. He was doing well, Eric decided, to hold his own here. With an inner start Moss realized he was proud of his son. Naturally he did not let it show. Neither of them would have known how to handle that.

The arrival of their food and wine provided an easy end to the career discussion, and they enjoyed themselves comparing notes about wine—another surprise to Moss Sr., and almost as delightful as the discovery that his son could make him proud. Midway through an animated discourse on the joys of a white from a little vineyard near Trier, Max was interrupted by a young sergeant from the reception area.

''Sir? Lieutenant Moss?''

''Yes?'' Max said, slightly annoyed.

''Uh, sir, you've got a call. Priority, I'm afraid.''

Max rolled his eyes at his father. ''Excuse me, Dad. Back in a flash. Probably something about a form I left unsigned. You know.''

''Sure. I know. The wine'll keep.''

He watched Max carefully fold his linen napkin and

leave the table, the picture of grace. The unexpected pride the older man felt threatened to burst his necktie, so he attacked the salmon savagely.

Max took the call on the club manager's personal line, which had a scrambler—a concession to the many high-priority calls that came to patrons of his club from nearby Washington chieftains.

"Lieutenant Moss," he said, rather more brusquely than usual.

"Sir? Sergeant Phillips here. I have Major Jackson holding. One moment, please."

Max waited. The next click brought Bob Jackson.

"Max?"

"Yes, *sir*," he replied, emphasizing the sir for effect. He knew Bob would hate it. The marine brought his laid-back Louisiana life-style to everything.

"Shit. Listen, things are goin' down fast here. Something's up—I haven't got the foggiest what, but a whole slew of assignments came down about an hour ago."

"Mine?"

"Yours. Uh—I didn't think it's what you expected."

"You mean I won't get to go to Kuwait?"

"Cut the crap, Max. No, I mean worse than that."

"Can you tell me now?"

"Sure. We monitor all the lines—this sucker's clean as a whistle. How about a guess?"

"Come on, Bob. Give me a break."

"Okay, I'll give you a hint. Think Europe."

"Oh, no."

"Yup. Right back in the fire, kiddo. Sorry. I tried my best. But Jesus, things are really screwy around here. Nobody has any idea what the hell's happening. Talk is they're closing down—well, never mind. We can discuss that later. Anyway, I presume you know what I'm talking about?"

Max stared out the window, not seeing the club parking

lot or the manicured lawn, now being soaked by a typical late-summer Washington thunderstorm. He felt numb, like a World War I doughboy being ordered back into the trenches after months in the mud. Or like a bomber pilot being sent back to make another fifty missions. Or like what he was—a specialist in East Germany being sent back there.

"A certain baronial mansion?" he said considerably more calmly than he felt.

"Right. Drop by tomorrow, and we'll get started on the details. They expect you, ah, *soonest*, shall we say?"

Max mumbled an assent and hung up.

His father beamed at him as he walked back to the table, but the pallor on Max's face slowly erased the smile. When Max had sat down again Eric said gently, "Well? Administrative problems? Laundry ready?"

Max smoothed his napkin in his lap and studied the half-eaten crepe in his plate before he answered. His features had closed in again.

"New assignment," he said finally.

"Oh? Good one?"

"Bad one."

"Ah." His father laid his fork down. "Not career-enhancing, eh?"

Max smiled wanly. "Hardly. I'm going back."

"Back. Back to what?"

"Potsdam. The Mission."

Eric Moss tried to think of something to say. Nothing came to mind. Max sat still, his hands in his lap, focused on something over his father's left shoulder. The elder Moss considered the ramifications of the assignment. There were many reasons for not sending Max back to Potsdam.

The military reasons were obvious; for starters, if you had a choice, you didn't ever send a man newly commissioned from the ranks back to those same ranks; it made life difficult for everyone, especially those with whom the new officer was friends. "Fraternization" was what the military called social interaction between officers and enlisted men, and although it was a given that at an elite, specialized unit like the USMLG fraternization would be impossible to avoid, no good could come from forcing the issue by jamming an ex-noncom down the throats of the men of the Mission so soon after he had left.

Then there was the reaction of the Soviets, who could be expected to take a very dim view of the reintroduction of the man who had professionally humiliated them. No formal protests would be lodged, but the significance of the assignment would not be lost on the Group of Soviet Forces Germany command or the GRU, the Soviet military intelligence agency. No matter how you cut it, Max's life was not going to be easy in Potsdam.

Eric Moss sought hard for something to ease the situation. And still nothing came to mind.

Max shook his head finally and smiled bleakly. "Well, everybody's career has to start somewhere, right?"

Eric recognized the strain in his voice, the tension that made the little scar on his chin turn white. He understood all too well. Like every other officer, he had himself taken such phone calls, and had himself been forced to look for silver linings in such dark clouds. Like combat, it was part of the professional military life, and like combat, it had its traditional rules and taboos. Eric Moss observed them by filling his own and Max's wineglass. He carefully replaced the bottle in its cooler and raised his in salute.

"Potsdam, Lieutenant Moss," he said gravely, looking his son squarely in the eye.

Max raised his glass and his little smile slipped off his face.

"Potsdam, General Moss," he said, and, eyes locked, the two men put their glasses to their lips.

──────────────── FOUR

The Soviet guard saluted slowly, almost insolently. Normally Muth would have ignored the all-too-familiar gesture of near contempt. Today he was in no mood for it. Instead of raising his hand to his highly polished visor, he simply stared at the youngish Red Army soldier. He gave the man the classic once-over while the corporal held his salute. A Kalashnikov was slung over his left shoulder, and on his greatcoat was the patch of the elite 11th Infantry, a Guards division.

The pale, slender features of the young corporal froze as he realized his mistake. He straightened and snapped in Russian, "Good morning, Comrade Colonel. You have authorization to enter?"

Oberst Oskar Muth returned the boy's salute, using his position to best advantage to intimidate. The height of the armored car's observation step enhanced that position. He waited a moment before answering the standard challenge. Beside him, his driver stared straight ahead, his features carefully blank. He could not hear the idling engines of the other six BTRs of A and B platoons, but he knew they were there, strung out on this little gravel road like gray-green beetles. The stink of their diesel exhausts filled the crisp forest air.

"Of course," he said at length. He plucked his map case from the seat and withdrew his orders. Handing them to the corporal, he nodded to the weather-beaten guard shack just beyond the red and white striped pole blocking the single-lane road. "Your officer will want to see these, Comrade Corporal."

The young Russian took the papers, saluted smartly, and turned on his heel, hurrying to the shack. Muth slipped down into the warmth of the armored car's cockpit. His driver continued to stare straight ahead. Through the open driving ports they watched in silence as the papers were handed to a shadowy figure in the shack. A moment later the corporal stepped out and fell in beside a Soviet officer, still buttoning his gray greatcoat. Even from a distance Muth read his red collar tabs clearly. As they approached he stood again, timing it so he arose just as they halted near the right side of the big BTR-50's prow.

"Comrade Colonel, I am Captain Voyodnev. We were of course informed of your scheduled arrival. Do you need any assistance before you proceed to your exercise area?"

Muth waved a return salute. "No. Thank you, Comrade Captain," he said in his best Russian. "Everything is optimal."

The captain nodded. Muth picked out the telltale signs of the typical Russian alcoholic: puffy red eyes, broken veins in the face, burned-out voice. The man couldn't be more than 35 years old, he thought. What terrible career miscalculation could have deposited him here, only a few dozen kilometers from the Czech border, running a tiny guard detachment that watched over hundreds of acres of mountains and dense forest? He shrugged to himself. It didn't matter; all that mattered was that they were on time.

He returned the captain's salute and looked back at his little column. Frankel stood in his BRDM, watching. Muth waved the go-ahead signal, and as the captain motioned the guards to raise the pole, he sank back into the car. His driver looked at him.

"Yes, Marcks, now. Go ahead."

The gears ground as he engaged first, and the six-ton armored car lurched forward. Muth glanced in the rear-facing periscope and saw the clumsy outlines of Frankel's BRDM close behind. One little knot of tension inside him dissolved. So, he thought, one more hurdle is cleared. The reality of it all was hard to grasp.

As he thought about how far he had come since Schoener had first contacted him—could it have been only eighteen months ago?—the entire enterprise seemed dreamlike again. The cold morning wind funneling through the open driving port stung his unprotected face, and he drank in the bitter wind like a drowning man gulping desperately for breath. He closed his eyes as the BTR jerked and bounced up the narrow little road, shutting out the brooding pine and spruce trees crowding in on the gravel track. It would take them another twenty minutes to reach their bivouac area. It occurred to him as he swayed with eyes closed in the cockpit that he could use those minutes to call off the whole affair. Only Frankel would know. At least, only Frankel of the men here. There was always Schoener.

Schoener. What did he really know of the man? How had he managed so decisively to rearrange Oskar Muth's life? The thoughts were old familiar paths winding through memory, fantasy, and reality, leading nowhere. Except to this moment, this commitment. As he had done so many times as he lay awake at night in his lonely bed, Muth replayed the mental tapes of Schoener's sudden emergence into his life.

It had really been a re-emergence. They had known each other back in the days when Leipzig was still a shattered, occupied city in which the fight for mere existence controlled everyone. Both of them were war babies, of course;

Helmut was slightly older, born in March of '44, three months before Oskar, in the same old hospital on Mannheimstrasse. Their families were not close, despite living only a few blocks from one another; Helmut's father was a railway worker, a man in a "protected" profession, while Oskar's father was a Panzer commander who had disappeared into the wastes of the Ukraine the same month he'd been born. Muth's mother had been loath to admit that her husband was dead, so she kept up appearances; after all, she was a Berlin University graduate, a major's wife, of good family. Schoener had no such distinction in his family; but at least he had a real family.

While the war lasted, such things apparently still mattered. But when the Russians came everything changed. They made a worker's hero out of Helmut's father, an example of the New Man, while Oskar's mother was scorned and raped. He learned of it long afterward; it apparently happened while she was on a food search when he was two. They said it changed her, and she became ruthless. He couldn't tell; she was always just Mother to him; silent, bitter, uncommunicative. But she never failed in her conviction that his father—also named Oskar—was still alive in some Siberian prison camp. She never remarried, but struggled to raise him on the wages she earned as an elementary-school teacher.

It was after the Rebellion of 1953 that Muth first came to be aware that Schoener was different from the rest of them, scrabbling for food, for clothing, for anything. Helmut had not seemed as electrified as the other boys at the news of the riots spreading like wildfire from East Berlin. He hung back when they excitedly planned fire bombings of the Russian garrison and sabotaging of the Russian commissioner's car. Of course they never did any of it anyway, but Helmut distanced himself from the others that day. He was never invited back into the circle again.

Perhaps that was why he joined the Young Pioneers,

then the Free German Youth. Perhaps that was why he never apologized for the perquisites they handed his father as a model worker—the extra food, the bicycle, then the ticket to Leipzig University that Helmut found himself with after he had made his Abitur.

Muth struggled through his own Abitur and never even considered university studies. He knew he was destined for the Army, and so, when he kissed his mother good-bye that day in 1963 and went off to catch the bus to camp, the silent nod he gave to Helmut Schoener at the bus stop was the last time he saw him for more than twenty years.

And then Schoener disappeared, not just from the university, but from Leipzig itself. The rumor mill claimed he'd defected, like so many. Trained by the war and then the Occupation not to pursue too closely the fates of people who vanished, Muth simply wrote him off and got on with his own struggle. It took him to the infantry, and it wasn't until the strange events of his own career entangled him with intelligence work that Schoener's name even came back to him.

The revelation had come in a buff file folder. As deputy inspector for Military District III (Leipzig) in Administration 2000, the secretive organization whose responsibility it was to ensure the reliability of all People's Army officers and men, Muth spent most of his days in the drab Leipzig HQ of the Ministry for State Security. He had not asked for the change from the life of a field infantry officer; they had simply plucked him out of it and assigned him the job. "The needs of the state come first," they'd said, and just like that he was consigned to a desk in a grim little office originally intended for some Imperial tax inspector. Every few hours a severely dressed secretary would knock politely, come in, and drop more file folders on his desk. His job was to open them, answer the questions his superior had noted on the multiline memorandum clipped to the file, and pile them in his Out box. He had been at it for three years when one of the file folders reintroduced him to Helmut Schoener.

His eyes still closed while Marcks swerved the awkward eight-wheeled armored car around the larger ruts in the road, Muth could recall the strange feeling he had when he opened the folder and saw the photo staring up at him. The man in the picture was middle-aged, but there was no doubt it was Helmut Schoener. He blinked and then slowly read the memo.

Schoener had become an agent for the Ministry's Administration for Reconnaissance, the German Democratic Republic's powerful covert foreign intelligence branch. His controllers had tapped him early to "defect" to West Germany, where he was guided through a series of schools and jobs until he was placed in the Luftwaffe. He had enlisted as a noncom for his mandatory two-year hitch, gotten out, entered Bonn Technical University, attained his electrical engineering degree, and reentered the Air Force, now as an officer specializing in the burgeoning field of computers in electronic intelligence. At that point the Soviets had decided that he was too much an asset to leave to the Germans, and had co-opted his services, commissioning him a captain in the GRU. It was quite a plum for Helmut; he held rank in three services—the West German Luftwaffe, the East German Administration for Reconnaissance, and the GRU. As he read Schoener's thick file, Muth felt a swift pang of envy. The scrawny, silent loner had become a hidden hero while he, Muth, wasted away deep in the bureaucracy.

But all was not perfect with "Peter," as he was known to the GRU and MFS. That was the reason for Muth's reading of the otherwise top-secret file. A tip had been given somewhere in the network that Schoener was not performing properly. There was, as always with such cases, the strong possibility of double-cross. Therefore, a detailed security check had to be pursued. There was so far no proof of actual wrongdoing, but neither the Ministry for State Security nor the GRU took chances. Muth's part of the investigation was to track down Schoener's cohorts from his Leipzig days who might be in the Army, the local Ministry of the Interior Alert Units or Combat Groups, and discover any contacts any of them might have had with him recently.

It had taken Muth only two weeks to discover that nobody on the list had so much as heard from Schoener. His father had disowned him; his mother refused to talk about him. He had no other family in Leipzig or elsewhere. Muth somewhat regretfully wrote a detailed report that cleared Schoener, closed the file, and sent it on. In the ensuing weeks he did not entirely forget the matter, but it sank from his sight.

But then on that rainy Thursday he had been called to his superior's office. He arrived expecting to discuss some administrative matter, was ushered in, and found himself eye to eye with Helmut Schoener. He was in mufti, dressed in nondescript civilian clothes. He could have been a postal clerk. Muth had been stunned into momentary silence. Schoener had smiled thinly, and his superior, Oberst Macklinberg, obviously had savored the moment.

"So, Oberstleutnant Muth, you do not know this man?" His tone was mock-serious.

For a dizzying heartbeat Muth wondered if Schoener was really under arrest, or suspicion, and if this was some sort of trap. He considered lying, then realized that Schoener would hardly have been brought to the administration HQ were that the case—he would be in the dank cells of the so-called sanitarium four blocks away.

"Of course, Herr Oberst. How are you, Helmut?" He stuck his hand out in greeting. Schoener had taken it in his bony, cold, clawlike hand and squeezed perfunctorily.

"Good, Oskar. And you?" His voice had not changed much. A little deeper, maybe, like the lines on his face.

Muth looked him over carefully. As always, his eyes were guarded, impossible to read. He was pale, gaunt, with thinning, receding hair. Hardly like an officer in the GRU, he thought.

"Oberst Schoener is here secretly," said Macklinberg, "for conferences. While he is here he will be referred to as Klaus Meyer, an architect. However, since you two are old friends, I thought you might enjoy a meeting." Macklinberg glanced at his watch. "Damn. I must go to lunch with the generalmajor. I trust you two can find your own?"

"Of course, Fritz," said Schoener. Fritz? thought Muth. First-name terms with the head of Administration 2000? His estimation of Schoener's standing went up several notches.

"Yes. Well, Helmut, see you at two. Until then, the *hofbräu* is good down the lane. Oskar knows it well." With that the colonel opened the door and bade them leave.

Muth followed Schoener out, and as Schoener collected his raincoat from the secretary, Muth said, "It's been a long time, Helmut."

Schoener made no attempt at light conversation. His smile had disappeared. "Yes. Shall we go?"

Lunch had been mostly silent until they reached the coffee. The *hofbräu* was jammed with people. It was smoky, noisy, almost impossible to converse in. They were crammed at a tiny round table, their wurst dishes still awaiting the harried waiter's attention. Schoener slowly stirred ersatz sugar into his thick black coffee, staring at the crowd at the bar. As he withdrew his spoon he looked Muth in the eye for the first time.

"Things have changed, Oskar. Have they not?"

Muth's defenses immediately went on alert. "Well, yes, in some ways."

Schoener snorted, looking around. "In all ways. You know I work in the West?"

Muth resisted the impulse to dart glances around to see who might be listening. "Helmut—!"

Schoener tossed the spoon down on the table. "Don't worry, Oskar. Nobody can hear us. I know. It's my job to know, you see? I'm a spy."

Muth shakily raised his cup to his lips. "Yes. Well," he said after he drew on the dark coffee, "maybe so. But it can't be good to speak of it in public."

"The public is the best place. But never mind. Are you surprised to see me?"

"Yes. Very."

"Good. I presume, since you were asked to review my file for possible treason, that you know the details of my work?"

Muth set the cup down. He looked at Schoener and said nothing. Schoener's expression didn't change. He seemed to be speaking without movement of his lips.

"I thought so. Now, I haven't much time, so I will be blunt, perhaps more blunt than I should be. Let me begin by telling you what I know about you. I know about Hannah. I know why she left you, I know how that affected your work in the infantry, I know about Michael's failure in school, his drinking, and his jail record, I know about Margot's activities with the so-called subversives in the university. I tell you all this to save time. You understand?"

Muth sat frozen. He stared, his mind numb.

"Now, let me ask you something. Are you happy?"

A reflexive laugh erupted from Muth. "What?"

Schoener did not smile. "I take it that means no."

"Who is happy these days? Who was ever happy?" countered Muth. He felt himself gripped by a fever. The crowd seemed to close in on him. He glanced around after all.

"You know who is to blame?"

"What the devil are you talking about? What do you mean, to blame? For what?"

"For Germany? For what has happened to us, Oskar. Listen. I know about your work for A-2000. I know that you have let off at least five offenders in the last year because you agreed with them. Three of them should have been shot, the other two sent to prison. Yet you arranged for them to escape punishment."

"Impossible. I do my job—"

"Yes. And very well, most of the time. Don't worry. The dolts in your building couldn't find this out in a thousand years. I tell you this to save us both time and effort, don't you see? Now, the question is, how willing are you to help?"

"Help?"

"Don't go stone-faced, Oskar. I need your help. To change things."

"I won't spy."

"I wouldn't ask you to."

"Then what?"

"More. Much more. Something right down your alley. Action."

Muth finished the coffee and carefully set the cup precisely in the center of the saucer. "You have lost your mind, Helmut. There is nothing anyone can do now. The world is as it is. None of us can change that."

"Wrong, Oskar. The world is as it is because there are half a million Russians in our country. Not to mention as many Americans, Frenchmen, and Britishers."

In spite of himself, Muth was engaged. "They have always been here."

"No. Not always. Only since the end of the war. Do you suppose they will be here forever?"

"Who knows? It's not my problem. I am an infantry officer. Let the politicians solve it."

"Are they solving it?"

"Why ask me?"

"Because you work in A-2000. You see the inside of the Army through its rebels, the nonconformists, the troublemakers. Tell me, are the numbers not growing? Is the dissent stilled? Are the defections slowing?"

Muth scowled. "You know the answer."

"Yes. I know." He paused. The waiter fought through the crowd, grabbed their plates, and was gone before they could ask more of him. Schoener leaned across the table. "Tell me, Oskar, do you think of yourself as a good socialist?"

"I am an officer in the Army."

"That's no answer."

"Well, I belong to the party."

"Of course. So does everyone. Answer the question."

"I don't know. Why do you ask these pointless questions?"

"To find out whether you are German or not."

Muth frowned. "What? Of course I'm German."

"Not *East* German?"

"Of course not. Just German. What the devil are you driving at, Schoener?"

"The future, Oberstleutnant Muth. The future. Think about it. We'll meet again in two months, and talk some more over lunch." And with that Schoener had abruptly shoved his chair back and made for the door.

Muth, caught by suprise, struggled to follow him. But by the time he made it through the crowd, Schoener had vanished again. When Muth met with Macklinberg the next morning for his usual eight o'clock briefing, neither man mentioned Schoener. It was as if he never existed. Only the memory of his words remained.

But that had been enough. Over the next weeks Muth chewed on them, relentlessly replaying the conversation in his mind, trying to discover some reason in the affair. The more he had thought about it, the less any of it made sense.

It wasn't as if he were not politically aware. What German could not be? But facts were facts. He knew them all well enough to know the futility of lunchtime discussions over coffee. His own department ruthlessly stamped out deviations from the safe party line. There was absolutely no chance of doing anything about the problems Schoener hinted at. A half-million Russians in the country? So what? It might as well be a million, two million. No organization existed to oust them—and Muth well knew it. Foreign intelligence people had been unable to do more than nibble at the status quo for years. All the intrigues of the Americans, British, Israelis, and others had managed to do little more than keep German and Soviet counterespionage units in top condition. Muth had been puzzled by it, once, when he realized how little actual effort was being expended in anti-GDR work. Then he recognized, at last, that the NATO people were almost as eager as the Soviets to keep Germany divided. It explained a lot.

Oskar Muth knew, once he had formulated the thought, that he would never pursue its consequences. As Schoener had intimated, they had broken whatever aspirations he had; Hannah, the party, the Army. He was unashamed the day he realized he had become a graying, middle-aged bureaucrat who had probably reached the apogee of his career in Administration 2000. He knew he was considered safely neutralized by his colleagues in the Army and by the Army itself. He knew, but did not care; the energy had left him. He was prepared to be philosophical about it.

But Helmut Schoener had not been content to be philosophical. He had not been content to cultivate a solid career in the service of the party. Nothing about Schoener was overtly charismatic, but the intensity that burned like a bright flame within him, the ferocity that he usually kept bottled like some rampaging genie until he wished to unleash it, as he had at the time of their first meeting, somehow mesmerized Muth. He hadn't recognized it at first, but as the months had passed, Muth couldn't get the meeting out of his mind. Despite himself, he was electrified by the hints Schoener had left. Action, he had said. What kind of action? He lay awake night after night, listening to the street noises of Leninstrasse outside his bedroom window, letting his imagination run free. *What kind of action?*

The left front wheel of his armored car suddenly dropped into a ditch, and Muth grabbed for the well-worn steel rail bolted to the dashboard. The BTR lurched sickeningly, but Marcks, as usual, was in control. The muscular Saxon sergeant rapidly jammed the gear lever into low and swung the wheel hard. The clumsy car groaned and churned through the bottom of the meter-wide ditch, filling the still forest air with fumes and noise. Once on the other side of the ditch, Marcks rolled to a halt. Ahead lay an even smaller road—two ruts, really—that wound through the primeval forest. Marcks looked questioningly at Muth.

"Correct, Marcks. Keep going. We're almost there," he said. Muth pulled the map from its case and checked it. Less than a kilometer through this grim stand of trees would be a meadow big enough for him to bivouac his people. For the 62 men of his two platoons, the camp would simply be another familiar part of the life he had accustomed them to, a welcome end to a day of travel, first by rail from the base, then by BRDM and BTR to the bivouac. But for Muth the bivouac was part of an answer—an answer to his question to Schoener, and to his deadened existence as a drifting bureaucrat. What kind of action? Schoener had said. This kind, my friend, this kind. And when he began to speak, Oskar Muth lost himself in the promise of a life with meaning.

It had begun in a *hofbräuhaus*. And it would continue

from this grassy meadow. Muth allowed himself a tiny smile, a mere fragment of the hot current that shot through him as the last vestiges of dreaminess fell away with every meter that the armored car rolled into the glistening wet grass of the meadow. This was no dream. This was reality. This was, at last, action.

——————————————————————**FIVE**

CONFIDENTIAL
NOFORN

Date: 031588
To: MG Henry, DCO/NATO-3 (US)
From: COL Gonzales, PA/NATO-2 (US)
Subject: BG von Grabow

1/Pursuant to your request for a backgrounder on
Luftwaffe Brigadegeneral von Grabow for your meeting 032188 re NATO airspace AOI/R, I tasked my
office for extraction of key personal/professional data.
Sources were standard Luftwaffe bio and US data
assets.

2/Full name: Friedrich von Grabow. DOB: 021335.
POB: Grabow Gutshof, near Schwerin, Staat-Mecklen-
burg. Parentage: father—Otto von Grabow, mother—
Klara von Grabow (von Schenk). Father was Gutsherr
(equivalent to English country squire); family business was the Gutshof (estate) —income from animals
and crops. Father not in Nazi Party 1933–45; due to

43

disability caused in WWI, excused war service. (WWI
service: cavalry officer. Retired as captain: Iron Cross,
earned at siege of Paris.) Postwar, father and son
expropriated to W. Germany (Emden) as "undesir-
ables" in GDR (1952). Mother killed by Allied bombs,
112344. Father established as Mercedes-Benz agent
in Emden (1953); son attended St. Josephus Acad-
emy (nr. Emden) until Abitur (no US equiv.—between
high-school diploma and college degree); 1955.

3/Career profile: joined Bundesgrenschutz (border
forces) 1955. Reached corporal by 1957; same year,
received requested transfer to Bundeswehr. Offizier-
schule 6/57; commissioned lieutenant 10/57. Transferred to Luftwaffe, 1/58. English language instruction,
Uetersen (for pilots only); preflight and primary, same
school. To Luke AFB, AZ, 11/58, trained as F84F
pilot. To FB-3 at Buechel as line pilot and sqdn A-2.
Luke AFB, 4/64 for F104G transition training. Staff
officer school, Neubiberg, 8/65. Fuehrungsakademie
(general staff course), Hamburg-Blankenese, 11/65–
12/67. A-2 at 4th Air Def Div, Kalkar, 1/68. CO,
Fliegende Gruppe 23 at FBW36, Rhein/Hopsten. Observer atch to HQ, PACAF (USAF), 2/73–9/73 (toured
all SEA facilities; flew 9 combat msns over North VN
with various fighter-bomber sqdns). Wing commander,
RW71 (Richtofen), 10/73–2/78, Wittmund. Luftwaffe
A-3 Ops at GAFTAC (German Air Force Tactical Air
Command), Koeln. Air Attache, German Embassy,
Washington D.C., 5/80–6/83. Commander, Sector Operations Center, Goch/Uedem, 7/83–present. Command
pilot, 4400 hours logged, rated in: F84F, F84G, F86G,
F104G, F105, FB111A, F15A, Tornado, Jaguar, C130E,
Transall, EC135H, E3A.

4/Family: married 081061 to Monika (Steiner), in
Longuich. Wife's DOB: 091940. Ex-schoolteacher,

daughter of prominent vintner in Trier area. Children: son, Herbert, born 052762, currently attending Freie Universitaet, Berlin.

5/Personal: hobbies: hunting (fox/horseback), golf, sailing, chess (was Bundeswehr champion, 1956). Languages: French, English, Russian.

6/Staff notes: BG von Grabow was tapped for highest Luftwaffe command early—expected to be CIC before retirement; command style known to be remote but detail-oriented; all units commanded showed markedly increased combat readiness after his tenure; politically conservative; formed no connections with any political groups in FRG or USA; socially adept at all levels (regularly eats at EM and NCO mess at every unit commanded); only known personal problem is son's involvement with left-wing groups in Berlin (incl. "Hausbesetzer," the squatters who occupied buildings to be torn down and replaced with luxury apartments). Holds highest security clearances in NATO, Luftwaffe; up to Category clearance, US. Formed close friendships with many US officers due to extended stays in USA; known to be friendly force in NATO; has four times diverted attempts to reduce US effectiveness in NATO opns (cf, FOLs [memo 991, 081284], AOIs [memo 1230, 030985], 'first strikes' [memo 1466, 111285], 'special weapons security' [memo 1500, 020286]).

7/Summary: Bob, as you can see, since the issue for the conference is areas of interest/responsibility for the sector operations centers, I don't think "Freddy" will be a problem. Bill D.'s people say he supports us in the need to deepen the zones for our operations, and can be expected to sway the Brits, French, and Belgians, should they hang tough. Let us know if you need more.

SIGNED

Leonard D. Gonzales, COL
PA/NATO-2
HQ USF, Brussels 18

CONFIDENTIAL
NOFORN

SIX

"Here you are, sir. Thirteen-A Heldstrasse. That's the one on the left."

Max glanced out the window of the blue Chevy station wagon. The corporal idled the car slowly by the three-story apartment building. Moss looked it over. It seemed brand new, like the rest of the concrete apartment buildings on the street. The driver cursed under his breath. There were, as usual in this section of Berlin-Dahlem, no parking spaces. The one in front of Heldstrasse 13 was taken up by a shiny red Porsche 944.

"Sorry, Lieutenant. Too many Americans in this area, I guess."

"I guess so," said Max. Dahlem was the site of the U.S. Mission, a big complex of headquarters for the American diplomatic and military people in Berlin, and naturally for both security and convenience reasons every attempt was made to house Americans as close to the mission as possible. Since he was going to be commuting to the other Mission—the U.S. Military Mission in Potsdam, about five klicks away, over the Wall—Max didn't much care

where they put him. So the Army corporal's concern was
wasted on him.

"Look," Max said as the driver crept along Heldstrasse,
scanning vainly for a parking place, "don't worry about it.
Just double-park back there and I'll offload my stuff and
you can get back."

"Oh, no problem, sir," said the fat corporal. He grinned
and pushed his GI-issue glasses back up his nose. "I'm in
no hurry. Besides, I know what it's like, in-processing all
day. You must be beat, sir."

Max rubbed his cheek. The stubble was coming back
despite his having shaved on the C-141 over the Atlantic.
How many hours ago? Seven? Eight? It didn't matter.
When the big transport had nosed into the typical low
cloud over Berlin, Max had already been into that dehy-
drated, aching daze that comes at the end of a long military-
style flight. When the airplane had touched down, Max
had resisted looking out the window until the last moment,
and then saw the familiar outlines of Gatow airport.

They'd arranged the flight so that it arrived early in the
morning, and as Max collected his bags he knew that he'd
spend most of the day in what the military euphemistically
called "in-processing." Even for officers whose work was
"special," it required endless patience to work through the
myriad tiny details of signing in to a new station. Berlin
Command was no exception. The only difference between
this time and the last time he'd checked in here was that
his new rank bought him a few perks, such as a sponsoring
officer who'd taken care of as many of the more irritating
details as he could. But still, it had taken almost five hours
to grind through the inevitable bureaucracy. So the enlisted
driver's solicitous concern for his having to hump his own
bags up the short flight of stairs to Heldstrasse 13 irked
him.

"Yeah. Beat. So let's get it over, shall we? Spin this
sucker around and let me off back there." His voice

sounded gravelly even to himself. Normally he might be more friendly. But the corporal was right: he was beat.

The young driver ceased being ebullient. He nodded and accelerated the wagon to the end of the short street. Traffic crept along the cross street, and at the first break he nailed the throttle and hauled the Chevy into a tight U-turn. Max fought a thin smile. The kid wouldn't last a minute against the Vopos.

Across from the red Porsche he stopped and jumped out. Max unfastened his seat belt and followed, feeling a thousand years old. The corporal already had two of his bags. Max collected his B-4 bag and his hanging garment bag and followed him across the little road. They went up the short flight of entry stairs into a foyer with a row of mailboxes. The driver stopped at a door beside the elevator, and as the corporal fumbled with the bags and the key, Max noted the little brass clip above the doorbell, where a nameplate was obviously supposed to go.

"Who makes the nameplates for these?" he asked.

The corporal finally unlocked the door and swung it open. He shoved his glasses back up his nose and peered at the clip.

"Oh—nobody, Lieutenant. We stopped that after the bombing."

"The bombing?"

The corporal collected his bags and struggled through the door. A faint, closed, musty odor wafted out into the foyer from the apartment.

"Yessir. We've had a little problem with terrorists around here. Didn't they tell you? Anyway, we lost a couple of people over by the Free University."

"Ah," said Max. The Free University was only five blocks away.

"So anyway, sir, here you are. Manifest for the furnishings is here in the welcome packet—sign it asap, please, and return it to 2177—you've got the standard ninety-day essentials kit, and otherwise it's fully furnished and all yours.''

Moss hung his garment bag in the little closet near the door and looked around the apartment. Furnishings were sparse, but they were clean and serviceable. A tiny bedroom sprouted off to one side of the equally tiny living room, as did a bathroom, a kitchen, and another room that was set up with a blond-wood dinette. It resembled nothing so much as a smallish, pale imitation of a Holiday Inn suite in Columbus, right down to the institutionally nondescript coloring of the carpet, walls, and even the piece of art that hung over the beige couch. But it certainly beat a BOQ.

"Thanks, corp," Max said, making a final effort to smile. "Appreciate your help. Let me know if I can do anything for you."

The corporal smiled back, only this time there was a sharkish aspect to his features. Max recognized it as the garrison veteran's look, a mixture of cynicism, self-promotion, and I-can-get-it-wholesale arrogance. "Thanks, Lieutenant. Maybe I will. Anyway, your phone book lists everything you'll need. Good luck, sir."

Max waved and the corporal closed the door as he left. Max stood a moment in the center of the little living room, not really looking at anything, but feeling Berlin come back. He went to the window next to the couch and cranked it open. The view was of the building next to this one. He sank onto the couch and closed his eyes.

Slowly the odors, noises, and images were coalescing again into the familiar. Max inhaled and tasted the peculiar electric quality of Berlin's air. Here in Dahlem they were miles away from the big industrial estates in Spandau, across the Grunewald and the Havelsee. And yet Berlin's air, even on a wet March day like this one, carried the same kind of ionized charge that Los Angeles's smog delivered. Berlin was built on a huge sandy marsh, but it had none of the weighty air of an English city in a similar circumstance. The low cloud scudding quickly from northeast to southwest overhead was typical, and might have been one reason for the bright colors Berliners loved. Max thought of the brilliant red Porsche parked outside, and smiled. Then his eyelids drooped, the smile faded, and he fell soundly and firmly asleep.

He awoke with a start. Sensations competed for his attention. His neck ached ferociously. His left arm was numb. And it was all but pitch dark. He blinked and struggled upright, recalling where he was and why. He forced his left arm up to check the time. The luminescent dial glowed eerily in the darkness. It was nearly eight o'clock. He'd been asleep almost four hours. He groaned softly and stood up.

He switched on the lights, and with them his move-in mode. Since the apartment had been specifically arranged for single officers like him, it was easy. Within fifteen minutes he had all his gear stowed and was standing in the shower under a typically German fierce needle spray of hot water. When he had shaved and dressed in his wool slacks and white turtleneck sweater, he felt as though he'd been through a whole day. A quick glance through the little refrigerator's starter kit of food—which the Army supplied to every newcomer free of charge—made him wince. Somebody had thoughtfully stocked it with good old American delicacies, but none appealed to him, least of all the six-pack of Pabst Blue Ribbon. The most common beer in the military these days, it was known, in unintentional self-mockery of the military style, as PBR. Max grimaced and let the door close. He checked the time again. First things first, then out for some food downtown; God knew there was nothing decent in the Dahlem area. Too many Amis.

He flopped on the couch, plucked up the telephone

receiver, and dialed Christie's number, referring for the last two digits to his battered old leather notebook. It surprised him faintly that he'd forgotten her number. But then, it had been nearly a year and a half since he'd spoken to her. When he had been convalescing in Wiesbaden he'd imagined that he could take a month or so in England and simply be with her for a while. But no such luck, of course. As soon as they'd known he was going to recuperate without complications, they'd packed him off to the first of the service intelligence courses as though getting him out of Europe were of major strategic importance. So, despite his good intentions, he'd never called her. Or, he realized with a pang, written. Maybe she would understand. She always did.

The connection was finally made to Cambridge. The familiar double ring came and went, four times. Then it was answered.

"Four-six-five-double-four," said a cheery female voice.

"Hello? Christie?"

"Sorry?" said the voice. He realized now that it didn't belong to Christie.

"Oh—is Dr. Greenwood there? Christine Greenwood?"

There was a pause, the line hissed and crackled.

"No. I'm sorry. Dr. Greenwood isn't here. May I help you?"

"Uh—this is Lieutenant Moss. Do you know when she'll return?"

"Leftenant—Moss? Max Moss?"

"Yes, that's right. Lieutenant Moss. Max. Did she leave a message for me?"

There was another pause. Then the woman said, "Well, Leftenant, she doesn't live here anymore, you see."

"Ah. Of course. It has been a while. Am I to call her at a new number?"

Another pause.

"No, I'm afraid not. The opposite, rather."

"The opposite? What do you mean?"

"Look, this is rather embarrassing. I'm a former student of Dr. Greenwood's, and—"

"Sure, sure. I get it. But what's the message?"

The young woman on the other end took a deep breath. "Well, she told me that if a Yank named Moss called, I was to tell him to, um, piss off."

Max blinked. "What?"

"To piss off, I'm afraid."

"Right. Okay. Got it. Now, do you have her new number?"

"Yes . . . but she told me not to give it out, especially—"

"Miss, I've known Dr. Greenwood a long time. I'm calling from Berlin, long distance, and I'd really appreciate it if you'd help me straighten this out. Now, can you give me her number?"

The English girl's tone hardened perceptibly, and the steel that lay always beneath even the most genteel Englishwoman began to show through.

"As I've *said,* Leftenant Moss, she left strict instructions. So you see, even though I'd like to help, I can't. Sorry."

"Of course I can see. But—"

"Good evening, Leftenant."

Click.

Max listened to the buzzing line for a moment, then slowly lowered the receiver. Well, what the hell did he expect? He and Christie had been an item, on and off, for a long time. But always on his terms. He'd gone off that night in Cambridge, leaving her his prized Lotus as a kind of offering, compensation for his lousy behavior. Then, within the next two years, he'd been able to see her only once, when he'd been named team chief. And then—

Then another year and a half of silence from him. What could he expect? He conjured her image: medium tall, slender, long golden hair in tight curls, a sweet oval face with huge brown eyes that spoke of quick wit and ready laughter. How could he expect someone like that to wait forever for him, when he never promised her anything?

He couldn't. And he understood the piss-off message to be an eloquent farewell from her. Neither one of them was any damned good at good-byes. Christie had loved him; he knew that as well as he knew how he loved her.

In her own delicately ruthless manner she had understood his last year's silence as evidence of some fundamental emotional flaw in him, a flaw that stubbornly refused to go away. She had waited a long, long time. But there had come a day when the time ran out, when she felt, perhaps, her own time slipping away—time for a family, for a settled life—and ceased waiting. So she had told him to piss off, in absentia.

Max stared at the neutral beige wall and tried to swallow the message whole. But it went down like a lump of cold stone into his gullet. It was over. It *felt* over, for the first time.

He was suddenly ravenously hungry. Outside, the ululating wail of a Berlin police car cut through the usual distant traffic noises. A city was the best tonic. Especially this city, which lived a hair-trigger existence, surrounded on all sides by the grim pressure of an alien way of life. East Germany pressed up against the Wall like a horde of silent, gaunt prisoners, their physical and psychic hunger for the West an omnipresent pressure. So there was nowhere like Berlin to lose yourself in food and drink and manic escape.

Max jumped up, grabbed his tweed jacket, and was through the door, pulling it closed before he had time to think further. All at once he needed Berlin desperately. The door latched and he turned, shrugging into his jacket. Still turned inward, he almost knocked over the figure just coming through the foyer door.

"Bitte um Verzeihung," he said quickly, *"ich moechte gern*—oh. Sorry, uh, Captain."

The figure was a woman. An American Army officer who held a plastic bag full of groceries in her right hand, a leather attaché case in her left. Captain's bars gleamed on her raincoat and hat. A black purse was tucked under her left arm.

She regarded him calmly with blue-gray almond-shaped eyes. A sweep of straw-blond hair curved across her forehead, but she wore the rest very short. Tiny pearls gleamed on her earlobes. Her face was high-cheekboned, with a slightly pointed chin and strong jawline. As she looked Max over, her eyebrows arched slightly and her lips, which were wide and mobile, twitched into a tiny smile. Little dimples like half moons appeared as she watched him blush.

The moment stretched embarrassingly. Still slightly fuddled by his mood, Max fought to clear his mind, to make sense of the scene.

"Uh, I'm in thirteen A now. Max—"

"—Moss. Right. I know. Sandy Koppel. I'm in B, across the hall. Glad to meet you, Max."

Max grinned. "News travels fast around here."

"No faster than anywhere else. I'm at Potsdam."

"Oh. In that case, how about my giving you a hand with your groceries?"

"Great." She handed him the net bag, which seemed to weigh at least fifty pounds. Max took the weight with some surprise. She was shortish—about five-three—but obviously strong. He followed her to the doorway across from his. She set her attaché case down, reached into her purse, and withdrew her keys. Max smiled behind her back; she was the first woman he'd ever known who could pull her keys out the first time.

"Home sweet home," she said, and led him inside. Her apartment was a mirror image of his, so he took the groceries into the little kitchen while she peeled off her raincoat by the entry closet.

"How do you like your place?" she asked as she came into the kitchen. Max smiled at her. Even in her Army Class A uniform he could see she had a good figure. She also wore three rows of ribbons. Max guessed her age as around his.

"Can't complain," he said.

"Well, you could, but you wouldn't get anywhere. Finished in-processing?"

"About six hours ago. Barely had time to unpack."

She pulled out the vegetables and stuffed them into a tidy refrigerator. "Groggy?"

"Not anymore. Got a few hours sleep."

She straightened up and looked up at him, still smiling faintly. "Dinner plans?"

"None. Yet."

"Great. Let me take you out, Max Moss. How about it?"

Taken slightly aback, Max blushed. "Well—"

"I hate eating alone almost more than anything, don't you?"

"Now that you mention it, yes. Sure. Let's go. Only I'll take you out."

She shook her head. "No way, José. This is your official welcome-to-Berlin dinner, the one Charlie Kemp would've given you if he hadn't had to take care of Karen tonight."

"Charlie?"

"Kemp, Charles, bull colonel, U.S. Army. Your boss. Wife, Karen Anne. Now among the multitudes stricken by the Berlin Crud. Got it?" She waited for him to nod, then said, "Glad we got it clear. Booze is in the corner cabinet. I'll take a Cinzano on the rocks. You can have either a beer—German only, no PBRs—or a Cinzano on the rocks.

Haven't made it to the Class VI store since last week's party. Sorry.''

Before he could answer she had disappeared around the corner. Max looked around the kitchen and found the cabinet. He pulled out the Cinzano bottle. The Rolling Stones suddenly burst out from the living room. He smiled as he poured.

The Stones suited his mood perfectly. He sat on her couch and sipped his sweet Cinzano, letting the beat wash over him. Unlike his living room, Sandy's really looked as if it were intended for living. Somehow she had taken the same GI furniture and arranged and augmented it with deft little touches to make it seem warm and homey. He snorted to himself; the classic cliché: a woman's touch. The trouble was, it was true.

Sandy suddenly appeared. She plucked her drink off the coffee table and took a swallow. Out of her uniform she projected exactly the same aura; she was evidently one of those rare women whose personality couldn't be changed by clothes. She wore black suede pants tapered at the ankle, almost heelless black loafers, red stockings, a red V-neck sweater, and a black, hip-length coat in the latest European—that is, shapeless—style. By her dress she might have been a young, professional Berliner. But her merry, direct eyes and her carriage instantly branded her as American. She obviously knew, and couldn't care less.

"Ready?" she asked.

"Sure." Max gulped his drink and stood up.

He felt a little odd. This wasn't a date; this was one officer going out with another for dinner, at least ostensibly. The fine points of the etiquette were handled by Sandy, and Max was grateful. He had never worked with women before, especially women who were his equals or superiors, so he had only the vaguest notion of how to handle the matter of dinner. Everything about her spoke of a colleague; yet there was inevitably the issue of sex lying just under the surface. Max gave himself over to her, the junior officer to the senior. Yet because of his age and hers, the relationship was a little forced while they were in civilian clothes. All this ran through his mind in confused bursts as she shut off the stereo, left the glasses in the sink, and turned off lights in a single, efficient sweep through the apartment on the way to the door. In seconds, it seemed, they were back in the foyer.

"Taxi?" Max asked as she pulled the door locked.

"Nah," she said, grinning. "We'll take my car. C'mon."

Max followed, playing what'll-she-drive with himself. Although he no longer raced, he considered himself a connoisseur of cars and people and the matchups between them, and so it was his conceit that he could determine which was hers before they got to it. Heldstrasse was a short street, newly carved out of two old blocks of houses, and he scanned the cars jammed along its curbs under the bright mercury-vapor streetlights. Sandy clacked down the steps just ahead of him, and he thought he spotted it: a battered blue Volvo on the other side.

She stopped next to the door of the red Porsche and inserted the key. The electric locks snicked open. Max grinned ruefully.

"Yours?"

"Yup. Got the good one too. Took for*ever* for the weenies in the concession to figure out that I really didn't want an automatic, and that I had to have the Turbo."

She slipped into the driver's seat while Max buckled up. The engine caught on her first crank. Max, intrigued, watched her carefully. Most people do not start their cars properly; as soon as it comes to life, they start to destroy their engine by revving it before the oil has gotten to its vitals—plain, roller, and needle bearings. In any turbo-charged engine, care must be taken to ensure that the oil gets to the turbine bearings before the turbine is spun hard, or the crucial little device will eat itself. Out of the corner of his eye Max watched Sandy Koppel as she cocked her head, listening to the engine and keeping an eye on the oil pressure gauge. In spite of himself, Max was impressed.

"Had this long?"

"A year, about. Since I got here." She nodded almost imperceptibly when the pressure pleased her. "It's been a good car. Vastly overpriced, but worth it on the autobahns and out in the country." She snicked it into gear and turned to look over her shoulder. She grinned at him. "But I guess you know all about that stuff."

"A little," Max said. How much could she know about him anyway?

She pulled out and started off. The heat began to flow from the vents into the car, and the chill March weather receded outside the tinted glass. Max noted the spotless interior. The leather smelled as if it had been well taken care of; in spite of its citified life, this car reflected knowledge and care.

As he ticked off how different all this was from the cars driven by most of the women he knew, Max realized that he had always used their cars as a measure against even the women he had loved. It had somehow seemed fitting that no matter what their intellectual or professional attainments might be, they would inevitably have cars that reflected inability to cope with machinery on every level. They might be able to drive, but not to understand a car properly. As Sandy halted at the cross street, Max knew he had found somebody whose values and behavior challenged his unwitting prejudices.

"A little, my ass," she said at length, still smiling. "I've read the reports, Max Moss. And you're a little bit of a legend back there in Potsdam, you know." She allowed a truck to pass, then nailed the throttle. The Porsche squirted out into the heavy traffic on the busy Clayallee. "Sportsman 300 winner, Recovery jock, Christ—

even Nubs Pierce thinks you can drive. And that's saying something.''

Max blushed again, but luckily this time she couldn't see it. "Nubs. Jesus. How is he anyway?"

"Gone. Back to Razorback Central, I guess. Just like Ike Wilson."

"Yeah. I figured Ike would be gone."

There was a new overlay on the situation now. Koppel obviously knew his whole file, knew that until recently he had been an enlisted man. He had learned, long ago, to ignore his unease at his rise from the ranks, as unsought and unwanted as it might have been. But at times like this he wished fervently that he was just another trade-school graduate or an ROTC product, like the officers around him.

Koppel darted a glance at him. "Hey. How about the Istanbul Express? You know it?"

"Sure. Haven't been there in a long time. Great dolmades." He kept his tone as light as possible. The evening was not going to be as easy to get through as he'd hoped.

"And even better baklava. You got it." She dropped a gear and whipped around a slow Mercedes, then shot up an on ramp to the Stadtring. Two hundred fifty horsepower shoved Max back in the seat as the turbo spooled up to its maximum boost. He closed his eyes and tried to relax.

Sensing his mood, Koppel concentrated on driving. She switched on the radio, and they sped toward the restaurant in a tight cocoon of warmth and music, punctuated by the distant, muted whine of the turbocharger.

"There it is," Koppel said, inclining her head to the right.

Max didn't even have to look; he knew the district too well. It hadn't changed a bit. Jammed with people, cars, motorbikes, bicycles, garishly lit, vibrating like a guitar string. It was as close to Hamburg as Berlin got. The

Express lay off the main street and down a tiny alley. Sandy slowed at the entrance to the alley, peering down it. Of course, there were no parking places. She halted momentarily and then swung the nose of the car down the alley. Max raised his eyebrows at her.

"I have a little understanding with the cops." She grinned.

"I hope so. Last time I did this it cost me fifty marks."

She crept past the doorway to the Express, then stopped and reversed the Porsche back so that the tail poked slightly into the entry zone of the restaurant. She worked the wheel back and forth until the nose was tucked tightly against the flanks of a dilapidated Renault minicar parked along the wall. She glanced both ways along the alley, then allowed the turbocharger thirty seconds to spool down before she shut off the engine.

Max considered saying something about how the Renault had Essen license plates, about how the guy would probably simply climb over her car's hood to get into his, power his way out of his parking place, and tear off the Porsche's left front fender, lip spoiler, and bumper in doing so. But what the hell. It was her car. He got out.

Like the district, the Istanbul Express hadn't changed in the past year. Originally it had been a real Turkish hangout, a place for the working-class *Gastarbeiter* who toiled in the Spandau factories to come for a taste of home. When Max found it, the atmosphere had been filthy with dense hash smoke, the floor sticky with spilled sweet tea, the noise almost indescribable, a mixture of Turkish yelled at close quarters and discordant, nerve-jangling music pounded out by a disreputable band apparently specializing in obscure songs from the homeland, danced obscenely by a belly dancer whose seven veils all came off during her performance. It had been a dive, pure and simple. But it also boasted the finest Turkish food in the city, at prices that the working stiffs could afford. The inevitable result in Berlin, as in any Western metropolis, was swift and merciless gentrification. And now, in place of the chaos, a well-lit, clean, and appealing little restaurant lay beyond the veils over the doorway.

Max fell in beside Koppel as she brushed the veils aside. Soft background music wafted from a muted band. Well-dressed diners clustered around low brass tables, some sitting on little chairlike cushions, some simply sprawled, leaning on piles of pillows. White-clad waiters glided through the dimly lit dining room, turbaned and belted with dashing cummerbunds. Contrasting this scene with the one he had first encountered, Max always grinned. The captain approached, a small, oily man with receding hair, a weak chin, and obsequious eyes. He was dressed in a perfectly tailored dinner jacket with a red carnation. He had evidently seen too many Bogart movies.

Something about Sandy's stance and Max's distance from her alerted the captain to the need for caution. He stopped a few feet from them and flicked his oily smile back and forth between them, speaking not to him or to her but to them both. In Turkey there would be no question about whom to address. But this was Berlin.

"Good evening," he said in English thick with too precisely weighted syllables. "Is it dinner?"

"It is," said Sandy, staring him down. "For two. And, captain—my car is outside. A Porsche. Please inform me if there is a problem."

He nodded, then ushered them to a brass table. They sank down. Max peeled off his jacket. Sandy did likewise. He was unable to halt an instinctive glance at her breasts, and winced inwardly. Old habits die hard. If she noticed, she ignored it.

A turban and cummerbund appeared, asked if they wanted a menu, took their order when they declined, and slid away. The band grew a trifle louder, and a dancer appeared.

"Good moves, but lousy tits." Sandy smiled.

Max halted his eyebrows in time. He'd imagined that he was mostly incapable of surprise from women. He was obviously dead wrong.

Their drinks arrived. Sandy raised her glass to Max. "Welcome back, Max Moss."

"Thanks," he said, forcing a smile. The clear Turkish liquor went down like napalm.

She put her glass down and looked at him. "You don't sound too happy."

"I'm not, frankly."

"Why not?"

"Oh, you know. Onward and upward. That sort of thing. Coming back here is—"

"Just coming back. Got it. Still, there are worse assignments. Idaho, for example. Besides, at least here you know the deal."

"Well, not quite. I knew one kind of deal. Not this one. This analysis is a whole new ball game."

"*Tell* me about it." She grimaced slightly.

"You weren't born to the game?"

"Hardly. My old man was an infantry type. The Queen of Battles, and like that. So was I—for a while."

Max's eyebrows rose again. "Infantry? A woman? As in guns and marching and like that?"

"Yeah. Like that."

"How'd you pull that off? I thought the weaker sex was relegated to support work?"

"Special program." She glowered at her drink.

"Why'd you switch?"

She regarded him for a moment with hooded eyes.

"You know much about the Army?"

Max chalked one up for compartmentalized reporting procedures. She knew a lot about him from his files—but not everything. She didn't know about Major General Eric Moss, U.S. Army Retired.

"A little."

"Well, I knew a lot by the time they gave me a platoon of grunts. I knew about the problems I'd have as a female officer—I thought. But I was flatass wrong." She paused and took a deep pull on her drink. "I did everything better than everybody in the goddamn battalion. I could shoot better, march better, last longer on exercises, the works. My people always won any brigade competitions. And that's what got me."

"Let's see. The dame's too good. Get rid of her. Right?"

"Right first time. It got pretty dirty. They couldn't fire me, and thank God the honchos are so damn scared of being caught in pure prejudice that they couldn't just ease me out or cancel the program the way they used to, on no pretext at all. They tried to kick me upstairs—'perfect staff material,' they said—but when I refused, the boys got tough. They sent in the first team."

"And?"

She swigged again. "And they won. The guy was sweet, compassionate, tough, a superb company commander, intelligent. Robert Redford and Jim Gavin combined."

Max stared into his drink. Somehow he had lost the thread. But she was talking to herself now. He said nothing.

"The bastards planned it perfectly. They were all trade-school types, see? West Pointers stick together, and like that. So was he. Meticulous planning, perfect execution. Frontal assault was out, so they flanked me. Why am I telling you this?"

He shook his head. "Dunno. Why?"

"Maybe because I feel a little sorry for you. Christ knows you've been through the wringer. When Charlie told me that the exec couldn't stand in for him to meet you tonight, I thought it was pretty lousy treatment. But then I read your file. I think they're all a little afraid of you, Max Moss." She blinked. "Jesus, why the hell did I say *that*? Must be the booze."

"Must be." Warning bells began to go off in Max. She

looked tough, acted tough, probably worked like a demon. But she was desperately unhappy about something, and it weakened her when she drank.

She sat up straighter. "Erase the whole conversation, Lieutenant. Welcome to Berlin."

"Erased, Captain. Thanks." He lifted his glass again. She seemed to regain her sharpness a little too easily. Newly trained in understanding nuances of behavior, Max began to wonder if she was using the unhappy-drunk pose to flush out any of his weaknesses.

It suddenly occurred to him that he didn't even know what she did in the Mission. That made him think of Jaggard, the counterespionage trainer at Lowry. The question had been trust, and now to ensure it, how to obtain it. Jaggard had led them through five hours of discussion, then brought them to the ultimate truth of their work: trust was only a weapon. Nothing more. When you found yourself trusting someone—no matter for what motives—the weapon was aimed at you. She had somehow enmeshed him so that he was already trusting that her story was true. But he no longer had the luxury of such transactions. Jaggard had promised that with experience they would all build that understanding into their every waking moment. It was taking him longer than Jaggard might have approved.

"So," he said, "from the infantry to Potsdam. What do you do now?"

"Technology," she said.

"Ours?"

"Theirs."

"Sounds interesting."

"It is. How about you?"

"You read the file."

"I did. And it just says 'general duties.' "

"Well, then, general duties it is."

Their turban-and-cummerbund materialized. Before he served them, the waiter sprinkled rose water over their

hands, then offered steaming towels. He carefully placed
the dishes of diced lamb, couscous, and dolmades on the
table and set a big basket of bread between them. The
pita-style bread would serve as their utensils. Sandy grabbed
a piece and scooped dextrously into the couscous. Max
waited until she had a mouthful, then said, "About the
file. How come you had access to it?"

She swallowed and grinned. "General duties of my
own."

"Like?"

"Like security."

"Convenient."

"Yes, isn't it? Try the lamb."

He tried the lamb. It fell apart in his mouth, succulent,
not too dry, not too greasy. Somehow the Express had
survived gentrification and the expansion of its menu from
purely Turkish food to a vague sort of Mediterranean fare.
Sandy watched him savor it. She smiled.

"Good, huh?"

"Good."

She raised her glass again. "Welcome to Berlin," she
said.

"That's the third time you've said that," Max chided.

"Then I must mean it." She smiled broadly, still holding her glass up. Max raised his own and touched hers.

As they drank, the dancer finished her routine and was
rewarded by a scattering of polite applause. Max glanced
surreptitiously around at the patrons. They were mostly in
their thirties, professionals. He noted their expensive clothing, their open mannerisms, and healthy faces. They were
as different from the old clientele as could be imagined.
He stopped in mid-scan across a mirror and locked eyes
for a split-second with a man sitting alone, half-hidden in a
corner. In any other place it might have been anything
from an accidental contact to an expression of sexual
interest. But this wasn't any other place. Despite the

gentrification, despite the politesse and the light laughter, this was still Berlin.

Max glanced at Sandy. Her smile had faded slightly. She held his eyes with her own steady gaze, and nodded almost imperceptibly in the direction of the man in the corner. "Kaslov. GRU. Zossen. He likes the lamb too," she said.

Max felt his mouth go dry. Until now, this very moment, everything that had happened to him since he had awakened in that guarded ward in Wiesbaden had seemed almost unreal, as events piled one on top of another faster than he could absorb them. He shuddered suddenly, as if a cold draft passed across his neck. All the training, all the semi-unreal simulations of this moment snapped into blindingly sharp focus. Somewhere inside he had considered it all a kind of game. But the game had gotten serious. He was not in Colorado or Louisiana. He was in Berlin, where all games are serious, and looks kill.

He did not consider himself a brave man, but he was ashamed that his hands trembled. He felt as if he were in the locus of a dozen spotlights, accused of some crime and guilty of it. Accustomed to the hazards of the racetrack and the dangers of wild chases through the East German countryside, calm in the face of sudden death on wheels, he was unnerved by the reality in which he found himself. The simple words *intelligence officer* now seemed sinister beyond belief. He struggled to get his mind going, to recall all the right moves from his endless lessons. But all he could do was draw a shaky breath.

Sandy watched him intently. He knew, somehow, that she was measuring him. She still wore a smile, but it was overpowered by the look with which she held him. Suddenly the smile blossomed out again, and he fed on it hungrily.

"It's like your first combat," she said in the sort of

tones one might use to discuss a lawn problem, "but it passes quickly. Try the couscous."

His hand reached for the bread by itself, already trembling less. By the time he had scooped the couscous into the pita, the dreadful moment had indeed passed. It did not occur to him to wonder how she might know what a first combat was like. But later, when he lay alone in his new bed at Heldstrasse 13A, he suddenly remembered that the ribbon at the head of the three colorful rows of service decorations on her uniform tunic represented the Silver Star.

SEVEN

The idea from the beginning of the exercise had of course been secrecy, but by 2100, the battery commander was beginning to think they had been too successful. For four days he and his men had been operating semi-independently deep in the Hohenfels exercise area. His contacts with Brigade and AFCENT HQ had been, as planned, few and infrequent. The nine Pershing IIAs of Bravo Battery, 5th Battalion, 56th Field Artillery had been meant to slide out from under the noses of those Soviet spies outside the compound at Neu Ulm, and they had apparently done just that.

Not that you could hide the twenty-seven vehicles, nine officers, three warrant officers and 198 enlisted men of Bravo. No way. What you did was send both Charlie and Bravo out on the same day under secret orders. Once clear of the compound, Charlie would head north, Bravo south. And both would carry identical markings. Both would appear to be equipped with live nukes. In reality, only Bravo would have them, at least during this exercise.

It all made so much sense when the colonel had briefed it back at the casern. Morale had been high when they'd

69

left. The men enjoyed the secrecy. But four days of mud and rain and cold food had eroded morale to the point where efficiency had dropped dramatically. His guys were tired, hungry, and dispirited, and the captain commanding Bravo Battery knew it. So it was vital that the promised hot food arrive when it was supposed to. Of course it hadn't.

He peered out the door of the command van at his bivouac. A few tents clustered nearby were visible in the glow of the van's interior lights. But the rest were blacked out, as ordered. They were playing war rules in this exercise, at least until the planned dinner arrived. The CO had promised a hot-chow break for three hours before they'd have to go back to the routine. That had been four hours ago.

The captain looked through the sheets of chill rain to where he knew his launchers would be. The forest at Hohenfels was perfect for a Pershing battery; the pine and spruce were spaced just right to fit one of the big German MAN erector-launchers into a little clearing. The cables from his nine missiles snaked back through the dark mud to this van, plugged in and ready to carry the launch message and target coordinates anytime. Naturally this being exercise time only, even though the missiles were armed, the protective action link codes would remain secure and unused in the command safe. And without the nine-digit PAL sequence, the Pershings were just so much solid fuel and wiring. His boys had done well; they'd sited, erected, and simulated a launch against Czech targets already today. Not only that, they'd "captured" a "hostile" patrol that had sniffed them out, so that the OpFor CO still didn't know exactly where in this god-forsaken 30,000 acres of mud Bravo was. And still no chow.

The rain dribbled stubbornly onto his Kevlar helmet liner, making a noise like someone urinating onto a tin roof. He sighed and stepped back inside the van. One of the warrants at the command board asked if he wanted to call Brigade to verify the chow. The captain told him to keep radio silence. Then he told him that war was hell. The warrant didn't smile. Like everybody else in the battery, he slept in a cold tent too.

The battery commander studied the situation map behind the Lucite pane. The opposing forces were studded all around his bivouac. His assignment was to evade contact as long as possible, launching on coded messages from Brigade. This was supposed to simulate the real thing, in which everybody from SACEUR down figured that the Soviets would slam into the 7th Army and scatter its elements like tenpins, despite the armored boys' best efforts. The plan was to use the various elements' mobility against the juggernaut while a second wave counterattack formed up. They called it the "everybody works, everybody fights" scenario. Cooks, clerks, the works. So his missile battery was supposed to operate as though his boys were guards, grunts, and crack commandos all in one.

So far it hadn't been too bad. They'd been able to maneuver much more swiftly and quietly than he'd thought possible. The troops had gotten into the spirit of the thing. But enough was goddamn well enough. The food they'd carried in on their spare five-tons was about to run out. Just like everybody's spirits.

In the manner of all field commanders, the captain worried about his pickets. He had fifteen men detailed from his three firing platoons to stand guard duty. He knew they'd be trying to shelter beneath trees, huddled in ponchos, wondering what the hell they were doing there. He had a slew of good NCOs, but they couldn't keep these guys up for the games forever. The young captain sucked in his cheeks and wondered where the food wagons were.

He should have wondered why ninety-eight Germans were gathering on a farm near the perimeter of the Hohenfels exercise area, only five miles from his bivouac. But he didn't know about them. He didn't know that they were donning Bundeswehr combat uniforms even though most were not in the German Army. He didn't know that they carried nerve gas projectors. And he certainly didn't know that they had code-named his bivouac BLOOD.

EIGHT

Monika and Frau Hassan cleared the table as Friedrich von Grabow reached for his cigar. At the other end of the table Helmut Schoener sipped cognac. Von Grabow clipped the end of the small cigar and examined the result critically. Behind him, in the kitchen, Monika scolded the maid lightly as the two handled the after-dinner logistics. Von Grabow smiled at Frau Hassan's terrible *Gastarbeiter* German.

"Shall we sit near the fire?" he asked Schoener.

"Excellent," replied the colonel.

They stood almost simultaneously and went to the adjoining room. It was a kind of den, a cross between an office, a library, and a drawing room. A cheery fire crackled and spat in the big fireplace. Like the house itself, the fireplace was a survivor. When the British tanks had ground through from Holland in 1945, they had somehow missed this century-old country squire's home. Von Grabow had fallen in love with it at first sight when he'd been transferred to command the sector operations center at nearby Goch. Originally the owners wanted only to lease it, but he had managed to wear them down until they'd finally sold it to him. It looked, smelled, and felt like the home near Schwerin his family had been forced to leave.

Von Grabow settled into a modern leather armchair. Schoener stood for a moment by the fire, warming himself. Both men wore civilian clothes; Schoener, a nondescript gray suit over a white shirt and dark blue silk tie; von Grabow a blue double-breasted blazer above white flannel trousers. His cream cotton shirt was open at the neck. Von Grabow lit his cigar and closed his eyes while he drew deeply on it. He rolled the smoke around his mouth and loosed it in a slow, lazy stream.

"A good one, Herr Schoener. Thank you."

"My pleasure, Herr General. There is nothing like a Cuban. Or so I'm told."

Von Grabow smiled at him. "Good old Schoener. No nasty, fouled lungs for you, eh? Well, you're right. It is a terrible habit, but one I can't break."

The fire hissed and popped. Neither man spoke into the silence; neither felt the need. The enormity of their undertaking created a bond between them that transcended small talk.

Schoener cupped the cognac in one hand while he glanced at his digital watch.

"They'll be in position now," he said.

"Yes. I expect so." Von Grabow pulled on his cigar again. "It's a filthy night."

"Perfect."

"Yes. Perfect. But still filthy."

Silence again filled the little room. Von Grabow's wife, Monika, knocked lightly on the door.

"Freddy? Helmut? Coffee?"

"Of course. Thank you, *liebchen*." She nodded the maid into the room and stood for a moment near von Grabow. He looked at her and marveled again at his good fortune. She was still slender, still elegant, still darkly wonderful.

"Would you boys like to be alone?" she asked, her eyes twinkling.

"For a bit. Maybe an hour or two. You understand?"

"Of course. It's always work with you two. Sometimes I wonder if the Air Force knows what it's got with the pair of you."

Schoener shot a glance at von Grabow. But the general was grinning wolfishly.

"Probably not. If they did, we'd both be wearing four stars by now. Will you tell them for us?"

"No. You both seem to be doing remarkably well on your own. Instead, I'm going into town with Frau Hassan. She needs a ride tonight. Her husband has to work. So, Helmut, good night. And thank you for coming to dinner."

Schoener bowed and smiled. "No, Frau von Grabow. Thank *you*. As usual, the company and the food were superb."

It was their ritual exchange, but neither felt compelled to change it. Monika dimpled and kissed von Grabow lightly, then left. She closed the door snugly behind her.

A sudden shift of wind brought the rain hard against the den window. Schoener's smile disappeared. It was a filthy night.

"Does she know?"

Von Grabow rolled the cigar reflectively between his fingers. "If you mean does she know the whole plan, no. Of course not. But if you mean does she know something is going on, without a doubt. She sometimes seems telepathic to me. But don't worry, Helmut, the details are safe. I am a good security risk."

Schoener didn't tell him what he had learned the hard way over the years. He didn't tell him that no man is a good security risk. That the fundamental belief of a security officer was that everyone would compromise every secret at the most inopportune time. Instead, he shrugged.

"So everything is on for the flight tomorrow," he said.

"Yes. Ops called to verify everything. We're to be there about 1600. Takeoff at 1800. Everyone is ready?"

"Poised, both land groups. And Wilhelm reports the air group maintains security. Everyone is ready. Not a hitch in sight—yet."

"Always the suspicious Red. They trained you well in Karl-Marx Stadt."

"A good thing, too, or we'd still be daydreaming."

"Maybe, Helmut. But give some credit to the Amis for their excellent computer."

"Professor-Doctor von Scherenberg at Stuttgart might put it another way. In fact, I'm certain he would. He'd give the Amis credit for sparking our own computer work. No more than that."

"Ah, well. A chauvinist Red at that. Well, whoever gets the credit, so far the result has been almost unbelievable." Von Grabow took another long pull on his Havana. The rain lashed the thick old glass windows. Schoener sat down next to von Grabow in the velvet wing chair.

"Have you ever considered, Helmut, the ramifications of what we have done?"

"Of course, Herr General. Politically—"

"No, no. I mean, organizational ramifications."

"I don't follow."

"Think back to your staff courses. Think about *our* staff people, each of whom is convinced that without his personal attention to every detail of planning and order execution, nothing can possibly happen. Then think of how far we have come with only ourselves and your computer."

"Computers, Herr General. Plural. No single computer would have been sufficient, or secure enough."

"Whatever. You see my point?"

"Perhaps. You mean we have replaced an entire general staff? That may be unfair; we, after all, are undertaking only one operation."

"You surprise me. Defending the general staff? Still,

grant that this 'one operation' has ingredients complex enough to warrant full staff participation. Consider the matter of recruitment, for instance. How many files did we probe in coming up with our three groups? How many— what's the damned computer term—*sorts* did we wade through? And how many deep background checks did we pull?''

"Many, of course. More than I can recall. Ten months worth. But these weren't active staff matters, only personnel details, security work. Even in the Soviet system it would be the work of two or three officers at most.''

"Herr Schoener, you spoil everything. I wish only to savor our success so far before the plan unfolds. I wish only to gloat that we have accomplished what our colleagues, so intent on their damned careers, could never even imagine doing. It is selfish, I admit. It is even silly, and counterproductive. After tomorrow evening, no matter how it goes, our lives will never be the same. You know the odds against success; your computers never let us forget them. So let's taste the fruits of our little victories in case the big one eludes us.''

Schoener said nothing. His usually inexpressive features remained so. He sipped his cognac and stared at the fire.

"You know," said von Grabow, speaking softly into the dancing flames, "I am a German general. Yet I have never commanded troops in a battle, never stood on a hill, figuratively or literally, and watched boys from Saxony and Schwabia and Stettin march to any kind of destiny at my order. This is the result of *Innere Fuehrung*. Because of inner leadership I was born in Germany, but raised, professionally speaking, by Americans. I am an American creation. A eunuch German general. I have uniforms, I have a command, I even have personal battle honors from Southeast Asia. But I have never stood on that hill." He stared hard at the glowing tip of his cigar. "Until tonight."

Schoener remained silent, not merely out of courtesy.

The gulf between him and von Grabow in some places was unbridgeable. The general spoke tonight as a Prussian— which he was, by blood and tradition, no matter how modern his education and environment. The Reds had kicked his father and his family off the estate near Schwerin after the war. Being tough, resolute, and German to his fingernails, the elder von Grabow had done what he had to do to establish himself in West Germany. He had, after all, learned to take it at Verdun, where the French machine-guns had decimated his troop of cavalry and ripped his left leg from his body. His son, who traditionally would have inherited the estate, had become, also by tradition, an officer. It could even be argued that the branch of his service—the Air Force—was the new cavalry. Von Grabow was elite, an aristocrat in bearing and background, no matter what his father's business. Everyone who met him— everyone German, that is—knew that. Freddy never tried to use rank or background against anyone—and that only enhanced his standing.

But Helmut Schoener was a workingman's son, a city boy. He had grown up jeering aristos, then actively working to root them and the bourgeoisie out of the country. Yet the more he tried to be a zealous Communist, the less it worked. Things were not better in the People's State. They never improved, no matter how many people's enemies were liquidated. The final blow to his faith had come when he almost accidentally had tapped the Interior Ministry's secret personnel computer banks, and had seen for himself how the party leadership worked incessantly to establish itself and its heirs as the new aristocrats. You read about that sort of thing in the West, of course, but you never believed it. You simply assumed, as a real Communist, that corruption existed everywhere, and that it had to be eliminated. Propaganda was propaganda. But when your own records told you that the corruption was not just incidental, but central to the government, you had to open your eyes.

It hadn't been easy. He had been afforded the highest honors as a people's agent. As he grew older, and better at his work, perhaps he had lost a little of the burning, ideological fire that led him to it in the first place. Perhaps in the end it was only his ego that kept him at it until even the Soviets adopted him and made him one of their elite agents. And perhaps all that was groundwork that made his defection of faith inevitable.

There had not been a sudden realization, an agonizing *cri de coeur*. Through those years in the late 1970s he had continued to work steadily, carefully, and profitably for the men in the Kremlin and East Berlin. But gradually he was no longer able to win the arguments with himself. Gradually he was stripped by his own dialectics of his beliefs. Until one day he was naked. Von Grabow would never know the feeling. He was cloaked in invulnerable layers of tradition, steeped in Germanness beyond politics and ideology. But Schoener one day found himself alone in a way that he'd never experienced before.

He had tried to ignore it, of course. No middle-aged man likes to admit that his world order is not right. No matter what his material surroundings, he wishes to be philosophically comfortable, his inner life furnished with the familiar. This was why so many revolutions were led by men who, if middle-aged, had reached their revolutionary ideals long before; it was a well-known axiom that it is easy to radicalize a youth, a woman, or an elder, but almost impossible to do so to a well-fed middle-aged man. But here he was, midway through two careers—both successful—unable to believe in either one.

Had von Grabow not entered his life at that period, perhaps he would simply have drunk himself into oblivion. Or made a fatal error and been caught by the West. As it was, a chance dining-in ceremony at a fighter-bomber base officer's club had changed his life—and the general's too.

The talk at the bar and the table had been typical pilot stuff, mostly the harmless braggadocio that infects all aviation establishments. Pilots, after all, are eternal juveniles, endlessly fascinated with their toys and their play. Friedrich von Grabow, presiding over the dinner, joined in at appropriate times, as jocular as necessary, as remote as the commander must be when that was necessary too. As the evening dragged on, Schoener had found himself, as always at such affairs, standing alone. What had he to say to a bunch of pilots? But von Grabow had spotted him on one of his orbits through the crowd, and had chosen to speak to him.

Schoener had clicked his heels and bowed as the general approached, as protocol demanded. Von Grabow had inclined his head and raised his glass.

"Your health, Herr Oberst," he had said pleasantly.

"And yours, Herr General," Schoener had replied. They drank with eyes locked, again as protocol demanded. When he'd lowered his glass, von Grabow had clearly noted Schoener's lack of pilot's wings. He had swept his hand around the room.

"Not one of the boys, eh?"

"Hardly, Herr General. I get airsick easily."

"If that were a disqualification, many of these self-proclaimed aces would be grounded too," von Grabow had said, smiling.

Just then two young lieutenants began arm-wrestling. They sat amid noisy support from their squadronmates at the crisp linen table, and swept the expensive china and silver aside. Schoener and von Grabow watched, Schoener impassively, von Grabow beaming. The general had looked at him strangely.

"You don't approve, Herr Oberst?"

"It's not my place to approve or not, Herr General."

"Such things are a matter of tradition with pilots in this wing, you know."

"Of course."

"So. You don't approve of tradition?"

"Some traditions, Herr General."

"And which are those?"

That had been the beginning. Schoener watched the flames in von Grabow's fireplace eat a pine log, little by little, and realized that he had been eaten the same way. The match that had set him afire had been tradition. He had found himself engaged in a discussion with a transplanted Junker about tradition. Had he not been in the trough of his disbelief, he would never have dared. Yet somehow, the booze, the heated play of the drunken pilots, the demands of protocol, drove him on. He argued too long, too pointedly, for cocktail chat. The general had not been fooled when Schoener, his usually well-oiled internal alarms finally ringing, had sought a way out with a graceful exit line. Instead, he found himself accepting an invitation to lunch with the general. And then he was having regular meetings with von Grabow. One day it dawned upon him that he had been recruited.

It had been an odd feeling. He was a loner, a wolf who prowled by himself. Yet he had been captured and converted by one of his intended victims. Over the months of genteel, oblique discussions, he had found himself stripped, layer by layer, of his values. Until he reached the simple facts of his own Germanness.

They had been sitting in this very room, but on a hot summer's night. He had long since realized that von Grabow was not, as his secret computer probes had insisted he was not, an agent trying to turn him. He was just a German like himself. So Schoener participated in the discussions, and his controller in Moscow delightedly encouraged it. They expected him to suborn von Grabow.

Instead, that night while they sat in the semi-darkness,

the warm breeze blowing through the window that now kept out the cold rain, they had converted each other. The question had been of Germany, naturally. Was it a culture or a state? If the former, it mattered not, as the East German ideologues claimed, whether Germany was one state or nine, divided or whole. But if it was a nation, then its people would never be fulfilled culturally until it was reunited.

The discussion had not been linear. Von Grabow had begun by talking about his faint memories of Mecklenburg and Schwerin, of the fat cows, the wonderful pigs, the fine horses on his family's Gutshof. Barley, wheat, rye—these were the eternal verities. The pews his family had occupied for generations in the church. Schoener had talked about Leipzig. His father's job as a railway worker. The food lines. The riots. The Volkspolizei. The sudden change of the teachers in the 1950s. Then he had fallen silent.

When von Grabow had spoken next it was about Herbert, his only child. He had grown up living all over Germany, had traveled the world. He was a good student, and now attended the Berlin Free University. But he seemed to speak a different language from his father. It was not just his hair. It was not just his invective against the Air Force. Freddy could understand those as typical youthful explosiveness. What bothered him was that Herbert had absorbed, apparently, none of the traditions of his family. He and his friends were totally ignorant of German history. He was not pro-West or pro-East; as far as von Grabow could tell, he was politically neutered, an anarchist. He seemed to believe that no institutions were worth saving, that mankind was doomed to extinction as a failed experiment. When von Grabow had first heard these he had naturally dismissed the notions as classically adolescent. But Herbert was now at the university, with older boys, most of whom seemed to be somewhere to the left of the most extreme Green Party theorists. As the general spoke softly about Herbert, Schoener could sense the anguish of such a man for such a son. A lost son.

Who was to blame? Von Grabow took it on himself, of course. But there were others—the people who abstracted Germany to be something other than a nation with proud traditions. The people who wished to bury the past because of the Nazi stain. The people who profited by the continuing division of Germany, who feared the power of a reunited state. Once you became attuned to it, von Grabow had said that night, you could hear the propaganda everywhere, a continual stream of pressure to abandon the past, to cast off Germanness. The most receptive were the young, who heard it all not as rejection of Germany but embracing of the world.

Schoener listened as if to a mental patient. He was unable to conceive of having a son at all, much less to having a son stolen by an unfathomable force. He understood von Grabow's interest in the nature of Germany to emanate partially from his son's defection. And that interested him in an abstract way. But what electrified him was the sense that those same pressures had been working on *him* since his own childhood. Every German understood that the division of his nation had been politically motivated, the punishment of the losers by the winners. But few sensed the wellsprings of continuing pressure to remain divided as did Friedrich von Grabow. As he talked, calmly and slowly into the hot night, Schoener had seen, as if by a flare, the truth of his beliefs. Germany was not an abstract culture. It was a nation, and by rights ought to be. Whether its political system ought to be democratic capitalism or socialism was not the issue; the issue was separation.

Or, rather, reunification.

As a topic of conversation in Germany, it had long since become an old standby. Despite its explosive overtones, it was a socially "safe" subject. Except among the higher-ranking Western military people. The higher one rose, the less one said about it. Schoener and von Grabow had both experienced the reasons; first, there was the possibility of somebody in the press getting hold of something incautious an officer might say, either pro or con. But more telling was the knowledge that most colonels and above had of the futility of such talk.

If one was privy to NATO war plans, if one knew some specific, secret national plans, and if one had any kind of imagination at all, one quickly came to the conclusion that German reunification was a conversational topic and nothing more. Nobody—but nobody—inside or outside of Germany in the halls of power, military and civilian, considered reunification even remotely possible. The reasons were the divisions.

Not social divisions, or political divisions, but divisions of infantry and armor. The British, French, Americans, and Russians had turned Germany into a huge combination buffer state and garrison. No matter what else had changed since 1945, that had remained constant. And as Bundeswehr and Luftwaffe officers rose, and were exposed to the war plans, they all eventually came to realize that the next war was scheduled to begin and end within the borders of East and West Germany. Some grew bitter about it. Some ignored its implications. But all saw the futility of reunification rhetoric in the face of such unanimous Big Four planning.

All except Friedrich von Grabow. When he had realized that he was training and planning his people for a war that would devastate his homeland in order to spare someone else's, he had instantly rejected the implications. Most officers slid past them, hoping for peace and a comfortable career. But von Grabow, stunned by the enormity of the Big Four's indifference to the fate of his nation, probed gently, insistently, and unremittingly for more and more war-plan data. The more he knew about British, French, and American contingency planning, the more appalled he became.

Schoener never shared his emotions. He had been too cynical, since he had access to the secrets von Grabow never saw, and knew that neither the Russians nor the Americans were likely to die for Dresden, but that each would expect—demand!—their Germans to die for Detroit or Dromovsk. It wasn't until that hot, sticky night near Uedem that Schoener was able to put his long-ignored knowledge together with the issue of unification.

Who will do something? von Grabow had asked in the muggy darkness.

Who indeed? he had responded. Not the politicians. East and West, they were intent careerists. Such men do not do things. They talk.

The Americans?

The British?

The French?

The Russians?

Who?

Nobody. The Greens were the most radical force in Germany. But their party was already showing signs of decay and dissension, their coalition based on too fragile agreements between warring interests. The military was too docile, still too cowed by guilt for World War II to act independently. No effective underground existed in either section of the country; the forces protecting the status quo were too efficient.

Who?

I, von Grabow had said at last. I must do something.

What? Schoener had asked.

Something, said von Grabow. Someone must do something.

An officer's revolt?

No. The careerists are not risk-takers. And the young ones don't care.

A blackmail operation against key political leaders?

No. No single individual or even political party can accomplish the changes.

But would the people support doing something?

Yes. If you know how to feel it, it is there. Not in everyone. But in enough. They will not rise against the foreigners in the West because they are comfortable, and afraid of change, and guilty. They will not rise in the East because they are afraid, period. Someone must lead them, guide them to the action. Then they will come together. Germans are not cowards. But they do require a jolt sometimes.

A jolt. Schoener sweated in the den. Next to him in the dim light a Luftwaffe general was talking treason—or something. Maybe not treason. A family man, a man known as a fast burner in his career, a man whom nobody would suspect of harboring such thoughts. And he was telling a GRU agent about a jolt.

No, he wasn't. He was telling Helmut Schoener of Leipzig about a jolt. One German talking to another.

And before he knew it, Helmut Schoener of Leipzig was helping to plan the jolt. Caught up in it, utterly transfixed by the notion of it, completely overwhelmed by the historical inevitability of it, he lent his entire being to the jolt. Better than that, he let the secret computer network he infiltrated like a silent electronic snake work on it.

And it had suddenly taken shape, within two months. At first, von Grabow and Schoener had been wary of each other, proceeding as if simply war-gaming. The crucial day had come when he had asked the right question of the artificial intelligence computer at Brussels, into whose most secret innards he had penetrated via the powerful SOC mainframe. The question was: What single action was necessary before Germany could be reunited?

The answer was: Removal of all foreign troops.

Schoener had stared at the glowing green tube, reading

and rereading the single line. Well, of course, he'd thought. The computer doesn't know any better; even the top-secret program he was running would look only for simple answers. But then he thought about the multiple layers of sophisticated programming that had gone into the computer, and realized it was giving him exactly what he wanted. The next question was: How can the troops be removed without warfare?

The answer took less than a second to appear.

Threaten the Allies, the computer had said.

How? he asked.

Nuclear blackmail of key strategic cities.

Already in operation, he had typed out angrily.

Incorrect statement, the computer had rebuked him.

Explain.

Threat now exists as implicit part of NATO/Warsaw Pact stalemate. Needed threat for desired result must be direct, immediate, and imposed by superpower's own weapons turned against own clients.

Problems, he had typed. 1. Warsaw Pact is invention of Red Army to maintain semblance of cooperation among so-called client states: does not exist as a real politico-military entity. Therefore WP leaders powerless in event of Soviet action. 2. Soviets have already demonstrated complete disregard for views of clients.

Incorrect statements, spat back the computer. New situation in Central/Eastern Europe exists (see Report COSSACK, file name KOALA). Erosion of leadership in USSR Politburo now gives probability that combined Warsaw Pact leadership would outface Soviet views in any situation except mass revolution or defensive combat. (See Report GLOBULE re command and control, intra-WP forces.) Effect is inability of USSR to act unilaterally to impose will on WP states in ultimate crisis short of items named above, if desired Soviet action is contrary to interests of grouped WP powers.

Does Politburo know this probability? he typed.

No. KGB Section Two study indicating probability not released for Politburo/Defense Council consumption.

Reasons?

1. Report remains trump card for M. M. Ganinov, Deputy Secretary, Second Chief Directorate, GRU. 2. Disinclination of Politburo leaders to believe possibility of changed center of power in Central/Eastern Europe. 3. Disinclination to believe emergence of powerful new national classes in client states would affect power base. 4. Disinclination to believe ineffectiveness of Red Army in large-scale reprisal actions against coalitions of WP states.

But the Warsaw Pact clients do now have that power to shift Soviet policy despite Politburo beliefs otherwise?

Yes.

Do WP clients know they have the power?

No.

1. State probability of WP clients threatened as noted above demanding Soviet withdrawal of troops rather than acceding to Soviet willingness to allow destruction of threatened cities. 2. State probability of Soviet accession to their demands.

1. 75 percent. 2. 52 percent.

State probability of immediate Soviet counterattack given above scenario if WP leaders not involved.

96 percent.

At first, Schoener had not known what to do with the computer's projections. Conventional wisdom among intelligence people on both sides was that the military and civilian leaders of Poland, East Germany, Hungary, Bulgaria, Czechoslovakia, and Romania would never confront their puppet master. The reason was always considered to be obvious: the enormous weight of Soviet armed might in each nation precluded national independent action, and nobody knew that better than the leaders. In any crisis, the Warsaw Pact actually dissolved, and its contingents became elements of the Red Army, commanded by Soviet officers. Yet this computer suggested otherwise.

It had to be taken seriously. It was the most powerful artificial intelligence in Europe, supposedly impenetrable, and had access to data from all the participating states—which was all of NATO. A fierce, bitter battle had been fought entirely in secret years before by key national agencies whose governments wanted them involved in feeding the computer; the battles had been straight-out turf wars. A certain amount of sharing was thought feasible, but no national intelligence agency wanted its real secrets shared with anybody. Yet a victory had been won by the NATO believers, who hammered away at the GIGO problem until successive erosions of the agencies' stonewalling by insistent government pressure finally resulted in a useful NATO computer. By pointing out that in a real crisis a NATO commander would have to have immediate, on-site NATO computational power rather than tenuous links to other national assets, and that if the agencies sandbagged the NATO computer with bogus, old, or low-level information, the NATO command would be subject to the "Garbage In, Garbage Out" problem. Given the increasing likelihood of a NATO war being fought with nukes, nobody wanted a NATO commander making a critical decision with a second-rate computer. So the national intelligence agencies finally began feeding the required data to the secret computer in Brussels. They all believed that they maintained the tightest possible control on access to it.

No printed references to it existed anywhere. No direct telephone connections could be made to it. It used the most sophisticated energy-tracing detectors in the world to identify times and durations of use. But even their computer's builders had warned them that no computer can be made 100 percent proof against "worms," as the specialists called invaders who left no tracks after they'd slipped into the computer, used it, and then erased all traces of their entry and exit. The most they could promise was 99 percent proof. They had to accept the faint chance that someone might succeed in breaking in. Because NATO desperately needed the computer, it did accept the chance. And someone—Helmut Schoener—had broken in.

Von Grabow had been as skeptical of the computer's identification of the way to force a troop withdrawal as Schoener. He understood the thinking of his colleagues in command of NATO forces, especially those in the British, French, and American elements that would be affected. He had snorted at the whole notion. But it lodged firmly in his consciousness, and he continued to mull it over. The more he mulled, the more ways he found for his colleagues to do precisely as the computer had predicted.

The matter boiled down to judgment about behavior. To get result A, apply stimulus B. That worked with planaria in Petri dishes. But how to affect behavior of whole staffs, whole command echelons, whole national leaderships?

Once he and Schoener had admitted that the computer might be right about the possibility of such a move, they realized that only a supercomputer like the one in Brussels could analyze the huge amount of data necessary to understand the nature and extent of the kind of stimulus and response on such a multinational, multilayered scale. A man thinks of a nation, inevitably, as a collection of data points congealed around his own beliefs about the characteristics of the national leadership and people; and when all of those data points are ruthlessly set down, the man recognizes how finite, how pitifully few they are compared with the scope he imagines they cover. A computer, well-programmed and well-fed, has no such limitations. Its data are not compromised by preconceived notions, and it draws, when properly asked, objective conclusions about stimulus and response.

Once he learned to ask the right questions, von Grabow managed to extract from the computers the detailed background for the behavior he needed to extract from his potential opponents. As he became more enmeshed in the idea, it was more and more difficult for him to maintain full interest in his real jobs. Finally, after the plan had been roughed out, he forced himself to turn over all the detailed planning to Schoener, whose role at the SOC gave him the time and excuses needed to continue the process.

After the awesome power of the computers available through Schoener's deft worming was tapped, problems solved themselves. No printed records were made of the plans as they unfolded. Everything was stored in various computer memory banks, accessible only to Schoener. If he had died or disappeared during the planning phase, von Grabow would have been helpless; he knew nothing about the computer work except that Schoener somehow did it.

Recalling the months of frantic, secret worming, Schoener allowed himself the ghost of a smile. As it had emerged, the plan caused them both concern.

Too complex, von Grabow had muttered when it fell together.

Too dependent upon key people, Schoener had grumbled.

But time after time, simulations showed that as they refined the nuances, the plan worked. Neither man completely trusted the computer at Brussels; NATO people had a way of disbelieving their own rhetoric that was unsettling. So they ran the key elements through the Group of Soviet Forces Germany computer at Zossen-Wunsdorf over a week of intensive intrusion. In itself, Schoener's invasion by way of land line was a triumph of electronic espionage worthy of a Western author's attentions as a thriller. But what they cared about was that even with its much less sophisticated programming, the Zossen planning computer also verified the potential of the too complex, too dependent plan.

Until things had actually begun to happen, it had all seemed dreamlike to Schoener. Perhaps even von Grabow had nights when he lay awake, wondering if he was losing his mind to be involved in such a thing. Schoener studied the general in the flickering firelight. He knew everything that could be written down about this man, and an enormous dossier of things that could not. Yet Schoener never knew whether von Grabow felt the things that Helmut Schoener felt. When Schoener had finally told von Grabow he was working for the Soviets, he had not known what to expect. It had been an admission he'd made after they'd reviewed the rough plan, and had come out almost by accident when he'd mentioned that the way to check it was to run it through the Zossen computer. Von Grabow had said nothing. He'd smiled and asked if Helmut thought the connection would prove embarrassing. Just that. Embarrassing.

What the hell were you supposed to think of a general who smiled at you when you told him you'd been working for his enemy for your entire military career? Von Grabow had leveled those calm blue eyes at him and pinned him to the chair until he'd answered. No, he'd said. It would not be embarrassing. Because he had far exceeded his authority to snoop in computers, he had long ago penetrated the East German and Soviet key computer nets. He knew what they thought *they* knew about him. He could easily control their control of him, because he had access to their precious databanks—and they did not know it. Von Grabow had smiled again and nodded. And that had been it.

Little had shaken Schoener as much as that exchange. To a military man, a spy was like the pig who fucked your wife while you were at the front. He was the filthiest form of life, dirtied by his work even when it was done for the highest reasons. The civilians never understood that. They glamorized spies. Made them into heroes. Likewise, the politicians. But not the spy's brother officers. Even in the modern world, in which values were eternally questioned, the spy was a pariah. Yet this quintessential soldier had accepted his confession as if he'd only admitted that he was a week behind in his officer's club dues. Schoener was chilled to the bone by his reaction. He had thought himself ruthless, but in the genial von Grabow he had suddenly seen the soul of steel that characterized so many German leaders.

In a way, it had settled something for him. The plan required that the commander be not only willing but able to launch the missiles that would vaporize millions of people, that could easily touch off the last world war the Earth would see. As the abstract nature of the plan had unraveled, as Schoener had begun to see the awful reality inherent in the plan, he had wondered: Would von Grabow be such a man? He knew that he himself could never do it. But von Grabow?

That night von Grabow had answered him eloquently. The quick smile, the question of Schoener's embarrassment. Brigadegeneral Friedrich von Grabow had made up his mind. Nothing—not the fact that his co-conspirator was a spy, not the possibility that he might have to kill millions of people—*nothing*—would stand in the way of his fulfilling what his mind had created. Thus had the crucial juncture in the life of the plan been passed. A look, a smile, a question. A certainty.

From then on the operation had lived. What shall we call it? Schoener had asked.

Von Grabow had smiled again, that German smile of inexhaustible determination, of calm in the face of fury. Prince von Bismarck has already named it for us, he had said.

How? Helmut had asked.

At the Reichstag that day in 1862, von Grabow had said. Bismarck told them the question they faced couldn't be answered with speeches. Only with blood and iron.

So? Helmut had asked.

So the plan is Operation Blood and Iron. Blood for the Western target, Iron for the Eastern.

Appropriate, Herr General, Schoener had said, seeing in a flash just how appropriate it was that one Prussian should continue the struggle begun by another more than a century before. It was symmetrical. It was necessary and sufficient. It was German.

And because they had found and trained the men who crouched this night with weapons in the cold rain on both sides of the barbed wire border, and because a handful of other men were preparing themselves for similar action aboard a certain U.S. Air Force electronic warfare aircraft, it was all about to become reality.

Helmut Schoener set his empty cognac glass on the chairside table. He glanced at Friedrich von Grabow, whose cigar had burned down to a stub. Their dinners were digested, their thoughts collected. The fire smoldered, almost out. The time for reflection was past. Schoener got to his feet.

"Herr General. It is time—"

Von Grabow silenced him with an upraised hand. With the other he slowly rolled the cigar stub between his fingers, looking hard at it, his features composed but intense. Suddenly he stood in a single, fluid motion. He flicked the cigar butt into the fire and looked at Schoener. The lamp in the corner threw his face into sharp relief. His American drinking buddies would not have recognized the face. It was granite, and the eyes that pierced Schoener were glittering marbles.

"Yes, Oberst Schoener," he said in a voice like a glacier grinding mountains to gravel, "it is time." In seconds he was through the door and shrugging into his Luftwaffe raincoat. Schoener followed.

Behind them, on the hearth, there were only ashes.

NINE

"Hey—what happened to the motel?"

Sandy Koppel walked a step past Max, then turned back to him. She grinned as he looked at the large garden.

"Gone."

"Obviously. But why?"

"Who knows? Maybe the Russians cut a deal. Ask your boss."

Moss shook his head. So much had changed at the Mission in so short a time. He rejoined Koppel as they walked from the parking lot to the entrance to the United States Military Liaison Group's Mission in Potsdam. Because Max had slept in the small nearby barracks they'd tagged the Missionary Motel, its absence jarred him.

Koppel was right. Only the CO would know what had happened, and why. Max unbuttoned his raincoat in the foyer and wondered how he'd get along with Colonel Charlie Kemp. Sandy waved at him and went to the stairs. She worked on the third floor, among the technical paraphernalia of the electronics guys.

Max straightened his tunic and walked over to the CO's office. Like the rest of the main floor, it had not changed.

In fact, except for the guest book, the hidden microphones, and the flowers on the table in the drawing room, not much had changed on the main floor since World War II. This floor was the "public" floor, where Soviet visitors were "entertained." Sometimes they were allowed into the CO's office. Under Colonel Martin that hadn't been too common. Perhaps Charlie Kemp would be different.

The secretary stood when Max went into the outer office.

"Lieutenant Moss?" Like Martin, Kemp used a military secretary, a male clerk. This one, too, was new.

"Right, Sergeant. Time to check in with the CO. He in?"

"Certainly, sir. Wait one, please." He knocked on the thick old oak door behind him and went in. Seconds later he reappeared. "Go on in, sir."

Max walked past the sofa he'd spent so much time on and back into the office that had changed his life. He tried not to think about it, or about what it had meant. It was just another office.

He stopped in front of Kemp's desk and came to attention. "Sir," he said, "Lieutenant Moss reporting—"

"Knock it off, Lieutenant. Relax. Glad to meet you."

Max relaxed. So the old man wouldn't be a tiresome tyrant. What was he exactly?

Tall, for starters. At least six-three. Skinny, with a huge Adam's apple. Blond hair cut to a burr. Deep-set grayish eyes. Big, rawboned hands, one of which he stuck out to Max. And an infectious grin.

"Sorry I couldn't make it for dinner last night, but I figured Sandy would stand in pretty good." Max shook his hand and grinned back.

"She did, sir."

"Hell of a fine officer, Koppel. Knew her dad. Anyway, Karen Anne had one badass cold, so I played nurse all night. Drove her crazy." He waved to a chair. "Siddown."

Max sat. He did not mentally replay all the conversations he'd had in this room. Instead, he concentrated on reading the clues the new CO gave about his character. The Army made part of it easy; the ribbons he wore told of a long and decorated combat career. He also wore the coveted Combat Infantryman's Badge, available only to men who won it in combat.

"Coffee?" Max shook his head. Kemp nodded and flipped open a file folder. Now it comes, thought Max.

"Expect you're less than thrilled to be here," said Kemp. He didn't wait for a reply. "Well, I'm sympathetic, but that's life. Important thing is, I've got you now, and we can really use you."

Max lifted his eyebrows. "Sir? My orders read only 'general duties.' How will you use me?"

Kemp swiveled his chair to look out the big window behind his desk. It opened up on the Havelsee, now bleak and gray. "Goddamn Russians used your little episode to demand a few changes. They got 'em, too, since nobody was too eager to upset more apple carts. Result was we lost six slots and the motel. We're back to pre-'73 staff levels and working arrangements. What that means is I haven't got enough people to cover the ground. So everybody wears five hats. What I want you to do is guide the Recovery people operationally and work as a utility infielder. Your file tells me you haven't got an intel specialty. That right?"

"Right. I was supposed to be field-trained for further work. So far all I've got is the freshman course."

"Well, what with your background here, that'll be plenty. What I'll need from you is analysis at the weekly Berlin Command briefings, and a lot of input at the daily stand-ups here. We're pretty informal about that. We meet every day at 0800 in the main drawing room. That okay with you?"

"Uh—sure, Colonel. Of course."

Kemp flashed a lightning-quick grin full of crooked teeth. "Good. Well, let me take you around and give you a chance to meet the folks. Everybody here is new, right down to the stable boss. Any questions before we go?"

"No, sir."

"Okay, let's hit it. You're in for a long day. Wouldn't even think about going back to Dahlem until 2000." Kemp stood and made for the door. Max followed him. At the door Kemp grinned wide again and stuck out his hand once more. "Glad to have you aboard, Max. Mean it."

Max shook the huge hand again. "Thanks, Colonel. Glad to be back." As he said it Max realized suddenly that it wasn't a lie. He followed the colonel through the door and something slipped quietly and permanently behind him.

TEN

By mid-afternoon the rain had slackened to a steady drizzle. Occasional squalls gusted in from the northeast. Right out of Poland, thought Muth. Fitting, somehow.

One of the launchers of the battery was visible even from the road. Muth frowned automatically. Lousy siting procedure. Even though they were all buried deep in a restricted area, and this road was strictly off limits to everyone who wasn't wearing the right uniform, no good missile commander gave his site away unnecessarily.

His armored car rounded a bend, the tires squishing in the gooey mud that had been the road. Another of the ubiquitous barber-pole bars blocked the way. Another of the Red guards stepped from under a makeshift shelter and advanced. His face was a washed-out pinkish blur under his helmet and poncho. He stepped to the driver's side of the BTR.

Muth sighed and popped the hatch. Water cascaded in, as always finding the holes in his raingear. He stood up.

The guard saluted. "Good afternoon, Comrade Colonel," he said.

Muth snapped a return. "Yes. I have an appointment with your commander. Fifteen-thirty."

"Ah. Of course, Comrade Colonel. With Major Konstantin?"

"Obviously. He is your commander, is he not?"

The miserable kid stiffened. "Yes, Comrade Colonel. Please continue. Through the gate, then down fifty meters and left along the second firebreak. You will see the command post." He stepped back and saluted again. The gate rose as he did so, lifted by another guard at the end of the pole. Muth sat down again, clanging shut the hatch. He nodded curtly to his driver.

Water streamed off his slicker and pooled at his crotch and feet. The heater of the BTR spun at full blast, but as usual only a trickle of heat came through the battered metal vents. For a people who lived in perpetual winter, the Russians seemed to delight in building vehicles with lousy heaters. Muth turned back and looked at Frankel, who sat next to the zampolit, looking glum. Muth couldn't blame him.

"Well, we're here, more or less. Warm enough for you, Felix? How about you, Comrade Stoltz?"

Felix just looked at him. Stoltz beamed, just like the asshole he was.

"Fine, Comrade Colonel, just fine. I look forward to meeting our brothers in arms at, er, the front."

"Of course," said Muth. What else could he say?

He turned back to look out the driving port again. Rumor had it that the NATO people were spared political officers like Stoltz. Such a thing was almost unimaginable. For as long as he'd been in the Army, Muth had been subjected to almost daily bullshit from zealous crazies like Stoltz. The Russians tagged them *zampolits*—a contraction of their Russian category title—and whenever any legitimate soldiers said the word it was with contempt. At least when the zampolit or his paid informants were out of hearing. The fact was that every unit bigger than a company had one attached like a parasite. And when you finished the day's work, dirty, bone-weary, too tired even to think, these bastards would drag you over to their little display areas and lecture you about Lenin. Like most infantrymen, Muth had long ago learned the trick of catching up on rest while appearing to listen intently.

But Stoltz was more than just another zampolit. This cretin had been assigned specifically to his group. It was part of the price he paid for being a little too imaginative in building the unit.

At Schoener's suggestion he had argued the case for pulling all the worst political troublemakers out of their own rehabilitation units, putting them together in a single company. A punishment company, really. They had been startled at first, but his boss understood, or thought he did, since he knew that Oskar had never been happy stuck in an office when his vocation had been in the field. Oskar had convinced him, over a week's gentle barroom persuasion, that his reasons for suggesting this were simply to get back in the field where he belonged. He had led his boss to understand that he couldn't care less about the rehabilitation or otherwise of some politically incorrect soldiers, but he would ensure, as a matter of payment, that they were in fact rehabilitated if humanly possible. That was the quo for the quid in the deal. He knew, he'd said over vodkas, that he'd probably never get another real field command. But he'd like one more chance with something like this.

His boss was sympathetic. And because he held influence with certain ministry officials, his sympathy quickly became approval for Muth's notion. Besides, as Muth had seen in the little glint in his eye when he'd understood the plan fully, if Muth actually did succeed in rehabilitating some troops with this plan, then his boss could and would garner all the official credit for himself. If not, then it was all on Muth's head.

There had been no trouble from the ministry types. He'd been asked to brief his plan three times, to different officials, each time with obvious success. Everybody liked the idea. Put all the rotten eggs you can in one basket. Make them work together as an infantry unit. Train them incessantly. Work them like animals. House them in special, secluded quarters. Then let exhaustion and ideological defeat take its toll. Much better, said the ministry types, than simple punishment in work battalions or confinement in insanity camps. This way you might actually save a few soldiers.

So Muth found himself one day commanding a company of sullen dissidents. They ranged in age and rank from young privates to grizzled sergeants and middle-aged officers. They were in for everything from slapping an officer to black-marketeering to political deviation. They were short and tall. They were apparently diverse. But two things ran as a common thread among them. They were all German. And they had been specially picked by Oskar Muth and Helmut Schoener.

He formed three platoons with them and began working them ruthlessly the first day. And at the end of it he subjected them to their first of many sessions with Hauptmann Stoltz. The ministry had insisted on picking its own political officer. As far as Muth was concerned, the more egregious a jerk he was, the better. And Stoltz was a classic jerk.

He actually believed the tripe he spewed. He exhausted himself and the troops in spewing it. As Muth had suspected, the effect on these marked men was invisible at best. They were good soldiers—as he had expected—but lousy Communists. That drove Stoltz to greater efforts, and drove Muth's plan forward.

Until now, finally, the end was in sight. The driver slewed the BTR into a parking area next to the command trailer, a big green box, about twenty meters long by four wide, raised on jacks. It stood in the center of a little clearing, surrounded by parked vehicles and a lone ZSU-23 antiaircraft gun. A trickle of smoke curled from a nearby tent. Thick black cables snaked from the underside of the trailer out through the brush and dripping trees. A small cluster of antennae stood on the roof of the trailer. One oscillated to and fro quickly. As the driver shut down the engine, Muth heard it: whzzz-click, whzzz-click. Somewhere to the rear of the trailer somebody shouted something in guttural Russian, and somebody else shouted back. It was a typical Soviet Strategic Rocket Forces forward missile site.

The door to the trailer banged open suddenly as Muth and his officers were clambering out of the armored car. Muth peered through the rain to see who stood silhouetted in the bright light of the command trailer.

"Oberst Muth?" called a voice in heavily accented German.

"Yes, here," he called back in Russian.

"Ah! Good. I am Konstantin," the figure bellowed, this time in Russian. The thick tones of the Ukraine, ladled onto the words as if they were syrup, identified Konstantin's background. Muth nodded. So far, exactly as Schoener had predicted.

He and his officers hurried to the door. Konstantin, a huge, bearlike man with a bristling black moustache, grinned ferociously and waved a sloppy salute. So much for Muth's outranking him. The Red Army still believed that any Russian always outranked any German, no matter what the manuals said. Muth waved an equally sloppy salute. He'd learned long ago to take the implied abuse.

"Come in, Comrade Colonel! We have drinks for you and your men." Konstantin stepped back and waved them in. A blast of heat met Muth as he entered. Inside, as he'd expected, the trailer was a mass of electronics. Three men sat at consoles at the far end, staring intently at cathode ray tubes flickering with numbers. They were separated from the door by a partition, half glass, half steel, which held a door, now closed. The entry section of the trailer resembled a small office, but still was crammed with electronics and communications devices. Behind the entry area, to the right, was another wall, and an open door, to which Konstantin was pointing. Muth shook off his raingear, handed it to a silent corporal, and walked through to the compartment indicated.

It was not the Grand Hotel, but compared with the miserable tents in which the two hundred men of Konstantin's battery slept, it was paradise. A small table had been set up in the center of the little room that contained the bed, a desk, a little refrigerator, and a bank of telephones. On the table stood three big bottles of Russian vodka and five glasses. It was clear how Major Konstantin planned to celebrate Muth's courtesy call.

"Sit, please, Comrades. Here, Colonel." He gestured vaguely toward a folding camp chair. Muth removed his hat and sat. He forced a smile as Konstantin oversaw the seating of the zampolit, Frankel, and his own executive officer, a mousy little captain with a dour face. The Russian captain hovered behind Konstantin until a quick scowl hurried him to a vacant camp chair. Then Konstantin twisted off the cap on a bottle and began pouring.

The Russian major screwed up his face as he poured, clinically precise with each little glass. The rain picked up again, driving on the metal roof of the trailer in monotonous waves, reverberating through the little room. The murmuring of the equipment and the soldiers who served it down the hall filled in the silence. It all seemed perfectly absurd to Muth, but of course he remained impassive. As the ranking officer he had to instruct the others in the eternal verities of military rituals. And no ritual was so beloved by the Russians as the courtesy call, especially since it gave them an official excuse to drink, day or night.

For Muth it was an excuse to ensure that their last intelligence had been correct. Before he left he would make a ritual tour of the facility with the commander. That would provide the final guide to the assault. In the meanwhile he had to match the Russians glass for glass.

Konstantin finally finished. He held up a glass, looked at Muth, and said, "Comrade Colonel, the men of the glorious Fourth Battery, Seventh Battalion, 196th Rocket Brigade of the Soviet People's Strategic Rocket Forces welcome you and your officers. Here's to worldwide victory in the people's struggle against capitalism." With that Konstantin tossed the vodka down his throat.

Muth followed suit. The stuff slid halfway down, then scorched like all the fires of hell. He blinked and set the glass down. Before his hand was away Konstantin, grinning, was pouring another. Muth knew what was expected of him.

He scraped back the little chair and held his glass solemnly out in front of the group. "My officers and I thank the commander and men of the glorious Fourth Battery, Seventh Battalion, 196th Rocket Brigade for their brotherly hospitality, and salute them and the Union of Soviet Socialist Republics for their eternal struggle against the capitalists. To victory," he said, and tossed the vodka into his gullet. This one went down smoother, but he still blinked. When his eyes cleared, Konstantin was beaming.

The next hour was predictable. More toasts, more drinking. More boasting about the unit's astounding prowess. Little realizing that Muth—a mere infantry commander—knew all about his rockets, Konstantin filled the increasingly stuffy little room with details of his battery. Occasionally he would stumble on a technical point and shoot a glance at his adjutant, who would provide the missing words quickly, precisely, and emotionlessly.

Frankel and the zampolit soon had the glazed look of schoolchildren kept too long at the blackboard. But Muth continued to urge Konstantin along, asking a question when he or his number two seemed to run down. Finally even Konstantin had had enough vodka, enough of the briefing. He stood shakily and waved toward the door.

"Comrades, let us go outside. I will show you the pride of the Strategic Rocket Forces." He knocked over a chair as he lurched to the door. Muth suppressed a smile. There was nothing more pathetic than a Russian who couldn't hold his liquor. They all prided themselves on the ability to drink any German under the table. Few could. This one couldn't.

They clattered down the metal stairs and wobbled out into the drizzle. Konstantin pursed his lips under his huge moustache and tried to concentrate. The effort obviously cost him. Muth stood mutely nearby and continued to work on hiding a smile. Frankel gulped air in huge drafts. Muth scowled at him. He stopped.

"Yes," said Konstantin. "Of course. The first section. This way, gentlemen." He straightened and began to walk along a muddy path, following one of the ankle-thick cables that spewed out of the belly of the trailer. Muth walked next to him, flicking glances this way and that. So far nothing had been changed from the latest intelligence Schoener had provided.

They visited only three launchers before Frankel was violently ill into a bush. Konstantin took the opportunity to ask Muth if he had seen enough. The Russian wasn't looking too well himself, with the characteristic greenish pallor that accompanied the DTs of the serious vodka drinker. Muth smiled his assent, and they returned to the command trailer. Muth had indeed seen enough. The camp was precisely as Schoener had promised. Not so much as a cook's tent had been shifted.

At Muth's armored car the Russians made much ado of saluting and thanking them for their brotherly visit. Muth reciprocated, then barked at his people to climb into the car. The scene would have been comic under different circumstances. But Oskar Muth did not imagine that because their commander staggered about like a drunken clown these two hundred Russians would be easy prey. His predecessors in the Wehrmacht had made much the same mistake in judgment, and it had cost them their lives and those of millions of Germans. In fact, his reading of Konstantin and his situation disclosed that the Russian was a favored commander, given an important rocket battery as part of his career climb. Schoener's pirated files had shown him to be a shrewd character, Party progeny who was expected to do well, and no doubt would.

As his driver churned the dark mud outside the command trailer in an attempt to turn the big armored car around, Muth, in a way, felt a little sympathy for Konstantin, as one officer for another. Whatever would happen tomorrow, his career would suffer, and all that scheming, all that nauseating toadying to the inspector generals and the corrupt party bosses would do Konstantin absolutely no good at all. By the time the signal "Bismarck Lives" would go out to Muth and his people in a few hours, Konstantin's career would be finished. At least, if everything went according to the plan.

Muth winced as a big pothole dropped the right front wheel of the BTR, and he swayed forward and hit his head on one of the damned protrusions that the Russians built maliciously into every vehicle they designed. He rubbed his forehead and cursed under his breath.

Nothing ever went according to plan, of course. And between Schoener's signal and his success reply a lot could go very wrong. Especially since he had two major hurdles to clear before the plan could even be attempted. The first was vomiting into the scuppers behind him. Stoltz the zampolit had no more stomach for vodka than for his mother. But that didn't keep him from being a major threat. And then there were the men themselves, now sitting miserably in their tents, cold, tired, and wet. They had to be his instruments. They were highly trained, very efficient infantry assault troops. But they did not know why they were really being trained. They still believed that he was acting as all other officers in their experience had acted: blindly, ignorantly, for the state. He glanced at his watch. He had only a few hours left to turn them into his allies. Everything depended on that.

ELEVEN

They pulled out all the stops for the briefing. Von Grabow, Schoener, and his seven crewmen had greeted their USAF hosts and been offered the obligatory coffee in plastic cups after they had been ushered into the luxuriously appointed executive briefing room. Then the lieutenant colonel who was the E3G program officer slipped into a presentation as slick as anything Madison Avenue could offer.

The show began, as always, with a projected slide of the program's logotype. In this case it was a stylized Boeing E3G with a huge plus sign behind it, making it seem like a German Air Force cross—a clever sales trick already, mused von Grabow. Then the colonel began to speak from his podium in nearly perfect German about the meaning of the enhancements program for the German Air Force. He traced the history of the airborne warning and control aircraft deployed to Europe, highlighting the development of the original E3 from a commercial four-engine Boeing 707 airliner to the unique machine that had transformed warfare. As he spoke, photos and movie clips appeared on the screen behind him, underscoring his points. Von Grabow recognized most of them; he had sat through this kind of sales pitch in Washington and Brussels so many times, he could recite most of the lines in his sleep.

The idea was simple enough. The original Boeing E3A was built on a transformed airliner airframe with a huge rotating radar dish mounted above the aft fuselage. With the thirty-foot dish, an E3A flying at only 29,000 feet could see, track, and target tiny airborne or seaborne objects as far away as 230 miles. And that had been just the first version. Intensive improvements were carried on ceaselessly, until the current USAF-deployed versions were capable of almost incredible targeting and tracking. But Boeing—and, indirectly, the U.S. Defense Department— were after more. They wanted every reliable ally to have their AWACS, so they sold NATO eighteen aircraft.

The problems became apparent at once. The NATO aircraft used European electronics. Naturally that meant that the issue of which electronics became a highly political one, and the aircraft, although formidable, were simply not as good as they should have been. So, responding to quiet, and unofficial but persistent German Air Force requests, the manufacturer had come up with a special version for the Luftwaffe only. Its changes were not just in its avionics but also its engines and airframe.

The new version was tagged the E3G and was capable of loitering on station for a full twelve hours, thanks to its new Rolls-Royce–General Electric turbofan engines. Furthermore, its sensors could spot the kinds of threats that mattered in central Europe: things moving not just in the air but on the ground as well.

The program officer halted his discourse for a film clip showing the E3G working against a tank concentration; the film cut from the command console in the aircraft to the ground, where "opposing" tanks rolled through heavy forest, then back to the console, where they appeared as ghostly blips, each carrying an ID number. The sophistication in the E3G wasn't just in its sensors, but in its computers, which digested the raw sensor data and transformed it into usable, identified target information. Thus could the airplane's awesome computer-sensor combination differentiate between a half-track and a main battle tank, or between a jeep and a sedan. Programmed into it were the details of every military machine known to the programmers, and quite a few civilian machines as well.

In spite of himself, von Grabow was impressed. Schoener had warned him all about this, of course. But still, such a machine could transform the battlefield commander's problems, which always revolved around knowing what the devil the enemy was up to. With this weapon—for a weapon it was, even though unarmed in the conventional sense—a commander would have a ninety percent certainty of the facts on the ground, sea, or air before he committed his forces.

The program officer flicked through the systems descriptions of the airplane, stressing that the complicated details were available in the manual. Then he finished with more film, a swelling musical finale, and the logo. The lights came on. Von Grabow suppressed a sudden urge to applaud. The Americans always knew their Hollywood stuff.

The U.S. Air Force brigadier general who was his host turned to von Grabow.

"Well, Freddy, what'd you think?" Von Grabow had knowm Marty Donaldson for nearly twenty years. They'd trained together as young fighter pilots at Luke AFB.

"Impressive," von Grabow said. "But it's not the technical problems, it's the political ones."

"Yeah, I know. Believe me, I know. Anyway, once you fly this sweetheart, you'll buy it." Donaldson seemed about to say more, then clamped his mouth shut. Around them their officers were collecting flight planning materials, since the actual flight briefing was next. Donaldson winked at von Grabow. "Back in a flash," he said, and rose to his feet. He gathered up a colonel seated in front and stepped to the podium. The murmuring stopped.

"Gentlemen, welcome to Frankfurt once again. I think you'll all agree, based on Colonel Jackson's briefing, that the airplane is damned impressive. But I guarantee that compared with flying the little thing, looking at Lucky Jackson's slides is like jerking off when you have Sophia Loren for a bedmate." A discreet chuckle ran through the audience. "Anyway, we're scheduled out on the ramp for a 1900 takeoff. So I'll turn the floor over to Colonel Garcia, who won't make any more tasteless jokes."

The small colonel stepped up to the microphone. Unlike the general, he wore a standard issue flight suit.

"Good afternoon, gentlemen. Welcome to Yellow Rose Five. That's our mission designator. Now, if you'll give your attention to the screen behind me, I can brief the actual flight." The room darkened again, and the screen lit up with a standard tactical navigation chart displayed, with colored flight-path legs and times called out. Garcia painstakingly went through the plan, and von Grabow knew his mission specialists were diligently scribbling everything down on their Form Nines. His eyes were drawn, as if by magnets, to two spots near the corners of the tac chart. One was in East Germany, one in the West. Unmarked now. But later, who knew? Perhaps monuments would rise there. Or perhaps only ashes would remind anyone of what Yellow Rose Five was really about.

Garcia wound up his spiel and asked for questions. There were none, not from the eight USAF crewmen or from the nine Germans. He noted the time and asked everyone to be present for the ramp ride to the aircraft in twenty minutes. The briefing dissolved. The German and American crewmen gathered their gear and assembled in small groups, chatting, drinking coffee, looking and acting as all aircrewmen do. There was no sense of nerves in the air; the Americans knew their airplane, and knew it would

impress the Germans. And the Germans—von Grabow
smiled as he picked up his helmet bag and flight paraphernalia bag, thinking of the seven hand-picked, carefully
questioned, ever so gently recruited Air Force officers now
trading banter with their American counterparts. The Germans, he thought, would do just fine. He nudged Schoener
and nodded almost imperceptibly at the men talking with
the Americans.

Schoener glanced at them and continued gathering his
flight equipment. He did not return von Grabow's smile.
As the moment of truth grew nearer, von Grabow grew
calmer. Schoener grew more agitated. He was used to
working alone, ferreting out secrets, worming through systems, enjoying the solitary pleasures of the predator. He
was not used to this kind of dependence.

The seven men here were vital; otherwise they never
would have been recruited for this mission, never told the
near-truths that they had been told. At least not if Helmut
Schoener could have anything to do with it. He saw them
not so much as assets as potentially disastrous liabilities.
Each time he and von Grabow had made a tentative approach, he had sweated bullets. No single man knew more
of the plan than he had to. They used the best-proven
systems for compartmentalizing each man's access to their
secrets, but still Schoener worried.

These were younger men, two with families, none with
the kind of drives that worked within him and the general.
He had been skeptical of their reasons for accepting the
challenge to join the effort. But the same recruiting techniques that had worked so well for the ground commanders
had worked with these men; beneath their contemporary
European mannerisms they were German. They were prod-
ucts of a tortured culture, and they were as contradictory
as it was. None of their friends and colleagues, perhaps
even none of their families, would have believed that each

of them was about to undertake something wholly outside the realm of their experience.

Yet even Schoener had eventually to admit that it was this adventuresome aspect of the plan that attracted them as much as the potential payoff. There was in Germans a certain wildness, a determination to go precisely where common sense dictated not going, that found form in the legions of solo German youths found in every remote corner of the world, traveling for the sake of traveling. To see for themselves. To endure. To experience. To do the forbidden.

As he had pored through these men's dossiers, no single common element seemed to emerge—save this penchant for personal daring. The bureaucrats who had fashioned the new German armed forces under the guns of the Allies had sought to gut the old military traditions, to make impossible the values that had allowed Hitler to squeeze the Army like a lemon while its leaders writhed impotently within the grip of their own prejudices and training. And so they had; the new Bundeswehr was a potent armed force, but nothing at all like the Wehrmacht. Those bureaucrats thought they had ensured that no rising of German militarism was possible, and again they were right. Palace revolts, takeovers by juntas—these were not available to a German schemer. But what a daring German planner might tap was the eternal German daring.

Seven stood now sipping hot coffee with their American counterparts. Two pilots, five electronic warfare officers. They ranged in age from twenty-nine to forty-two, in rank from captain to lieutenant colonel. Schoener forced himself not to think about how any one of them could destroy the whole operation. People were necessary security risks. They could not be controlled effectively by fear; he had learned that the hard way from his trainers at Karl-Marx Stadt, although they believed they had taught the opposite. Nobody bears the burdens as willingly or fights as fero-

ciously as the man committed to an idea. And he and von
Grabow had carefully committed these seven young men
to the idea of a freed, reunited Germany. At least he hoped
they had committed them.

The answer would be known in less than six hours. If
one of those seven coffee-drinking aircrew were really
working for someone else, if all of Schoener's agonizingly
secret security checks had been for naught, they would all
soon know. He felt a million years old as he watched von
Grabow slap Donaldson on the back in the best old-boy
way and whisper something doubtlessly dirty in the American's ear. Donaldson's guffaw filled the briefing room,
and all the aircrewmen turned to grin down at the two
generals by the podium.

Not one of the boys? von Grabow had asked him that
night. No. Not now, not ever, probably. But while boys
may fly fighters and arm-wrestle on wine-stained linen,
they don't orchestrate revolutionary changes in human affairs. That is a role, he thought, for men. Whether it was a
role either he or von Grabow were properly cast for, he did
not know. But the curtain was about to go up, because
Yellow Rose 5 would leave the wet Frankfurt concrete in
twenty minutes.

The time for ruminations, for worrying, for double-
checking, for final planning, for *anything*, was done. All
that was left now was action. Schoener looked down into
his black coffee. He knew he ought to drink it. He would
need the caffeine. But the smell nauseated him. His stomach spasmed, and he tasted bile behind his molars. He
clenched his teeth and downed the coffee. When he set his
cup down the crewmen were drifting out toward the ramp.
He sucked air, dropped the cup on the floor, hefted his
heavy flight bag, and followed them. At least by concentrating on his roiling gut he could avoid thinking about
everything that could go wrong.

Walking along the brightly lit corridor of the operations

building, another flight-suited figure among the dozens who clumped up and down the halls, he fought with his gut. When somebody opened the double glass doors out to the ramp and he stepped into the cold, rainy twilight, it all suddenly stopped. The nausea, the headache, the fears.

Standing floodlit across the field was the dull silver shape of the new E3G. Its radome rotated slowly as antlike figures scurried around it, preparing it for takeoff. A fuel truck pulled away, heading out of the floodlit area back into the rainy darkness. Ahead of him the men waited impatiently to climb into the warm crew bus. He stood rooted to the spot and stared at the airplane, feeling the cold wash him free. A hand took his left elbow.

"Let's go," whispered Friedrich von Grabow. "No time for airsickness now, eh, Helmut?"

Schoener nodded mutely. Then he was in the bus, von Grabow was sitting next to him. The pneumatic double doors hissed closed and the bus lurched toward the airplane.

There was no more time for anything. Especially airsickness.

TWELVE

The commander lifted the flap of his watchband. Rain dripped down through the slit of his poncho and splattered on the watch crystal. The time glowed in the dark. He carefully reseated the flap.

Next to him his radio operator shifted uneasily, trying to find a comfortable way to huddle on the wet pine needles. He fiddled with his radio settings, checking the squelch control for the hundredth time. Inside his helmet his earphone squawked with the bleeps and squeals of the short-wave band. The commander nudged him.

"Anything?"

"No, Herr Oberst. Nothing."

"It's early yet."

"Yes, Herr Oberst."

Helling lifted the edge of his poncho. Nearly a hundred men were scattered around him within fifty meters in every direction. All except the guards were huddled like him under dark ponchos and dripping trees. He wondered about the canisters. He always wondered about the canisters. The stuff was supposed to be good. But it had been far too easy to steal it from the American stockpile near Neu Ulm. He knew American security was lousy. But five canisters of their most potent, undetectable nerve gas had been lifted from them with less trouble than he would have had in stealing a VW with the keys still in it. Being a thorough commander, this bothered him.

He was also bothered by the ease with which they'd penetrated the Hohenfels exercise area. Yesterday afternoon he had rendezvoused with his men near a friendly farm. There they had spent the night, then changed from civilian clothes into their battle dress. Bundeswehr battle dress, naturally. Then he had marched them out into the rain and along the Hohenfels perimeter road in company order as if they belonged there as part of the planned exercises. It had worked. The American MPs in their jeep had passed them and ignored them, even though he was prepared with all the proper documentation. After that it was easy to slip into the dense, wet underbrush by the peri-road and head for this jump-off spot only two kilometers from the target.

Too easy. All too easy. Everything had worked according to plan. It bothered Helling, as it bothered all commanders when everything worked.

He flipped back his hood, pulled out his pair of mini-nightvision goggles, and scanned the area. His people were well camouflaged, their ponchos doing their jobs as thermal insulators, hiding well the telltale heat of a human body. Anyone doing the same on this filthy night would see nothing worth reporting. He flipped the lens hoods down and replaced the goggles. There was nothing to do now but wait.

The waiting was over. Oskar Muth did not need to check the time. He knew it all too well. It was time to see whether this bizarre plan would work. He ran his hand through his thinning hair, pulled on his cap, stood, and tugged the tails of his tunic tight. He adjusted his 9mm

Makarov in its shiny brown leather holster. Now or never, he thought.

He stepped outside his tent. The rain had again abated slightly. In the darkness the lights of his men's fires and tent lamps gave the bivouac an almost homey quality. He called for Frankel. The exec appeared at the mouth of his tent, only a few feet away.

"Herr Oberst?" He, too, knew a little of what was at stake. It had been impossible not to let him in on some of the details.

"Please assemble the men."

"Here? Now?"

"Yes. Immediately."

"And—guards?"

"None. I want everyone here. No exceptions."

"Done, Herr Oberst."

"And Frankel—arrange some light here. I want to be able to see them."

"Of course."

"One more thing, Frankel."

"Yes, Herr Oberst?"

"The zampolit?"

"He left an hour ago, as you directed. To visit the second platoon at its bivouac."

"Good. Thank you, Frankel."

Muth went back inside his tent. He knew Frankel; the man would have them lined up outside, with electric lights shining exactly in the right places, within minutes. Muth sat on the edge of his camp bed. The odor of wet canvas permeated the tent. Motor rifle troops rode in vehicles, but they lived on the ground, just like all infantry throughout all time. He made his mind go blank. The effort paid off; Frankel stepped inside his door in what seemed to be seconds. He was wet and haggard-looking.

"Herr Oberst?"

"Yes."

"All is ready, sir." He glanced back out the open tent flap. Muth heard the telltale shuffling of clothing and boots. His company was assembled. Or at least, the two platoons he thought he might trust were assembled.

Muth followed Frankel outside. The rain had stopped entirely for a moment. Frankel had arranged the armored cars so that their headlights and spotlights shone down into the area where his men stood in ranks. A few shone directly at him. He squinted slightly. The effect was eerie. A generator somewhere banged away, driving some pair of lights. Frankel waited for him to clear the tent, then barked, "Attention!" The men stiffened to attention.

"Stand easy," Muth said. They relaxed a little. His breath condensed slightly in the air as he spoke, outlined by the headlights. He had rehearsed this a thousand times, but his throat was dry as dust now. Neither he nor Schoener could predict what would happen next. It was all a gamble. But there was no choice.

"Men of the first and third platoons. I have called you here because you have an opportunity no soldiers in the Nationale Volksarmee have ever had before. I will tell you of this opportunity in a few moments.

"First, let me summarize your situation. Each of you has been placed in this company for a final attempt at your military and social rehabilitation. That much you know. Each of you came to me as some kind of misfit in the worker's state. That much you know all too well. Some of you are young. Some are older. Some held high rank—we have ex-captains and ex-lieutenants here, as I'm sure you know also.

"You have been with me more than six months. We have worked hard at our military duties. You know and I know that you have become superbly trained infantry shock troops. You have seen yourselves that this is true in the few maneuvers we have been permitted with combined forces." He paused, scanning the crowd of faces. They were impassive. Some looked at him. Most simply stared blankly ahead, the perpetual not-me look of the professional soldier. They had heard too many speeches.

"All this training has not just been for the benefit of some fat cats in Berlin. It has not been so that you will somehow be drained of your revisionist thoughts by exercise. It has not been so that some zampolit could brainwash you when you were too tired to resist." A few glazed eyeballs focused on him. This kind of speech they had never heard.

"We have worked this hard, training at silent assault, because there is a target we must take. But it demands your volunteering to take it. The Army is not involved. The state is not involved. It will be up to you, as free men." He had them now. He drew a deep breath.

"It is time for the foreigners to leave German soil. It is time for Germany to be reunited. It is time for all Germans to decide their own fates. The crimes of the fascists have been paid for many times over. You men will be the ones who can make this happen. But only if you choose. Shall I continue?"

When he and Schoener had planned the scene and the speech, they had thought that at this point some men would cry for him to continue. But they had recognized that these men, victimized, brutalized, bludgeoned to silence, might consider it all simply another trick to draw their real allegiances out so that they could be further bullied. And so when nobody said anything, Muth was prepared.

"I understand. This could be a trick, you think. And you might be right; that is the sort of despicable action we have all come to expect from the state run by Russian puppets. So I will continue, to prove it is not a trick.

"The means by which we few can affect history is as follows. You all know that this afternoon I visited a Russian rocket battery. This battery is only a few kilometers away. It consists of nine SS23X rockets mounted on mobile launchers. The battery is manned by two hundred soldiers, all native Russians. We can assume the rockets, are targeted on Western military and civilian targets of high importance to the state.

"We will attack this battery in a few hours. We will take it intact, using the tactics we have worked on ceaselessly over the last months. Once we have the battery under our control we will signal that we have it to a controller who will be flying over the West zone. A similar attack will take place on an American battery in the West. The controller will then alert us to the success of the attack, and we will retarget the rockets against nine cities on our side: Prague, Berlin, Budapest, Bucharest, Warsaw, Sofia, Moscow, Leningrad, and Kiev." Finally the group stirred. Their shuffling was eloquent.

"Why do this? Simple. We know what language the Russians understand. Force. Or rather, threats. We will threaten these cities with destruction. To save them, we ask only that they leave us. That they withdraw all their armed forces from German soil." He looked around the ranks of men. "Now. Questions?"

The first came from one of the ex-officers. "Comrade Colonel. Assuming, just for the sake of military argument, that this could be done. Why would the Russians not simply counterattack? In this forest alone there is at least a motor rifle brigade and a tank battalion. Why would these forces not immediately retake the battery?"

"Because of the airborne commander. As soon as we have the battery he will broadcast a message to Warsaw Pact leaders and Soviet military headquarters at Zossen-Wunsdorf informing them of the takeover, the threat, and their required response. Naturally their first thoughts will be of counterattack. But they will be forestalled; the airborne commander, you see, has precise knowledge of all air, sea, and ground activity within five hundred kilometers of the batteries. Nothing significant can move within that radius without his knowledge. Therefore, he will simply tell the Russians that if he detects so much as a MiG movement, he will order a launch. And believe me, Comrades, we will launch. More questions?''

Another of the broken officers spoke up from the rear ranks. ''Comrade Colonel. The requirement that the Soviets withdraw. Even assuming they agree, how long do they have to do so? How long must we—uh, that is, assuming one did this, purely as a matter of military discussion—how long must one hold the battery?''

Muth sucked in his cheeks. He had agonized over the same point. He knew only a little of logistics as a science, but he had seen enough massive troop movements to sense the potential for huge snarls in the exodus. Schoener had assured him that he had run the programs a hundred times to compute not just the desired but also the possible, the realistic response times.

''They will be given twenty-four hours. No more.''

Suddenly the questions tumbled out.

''But Comrade Colonel,'' a reedy voice yelled, ''what's to keep them out? One little rocket battery?''

''No,'' he barked. ''Once all of Germany is united, once we are free of all troops, they will not be strong enough to risk a major war with us—or with the West—to retake their lost garrisons and equipment. The conditions will demand that they leave all hardware not hand-transportable here. They will be gutted.''

''And the Czechs? The Poles? The Hungarians? The Romanians?''

''With Germany gone, they will not support an attack. The time has come for all nations to throw off the yokes of the foreign powers. Germany will lead the way. The others will refuse to attack.''

Silence suddenly descended upon the chilled scene. Their breath condensed in a cloud over their heads. The lights painted everything in stark shadows. Men's eyes flashed. The crucial point had come. Muth sensed it. These men— cold, hungry, victimized—wanted to believe that something fantastic had indeed overtaken them to spare them further years of toil and agony. They wanted desperately to believe in him and his phantom airborne commander, his fantastic plan to liberate their homeland. But they were still too cautious. No one had admitted anything yet.

Muth was growing desperate himself. He had hoped that he might have persuaded them by now. He had hoped that one of the ex-officers would have stepped forward to declare himself, thus bringing others forward. In his endless rehearsals for the scene it had happened thus. But not tonight.

"Men," he said at length, "Germans, I ask you to believe me. This is not a trick. By speaking to you thus, I do not ask you to risk yourselves; indeed, I am the one at risk. I put my trust in you now. Will you join me?" He knew as soon as he had said it that it was all wrong. The timing was wrong, the words were wrong. He was not an impassioned speaker, just an infantryman. He had no skill with words. His heart pounded. His mouth was dry.

"Have you not heard enough?" he said.

Before anyone else could say anything, a voice from the far rear ranks yelled hoarsely, "Yes! *I* have heard enough! And I call upon these loyal soldiers to arrest you and your co-conspirators immediately, in the name of the state!" Muth stood rooted to the spot. The voice belonged to the zampolit, who was supposed to be safely out of the camp tonight. He glanced at Frankel, who returned his look with round eyes. Muth fingered his holster.

The men around the zampolit edged away from him. No more-hated man existed for these soldiers. Yet they were confused. What if the whole affair had been staged? they wondered suddenly. What if this were the elaborate loyalty test they had feared at first?

Muth came alive. "Soldiers! Germans! Arrest me and you destroy your country's future. Grab the zampolit!" He pulled his Makarov from its holster. *"Now!"*

Two seconds ticked by. The zampolit struggled to drive through the mass of men. He opened his mouth to yell something, but a strong, callused hand clamped over it. The other pulled his left arm behind his back. The hands' owner, a twenty-year veteran, once a sergeant, now a private, marched the thin political officer forward. The ranks parted. The zampolit's eyes rolled in fury and fear. He struggled to free himself. But the big ex-NCO duck-walked him relentlessly forward. He stood in front of Muth and looked hard at him.

"Herr Oberst," he said, deliberately using the German rather than the Soviet expression, "I have some scum for you. Maybe this is a trick. Maybe not. But I'm fed up with the horseshit this bastard has been stuffing down our throats. You can shoot me now if you want." The big soldier thrust the zampolit down to the mud and stood defiantly in front of Muth, his arms dangling.

The zampolit struggled to his feet; he spit muck from his mouth and screamed, "Yes! Yes! Oh, I promise you, pig, you will be shot!" He reached for his own holster.

Muth raised his pistol. The ex-NCO squared his shoulders and looked him defiantly in the face. The headlights threw his craggy features into sharp relief, rendering him granite. His eyes stared coolly into Muth's.

Muth's Makarov barked three times. The last two were unnecessary. The zampolit's head turned to a pulpy mass as the heavy slugs ripped through flesh and bone. The old soldier stood, unflinching as the brain matter and splinters of skull spattered along his right side.

Muth lowered his pistol. The veteran ignored the body that quivered in the mud beside him. He drew himself up to attention and snapped a salute.

"Herr Oberst. Ex-Feldwebel Steiner awaits your orders. I wish to volunteer for the mission."

Muth holstered his pistol and solemnly returned his salute.

"Feldwebel Steiner. Thank you. I am honored." He looked beyond Steiner to the mass of men, frozen into silent clusters. "You see, gentlemen. This is not a trick. I ask again for volunteers. Will you join us?"

The shout began in back. By the time it reached the front ranks it had become a cheer. It was the raw voice of liberation.

THIRTEEN

Precisely at 1859.30, Yellow Rose 5 rolled. The American pilot caressed the four throttles forward at the end of Frankfurt's Runway 07R, and 165 tons of E3G slowly gathered speed in the rainy gloom. Each of the four huge, high-bypass GE/Rolls-Royce turbofans spooled up to its maximum thrust of 25,000 pounds. The thirty-foot radome accelerated from its ground rotational speed of 0.33 rpm to 6 rpm. The co-pilot's left hand shadowed the aircraft commander's right hand on the throttles as the pilot advanced them. He called out V speeds as the digital display on the cathode ray tube before him came alive.

"Eighty knots."

"Ninety knots."

"One hundred knots."

"Go/no-go coming."

"One hundred ten. One hundred twenty. One twenty-five. One thirty. One forty. Rotate."

The pilot gently eased back on the yoke, and the nose lifted gracefully into the murk. A second later the wheels left the ground.

"Gear up," called the pilot.

"Gear coming up," replied the co-pilot. "All green. Up and locked."

Friedrich von Grabow, seated behind the pilots at an observer's station on the flight deck, glanced at the flight timer that had begun to record elapsed time when the airplane left the runway. He subtracted the few seconds since takeoff as the aircraft commander stabilized the Sentry G in its right climbing crosswind turn, made to avoid busting the buffer-zone airspace just to the east of Frankfurt. Takeoff at 1900.01. These men knew their stuff. The aviator in him reveled in the precision, the economy, the grace of their moves. He was a fighter pilot by inclination, but he had to admit that the coordination of an entire crew to launch and fly such an airplane was in itself a challenge, and when executed well, a reward. Like so much of the pilot's world, it was an undiscussed reward.

But as the airplane gained altitude, von Grabow's shared relish of the rituals of flight diminished. This was not just another routine mission. He sighed inwardly and focused on the demands of the real mission plan.

The American pilots, busy with setting up the initial courses, negotiating with the ground-based air traffic controllers for better step-climb altitudes, navigation fixes, and position holds in the jammed airspace over the industrial heart of West Germany, ignored him as he unstrapped. The navigator, seated across from him on the starboard side of the flight deck, caught his eye. A tall black captain, he stopped his scan of his instruments to smile at the general. The noise level in the pressurized cabin dropped as the co-pilot pulled back the throttles to cruise-climb settings.

Von Grabow made his way back through the flight deck bulkhead to the main communications station, just behind the flight deck itself. The comm man ignored him. Immediately behind the radio stack were the computers, whose operator/monitor faced a fuselage-mounted display domi-

nated by two large cathode ray tubes. Von Grabow halted
briefly to peer at the hieroglyphics stuttering across the
screen of the leftside tube. As always, they meant nothing
to him.

He continued back along the carpeted aisle to the two
banks of multipurpose consoles and their operators. These
were the heart of the AWACS airplane; each of these
seven consoles could reach into the powerful computers to
find, arrange, and display any desired data from an accu-
rate terrain map of the ground below to the positions of
every major airborne, seaborne, or, in this new Sentry,
groundborne vehicle. The American operators were busy
with their warm-up procedures, checking everything. The
duty officer nodded to him as he passed his station on the
way aft. The deck angle steepened a bit, and he grabbed a
side rail near the life raft stowage area, about at mid-
fuselage. The E3 was more than fifty meters long, and it
seemed as you walked down the side aisle that you could
see all of it. In some ways it was like a commercial
airliner; it had softly glowing fluorescent lighting along its
ceiling, and the same gray-white textured plastic walls
reaching down to the same tight-nap carpeting. But the
steel-gray seriousness of everything belied those impres-
sions. And so did the crew rest area.

He walked through the open curtainway into the rest
area. His men were seated in the three rows of standard-
issue airliner seats, all facing aft for safety. Their flight
bags were stowed neatly in a big fuselage-mounted box,
secured by nylon netting. They seemed completely calm.
The briefed plan for the Air Force mission called for them
to remain here until the airplane was at altitude; then the
duty officer would begin their familiarization training. Each
man was allotted a station, a task, and a controller. The
pilots would go forward for flight-deck work, he would sit
at the mission commander's console, Schoener at the duty

officer's station, and the others at the multipurpose and communications consoles.

Von Grabow stooped to speak to Schoener. "Canisters?" he asked quietly. The distant whine of the engines almost drowned his words.

"Checked. Every man is ready." Schoener reached into his flight suit's breast pocket and withdrew a small, pencilsize silver canister. A tiny window at the top showed a green tag.

"Good. Let's go forward."

Schoener unbuckled his harness. He fell in behind von Grabow as the general went back through the curtainway. The console operators and duty officer were still intent on their tubes and procedures. The deck angle flattened. They were near their cruise altitude. The big Boeing climbed at something less than 1500 meters per minute at maximum gross weight, so it was taking a long time today to climb to their mission altitude of 11,000 meters.

Von Grabow halted behind the communications officer, whose back was to the aisle. He hunched over his console's desk, staring blankly into space beyond the digital readouts on his overhead unit, concentrating on the electronic ether. Schoener tapped him on the shoulder. Surprised, he swiveled his seat around and pulled off one earphone. He nodded at Schoener and addressed von Grabow.

"Ah—sorry, General. Didn't see you, sir. What can I do for you?" He was a youngish Air Force captain, with thick glasses and a blond crewcut.

"I wonder if you could get a message off for me, Captain. A personal matter."

The captain pursed his lips and darted a glance at the mission commander's console around the corner. "Ah, well, sir—"

"Perfectly okay, Captain. We do it all the time on our E3s. And you can log it."

"Well, okay, General. Sure. Here. Write down what you want sent, how, and on what freq." He handed von Grabow a message form. Von Grabow waved it to Schoener, who took it and swiftly jotted down the information. He handed it back to the young officer.

"Hmmm. Shortwave, huh? Plain language? And—exactly at 1915?"

"Correct, Captain."

The American obviously wanted to ask more. But a general was a general. He was on board. He was given the run of the ship—the "old man" had made that clear. So he must have authority. The captain shrugged. "Sure thing, sir. It'll go out on time."

The general smiled winningly. "Excellent. Thank you, Captain." With that he turned and headed for the flight deck, followed again by Schoener.

The captain checked the time. 1911.46. He flipped open the comm log and carefully noted the details of the general's message. In the Comments section he even more carefully noted that he had been ordered to send it by a foreign national whom he assumed had authority. A man had to make a point of covering his ass, he thought.

At 1913 Yellow Rose 5 was at altitude, on station, ready to begin its familiarization training.

At 1915 exactly the young captain selected the appropriate shortwave frequency, listened to the channel briefly, cleared his throat, and said, "Bismarck lives. I say again, Bismarck lives." After he spoke he listened once more to the frequency and heard nothing but the usual shortwave background. He repeated the message and shrugged again. Who could figure out the Germans?

The radio operator sat bolt upright. He touched the sleeve of the commander. "Herr Oberst," he whispered hoarsely.

"Yes?" The commander leaned forward. In the gloom

he could hardly make out the operator, his radio, or its whip antenna.

"Bismarck," said the operator.

"On time?"

"Exactiy, Herr Oberst. On time."

The commander sat still for a moment. He pulled back the flap of the dripping poncho. The rain had finally slacked off. But it was still bone-chillingly cold.

"Pass the word to the section leaders. Prepare to advance as planned on my notice."

"Herr Oberst." The operator selected another channel and spoke into his mike.

"All acknowledge. Ready to go, sir."

The commander stood up. Water cascaded down his poncho. From under it he pulled his FN 9mm pistol. The radio operator stood awkwardly to join him. The commander looked around, but his men were invisible in the fog and darkness. He thought he heard a faint rustle nearby. The snicking home of a weapon bolt.

"Execute," he said quietly, and moved forward over the lip of the sodden hollow in which he'd spent far too much time waiting. The radio operator whispered into his mike again and hurried to keep up.

Muth vibrated as if he'd drunk too much coffee. In the dim red light of the BTR's simple radio panel, he held out his hand as steadily as he could. It twitched oddly. He dropped it before the driver noticed.

The headphones poured the hissing, crackling background noise of the shortwave band into his ears. He checked the frequency for the tenth time. He checked the time. Then, suddenly, the words came. And were gone. He blinked. Had he imagined them?

No. They were real. He'd watched the signal-meter needle peg itself for a few seconds as the powerful American transmitter boomed out its message.

Muth's heart pounded. His palms went wet. His mouth

went dry. He made his shaking hand select another frequency.

"Viktor One. Viktor Two. Do you read me?"

"Viktor One. Affirmative."

"Viktor Two. Affirmative."

"Viktor One and Two. Advance. Repeat. Advance. Acknowledge."

"Viktor One. Advancing."

"Viktor Two. Advancing."

The headphones were silent again. Muth peeled them off, looked at the driver, and said, "Wait for my signal on channel five. If you don't get it in fifteen minutes, you're on your own." Then he lifted the armored car's cold steel hatch and levered himself out into the darkness.

Next to the car, Steiner waited. Muth dropped to the ground beside him and almost lost his footing in the mud. Steiner steadied him. Without being asked he handed Muth his AKM automatic weapon. Muth took the AKM, checked it by feel, and started for the trees. Steiner fell in alongside him.

At 1918 the American duty officer went aft to ask the Germans to join him. They stood and followed him up the aisle. As they crowded into the console area the American operators stood. For just a moment nobody was sitting down, and each American stood next to a German. Helmut Schoener, standing next to the duty officer, suddenly said, "Bismarck" in a clear, commanding tone, breaking through the friendly chatter of the Americans as they made way for the Germans to take the stations.

The scene froze. Each German pulled the little silver canister from a pocket and firmly pressed it against the arm or leg or chest of a nearby American. By the time the Americans reacted it was too late. One by one they succumbed to the nerve agent forced into their bodies by the compressed air in the canisters. In three seconds they all slumped to the floor, unconscious.

Schoener waved to the men to drag them back to the crew rest area. He hurried forward to the comm section. The young captain had heard none of it. He still worked his procedures, staring intently at his cathode ray tubes. So he never saw Schoener or the canister that briefly touched his shoulder. He fell forward onto the little table, senseless. Schoener checked his pulse, then swiftly went around the radio stack. The data systems operator glanced at him. Schoener grinned back.

"On schedule?" Schoener asked.

The systems officer pulled one earphone off his head, still smiling. "Sorry, Colonel, what? Couldn't hear."

Holding his smile, Schoener edged close. As if mocking the man's inability to hear, he bent low, cupped his right hand, and said, "I wondered if everything is on schedule." With his left hand he fired the canister into the man's neck.

A look of surprise flashed over the operator's clean-cut features. Then he went limp. Schoener steadied him against the straps of his seat and turned to the flight deck.

Von Grabow and the German pilots had done their jobs. They were already struggling to get the Americans out of their positions. The navigator slumped against his console. A little trickle of blood ran down his neck. Schoener lifted his eyebrows at it while he unbuckled the straps. Von Grabow heaved the pilot to the side of the fuselage and said, "He caught on a little too quickly. Wolf had to deal with him."

"But he's alive?"

"Of course. Sedated, like the others. Here, help us."

Schoener grabbed the pilot's arms and started through the bulkhead. One of the Luftwaffe pilots took his feet while von Grabow and the other pilot quickly checked the autopilot. In the main aisle Schoener gave his end of the unconscious pilot to one of the junior officers and went to the duty officer's station. He donned a headset and plugged it into the intercom.

"Schoener here. All stations, check in."

One by one the operators came on line. Within a minute the critical functions were all manned. The American crew lay in the bunks in the crew rest area, securely strapped in. The nerve agents would keep them unconscious for at least twenty-four hours. Schoener listened as each man checked in, then said, "Herr General, are you on the system?"

At the mission commander's station near the flight deck von Grabow toggled his intercom. "Yes, Oberst. Men, you have done superbly. No one has been injured. Our situation is this. We have full fuel, and we are ready to proceed. I assume you are ready also?"

The response was gratifying. Still excited by their take-over, his Luftwaffe people were ready for anything.

"Good. Then we proceed. You each have your tasks. Communications, let me know the instant we have confirmation from Blood and Iron. Oberst Schoener, you are in charge. Good luck to us all. And—remember, all of you. Germany's future is in our hands." He toggled off and removed the headset. The clock read 1923.27. He sat still for a moment, listening, feeling. The airplane vibrated ever so slightly, the tiny tingle of aluminum shaken by the roaring fury unleashed by jet engines. Up here, far above the clouds, all was peaceful, seemingly unchanged. Below, he knew, it was different.

The nerve gas rolled through the American battery unde-tected. The men had finally been fed. They were full of hot food, they were exhausted and cold, and they were simply not playing the game. The guards were as sluggish as the off-duty people. Even if they'd been alerted to the presence of the gas, they would have reacted too slowly. As it was, the gas penetrated the open areas within three minutes, and because the CO had left the door open in the command vehicle, defeating the built-in filter system, it took out the CO, his deputy, and the duty comm man within the next minute. By 1927 the Pershing IIA battery was manned by unconscious Americans.

Helling advanced cautiously, hardly believing his luck. The little radio built into his protective mask told him that the luck was genuine, as one after another of his men discovered the knocked-out Americans. There was no resistance. He reached the command vehicle at 1931. The detectors they carried registered radically diminished levels of the gas. He ripped off his mask and detailed his men to clean up the mess. His own comm operator took over the console. Because of the endless joint training between the Americans and Germans, and because the Germans operated their own Pershing IIA batteries, he knew the system well. He selected the secure narrow-band voice channel previously determined.

"Ready for transmission, Herr Oberst," he said. The colonel paused in checking the missile-status reports left on the command console.

"Send the signal then," he said.

The comm operator keyed his mike. "Hello Bismarck. Hello Bismarck. Do you read?"

Eleven thousand meters above and one hundred kilometers northwest, the E3G's radioman jerked. "Bismarck here. Go ahead."

"Bismarck, this is Blood. All in order. I say again, all is in order at Blood."

"Affirmative, Blood, understand. Stand by." The airborne radioman flipped his audio selector to intercom and toggled Schoener's switch. "Sir, we have Blood," he said. Schoener nodded. "Excellent. I'll tell the general. Anything from Iron?"

"No, Herr Oberst. Not yet."

"Let me know soonest."

"Of course, Herr Oberst." The radioman reselected the Iron frequency. Nothing came over but the UHF white noise.

If Muth had had things his way, the assault would have been early in the predawn hours. As it was, not enough of the Russians would be drunk. Their only hope would be surprise. It was axiomatic in such commando-style attacks that if you didn't capture your target within a short time of the general assault, you were finished. Especially if the enemy had superior forces on call. And this SS23X battery certainly had that.

Yet so far things were working well. He crouched under the branches of a spruce and listened to the reports of his knife men. The outpost guards were silenced without trouble. Too many months of inactivity had dulled their edge.

Another report came through. The most important one. They had eliminated the command-trailer personnel. Silently. His teams now moved through the tent area and the rocket guards themselves. He motioned his radioman and Steiner forward with him.

Suddenly, somewhere to the left, an automatic weapon chattered out its whole clip. It was instantly answered by two or three more. Muth cursed under his breath. It had been too good to be true, of course. Somebody had to screw up eventually. But at least the Russian commander was out of it. He cocked his AKM and ran forward.

All around him weapons stuttered into life. They all sounded alike because they were. All Warsaw Pact armies used the same weapons. But as a precaution his people fired green tracer to keep from engaging one another. The Russians used red tracer. As he broke into a cleared area by one of the rocket launchers he stumbled over a body. He recovered his balance and ignored the body.

"Radio!" he barked.

The mike came out for him.

"Frankel! What's your situation?"

"Herr Oberst. We have almost all the battery out of action. Just one little group on the north side, by rockets three and four. They're stubborn."

"Make it fast. I don't want this to go on any longer than it must."

"*Jawohl,* Herr Oberst!" Frankel got off the line. Muth handed the mike back and surveyed the scene over the edge of the launcher's massive fenders. The tracers were now mostly green. He waved to the radioman and Steiner and ran around the launcher, making for the command trailer. In the erratic light of the few camp lamps left burning, he made out more and more prone figures. His people seemed to be nowhere in sight. He rounded a stand of trees and saw the command trailer, well-lit inside. Figures scurried in and out, carrying bodies. By the time he pounded to a halt outside the door and confronted a startled soldier on guard, his legs ached and his heart sounded like a cannon in his ears. He was getting too old for hundred-meter sprints.

"Report!" he said, gasping for breath.

"Herr Oberst, the captain left to take care of the northeast problem. Former-lieutenant Kollsmann is inside."

"Good. Stay here. Steiner, go see if you can help. Radio, come with me." As he wheezed up the steps he thought he heard the firing dying down.

Considering that his men had killed four Russians inside the trailer only a few minutes ago, things were in good shape. A fair amount of blood was slung here and there, but that was to be expected. Kollsmann directed the clean-up crew crisply, efficiently. He saluted when he saw Muth.

"All is in order, Herr Oberst," he said tonelessly.

"Good. As of this moment you are reinstated as a lieutenant. I want a body count. No one must escape. Go."

Kollsmann grabbed his AKM and clattered out the door and down the steps.

Muth wondered for a split-second about Konstantin. Had he been asleep, drunk, when his men had killed him? He brushed the thought aside. There was too much work to do.

"Radio," he snapped.

"Sir."

"Get on their set, on this frequency, and get ready to contact Bismarck." Muth handed him a scrap of paper with the frequency.

The radioman slipped out of his backpack, jumped in front of the comm console, and turned the black selector and frequency knobs to the desired settings. In a moment he had the earphones and microphone settled on his head. A little blood lay unnoticed on the console. "Ready, Herr Oberst."

Muth riffled absently through the papers on the console. He couldn't do anything until all was secure. The firing in the area wouldn't alarm anybody. All the units that might hear it knew his people were there for extended joint maneuvers, and the Soviets made a fetish out of night attacks. But nobody could be allowed to escape. When Schoener had been helping him plan all this, he had mentioned that the man taking the Ami battery would have gas. For a moment he'd envied him. But his people couldn't have trained properly with gas; it was considered too dangerous for such unreliable troops. So it had to be the old-fashioned way. A commando ground attack.

He realized that the firing had been stopped for some time. A moment later Frankel appeared at the door and said, "Herr Oberst. No one escaped. We have accounted for everyone."

"Any of them wounded?"

"Fifteen. All killed."

"Our casualties?"

"Nine. One dead. The rest minor. It went exactly as we had planned."

And so it damn well should have, thought Muth. He looked at his watch. 1940.

"Excellent. Tell the men well done. Establish your guards. Begin the rocket set-up procedures as we discussed. These instructions will guide you. Orders for your guards are to shoot at anything that moves outside their perimeter. No exceptions. Until I say so, nobody gets in, nobody gets out. Questions."

"None, Herr Oberst. We should have the bodies stored in the designated tent within ten minutes. The launchers will be ready in twenty."

"Good. Stay in touch on channel eight." Muth dismissed him with a waved salute and turned to the radioman. "Now. Contact Bismarck now."

"The message, Herr Oberst?"

"A short one. Just tell them Iron is ready."

"Iron?"

"Iron. They'll know what it means."

When he got the word from the communications man, Schoener slowly pulled off his earphones. He stood up and left the duty officer's console, headed for the mission commander's station. When he arrived von Grabow regarded him gravely.

"Well?"

"They've done it, Herr General. Iron is taken."

"My God," said von Grabow finally. "My God. We've pulled it off, Helmut."

The blood began returning to Schoener's face. The dizziness cleared. He realized with a start that the general had addressed him by his Christian name. "Yes. But now the hard part comes." He glanced at the console clock. "It's now 1942. We should have both batteries ready by 2015. Then we can start."

"Almost exactly according to plan."

"Yes."

"Seems too easy, doesn't it?"

"Yes."

"It troubles me too. But God knows we worked hard enough on the variables. Perhaps this is the one plan that every officer gets to have executed properly."

"Perhaps."

"And maybe, Helmut, maybe this time God really is on our side." He tried to say it with a smile. Schoener remained impassive, but his mind whirled. It had all happened so quickly. He looked for the right thing to say. But of course the wrong thing came out instead.

"Maybe," he said.

━━━━━━━━━━━━━━━ **FOURTEEN**

"Phone, sir."

"What? Dammit, Henderson, I told you I wasn't to be disturbed. Have General Miles take it."

"Sorry, sir. Flash priority. Category clearance. Has to be you. I've got the portable here."

"Well, who the hell is it?"

"Luftwaffe, sir. Von Grabow, brigadier general."

General Wade C. Morse, U.S. Army, glared at his aide. The young lieutenant colonel had been a fine choice. He spoke five languages, held the CIB, was an 82nd Airborne Master Blaster, understood politics better than most of the nitwits who ran NATO, and had kept Morse's schedule coherent. But the son of a bitch still irritated the Supreme Commander, Allied Forces Europe.

Morse glanced at the head of the long table. The elderly, dignified prince had noted his aide's smooth entry into the glittering hall. He held Morse's eye and nodded his understanding. Morse bowed slightly, muttered his apologies to the stunning young woman in a low-cut white gown to his left, nodded to the prune-faced UNESCO chairperson to his right, received a frosty stare in return, and slid away from the table.

The people packed into the palace's dining room hardly noticed. He wouldn't miss the usual European natter of this group of sixty semi- and demi-important Europeans. But he would dearly miss the chow. He tried not to think about the incredible *filet d'esturgeon fumé à la Muscovite* that was just now being served. There would be another such dinner. There always was.

He strode out of the high-ceilinged dining room through one of the side doors, flanked by the lieutenant colonel. A liveried footman swung wide the gilded door. The aide turned left immediately. They crossed the rich carpeting of the sumptuously appointed anteroom and entered a small adjacent office. A huge American MP stood guard at the door. He snapped to attention as the general and the aide stepped through.

Inside the oak-paneled library-cum-den the aide had set up the temporary command post that followed the general everywhere. It resided mostly in a big black aluminum case, and consisted of a master multiband transceiver and scrambler, a flimsy-fax telecopier, two narrow-band secure voice telephones, and the daily documents. The aide handed the white phone to Morse.

"Morse here," he grated. The old oaken walls absorbed the edge of his voice. The aide stepped back slightly. Morse's physical presence was impressive even when he was smiling. When he glowered, as now, it was best not to be too close. He seemed to swell from his normal six feet two to about nine feet, and his barrel chest threatened to pop the many medals from his dress blue uniform.

"Wade. Thank you for coming. I know the prince's *filet d'esturgeon* is delectable. This is Freddy von Grabow."

"Von Grabow. Jesus. Damn right his fish is good. I hope you've got a good reason making me miss it, General." The aide caught the nuance that the German Luftwaffe brigadier general couldn't miss. When Morse got formal with junior general officers, it meant he was really angry. Especially when the junior generals were men whose company he enjoyed socially.

"The best, General. I'm about to present you with a situation. You're familiar with the E3G?"

"E3G. Oh. The new AWACS. Of course."

"I'm calling from it. We're at, ah, thirty-five thousand feet, over the Moselle."

"Great. Why the hell is that a situation?"

"Because I've commandeered the airplane. The American crew is sedated."

Morse blinked. He opened his mouth, then closed it slowly. He glanced at his aide and nodded toward the recorder. The aide pressed the auto-record switch. He lifted the listen-only receiver and then his eyebrows. Morse nodded.

"So. You stole an airplane. Congratulations. You guys get drunk or something? Trying to prove we've got lousy security?"

"No. We also have Battery B, Fifth Battalion of the Fifty-sixth in our hands. You know what that means. Nine Pershing IIAs with reloads. And we now control a battery of SS23Xs near the Czech border on the other side."

A vein swelled on Morse's temple. "Nice. What do you mean 'we'? Who's 'we'?"

"My organization. No political affiliation. Just Germans. Now, time is going to be short, General Morse, so I'd like to get to the point of all this."

"I wish you would." Morse's voice had gone smooth as silk.

"I imagine right now you're thinking that the most likely cause of this call is not that I've done the things I mentioned. I imagine that you figure I'm simply insane. I know I would think that. So to demonstrate that what I say is true, please ensure that your fax is on auto."

Morse inclined his head to the aide. The lieutenant colonel checked and nodded.

"It's on."

"Good. Now, you know and I know that only a few key people can access your fax directly. We don't need to go into who those people are. But the point is that you don't get in unless you've got the numbers. We've got the numbers. And we've got something else. I'm going to send it to you now. Please scan it as it comes out and stay on the line. Ready?"

Morse chewed his cheek. What else could he do? "Sure. Fire away."

Four hundred miles east and seven miles high, von Grabow turned his intercom selector to the computer operator's station, where Schoener awaited his call. "Helmut. Send it."

Schoener toggled his intercom, said "Affirmative," and pressed an illuminated key. It ordered the powerful transmitter of the E3G to select a preset frequency and send a coded burst transmission to the Sector Operations Center at Goch. The transmission was received by the mainframe data processor, translated immediately as a data command that activated a secret program, and the program was run. The operator on duty at what had been Willi Vogel's station gaped in astonishment as the computer cleared his screen, apparently took command of itself, and instigated a series of communications and control actions that resulted in the top-secret Brussels mainframe computer itself acting as an unwilling accessory to the SOC computer. In seconds the program that lay locked in the Brussels computer's labyrinth memory was fed to a remote transmitting site in Belgium, sent via narrow-band secure data link to the transceiver sitting on the desk in the prince's oak-paneled office, and the fax began to print out a message at the rate of 150 characters per second.

Morse peered at the flimsy paper and the spidery characters as they whirred out onto the paper. He slowly put the phone on the desk and sank into a chair, mesmerized.

TO: COMMANDERS OF AMERICAN, BRITISH, FRENCH, AND SOVIET FORCES NOW OCCUPYING GERMANY

FROM: FRIEDRICH VON GRABOW, BRIGADE-GENERAL, DEUTSCHE LUFTWAFFE

SUBJECT: DEMAND FOR WITHDRAWAL OF ALL AMERICAN, BRITISH, FRENCH, AND SOVIET FORCES FROM GERMAN TERRITORY

1. YOU ARE DIRECTED TO WITHDRAW ALL YOUR FORCES FROM "EAST" AND "WEST" GERMAN TERRITORY.

2. WITHDRAWAL WILL BEGIN AT 0830 TOMORROW. YOU WILL HAVE NOT MORE THAN 24 HOURS TO COMPLETE WITHDRAWAL.

3. ALL MILITARY EQUIPMENT NOT HAND-TRANS-PORTABLE WILL BE LEFT IN SITU.

4. UNTIL WITHDRAWAL OF ALL OCCUPYING FORCES IS COMPLETE, NUCLEAR MISSILES APPROPRIATED FROM U. S. AND SOVIET FORCES WILL REMAIN AT READY-LAUNCH STATUS, TARGETED ON NATO AND WARSAW PACT CITIES.

5. AT THE CONCLUSION OF TOTAL FORCE WITH-DRAWAL, THE MISSILES WILL DOWNGRADE TO READY STATUS.

CONDITIONS AND EXPLANATIONS:

1. Definitions.
   A. "Forces" in this context means all combatant personnel, ground, sea, and air. Dependents and civilian-contract employees not assigned overt or co-vert combat roles are excluded.
   B. "Withdrawal" means "permanent withdrawal,

by whatever means chosen, beyond the physical boundaries of the Federal Republic and German Democratic Republics of Germany."

C. "Begin the withdrawal" means "the physical movement, at the highest possible speed, no later than this time."

D. "Hand-transportable" means "capable of being moved by a single soldier without mechanical or other aid."

2. Conditions.

A. Logistics.

I. GAF BG von Grabow has available multiple, computer-proven withdrawal plans for all forces affected. In the event commanders are not able to produce such plans themselves, BG von Grabow will make the required plans available. Repeated and exhaustive simulation on the Brussels and Zossen computers has demonstrated feasibility of the demanded withdrawal within the time frame required. Therefore, logistical difficulties will not be permitted as reasons for noncompliance.

II. All communications between the forces involved and BG von Grabow will be on these channels (use today's frequency guides):

US—channel 9 (alternate: channel 8)

British—channel 6 (alternate: channel 5)

French—French Air Force channel 7 (alternate: FAF channel 8)

Soviet—Command channel 2 (alternate: GRU channel 1)

All communications will be via narrow-band secure voice link, unless otherwise arranged with BG von Grabow.

B. Nature of threat.

I. BG von Grabow is in command of an appropriated USAF E3G, now flying as USAFE Mission Yellow Rose 5. This aircraft is the command element of the forces controlling Pershing IIA missiles in Hohenfels and SS23X rockets near the Czech border. Sensor capabilities of the E3G are such that any undesired military activity within the sensor range of the E3G will result in a launch command to the missile site commanders. It is important that commanders of the involved forces understand that:

a. Any belligerent action by any force will result in immediate launches of all missiles;

b. The Pershings are targeted against Western cities and the SS23Xs against Eastern European cities, thus enhancing the ranges of each; and that

c. The launch sites are controlled by fully armed forces, which have retargeted and armed the missiles.

II. Verification of the above for maximum national efforts is obvious. BG von Grabow directs therefore that each force commander detail a single technically qualified officer to visit each site. That officer will be allowed free access to communications to report his findings, but will not be allowed to leave the site until withdrawal of all forces is completed. Details of travel to and access to each site will be transmitted when appropriate.

III. Final warning. In the event BG von Grabow is not convinced that full withdrawal is proceeding by any of the forces a/o 0800 tomorrow, civilian populations of the targeted cities will be exposed to broadcasts over national and local media describing the threat, its purpose, and immediate cause, which will be defined as leadership intransigence. This step can be expected to produce immediate civil disorder and ultimate breakdown of authority in the affected states. Verification of this can be determined by reference to Brusse's program Q:NAC11, and at Zossen through access to Ministry for State Security Secret File GDRNG.2A.

END OF MESSAGE

The fax machine whirred out the last line and quit. Morse let the flimsy fall behind the machine and picked up the phone.

"Is this some kind of *joke*, von Grabow? Because if so—"

Von Grabow's tone hardened. "General Morse. You do not have much time. I assure you, this operation is under way, and it is in dead seriousness. I assume you received the full message?"

"Apparently. But look, Freddy. Jesus. Even if I wanted to follow this—this *lunacy,* I don't have the damn authority. Man, you're talking about national defense policy. Nobody can authorize this but the President."

"I know. Clearly you'll have to get working on authorization, won't you?"

Morse started to yell something into the receiver, then forced himself to calm down. He looked at his aide. The colonel stood by coolly, listening, as if he heard such ultimata issued to the United States every day. Morse gathered his thoughts.

"Wade? General Morse? Are you there?"

"Yes, yes, I'm still here. Look, Freddy. I presume, since you claim to have worked all this through the computers—God knows how, and we'll have to look hard into that one—anyway, since you claim to have worked this, you must know that even in the strictest logistical sense, even if we agreed to this insanity, we'd be facing a move that would make the evacuation of New York look like a picnic. There's just no way we could manage it in time. Too many people. Too many questions. Too much—"

"Wrong, Wade. It will work. I can give you the plans, and all that is worked into each one—confusion, bungling ineptitude on the part of the petty officials involved, stubborn resistance by family soldiers, the works. You're not dealing with some half-cocked juvenile terrorist, Wade.

You're up against your own systems. They say you can do it. If you begin now, and cut through the red tape.''

"I'm not dealing with a terrorist? Really? Doesn't damn well sound that way to me, von Grabow. By the way, do your people know about all this?"

"Which people?"

"Your government, for starters. I assume they'll back you up. And the military. Command staff. Line officers."

"The government will be told what to do when all the forces have been told. Likewise the command staff."

"You mean you're on your *own*? You dare to pull this kind of harebrained, wise-ass stunt without some kind of authority? That makes you a goddamn outlaw no matter how you cut it!"

"My authority comprises about fifteen megatons of yield, General Morse. Your side's part of that would be nearly seven megatons, delivered to most effect. As you know, unlike the IA and the II, the IIA is virtually uninterceptible. Once they're launched, questions of legality are unimportant."

Morse shook his head, staring through the paneling. "You'd actually launch? You'd kill millions of innocent people? Just because of some grandstand play like this?"

"Millions of innocent people? There are none anymore. I direct your attention to the contingency OpPlan recently approved by your President. You must know about it. You signed it five months ago. It calls for a pre-emptive attack on Pact lines in case of continued intransigence over the space stations and the oil states. Aside from the hypocrisy of pledging no first use of nukes, aside from the subjection of my country to what the computers all agree would be total destruction—again!—*you* are talking about blithely subjecting millions of Europeans to another war. Don't talk to me about morality. And don't doubt my willingness to launch. I am a German. Remember your history." Von Grabow paused. "Now, time is very short. I must speak with the others. Get moving. I can assure you, if you do not push this through, if you try to counterattack this aircraft or the Pershing site, we'll launch immediately. Do you understand?''

"Yes. I understand. But I promise nothing. Except that you and your outlaws are going to wish—''

"There's no time for that, General Morse. I suggest you use your little remaining time to assemble your decision people and get your on-site inspection officers ready. They will need to see that we are in fact quite capable of independent launching, so that the predictable refusals to acknowledge reality by your politicians can be eliminated as quickly as possible. They will need to see, for instance, that we have circumvented your so-called protective action link. That we have reprogrammed the missile-guidance computers. And one more thing.''

"Yeah?''

"One of your bright boys will eventually figure out from the records of this flight that we have only enough fuel to make to about 0830 tomorrow. This is not an oversight in planning. It is another guarantee of our intentions. If you people refuse to take action—if any one of you refuses—when our engines flame out, we launch on both sides.''

"And if we play ball? How do you propose to run this whole little drama with no fuel for the next twenty-four hours?''

"You're going to scramble a KC-135 from Rhein-Main to rendezvous with me for in-flight refueling at 0825. We'll know by then whether it'll be needed. I suggest you don't try to play for those extra five minutes. It won't do you any good. If we've gotten to 0800 and I see insufficient evidence of your good faith, we will have sent the message to the people. That may take things entirely out of everybody's hands.''

"All right, von Grabow. Stand by. You are, by God,

going to hear from us. And soon. Out.'' He slammed the phone down on the desk savagely.

His aide replaced his receiver in the case. He waited while Morse glared at the wall. In the dining room a chamber ensemble began playing Mozart.

''Okay. We've got a lot of work to do. This bastard has a fistful of face cards now, and we have to play his game for a while. First, check his facts. Get Wiley and his boys on this immediately. Second. Assuming the SOB is telling the truth, we have to let the NMCC know about this, so stand by with a direct line to Washington. Third. Activate the command net with the Frogs and Brits. Let me know as soon as you can what the Reds are up to.'' He looked at his watch. ''It's 2025 now. I'm going back to tell the prince I've been called away, and collect Bernie Bernstein. Get my car, clear the route, and stand by to take off for the bunker like a striped-ass ape in, say, five minutes. I'm not going to run this freak show from a library. Got it?''

The lieutenant colonel had it. His young face was still impassive. But it was pale, and beads of sweat stood out on his forehead. ''The President, sir?'' he asked.

''Not yet. We'll get to him when we know the score. We have to keep this contained right now. And I mean contained. Freddy had that part right anyway. Get the cookie pushers involved with this and we'll all be sucking rads by noon tomorrow. Let's go.''

Von Grabow swiveled his chair away from the command console. The technical part had been easier than he'd expected. But the discussion—that had not been so good. Too much wasted time. Too much argument. The British would be easier. Air Marshal Sir Alexander Davey-Whyte was much less impulsive than Morse. And he knew him better, socially. Likewise Jean-Claude Deschamps.

''Herr General?''

Von Grabow flipped on his intercom. ''Yes?''

"How did it go with Morse?"

"He understands anyway. Let's proceed, Helmut. Contact the air marshal now. He is in London?"

"Yes. In his club."

"But he will have access to his command net—?"

"Yes. His adjutant is a member too."

"Excellent. Any problems technically?"

"None, Herr General."

"What about the Soviets?"

"I have already taken care of them, Herr General. A single call to General Colonel Konetsov in Moscow, and one to First Deputy Secretary Irgunin. As we thought, they both grasped the situation immediately. Especially when I told them of the other calls we planned to make."

"How did Konetsov react to one of his top agents double-crossing him?"

"He was clearly not happy. But he is a hard man. He did not reveal too much emotion. Besides, a GRU commander must expect such things."

"Did he threaten you?"

"Of course. But a GRU agent expects such a thing to follow a defection. It was mostly ritual. We dispensed with it quickly."

"They both received the printed message?"

"Perfectly. Konetsov was, as I thought, in the GRU command post. Their facilities are quite impressive. And Irgunin took the message through the Kremlin's Politburo communication center."

"Then the next call I shall have to make after Deschamps will be to Bonn. You have everything ready for that one to the Chancellor?"

"The whole file is in the aircraft's memory, ready for transmission."

"Then expect to do it in no more than fifteen minutes."

"Ready, Herr General."

"Get me the air marshal then." Von Grabow toggled

off his intercom and waited while the headphones hissed. Another dinner was about to be interrupted, and another general officer was about to have indigestion, he thought. It made him smile a little. Then the phone was answered by the air marshal's aide-de-camp. His smile vanished. And soon enough, so did the air marshal's.

────────────────────────────────FIFTEEN

Max confronted the steaming mug of coffee with something less than enthusiasm. It was after nine o'clock, and he had at least two more hours of homework to do. The coffee was not a luxury; it was a necessity. He sighed and sipped the scalding black go-juice, picked up a new file labeled MEMORANDA/MEETINGS AT GSFG HQ/ZOSSEN-WUNSDORF, and flipped back the cover. It was a thick file. Each page was covered with typescript. He rubbed his eyes and pulled the yellow pad nearer. So much for the excitement of intelligence work.

With the thick steel-reinforced door to the file reading room closed, the life of the Mission was inaudible. Max might have been alone in the old mansion. He wasn't. The Missionaries, as the two dozen military officers and enlisted people who worked there called themselves, lived a twenty-four-hour life. There were official shifts, but almost nobody paid any attention to them. There wasn't time, and there was too much work to do. When Max had ambled down to a late dinner more than an hour ago, there had been five other people wearily eating Frau Meissner's chicken in the baron's elegant dining room. Sandy Koppel had been one. She looked as flagged as he felt. Red-eyed, pinch-cheeked, with a crescent of hair falling over her eyes as if to chastise her for being a workaholic. Max slipped into the chair next to hers and grinned weakly.

"Good morning."

"Funny."

"You come here often?"

She eyed him bleakly. "Too tired for fun, Max. Back off."

"Sure. What're you working on?"

"Some guy on a Recovery jaunt spotted something that looked to him like a new damn version of the Tu-30. He managed to get one fuzzy roll of it with his motor drive before the Vopos showed up and escorted him away. We're doing analysis tonight before we send it to Fort Meade."

"Why not let the computer weenies enhance it?"

"Best computer's in here." She tapped her head. "Me and Jinx know what the hell to look for. The pukes at Meade just push buttons. They could look at a MiG and turn it into a Fat Albert and never know the difference."

"Ah." He nodded his thanks to the silent waiter who brought him a plate of steaming chicken. He eyed the pale flesh, the boiled sprouts, and the washed-out carrots with something less than relish.

"What're you up to? Still getting oriented?"

He forked some chicken into his mouth. No taste at all. He chewed and gulped mineral water.

"Yeah. I've got two choices it seems. Work all day and all night to get up to speed by Friday. Or work all day and all night to get up to speed by Friday."

"Democratic, that."

"Yeah." He worked through the food listlessly.

Koppel exuded exhaustion. She looked at her watch and groaned. "Damn. Gotta get back to it if I want to get any sleep at all tonight. See you, Max."

He waved as she left and kept eating. When he returned to his work in the locked file reading room, the stack had not magically reduced itself.

That had been more than an hour ago. He forced himself to focus on the dry, institutional prose, deliberately stilted and cautious, the work of cover-your-ass careerists. He never noticed when boredom became slumber. The pencil in his right hand slipped to the floor and his head lolled. He fell into deep, dreamless sleep.

Somebody was banging on a steel drum. He fought to awaken. No, it wasn't a drum. It was the file room door. He closed his mouth, opened his eyes, and swallowed hard. The banging was just somebody knocking. He glanced at his watch. Only five minutes? Impossible. He struggled to his feet. His left leg had gone to sleep, so he had to lurch to the door. He slipped back the latch and opened the heavy door.

"Lientenant Moss? You all right?"

"Yeah. Sure. What's the problem, uh, Johnson?" It was the black enlisted clerk who doubled as the messenger when he pulled night duty.

"Sir, the colonel wants you. Right away. In his office."

"Sure. Sure. Be right there."

Johnson looked dubious. But he left and Max closed the door. He rubbed a hand across his face and shook his head hard. Wake up, boyo, he thought. He hobbled painfully to the desk as the feeling poured back into his numb leg, and he winced as it turned from that icy sensation to momentary agony. The glamorous dangers of intelligence work. Eyestrain and phlebitis.

He shuffled the files back into order and stuck them into the file drawers, replaced the File Closed card, and signed out on the register. By the time he closed the door behind him his leg was alive again.

He cinched his tie and straightened his uniform as he walked slowly down the corridor to the stairwell. Passing the office Koppel shared with Jinx Morgan, he glanced in. Morgan was hunched over a light table, peering intently at a roll of film in positive format. He said nothing and kept going. Sandy was nowhere in sight. The walk from the third floor to the CO's office on the first woke him. He wasn't feeling great when he nodded to Johnson at the clerk's station and knocked on the door, but he wasn't feeling as if he'd swallowed a mattress either.

"Come in," the CO bellowed. Max went in. The bellow sounded serious.

"Moss. Siddown."

"Sir." Moss sat.

Kemp was in his mess dress blues. He'd left at five or so, Max recalled. Something must be up to get him back at this hour. He scowled, but didn't look angry so much as puzzled and a little worried. What the hell would it take to worry a man like Charlie Kemp?

"We've got a problem, Max. A big one. We—"

A knock interrupted him. "Come in!" he yelled. Koppel opened the door.

"Colonel? You asked—"

"Yeah, Sandy. Grab a chair. I was just getting started." Koppel nodded to Max and hauled one of the straight-backed chairs over from the wall toward Max.

Kemp eyed them for a moment, then referred to a notepad. "Well, hell. Here it is as I know it. Brown—General Brown, DIA deputy—called me while I was at a party in Spandau. I figured some Recovery guy had stepped in it again, but it turned out to be bigger. I got the whole story from NMCC when I got here, twenty minutes ago." He sat back in his chair and took a deep breath.

"About two hours ago a kraut general stole an E3. Yeah. Stole one, even though they have their own—no, don't ask questions yet, Sandy. Hear this out. Anyway, he and his guys steal this E3. Why? They need to have cee-three, that's why. For the Pershing and SS23 batteries their guys also took over." Kemp looked at them. "This isn't some kind of stunt apparently. Washington went into fucking orbit over this, as you can imagine, and they ran everything they could on this guy and his claims. Turns out, as far as they can determine, the son of a bitch actually does have the airplane, the missiles, and the people he claims he does." Max opened his mouth. Kemp held up a hand to stop him.

"What's he want? Simple. He wants our asses out of his country. Now. Not next month, not next year—tomorrow. He's holding a slew of cities hostage until we're gone. He means us, the Reds, the Frogs, and the Brits. Now. Before I let you ask questions, the reason you're here is that we have to send somebody to each site to verify his wild-ass claims about those missiles. Personally I figure the guy's on the level. If he could pull it off this far—steal a goddamn E3, take the American and Soviet batteries, as been verified—then it stands to reason the sucker can retarget the nukes. But to prove it we've been told to provide an expert to check out the Soviet battery." He paused.

Koppel sat up straighter. "No sweat, Colonel. I can be ready in five minutes."

"Great. But you're not going. Moss is."

"What? He just got here!"

Max flushed. But Sandy had turned a brighter red. Angry red.

"I know. But he has experience in the field, Sandy. You haven't."

"Oh, really?"

"Really. Look, I appreciate your gung-ho, but I can't risk you. Suppose things turn to crap? Suppose the Mission has to get really serious in quick-and-dirty analysis? You're our best—our *only*—expert on Soviet technology."

"Perfect reason to send me—"

"Wrong. See, the one who goes, stays. Until the play is over."

"How long is that?" asked Max.

"The kraut has given us until 0830 tomorrow to get cracking. Says, apparently, that if things aren't moving by 0800, he'll broadcast a warning to the threatened cities and let the people go crazy. So basically we got about nine hours."

"The inspector will be a hostage until then?"

"Correct. That's why I need you here, Sandy. But Max—you've handled this kind of stuff before. Right?"

Max swallowed. "Well, sort of."

"Good. Now, Sandy. You have to give Max all you know about these missiles. Guidance, arming procedures, the works. He has to be able to tell if they're really active or just a bluff."

She frowned. "I still think—"

Kemp glowered at her. "Cut the crap, Captain."

"Sir. Okay. As long as you're not playing it this way because I'm a woman."

Kemp got to his feet and put both arms on his desk. He leaned forward, the cords standing out on his neck. His eyes burned. "Let's get one thing straight, Koppel. As far as I'm concerned, women have no place in action. But that's just my view, and the Army's never asked me for it. So what's important to me is that the one officer I have who's experienced in staying alive and useful in the field be used there, and the other officer I have who's got a damn encyclopedia of Red hardware locked in her peabrain be used best here. I couldn't give a shit whether you're male, female, or morphodite. You got that?"

Sandy blushed. "I'm sorry, Colonel. It's just that—"

"Yeah. I know, sexist bullshit and like that. But we don't have time for any of it now. So let's get to work. A Russian chopper is picking up the other three inspectors. The Brit is from their Mission, likewise the Frog. The

Russian is coming from an intel bunch at the GSFG HQ at Zossen. You've got less than ten minutes to cram everything you know about SS23X procedures into Moss. Now—questions?''

Max leaned forward. ''Colonel. Where is the battery?''

''In the area of UR 33, 55.9. By the Czech border. Restricted zone, of course.''

''Do we have any data on the area?''

''Overhead views, topos. Some Recovery information. Not much.''

''A lot of Soviet people in the area?''

''Sure. Guards motor rifle regiment, this rocket bunch, and lots of PVO Strany choppers. Hind-Es mostly. Why?''

''Well, I'd just feel better if we could get some Recovery people down in the area. You know, just in case.''

Kemp pursed his lips. ''The kraut can see everything that moves with that damn E3. But maybe a couple of jeeps . . . yeah. We'll try for it. But we'll have to make sure they stay outside the PRZ. We'll set up freqs for help in case you need it.'' He looked at the grandfather clock ticking away. ''Before you leave I'll have more details from Washington, and specific policy instructions. But I don't think much is going to change. You go down there, contact me with your appraisal of the missiles' readiness, and sit tight until it's all over.''

''Got it. But, Colonel. One more thing. Is this guy for real? I mean, do you think they'd actually launch?''

''Who knows? But we're not talking about some raghead hick, Max. This guy's a German. Prussian background. And with one of them, anything's possible.''

''Including us getting out of Germany?''

''Don't ask me. I work for the government. Ask the government.''

Sandy chimed in. ''Seriously. Do you think they'd do it?''

Kemp picked up a chromed North Vietnamese hand

grenade. It had been tossed into his command car near Phu Bang many years before. The young Latino corporal who'd jumped to pitch it back out had stood up, ready to throw, and been cut down by AK47s from the side of the road. The grenade had fallen back in and Kemp had waited for it to go off, helplessly pinned under the body of the kid who'd tried to save him. The thing had hissed, then fizzled. He kept it to remind himself of certain facts that never changed. He traced its familiar shape absently with his fingers.

"I don't know. We've got to get out someday. We can't garrison this damn country forever. Maybe this is as good a time as any. It's not 'fifty-six anymore. The krauts can handle themselves pretty well. Better than we can, I think sometimes. And they're not afraid of the Reds."

"What do they think in Washington?" Max asked. His throat was dry. He was beginning to get the old pre-race jitters. He wiped his palms on his trousers.

"For a man with only ten minutes to swallow a manual on a missile, you're mighty curious, Moss. What do they think in Washington?" Kemp laughed hollowly. He tossed the grenade up and caught it. "Who knows? They think somebody else ought to deal with this maybe. Or maybe that it will just go away. Hell, I don't know." He set the grenade down and looked hard at them. "Get the fuck out of here, both of you. And Max . . ."

"Sir."

"Good luck. You'll need it."

"I gathered that."

"Then gather your ass out and get moving. We'll be waiting. And no heroics. A simple job this time. Okay?"

"You bet. My heroic days are over. I'm in this for the retirement, not the fun." His line fell flat even as he said it. But as usual he couldn't think of what else to say, and his mouth ran away with itself.

Kemp ignored it. He waved them out. Koppel led and

was through the door in seconds. They said nothing walking up the stairs to her office. The Mission's little sounds— the distant hum of the generators, the muffled electronic noises from the comm room, the remote bangs and clangs from the garage area, where mechanics worked to keep the Recovery stable in top condition—all seemed preternaturally important tonight. The rain had ceased its drumming on the windows and roof. A restless wind blew. Somewhere on the roof a loose antenna wire scraped against tiles.

"Most sensible people are about to go to bed," Max said as they entered the analysis room. Jinx Morgan glanced at him, peering through thick glasses. The Navy lieutenant was unpopular on ships because of his reputation for bringing unfavorable surprise inspections to them. But he'd been well liked at the Mission, where his expertise in photointerpretation was vital.

"Maybe," he said in his Georgia drawl, "but most folks know better than to take up this here kind of life. What'd the CO want?"

"You won't believe it," Koppel said. "And I don't have time to explain now. We have to pump Max full of SS23X. Now."

"Now?"

"Now." She hauled out a thick binder and riffled the pages until she came to the SS23 section. "The X model was included only last month. It's back here." She smoothed the pages and looked at Max.

"Ready to receive?"

"Fire away."

She grimaced. "Poor choice of words, Max. Okay. Guidance. You have to remember that—"

He tried to. He burned the stolen diagrams into his memory. He repeated, as he had been taught to, the vital facts, looking into her eyes, again as he had been taught.

And after five minutes the phone rang. Jinx picked it up, muttered "okay" into it, and replaced it.

"Johnson says CO says the chopper's on the approach to the backyard. Says Moss is to get moving. Anybody want to let ol' Jinx in on the secret?"

"No time, Jinx. Sorry." Koppel slammed the book shut angrily. "I don't care what he says. I should go."

Max buttoned his tunic. "Nope. He's right." He slipped off the chair and headed out the door. "See you in, um, well, I guess whenever," he said over his shoulder. "Thanks for the help, Sandy."

She grabbed her coat and ran after him. She pulled it on and fell in step. Above, the whop-whop of a big helicopter became audible. Max hurried.

Kemp met them at the bottom of the stairs. He handed Max a piece of paper.

"Frequency to call from the battery. We'll be standing by."

"And the Recovery guys?"

"Maybe. We're working on it. Use the guard channel if you need us."

"Thanks, Colonel. See you."

"I'll walk you to the chopper." Johnson handed Max his raincoat and hat. The helicopter drew closer. Its noise buffeted the Mission, and its bright landing lights lit up the rolling lawn between the back porch and the Havelsee. Max stood with Kemp and Koppel at the back door, waiting for it to land. It slowly settled down into the floodlit area, the ugly buglike contours of the Mil-24E suited perfectly to the flat green paint. A huge red star was painted on the loading door, which slammed open as soon as the wheels touched the wet grass.

Max jerked the French doors open and stuffed his garrison cap into his raincoat pocket. He hunched and ran out the doors to the chopper. A Red Army major wearing a headset knelt in the open bay. The big blades chuffed close overhead.

The major extended a hand to Max. He grabbed it and heaved himself into the helicopter. A second later the door slid shut and the major barked something into his headset's microphone. As Max struggled to get into the webbed canvas seat against the far fuselage, the chopper jerked into the air. He fell against the man in the next seat.

He was a British Army major, who regarded him coolly. He said nothing to Max, only inclined his head imperceptibly. Max secured his seat belt and nodded back. Conversation was out of the question, so he looked around the troop bay.

Three other men were strapped in the bay. The Russian major with the headset, who was settling himself into a seat by the door, a Russian captain, and a French major. Details were hard to make out in the dim red light, but Max tried to look them over carefully, if discreetly. Obviously the Russian major was part of the crew. The youngish, thin Soviet captain must be the inspector. He blinked behind round, wire-rimmed glasses, carefully avoiding eye contact with Max. He reminded Moss of Jinx.

Next to him sat the French Army major, who sat bolt upright, making his dark, high-collared semi-dress uniform with its striking gold trimming seem even more militarily impressive. He seemed to be about forty, with thinning black hair and a small, tidy moustache. He wore the French nuclear missile symbol—for a Pluton battery, no doubt—as well as some kind of jump wings. He had deepset dark eyes and a beetle brow, and turned away from Max's gaze after nodding a visual greeting to him in a remote sort of way.

The British Army major likewise swiftly averted his eyes when Max looked again at him. He seemed to be in his late thirties, and was in the distinctive brown winter wool of the Brigade of Guards. A dark beret was tucked

under his left epaulet. He wore two rows of ribbons, none
of which were familiar to Max. He was clean-shaven, tall,
and stocky, and sat board-straight against the side of the
fuselage, as if he and the Frenchman were engaged in
some kind of competition in military bearing, a matter of
honor between St. Cyr and Sandhurst, perhaps.

The noise of the turbines, the gearbox, and the rotor
overhead relieved them of any need to speak. Max settled
against the cold metal wall and stared out the tiny window
in the door across from him. Even at low altitude they flew
through occasional scud. The lights on the ground grew
sparse as they bored through the night, heading south.
Max tried to orient himself by reference to the lights. But
he was too tired, and they were too unfamiliar from this
angle. He closed his eyes. He had at least an hour's flight
ahead. He recalled the sage advice of his unconventional
combat instructor. When in doubt, sleep.

He tried, but was unable. It was hardly surprising. An
hour ago he'd been warm and comfy, staggering through
dreary reports. Now he was being lofted through the night
in a chilly metal box—the twin of one that had tried to kill
him not far from here, and not so long ago—on a lunatic
mission he hadn't really comprehended. Business as usual
at the USMLG. You always imagine that when something
like this comes along, he thought, you'll have time to
square your life away. Say the right things, get ready in a
planned manner.

But it never worked that way, at least not for him. The
chopper lurched sideways and then upward suddenly and
he grabbed a fistful of webbing on the seat to steady
himself. The British major rocked hard against him, and
for a moment Max saw a kind of panic in his eyes. So he
wasn't alone in being confused and scared.

The realization should have comforted him.

It didn't. And whatever waited for him on the other side
of the helicopter's plunge through the night was hurtling
closer at two hundred mph.

SIXTEEN

"Herr General."

"Yes?"

"Movement. Near the Polish border. Fritz picked it up."

"What elements?"

"Ground. No air."

"Remote it to me." Von Grabow pushed the cardboard inflight lunch box to the side of the desk. He keyed the button that would allow the scene now on Schoener's and Fritz's cathode ray tube to be repeated on his. A moment later an outline map of Eastern Europe appeared. Then a box-shaped blip flashed on the screen near the Polish-German border at Goerlitz.

"I have it," he said. "Composition?"

The scene changed. The area expanded many times until a detailed topo-style map filled the screen. The scale told him it was a 1:10,000 reading. The blip was resolved into many smaller blips, in different colors, each with a code number.

"The computer analysis suggests a tank brigade," said Schoener in his earphone. Von Grabow studied the blips.

Some moved faster than others. They all crept toward the border.

"Unit?"

"Best guess is Twenty-fifth Guards from Sorau. They're equipped with T-84s."

Von Grabow watched a moment longer.

"Get Konetsov on the line."

"Do you want me to speak with him?"

"No. The aged arteries of the Politburo allow its members to think only in narrow ways apparently. So I must speak with him. They must understand we are serious."

Schoener clicked off to contact the Soviet GRU commander. Von Grabow munched a piece of sandwich absently, watching the tanks creep toward the border. It couldn't be too pleasant inside them right now; it was raining, the ground must be soggy, and those eighty-ton monsters were the devil to steer in muck. Schoener clicked back on his headset.

"I have the general."

"Good. Switch to me." The line went from completely clear—the intercom—to one that hissed.

"General Konetsov."

"General von Grabow. You want?" The Soviet spoke German. Badly. Von Grabow decided to stay in Russian.

"Comrade General, you evidently have not understood our conditions."

"Why do you say this?"

"As we speak I am observing movement by a brigade of the Twenty-fifth Guards toward the German border. You were warned not to proceed in this manner."

Silence.

"A moment, General von Grabow. This is news for me. I must check. Please stand by." Konetsov's voice remained perfectly neutral. But von Grabow could imagine the fury he would feel if he had discovered that some other Politburo chieftain had decided to cover his bets by secretly ordering a brigade out in the name of the whole Politburo. It was a possibility he and Schoener had encountered in several of the computer simulations. He swallowed a bite and the tanks got closer to the border.

"Comrade General?"

"Yes, General Konetsov."

"My comrades deny any movement of Soviet resources. Your equipment must be malfunctioning."

"It is not, I assure you. Please understand. If the movement continues, we will launch. Penetration of the German border will result in the devastation of nine Warsaw Pact cities. There is to be no discussion."

"This is clear. It is why I tell you now we have no intention of testing your resolve. We believe you."

"Someone does not, obviously."

"Your equipment—"

"Is working perfectly, Comrade General. We have confirmation from all our sensors. Infrared, magnetic anomaly, radar, laser imaging, acoustic—all agree. You have a tank brigade moving on us. It will not be tolerated."

Silence.

"Instead of attempting to blunder through this crisis with outmoded, clumsy methods, General Konetsov, why do you not use the resources you have to accede to our demand? Surely you have already read the file—"

"The file does not exist. It cannot be read."

"I am assured it does. Therefore, since you choose to ignore the realities, you will deserve your fate. It is up to you."

"Von Grabow. It is not that simple. We . . . that is, some of us know. But there are problems. We cannot act so fast. And others—"

"Others are fools. Will you allow fools to bring on the destruction of your motherland? I will not. That is why I act now. The Great Patriotic War is over, Comrade General. It has been for five decades. New realities exist. A

Marxist would know this. He would adapt. Your choices are clear. Adapt or die.''

"A Marxist—"

"Should also know that the tanks are now less than one kilometer from our border. You have little time, Comrade."

Silence. Von Grabow sipped coffee. He felt strangely light-headed.

"Half a kilometer, Comrade," he said into the silence.

"Von Grabow. We will halt the column. Do not launch. Do you hear me?"

"I hear you. But until the tanks stop I will do what I must."

Silence. The leading blip stopped. Then the others halted. Some of the numbers next to each blip began changing. The heat signatures were altering. The tanks were shutting down their engines.

"We have stopped."

"So I see, Comrade General. You will do well to do the same with the infantry battalion to the north."

"The infantry?"

"The sensors are excellent. When the Americans care to, they build better even than we Germans. Don't try my patience, Comrade General."

"I will not. The orders have been sent."

"Good. Now, your inspecting officers should be in place within a few minutes, and then you will have their reports to back up what we say. After that you should not hesitate. You will have much to do, and little time to do it."

"Good-bye for now, General von Grabow." The line clicked. The carrier hiss returned.

Von Grabow switched to intercom. "Herr Schoener?"

"Herr General."

"Give your console to someone else. I need to speak with you."

"Of course."

Von Grabow stuffed the food back into the gray box and shoved it aside. Schoener showed up a moment later.

He looked haggard. Von Grabow knew he must look the same. Dark circles underlay his eyes, which were red and puffy. Stubble covered his chin in blotches. His flight suit was rumpled. He leaned against the outer databank wearily. Von Grabow removed his headset.

"It was close."

"Too close. I did not actually expect them to try it so quickly."

"There was the chance. We knew that."

"Yes."

"What are the odds now?"

Schoener rubbed his eyes with a handkerchief. "The same. The next data plateau will be the reports from the inspectors. All involved have by now established that our basic claims are valid."

Von Grabow ran a hand through his hair. "Have you monitored their action statuses?"

"Except for the Soviet Twenty-fifth Guards, normal readiness worldwide. Only slightly elevated signals traffic within the range of the relayed sensors. They have obviously kept the matter within the projected groups."

"The computer could hardly go wrong with that prediction. These men have built their careers on avoiding just such a situation. They have depended on their staffs to keep them away from a crisis of national policy in which they must act without delay. They do not want to rely on their own judgments in this. We know their initial reactions will have been incredulity, then anger and determination not to dance to our tune. The question is, can their specialists be effective at convincing them they must do as we say?"

"In America it is easier. There is a strong feeling among the cabinet that NATO is not effective, that it is time for the Europeans to solve their own problems. In

England, and France, and certainly Russia, as always, it is
fear of the reunited Germans that will struggle with their
geopolitical understandings.'' Schoener smiled weakly. ''Forgive me, Herr General. You know all this. We have been
over it so many times.''

Von Grabow smiled back. ''No need for apologies. We
are both tired. As soon as the reports are filed we can
expect a long period of scheming on their parts. Take a
nap then. I'll call you if I need you. It is a time of little
danger. Things won't heat up until dawn.'' His smile
widened. ''And there I go. You were the one who worked
all this out, and I lecture you.''

''It must be catching.'' Schoener grinned.

Von Grabow was relieved by the genuineness of his
expression. Schoener almost never revealed his true feelings. To do so in this situation was a good sign.

''So. Back to your station, Herr Schoener. The night is
young.''

Schoener blinked at the digital timer above the commander's console. ''2230. So it is. They should almost be
there by now in the West. And in the East, within ten
minutes.''

''You are tracking the helicopters?''

''Easily. Both continue to use their transponders as
directed.''

Von Grabow reached for his headset. Even with the soft
foam padding, after two hours they raised angry red areas
around his ears. He rubbed them. ''Good work. The men?''

''Fine. High spirits. They ate in two shifts, at their
consoles. All is nominal on the flight deck. Wolf reports
that it is a good airplane.''

''He would. Wolf loves anything that flies.''

''Unlike the general?'' Schoener smiled again

''Back to your station, Herr Oberst,'' von Grabow
growled in mock anger.

As he left; von Grabow gingerly replaced the headset.

The night was young. But it would be ancient before it was all over. And so would they all. He fiddled with the screen selector switch. Had they thought of everything? Had the computers? What was he not doing that he should? Somewhere someone was attempting to destroy him and his plan. Who? Where? *How?*

────────────SEVENTEEN

The Soviet pilot cranked the big gunship into a steep banking turn to the left. Max peered through the little hatch window across the troop bay. The helicopter circled 100 feet above a forest crossroads lit by the headlights of three vehicles. Nearby a red flare indicated the landing zone. After two orbits the Hind pilot executed a high-performance flare and landing. The descent was so sudden that Max had to gulp air to hold his dinner. In seconds the big chopper settled onto its gear. Instantly four spotlights from the sides of the clearing pinned the chopper. The glare dazzled everyone inside. The Russian major yanked the sliding door open. He waved Max out impatiently.

Unfamiliar with the Russian seat belt mechanism, Max fumbled. The Frenchman scrambled out first, heading into one of the lights as if he knew exactly where he was going. He hunched to clear the blades and scurried off away from the ship. Finally Max's cold fingers found the combination, and he clambered off, following the British major.

He didn't notice the cold at first, even though he still wore only his office clothing. He ducked his head and made for the place the Frenchman had run to. Head down, raincoat gathered around to stop its flapping in the rotor downwash, Moss almost ran into him. The Frenchman stood just outside the rotor arc, squinting around. Max straightened and pulled on his garrison cap. He realized that the other two had silently joined them. They stood, whipped by the cold, wet wind made by the chopper's turbines, and waited uncertainly. Nothing happened. They remained transfixed by the brilliant spotlight.

The engines of the helicopter wound up suddenly, and the pilot changed the blade pitch. Max turned in time to see the chopper take the weight from its gear slowly, then all at once jump from the ground. The round, impassive face of the Russian officer in the bay window stood out as the lights continued to track it upward a bit. Then it was gone, the whine of the engines masked by the huge blades. Its belly nav light disappeared quickly into the invisible overcast. Max looked back down just in time to see three of the four lights wink out. They continued to squint into the glare of the fourth.

"Diesen Weg, meine Herren," called a deep German voice from near the light.

They covered their eyes and stumbled forward across the knee-high wet grass of the little meadow. Max concentrated on keeping his footing. His thin socks were soaked, his ankles already freezing. He stumbled and fell a little behind the others. As he recovered his balance he caught a glimpse of something metallic behind him. He half-turned, still walking, and saw that the glint he had noted was the dull sheen of an AKM. Its owner and his partner silently paced the foursome from the rear. Max glanced at the soldier whose weapon he had seen. The man looked gaunt. In the harsh spotlight his features were almost skeletal. He inclined his head slightly and urged Max along by pointing ahead with his automatic weapon. Max caught up with the others.

All at once the light winked out, leaving them momentarily blinded. Flashlights snapped on ahead, and as the hot spots faded from their eyes they made for them.

"Here, gentlemen. Please. Beware the ditch. That's right. Now, please stand facing the personnel carrier." The deep voice, now hidden behind a flashlight, directed them to the flank of a BTR-60. They slogged over the ditch and found themselves standing on a half-mud, half-gravel road next to the eight-wheeled armored vehicle. Six flashlights contained them. A figure entered the circle of light.

"Who is senior?"

The British and French major exchanged looks. The Frenchman shrugged slightly. "I am," said the Brit. His voice sounded thin and reedy, quite unlike his rugged appearance. The distinctive cadences of the Guards were obvious.

"Good. Your name?"

"Findlay. Ralph. Major, Her Majesty's Guards. Look here—"

"Please speak when asked, Major Findlay." The figure—whom Max now saw wore captain's tabs in the NVA—checked a little notepad. "You are with the British Mission?"

"Of course I am. Why else would I be here?"

"A good question. Please tell me the current code sequence for your command post entry door, Major."

"What? I'll do no such—"

"Major Findlay. We do not have much time, and it will rain again soon. Even you will recognize that we must verify that you gentlemen are in fact from the missions you claim to represent. Please tell me your code. Now."

Findlay looked at the Frenchman, who ignored him. "Well. Ah, I believe it's four-six-one-nine. Yes, that's right."

The German held his notepad up to his flashlight. "Correct. Please go to the back of the car, where you will be checked for weapons and asked to enter.'' Findlay hesitated, then walked past the others. As he rounded the tail of the squat car its engine turned over and stuttered to life. Diesel fumes poured from the nearby exhaust.

"Sir? Your name?"

The Frenchman smiled thinly. "Ricard. Henri. Major. And my Mission has no entry code."

"Yes, Major. We know that. Please tell me the telephone number of your Chief of Protocol."

"Of course. That would be Captain Lescaux. He is on zero two three three."

"Thank you, sir. Please follow Major Findlay."

"Comrade Captain?"

"Kulikov. Pavel Pavelovich. Technical intelligence." The young captain pushed his glasses higher on his nose, ducking his head in unconscious deference. Nerves strained his voice. He dropped his hands and smoothed his brown tunic.

"Yes. Your safe combination, please?"

"Yes. My safe. Ah. Two—no, no. It's three–sixteen– twenty-seven–forty. Yes, that's it."

The German paused. "Are you certain, Comrade Captain?"

"Certain? Of course. Yes. Of course."

"We show it as two–sixteen–twenty-seven–forty."

Kulikov stiffened. "Then you are in error. It is as I have said."

"Yes. Thank you. Please go to the entry." He turned to Max, whose wet ankles had begun to go numb. The temperature was only in the middle thirties, but the cold was the wet European cold that seeped through the warmest defenses. Standing in mud wasn't a good defense against it. A shiver ran through him.

"Moss. Maxwell T. Lieutenant. U.S. Air Force. And I

haven't the slightest idea what any of our codes or combinations are. I just got here.''

"I see, Lieutenant Moss. But you can tell me today's NATO code for your Mission?''

"Sure. Pigpen.''

"Good. Join the others.''

His shoes threatened to stay in the congealing goo when he turned for the door. The German captain shadowed him, and a husky NCO frisked him efficiently. Since he had nothing to hide, they found nothing. They pulled open the hatch and he climbed in. Inside, it was warmer, but not by much. The Russian slid over to make room for him on the troop bench. Max found himself again facing his three compatriots. And again they studiously ignored one another. At least he knew their names now.

The captain climbed into the vacant seat in front and signaled the driver to move on. The gears ground and the big armored car lurched forward. Max reached down to massage his numb legs. By the time some circulation was restored they had reached their destination. The captain shouted back to them to prepare to disembark.

The hatches swung open and the four of them filed out. This time they were obviously in a major bivouac area. The roar of generators filled the air. People hustled in every direction. Floodlights illuminated a churned-up parking area for what was obviously a Soviet command trailer. More than a score of soldiers encircled them, weapons lowered but ready. The captain came around and said, "This way, please, gentlemen, to the commander.'' They fell in behind him obediently, and went into the trailer.

Inside, two guards kept them against the wall while the captain went to the rear of the trailer, through a security door. In a few moments he reappeared.

"Gentlemen,'' he said. "Oberst Muth, commander of the camp.''

It was a peculiar situation. Obviously the captain expected them to render military courtesy to the colonel. But to them he was an outlaw. The Frenchman casually peeled off his cap. Max followed suit. The Russian and Englishman remained covered.

Muth appeared and looked them over. He was tallish, stocky, and, like the others, wore mud-spattered battle dress. His gray eyes looked weary, his face drained of color and sagging. Lines etched around his thin lips spoke of deep bitterness. It was a familiar German face.

"Good evening, gentlemen. You are here to verify that the situation is as General von Grabow has presented it. To do so, you must verify several items. First, that we are in fact in control here. Second, that we have readied the rockets for launch on our—not Moscow's—command. And third, that we have correctly targeted and armed the rockets. After you have verified all this to your own satisfaction, you will be allowed access to our communications—under a monitor, of course—and will then be held for the remainder of the situation. Questions?" His German was swift, uninflected, and precise.

"I have one," said Findlay.

"Go ahead, Major," Muth replied.

"Where are the rocket troops from whom you stole this equipment?"

"Dead. Next question."

The Russian captain blinked. He shoved his glasses up on his nose again. "All dead?" he asked, incredulous. "Including Major Konstantin?"

"Yes."

"But there were almost two hundred men here—" the Russian ejaculated.

"Two hundred two. Yes. Gentlemen, there is little time. I suggest that you—"

"But," said Ricard, "how could you have defeated so many? How many men have you?"

A muscle twitched under the gray skin sagging over Muth's cheeks. A little color rose into them. "We have enough, Major. We lost a few in our assault."

"And whose men are they? They are dressed as Germans," said Findlay dryly. "We like to know with whom we're dealing, you see?" Even Findlay's German carried his reedy Guards drawl.

"They are Germans, Major Findlay. That is all you need to know. And to cut this line of inquiry off so that we may get to the serious business for which you have been allowed here, I will tell you how we took the battery. We used surprise, knives, and good intelligence. It was simple."

Max noticed for the first time that a good deal of dried blood covered the floor upon which he dripped muddy water. These guys were serious. The same thought must simultaneously have sunk in to the others. The tension in the trailer became palpable. Muth eyed them.

"I see you are beginning to understand. Excellent. Let us now go to work." He looked at Kulikov. "Comrade Captain. You are the expert among us here. I propose that to save time you conduct your investigation of the technical details while the others observe."

"Ah, certainly. Yes. A sound idea." The Russian obviously was fighting to control himself. His eyes were opened a little too wide, his nostrils flared, his breathing too fast. Muth took him by the arm. He almost jumped.

"This way then," said Muth, and led him toward the master consoles.

The others shuffled along. There seemed hardly enough room to breathe in the jammed corridor. Electronics were packed into every available space. Since many of the units worked with tubes rather than transistors, the master control area was hot and dry. Two soldiers sat at the master console. One wore earphones and ignored them. His shoulder patch identified him as a radioman. The other man seemed to be monitoring the status of the rockets, shown by a mass of nine duplicated dials and lights.

"Captain, you will undoubtedly notice the most important change here." Muth halted and pointed to a place on the horizontal element of the master console. Max realized he was indicating the element Sandy had called the CDS, or central data sequencer. It was really the linchpin of the whole system. Because the Soviets trusted nobody—not even their field rocket commanders—they ensured that launch could occur only when the Politburo decided it was time. The result was a kind of lockbox on the whole system. In effect, they took the Pershing IIA's protective action link idea a step further. In order to launch, a Pershing commander had to have that day's proper codes, which could come only from certain sources. And the two-man system common to American nuclear policy obtained there too. A single lunatic, the reasoning went, could not launch any Pershings. But there were ways for a Pershing commander to get the PAL in the event of totally disrupted communications. Not so at a Soviet rocket battery. Without a signal from Moscow to activate the CDS, nothing would work. The rocket's guidance computers couldn't be programmed, the warhead could not be armed, and the launch signal would be ignored by the processor in the launcher itself.

The captain went to the CDS and examined it. It was a small unit, no larger than a small radio, with two steel loop handles projecting from its top to enable removal and replacement. A big cannon-style plug hung out its bottom, into which was connected the umbilical to the rest of the command trailer's launch system. To prevent tampering, Sandy had told him, the CDS was usually welded shut, and reportedly had a booby trap built in to kill whoever might try to activate it without authorization—and, of course, simultaneously destroy itself.

This CDS obviously had not exploded when Muth had

tampered with it. Instead of resting flush with the console, it lay on its side on top of it. A half-inch hole had been drilled in the bottom, and another, smaller black box attached to something inside by three wires, a red, a blue, and a green one. Five red lights burned on the little box. A cheap Japanese cassette recorder was itself attached to the smaller box. It all meant nothing to Max.

But the Soviet captain, fingers hovering over the weird assemblage, began shaking. After a moment he stood up and confronted Muth. Sweat ran down his smooth young face.

"Do you realize what you have done?"

"Yes. We have taken control of the CDS from Moscow. We have fed new target coordinates into the master guidance computer with the cassette recorder."

"But—but this is impossible. I was told it was impossible!"

"Forgive me for pointing out the obvious, Captain. But it clearly is not impossible. Please verify for yourself. Check the status screen. Note the new rocket readiness states, and take particular note of the launch command now in effect. All we have to do is close one switch. They all go simultaneously."

Kulikov peered at a cathode ray tube screen in front of the seated, silent soldier. He reached past the man and turned a knob. The screen changed. He typed a few alphanumeric sequences into the keyboard. A light flashed above the screen, and in a moment green Cyrillic letters marched across it in the form of nine tables. On the left were the rocket identifiers. In the center were their statuses. On the right their target coordinates. They were all east of the battery. Two were south.

Kulikov slowly straightened up. He looked around the master suite. Blood spattered a few of the gray and black surfaces.

"It is true," he whispered. "True." He looked, dazed,

at the three others. "They have done it," he said in Russian. "Here"—he pointed to the fifth rocket's column on the screen—"here is Moskva." His hand dropped, limp.

"Shall we check the launchers, Kulikov?" asked Findlay. "I mean, what if all these fellows have is a good computer screen?"

Kulikov looked dully at the British major. "No. This cannot be faked. The rockets are armed, targeted, and ready. We need no more."

"Well, I want to see them," Max blurted out. Muth and the others turned to stare at him. "Sorry, Herr Oberst, but I've seen too many computers to be impressed with this one. I need to check the sharp end of the stick."

The colonel almost smiled. "Ah. The American stubbornness. Of course, Lieutenant. If you will turn, Captain Frankel will escort you and your comrades to each rocket." He held his arm up to usher them out. Since he was at the rear, Max exited first.

The tramp to the first rocket didn't take long. It lay just beyond the ZSU-23 antiaircraft gun, which, as Frankel pointed out, was now manned. He led the four through the dank, dripping trees to a nearby clearing. It was a matter of leaving the noise zone of one generator for that of another. As they drew nearer. Max heard the high-rpm clatter of a two-stroke diesel, then saw through the branches a lone mercury light. It shone on a pair of soldiers standing near an uncovered control panel on the flank of the huge green rocket launcher.

The group assembled around the panel. The soldiers eyed them and moved away a bit. One fingered his AKM.

Frankel waved at the rocket, which lay horizontally on its launcher. For all the untrained eye could tell, it was an inert mass of metal. Moss, cued by Koppel to check the three key gauges on the uncovered panel, saw that it was in fact very much alive. It would take less than thirty seconds to bring it to the vertical firing position and light it off. The knowledge chilled Max even more than the walk through the soaked woods. He looked at Kulikov.

"It seems ready," he said.

"It is," the Russian replied. "Do you now believe the master console?"

"Yeah," muttered Moss.

"Good," said Findlay in English. "Now we can get out of the bloody cold and wet, eh?" He turned to Frankel. "We've seen enough, Herr Hauptmann," he said ceremoniously in German.

Max tried to orient himself on the walk back to the trailer. It was difficult. The clouds obscured the stars. But when they reentered the command trailer compound, he guessed that the road to it from the main forest road ran approximately north-south. He noted three armored cars— BTRs, like the one they'd come in—and one armored personnel carrier, a tracked, new-style BMP-9, in the compound, but few soldiers. They were all at their stations apparently; Muth had to make a hundred men do the work of two hundred. He didn't envy them. No matter how easy their victory, they had fought a sharp battle. And yet they had to continue, to stay alert, on edge for another battle for—how long? Like Ricard, he wondered who they were.

Muth allowed them access to the transmitter one at a time. The British major went first, because of seniority. Max stood in the trailer corridor and eyed the guard. Like the others, he was gaunt and tough-looking. He had the look of the professional soldier who's been long on the front. Max smiled and asked him a question in German. The man just glowered at him. He was a stark contrast to the West German soldiers Max had encountered, and even to the few NVA types with whom he'd dealt. This man looked more like one of Rommel's veterans than a modern soldier.

He listened with half his mind as the others made their

verification calls. The words were different, but the sense
was the same. Yes, yes, they could do it, they had done it,
they would do it, each man said. Finally it was his turn.
He took the scrap of paper out of his raincoat pocket and
handed it to the radioman. He twirled the frequency knob
until he thought he had it. Then he handed the mike and an
earphone to Max.

Max squeezed the trigger on the mike. "Pigpen, this is
Hogcaller. Pigpen, this is Hogcaller. Over."

The reply was immediate. "Hogcaller, Pigpen. Over."

"Okay, Pigpen, is the boss there?"

"Affirmative, Hogcaller. Stand by." There was a slight
pause, then Kemp's unmistakable bass came on. "Hogcaller.
You all right?"

"No problems. Looks like they can do what they claim."

"You're certain?"

"Not just me. The Russian is sure too. They foxed the
lockout box. Seems like all they need to do is raise 'em
and launch 'em."

"How many?"

"Nine. With reloads."

"SS23Xs?"

"Yeah. As advertised."

Kemp paused. Max could hear the muffled noises of an
off-microphone conversation. Somebody was asking him
something.

"Hogcaller. What's the ground situation?"

"Again, as advertised. A lot of people on the ground.
Under the command of an Oberst Muth. NVA uniforms."

"And the Soviets?"

"*In* the ground."

"What?"

"Deceased."

"*All* of 'em?"

"That's right."

Kemp paused again. "Well, Hogcaller, hang tight. We understand your situation. Anything else?"

Max glanced at the radioman, who was studiously listening on his own headset. Presumably Muth would be too.

"Glad you understand my situation. I'll look forward to its recovery. You copy?"

"Recovery. Right. We copy, Hogcaller. We'll be waiting for you. But you be careful there, understand?"

"Understand, Pigpen. Out." He handed the mike and earphone back to the radioman.

The four stood uneasily in the command area. The guard covered them. Nobody knew what to do next. Then Frankel showed up in the corridor behind the guard.

"Gentlemen. This way, please." And once more they trooped down the corridor to the entry. Muth was nowhere in sight. Outside, they were herded to the new personnel carrier Max had seen in the parking lot. Frankel swung open the rear door and waved inside.

"I am sorry, but this is where you must spend the rest of the night. As you all know, everything will be determined by 0830 tomorrow. At that time, you will either be released to join your comrades in evacuating Germany, or you will be present when we launch the rockets. I am sure you will pray with me for sanity on your leaders' parts so that you will be able to leave these uncomfortable quarters for more pleasant duty elsewhere. You will find water and a little food inside. Once you are in we will lock the outer hatches with this padlock through the retaining brackets. There are blankets inside. They should keep you warm enough through the night. And now, if you would step in, Major Findlay?" He waited by the hatch while Findlay slowly moved forward.

"Not exactly according to the Geneva Conventions," he said, "but we seem to have little choice." He clattered around inside. Ricard and Kulikov followed, then Max got in.

As soon as he was in, crouched to clear the low ceiling, the hatch slammed shut. A metallic scraping and final, muffled click told him that Frankel was as good as his word. They were now locked in.

Max sat down on the cold troop bench along the right side of the vehicle. Red light from a single armored bulb was the only illumination. As Max's eyes slowly got used to the dim lighting he picked out details of the interior. Their cell was the troop section of one of the newest Soviet APCs, the BMP-9. He dredged the data sheet on it from his memory. It was a tracked vehicle, twenty-three feet long, seven feet tall, shaped like a wedge in front and a cube in back, with dual hatches for entry and exit. Unlike the other, older APCs, it had no firing ports for the ten troops who were expected to be inside during combat. This vehicle was optimized for survival on a nuclear battlefield, so the only openings were the hatches in the rear and the hatch forward, which allowed entry to the driver's and commander's area. The only furnishings were the steel benches, which lined both walls. A swiveling periscope poked through the roof. In effect, they were locked into a steel cell on wheels, ten feet long, six feet wide and five feet deep.

Findlay wrapped himself in one of the blankets stacked on the lefthand bench and handed the stack aft. "Might as well get comfy, chaps," he said cheerily, "we've got a long night."

Ricard wordlessly accepted the stack and pulled one out for himself. He handed the blankets across to Kulikov, who sat forward of Moss on the same bench.

"How about the forward hatch?" asked Max.

Findlay grinned. His teeth gleamed weirdly in the red light. "Already tried, Leftenant. No go. Another padlock, I'd guess." Kulikov was shivering. He hurriedly pulled off a blanket and handed the last one to Max.

Moss slowly unfolded it and peered around. The blanket

was thin, cheap felt. The cold oozed from every square inch of the steel in the APC. Already the air seemed fogged and stale with their breath.

"Hope they left the ventilators open," he muttered.

"Oh, they are always open except when under attack," said Kulikov. He sounded almost cheerful. But he blinked rapidly and shook. Not just from the cold, Max guessed. The guy was petrified. Well, who could blame him?

"You know this kind of vehicle?" he asked.

"Of course. It has not yet been exported. But it is common among our frontline units. I—" He stopped abruptly. "But this is secret information. I cannot tell you any more."

Max laughed hollowly. "Sure, Comrade. Let's keep up appearances, shall we? Let's play cold war while these gents start World War Three right next to us."

Kulikov scowled. "Please? I do not speak good English."

"Never mind, Comrade Captain," Max said in Russian. "My comments were not worth repeating." He tried to find a comfortable way to hunch against the bench and backrest without sucking its cold into his body. The blanket seemed not to help at all.

"It is late," said Ricard in English. "I do not know about you, but for me, this has been a long day. I will sleep now. Our part is done."

"Hear, hear," added Findlay. "Well said, *mon major*. I agree. Rotten business, this. But we've done our bit. Time for a wink or two. Right, Leftenant?" He grinned again from his corner near the forward bulkhead.

"Shouldn't we try to do something?" Max replied.

"What can we do?" stammered Kulikov. "We are locked in."

"Right," Findlay said. "Good thought, but no go. Have to be Houdini to slip this bloody box."

Max looked across at Ricard. He returned Max's gaze impassively.

"Yeah," Max said finally. "What *can* we do?"

"Wait," said Ricard. "We can only wait."

Nobody said anything in reply. There was nothing to say. There was only the cold and the stale, foggy air.

EIGHTEEN

1920 hours
Washington D. C.
White House Situation Room

The air was heavy with cigarette smoke. The twelve men around the big teak table sat in luxurious leather swivel chairs, but they were not comfortable. In part they were uncomfortable because Morris Levin sat at the head of the table. But the major source of the discomfort was their collective sense of failure.

Levin eyed them with ill-disguised irritation. He was a gangly man, all Adam's apple and elbows, who preferred professorial tweed over the smooth dark wool favored by his colleagues in the capital. He had survived as the President's special assistant for national security affairs in spite of it.

"Well, gentlemen," he said at length, "what shall we tell him? Have we any kind of consensus?"

H. Lawton Colby, down and left from Levin, doodled on his yellow legal pad. As far as he could tell, this whole affair was a no-win situation for him. When the pieces were being put back together, the first thing everyone would do is blame poor intelligence. Because he had recently orchestrated sweeping changes for intelligence, there was a good chance the fallout would get him. Lying low was the order of the day. He frowned at the doodle and went over some of the lines again.

"I see," said Levin dryly. "We in the national security staff usually are quite voluble. Tonight we seem speechless."

"Sir?"

"Go ahead, Brad."

Brigadier General Brad Dumfries, USMC, tapped out another Camel from his depleted pack before he spoke. He had the leathery face of the fighter jock, but his body was beginning to show the wear and tear of the demands placed on it. On one hand, Dumfries ran every lunch hour on the Mall, and on the other he refused to give up his Camels. The result was that he was, as his flight surgeon put it, "the healthiest damn emphysemic in Washington."

"Well, I'd just like to point out that this silence is natural, given the circumstances. We've verified everything we can. We've talked about—and dismissed—instant military response, as the Joint Chiefs suggested a few hours ago. We've already been in contact with the Soviets, French, and Brits, and they're as stuck as we are."

"I'm painfully aware of that, Brad. But the boss will expect something from us, and soon. I have an eight o'clock meeting with him, and we have to do *something*, for Christ's sake."

Dumfries sucked hard on a Camel and let the acrid smoke curl from his nose. "Why?"

"What? What do you mean, why?"

"Well, sir, consider a new possibility. As long as we concede that this von Grabow has all the cards stacked right—which our own people verify that he has—then we are in a purely reactive stance. There aren't any magic gimmicks that can get in there, change the force ratio he's got working against us, and pull the chain on his operation. But his weakness is time.''

Levin frowned. ''I thought that would be our weakness.''

''No, sir. I believe, unlike some people around here, that this guy will push the button if we don't play ball. But I also believe that he does not want to. All we have to do is give him a way not to, and we win.''

''And how do we do that without pulling our people out?''

''Stall. Claim technical foul-ups. He's a military man. He'll understand. And once we stall, once we have more time, we can work the problem better.''

''You mean, simply do nothing?''

''Right. More battles have been lost by rash action than have been lost by prudence.''

''Strange advice from a gung-ho marine, Brad. Besides, what about all that expensive hardware he wants us to abandon?''

''This isn't Iwo Jima. In fact, the way I see it, this isn't really a military situation at all. It's a pure policy problem, in which the costs and benefits are more up front than usual. The hardware is only part of it. And there's a precedent. Don't forget that we left billions of dollars worth of stuff in Vietnam. It's all useless without somebody to work it. So I wouldn't worry too much about the equipment. It's the troops who count.''

Levin jotted a note, then looked up. He sucked his teeth. ''You lost me on that one. Mind expanding it a bit?''

''Sure. See, in a way von Grabow's right. We all know that sooner or later this split-Germany thing is going to have to be resolved. All he's done is taken the most likely scenario and speeded it up a bit. He figures the place is going to be zapped eventually anyway, so why not gamble on making it happen now? A good plan as far as it goes. But the problem is, maybe we or the Brits or Frogs or even the Reds aren't ready to play this game now. Aside from the fact that we don't like having our policy made somewhere else, maybe it's just not good timing.''

Beale, the State Department man, cleared his throat. "You mean, General, that we ought to somehow take advantage of this to cut our European losses and run?''

Dumfries shrugged. "Only if there's advantage for us in it. And that's my point. Why not force him to drag it out a little so we can examine the possibilities better? One night just isn't enough.''

Levin cocked his head and drummed his fingers on the tabletop. "So, in sum, Brad, you figure we ought to take no overt action at all.''

"Well, it's all I can think of. He's got his people on a trip wire to launch those damn Pershings at us, and after reviewing his situation, I'd say we'd be fools to pull some Desert One stunt to change the odds. Sending the cavalry in just isn't going to cut it.'' He grinned suddenly. "Although, in case you wanted to, the Seventh Cav *is* up in Coburg.''

It was a tiny witticism, in any other setting not worth noticing. But it broke the tension and gloom in the room. Somebody chuckled, then someone else laughed, and there was a moment of general amusement. Even Levin smiled.

"No thanks, Brad. No last stands tonight.'' The smile faded. "Okay. General Dumfries has suggested that we examine—in the few minutes we have left—the option of stalling for time. I think he's got a case. Anybody else?''

Sensing his moment, Deputy Assistant to the President for National Security Affairs H. Lawton Colby sat up. "Sir, it seems fitting to me. It would tell the others that the United States is not an imperialist power out to militarily dominate anybody. It would give us more time. And it would give the renegade a new problem—and, like the general, I don't think he'd be foolish enough to launch just because we were having 'technical' problems." Colby finished with a confident smile.

"Good, Lawton. Thanks. Now, gentlemen, we have about fifteen minutes to work up a plan for doing nothing."

0045 hours
The Blue Room
Burleigh House
Kent, England

The Prime Minister was at that state beyond bone-weary. He had swallowed the little yellow pill two hours before, but it seemed only to make him more nervous. He was fast losing patience. He closed his eyes and imagined himself on his boat, the *Dolly Bird,* heeled hard into a beam reach, running down to St. Malo under a blue Breton sky and a bracing breeze. But the vision wouldn't stay put. The grinding reality of Burleigh drove it out. He sighed and opened his eyes.

The scene hadn't changed. Five men were arguing. As they had all night, since he'd called them here to work out their response to this absurd situation. He decided to break up the monotony of listening to these potentates squabble like schoolchildren.

"Mr. Blanchard. Excuse me for interrupting, but might I know the latest position of the Germans?"

Blanchard lowered his well-manicured hand with which he'd been making a point to the First Sea Lord. "Of course, sir. As far as I know, it has not changed."

The PM rubbed his eyes. "Pray give it to me again, would you?"

"Certainly. Um, here it is. The cable from Bonn reads, 'The President and Chancellor of the Federal Republic of Germany wish the Prime Minister and government of the United Kingdom to be assured that the activities of the former Bundeswehr personnel now operating in Hohenfels and in the stolen American aircraft are completely unauthorized by this government. The strongest measures are being taken to end this situation and charges of treason will be brought against the leader and followers of this group when they are brought to justice. In the meanwhile, as specified under the NATO and Bi-Lateral Treaties, the FRG will work in concert with the United Kingdom to bring this crisis to an end.' Signed by Chancellor and President, end of message.''

"Um. Yes. Very nice. Point is, do we believe it?"

Air Chief Marshal Davey-Whyte leaned forward and looked down the green felt table at the PM. ''Why, of course, sir. Intelligence—''

"*Bugger* intelligence, ACM, if you'll excuse me. All the millions we've poured into them has netted us exactly sweet fanny adam in this one, hasn't it?'' His eyes seemed to bulge from his head. His pulse pounded. He fought to calm himself. The bloody pills. It must be the pills.

Davey-Whyte pursed his lips. ''Well, PM, if you'll excuse *me,* this has to be the most brilliant bloody coup in the history of Germany. There's no way we could have foreseen it.''

"Yes. That's right. He's your friend, isn't he? Flew together, and that sort of thing?'' The Prime Minister peered out at him from hooded eyes. He slumped in a heap at the head of the table, his head resting against the backrest of the tall black chair.

Davy-Whyte stiffened. ''Yes. We did. And he is—was—my friend. But—''

"Oh, never mind, Alex, never mind. I'm just tired. And you're right, blast it. The bastard has pulled one off on us, no matter what happens. So let's get back to the problem. Which is, at present, in my view at any rate, whether the Jerries will support us or him. Blanchard?''

"Well, M16 say the military can be expected to back

him—if he wins. If he doesn't, of course, nobody will
know him. Standard German behavior.''

"Wait a moment. You mean we can't count on the
Germans to provide military support if we need it?''

"No . . . that's not it exactly. Quite complicated,
really. It seems that the best estimate is that a significant
proportion of the officer corps would in fact help von
Grabow—but only after he's won. Not before. So they'd
work for us until then. Somewhat like Ney and Napoleon.
Promised Louis he'd hang Nappy up in a cage when he
caught up with him—then simply took his whole Corps
over to his side the moment he laid eyes on the little
bandit. Same sort of thing here, the boys in analysis say.''

"The way I read this, it's quite simply up to us. The
original Big Bloody Four. I'd prefer to simply leave the
Jerries out of it for now. Any opposition views?'' The PM
scanned the five puffy faces. "Good. Now. I presume we
all do in fact believe we should attempt to remain in
Germany. May I hear your views?''

Davey-Whyte attempted a grin. "Well, PM, you can
certainly have mine, but you won't like it.''

"Umph,'' said the PM.

"I think we ought to use the excuse Freddy's given us
and get out. It's costing billions to garrison NORTHAG,
and 2TAF likewise. As we've seen time and again in the
last five years, the NATO deterrent is really a German
deterrent, backed up by us. With the space battle stations,
we've got a whole new set of rules to learn to live with,
rules we've tried to evade for a long time. The air war is
now a space war, and the ground war can't be fought
under plans updated and rebuilt over five decades. I suggest we get out, allow whatever is going to happen inside
Germany to happen, and simply adapt.'' He looked at the
others. "There. Somebody had to say it.''

"Indeed,'' said the PM slowly. "Indeed.'' He gazed

wearily around the table. "I presume," he said heavily, "you don't all agree with Alex?"

He presumed correctly. They all started talking at once. He closed his eyes and massaged his temples.

0048 Hours
Command Staff Room
Central Command Post
Armée de l'Air
Paris

"Twice before in this century we have been deceived by the Germans. Is this to be the third?"

"No, *mon premier*. I was not arguing for letting them disgrace France. I was suggesting we consider the potential for new alliances, more strength."

The gray walls of the secure command room echoed the general's words. The Premier seemed not to have heard him. Since the accession of his party and the re-emergence of the Gaullists as a powerful political force, such men as Jean-Claude Deschamps were not in favor with the new government. The Premier fingered the tiny boutonniere he always wore, a tricolor roundel. A knock interrupted whatever reply he might have made to the Air Force general.

"Come in," called the Chief of Staff. An Air Force captain entered, saluted, and handed an envelope to the chief, who nodded and waved the courier out.

"Another correspondence from the Americans?" asked the Premier. "They seem to think we cannot make our own bread without their direction," he sniffed.

The chief scanned it quickly. "No, sir. It is a status report. All our forces are ready for full mobilization, as you directed. We can move to a full offensive position within ten minutes."

"Good. No more Black Junes." The Premier relaxed

slightly. "Now we are not so vulnerable, gentlemen. And I must tell you, I am weary of bargaining with Germans. Perhaps, after tonight, we need never do it again."

The Minister of State glanced at Deschamps. Like the general, he was a holdover, a man whose portfolio rested with him solely because the new Premier acknowledged his pre-eminence in foreign affairs. He cleared his throat.

"If I may—?" he said.

"Of course," replied the Premier.

"Sir, I would like to state, for the record, that we believe it is best to discuss further the situation with this German. We believe he is serious."

The Premier's eyes lit up. "Serious? Of course he is serious, St. Denis! He is a *German*! The question is, are you serious?"

The minister gritted his teeth but tried to smile. "Naturally, sir."

The Premier folded his arms and settled back in his chair. Somewhere in the subterranean command post a klaxon sounded. He raised one bushy white eyebrow. "Then you will have to convince me, because it is my inclination, at this moment, to attack this madman with everything we have."

The minister momentarily lost his reserve. "For *Germany's* sake?"

"No!" blazed the Premier. "For *France's* sake!" He pounded the table with a meaty fist. "In case you have forgotten, it is for *France* that we sit here! It is *France* we serve! And *France* we must defend!"

Deschamps tried to catch the minister's eye. But the man was seized by the moment.

"And we do that, *mon cher premier,* by incinerating Paris?"

"No. We do it by doing the Americans' and Britishers' dirty work for them—as always! We do it by taking the initiative." The Premier slowly relaxed and sat back in his chair. "Unless, as I have asked, you can demonstrate that it is best to proceed otherwise."

The Minister of State likewise forced himself to remain calm. He preoccupied himself with the papers in front of him. "And so I will, sir. So I will." He looked at Deschamps, who shook his head. There was still a chance for sanity. Between them they might yet pull the man back from the brink. But it would be a long night.

0155 Hours
Room 33
Defense Council Bureau
The Kremlin
Moscow

Ganinov confronted the guard with his identification. The KGB sergeant of course knew who the Deputy Secretary was. But he elaborately checked the ID against Ganinov anyway. It was expected, he had been told. Ganinov stood patiently while the husky guard matched everything up. He handed the card back to the second most powerful man in the GRU and touched his billed cap.

"Thank you, Comrade Secretary. Please go in."

Mikhail Ganinov knew the room well. He had held many conferences here himself. But he had never been here as a Politburo member. He pushed through the door.

A large circular table dominated the windowless room. Four telephones stood on a small side table. Each of the ten seats at the table also had a telephone in front of it. Ganinov paused by the door to wait for the General Secretary to see him.

The pudgy man ignored him for a moment more. Then he jerked his chin toward the vacant chair nearest Ganinov. As he sat, Ganinov noted a conspicuous absence.

"Welcome, Mikhail Mikhailovich. You will see of course

that Comrade Konetsov is not here. To forestall your having to inquire, the reasons are complicated, the result simple. He has been purged. We cannot tolerate failure.'' He shifted his piercing blue eyes to the man next to him. Marshal Ulanov.

''The subject was pressure, Alexei Alexeivich. There will naturally be pressure when we refuse this madman's demand. Will we have significant trouble with our allies?''

The marshal, a heavyset, slow-talking man, laid his huge hands on the table. Like his face, they were gnarled. The marshal was of the old school.

''No,'' he said. He was also a man of few words.

''And why not, Comrade Marshal?'' asked Lebedev, who held the foreign secretary's portfolio.

''They won't dare,'' rumbled the marshal. ''Too many tanks,'' he added.

''I disagree,'' said Ganinov in his clearest, most forceful voice. He sat straight in his seat and looked calmly at the others. They regarded him with obvious surprise. He had not been expected to be opinionated. Simply present in a pro forma sense to represent the GRU.

''Ah,'' said the first secretary. ''Go ahead, Mikhail Mikhailovich. Enlighten us. I am certain Comrade Ulanov will be most interested in your reasons.''

''They are obvious to those who can see,'' he said.

The atmosphere charged slightly. Ganinov was going to challenge. None of the seven old men around the table really knew what to expect from this fifty-five-year-old. They all had dossiers on him, naturally. But one never knew. In these sessions it was always best to remember Beria's fate.

''First, the so-called allies you speak of are actually subject peoples, Comrades. They know it, and we know it. Second, their leaders, although schooled here and indoctrinated as best we can do the job, are not wholly Soviet in their viewpoints. It is, as Marx himself pointed out, human nature. But third, and most important, the organization we created—the Warsaw Pact—now is a pistol aimed straight at us.''

''No!'' growled Ulanov. ''We foresaw this possibility from the start. That is why at the top of each chain of command in the Pact there is a Soviet officer. That is why in a crisis the various Pact armies become, effectively, Soviet armies!''

Ganinov shook his head ruefully. ''You planned well. For the times. You did not reckon with a future in which the final confrontation would not occur until these Pact countries had developed their own brands of socialism. You could not have seen the insidious result of training not just senior generals in our strategies, but also young colonels. The result is this, Comrade Ulanov: It does not matter who is at the top of these mythical armies. What matters is who commands the battalions. And the battalions are commanded by young men who will not obey us if the German, von Grabow, puts his plan into effect.''

''You are wrong. But it doesn't matter, since we will simply crush any mutinies anyway. As we have done before.''

''So you have, Marshal. Nineteen fifty-three, 'fifty-six, 'sixty-two, 'sixty-eight, 'seventy-eight. I recall them all. And each time the use of force grew more and more difficult. Now, in this particular case, it is not just difficult, it is impossible.''

The first secretary leaned on one elbow. ''Really? And why is that?''

Ganinov pushed the stack of papers to the leader. ''It is all here. If von Grabow were threatening just the West, our 'allies' might stand with us. But not with his—*our*—rockets aimed at their cities. Not with his broadcast. Not with his phone calls to a few key men in the Pact organization. Not now. Now, if we ask for a mass attack, if we ask for the sacrifice of a few cities as the price for keeping

Soviet troops in Germany, they will rebel. And the odds are that they will combine, and they will use our own weapons, our own tactics, our own ideology to beat us." He fell silent.

"Defeatism," rumbled Ulanov. "At Stalingrad—"

"At Stalingrad everything was different, Comrade." The first secretary said it quietly, even before Ganinov could.

He was a shrewd man, thought Ganinov. Much shrewder than anyone knew. He was already outflanking Ganinov. He had picked up the thread and meaning of the bombshell Ganinov had dropped, and appropriated it. Even now, as the leader's beady eyes roamed the room, Ganinov himself was being turned into an asset, not a threat. For the first time Ganinov felt the slight twinges of intimidation.

The first secretary picked up the reports in his sausage fingers. "This is good analysis, Comrade. We thank you. But what do you suggest we do about the Germans? Surely you do not need a history lesson about them? You, whose father was tortured by the Gestapo, whose mother was raped and beaten senseless? How do we deal with Germans reunited?"

His tone was not rhetorical or mocking, Ganinov decided. He reciprocated. "The ultimate victory of socialism in Germany is inevitable and undisputable. But we have seen how expensive it would be to bring socialism to the Western sector by use of Marshal Ulanov's tanks. I suggest that in this crisis lies the way to final victory in the entire German culture. As long as the Germanys are kept separate, the enemies of socialism will prosper, by promising a war to regain the separated sections. Von Grabow is only the first, not the last. And the next time we face this situation it will be much, much worse for us. Because when this affair gets out—and despite Comrade Nishiny's apparatus it will get out—the people will know it is possible. The now dormant German nationalism will explode in our faces. We calculate that even if we are able to defeat von Grabow and retain our troop positions in the GDR, within eighteen months the seeds he will plant will ripen and we will face a harvest of terror from the entire German population. It is this I seek to avoid. The Germans cannot be conquered. They can only be neutralized by a social victory.'' The room was quiet. He had their attention. They did not resent his lecture.

''There are only two alternatives,'' Ganinov continued. ''Each has been verified by our planning computers. The first is to withdraw as demanded. The second is to attack just before dawn. Leading with the new Tupolevs, and then with everything we have.''

''And also with, as you point out here''—the first secretary thumped the papers—''the possibility, even with the Tupolevs, that we have only a shred of hope for a full victory amid the confusion?''

''With perhaps less than that if the aircraft are not wholly successful in their first strike. If the Germans then launch, and the situation proceeds as we fear, then you must count the final losses. The population. The arable land. The minerals. The cities. All gone, but not because of the Americans or Chinese. Because of our own 'allies.' ''

''If only our battle station in orbit were operational,'' whined Petrovich. ''The laser could—''

''Do nothing. We do not have the accuracy. We looked into that.'' Ganinov sat back in his chair.

Room 33 fell absolutely still, save for the labored breathing of the old men. The first secretary looked at them in turn.

''Withdraw. Or attack. Which is it to be, Comrades? In favor of withdrawal? Let me see your true thoughts.''

Ganinov and Petrovich raised their hands.

''And attack?''

The remaining six lifted their hands from the table.

''I see.'' The first secretary laid the papers on the table

and looked hard at Ganinov. His expression was marblelike, his corpulent features inscrutable. "I must study these, Mikhail Mikhailovich. I will need an hour alone. Until then, Marshal Ulanov, you will direct a general mobilization and will scramble the nearest Tupolevs from units closest to the stolen rockets to be ready for the attack. As I recall, even the closest ones will have to fly all night to be there by dawn." He stood. The others got to their feet too.

"But listen to me, Comrade Marshal. Do not force the issue. Do not allow your men to get too close, or too trigger-happy." He turned on his heel and stalked to the door, moving surprisingly quickly for a dumpy fat man. There, he spun again and fixed Ulanov with a look that froze him to the spot. "And remember, Marshal, Stalingrad was a long time ago. Longer than you realize, I think."

Ulanov only blinked at the closing door. He never had a riposte for the likes of the first secretary. But fifteen minutes later the combined forces of the Union of Soviet Socialist Republics—including a flight of the Tupolev Silent Killers based in Kazakhstan—scrambled to war readiness. For Ulanov, that knowledge was more satisfying than mere words.

─────────────────────NINETEEN

The problem wasn't that Max couldn't stay warm. The problem wasn't that he couldn't sleep. The problem was that, awake and thinking, he knew that he had a solution.

It was a problem because he couldn't do anything with the knowledge. He pulled the thin blanket tighter and hunched closer to the fetal position to preserve what warmth he could.

Soon they would be forced to huddle for survival like cossacks in a snowstorm. How long would it take? How long before these officers and gentlemen, these men playing out roles they didn't understand, comprehended their peril? Each man shifted miserably in a corner of the frigid steel cell now, suffering alone. Max knew from the moment he realized the danger of hypothermia that it would be up to him to suggest that they gather their warmth for mutual benefit. But he also knew that they would have to struggle for a while alone for pride's sake. Even the Russian captain, who'd shivered so hard at first the bench had shaken, now seemed resigned to his fate, whatever it might be.

Predictably Max's mind had gone into high gear as soon as he'd tried to slow his vital biosystems down for conservation of energy. The techniques he'd been taught in the high Rockies snapped right into focus. The only trouble was, his mind just wouldn't quit. Had it only been a few hours ago that he'd drifted off to sleep over a boring file folder?

It seemed impossible. Only now was the reality of all this sinking in, as his body heat was inexorably absorbed by the cold steel. He had to have a knack for getting into insane situations like this one. He sighed and immediately regretted it. The condensed breath hung like a gas attack in the air. He winced. His own breath tasted foul, as foul as the air in the BMP.

Getting out was the obvious move. But a few things militated against it.

Number one. The clear order from Charlie Kemp. Don't be a hero.

Number two. He'd have to have help. And these guys were obviously not the getting-out type.

Number three. Even if he did get out, there were too many armed, keyed-up people outside.

Number four. If he got past them, where would he go? What would he do?

Number five, and most important. What he should do, according to his duty, was one thing. But what he wanted to do was quite another. That one stopped him from action more certainly than any of the other items.

His duty was clear. Halt the German plan somehow. Your average gung-ho Green Beret would understand that easily enough. What he wouldn't understand is that Max really sympathized with the Germans.

He seemed inevitably entwined in this divided country. As a boy he'd lived here. And then as a Missionary he'd roamed the land at will. You couldn't do that year after year and not come to identify with the people who lived on it. For him Germany had become something more than just another duty station. Its people had become more than simply indigenous personnel. He sat in their bars and cafés, ate what they ate, read what they read, listened to their words, inhaled their air, lived an increasingly German life. He would never *be* a German, and had no desire to be one. But the country had gotten under his skin, willy-nilly.

Which must explain, he thought, why his personal view was that Muth and his boys deserved to win this one. He felt no nationalistic pride in this contest; that Muth's boss had stolen an Air Force airplane meant nothing to Moss. What counted was that von Grabow's raid might well give Germany a new lease on life. It might break up the vicious circles of the American-Soviet death dance, in which Max had been cast, somewhat awkwardly, as a member of the chorus. It had been easy for him to ignore the desperation of the dance at first. But then he'd picked up that damned canister of film, and been spun right into the center of the whirling, reeling troupe. What he'd learned from it had shaken him. It was too easy for the safeguards to fail. Too easy for one side or the other to set off events that could result in the whole nightmare of nuclear war finally coming true.

Most people, even most Air Force officers his age, had the luxury of simply not thinking about it. But Max had been responsible for interrupting the dance. Personally. And more important than the dramatic change in his career had been the significance of that fact. One man at the right—or wrong—place and time could change everything. For the better or for the worse. The huge, complex systems erected to satisfy the pride and policy of the superpowers seemed remote and invulnerable, but they were not. The more complex they became, the more they depended on predictable causality, and nothing is less predictable than a single man acting on his conscience.

Max rubbed his hands to bring feeling back. It didn't work. His feet were long since numb. They'd be warmer if they were in a miserable pup tent. Had any of the others considered yelling to someone to start the engine to bring heat in? Or had they all succumbed to the need to preserve dignity by just taking it? Even he had done so. If his face weren't so painfully cold, he'd smile ruefully at the little vanity.

And vanity also lay at the core of his belief that von Grabow was doing an admirable thing. He had to admit it. If some general had asked him to explain his belief that Germany would be better off a single, unified nation, and that the unification would be a stabilizing element for the whole world, perhaps leading even to a lessening of superpower tension, how the hell could he convince him? Generals, luckily, almost never asked lieutenants what they thought. Nor did politicians. Yet Max thought anyway. Or rather, felt, then rationalized his feelings.

His contacts with the Russians had taught him a lot about them. They were canny opponents. They were ugly, handsome, tall, short, skinny, fat, Slavic, Oriental, European, Muslim. He seemed to have been fighting these people his whole life. Yet even as he dodged their attacking helicopters and tanks, he was curiously unemotional about them. He had seen how they had brutally subjugated the territories under their domination. And men like Ike Wilson had felt the direct touch of their institutional, mindless viciousness. But the way they had sliced Ike's girlfriend up and dumped her in a Berlin trashcan was not uniquely Russian. As he had been exposed to the uses and techniques of terrorist tactics in Louisiana, Max had seen that such things were simply part of the way this war was fought. His people did it too. Shit! *He* would be expected to do it too. And that he would not was not at all certain, even to himself. It was the echo of the deadly dance's hypnotic tune.

But this chain of events . . . this might break the spell. Everyone in Europe was paralyzed by the thought that the two halves of Germany might combine again. Back in '84, when Kohl and Hoennecker were making the first, faint, tentative moves toward a real East-West German rapprochement, the Russians and French had gone berserk. Apparently you didn't have to be a World War II veteran to fear such a thing. Such was the power of the German myth that people dreaded the GDR and FRG coming together as much as they would two pieces of unstable uranium. The automatic assumption was that the inevitable explosion would occur. That some kind of German gene would force even the "nice" Germans to once again try to rule the world.

Max didn't think so. Some changes are irreversible. Like the Black Death that depopulated whole towns in the Middle Ages, the war had changed Germany forever. It was time to understand that. It was time to take the pressure off the pot that was boiling, mostly unseen, in the two Germanies. Von Grabow could make it happen. And Max wished he would.

But even as he thought it all through in the achingly cold BMP, he knew he would not act on his conscience this time. Not because he didn't want to. But because von Grabow simply did not have a chance. His plan was perfect, as far as it went. It depended on the Big Four's leaders seeing, understanding, and acting on the deep threat von Grabow held over them.

But it also depended upon their being able to overcome their own short-term interests. And Max had seen enough careerists to know what those interests really were. The result would be that someone—Russian, American, British, French—someone would try to take von Grabow on. Maybe it would be a commando attack. Maybe a "stealth" aircraft raid. Maybe some cobbled-up laser attack from the half-built space stations. But it would come. He knew the power of belief in power. Sitting in the secret briefing rooms of the Pentagon's F-Ring, or in Whitehall, some

general or politician would simply not be able to compre-
hend that the vast might at his beck and call could not be
used to solve this problem. And finally he would succumb
not to the entreaties of his advisors but to the urge to save
face, to *do something*. To *win*. And that would be it.
Game, set, match. Because they wouldn't really expect a
man like Muth to launch those missiles. Not really. Too
many years of thinking of Germans as clever industrialists,
as subject peoples, as *guilty*, would muddy their understanding.

But Muth would fire them all. Max knew it when he'd
looked into the man's face. And so would the commander
in the West, whoever he was. Sending the missiles might
be their last act; but they would do it proudly, remorselessly,
instantly.

The Russian captain coughed. It was a sickening, tuber-
cular sound. It urged Max to the action he knew he'd have
to take. He had to convince these men to help him do his
duty, even though he would love to be able to ignore it. If
somebody didn't do something, the missiles would surely
fly. That someone seemed to be him. Again. He shoved
himself upright, still clenching the blanket tightly.

"Listen, gentlemen," he said. His voice sounded squeaky.
He tried again. "Hey. How about it?" He spoke in English. It would help give him the tone he needed; he might
be understood in German or Russian, but he would not be
persuasive.

The British major mumbled, "Be quiet, Leftenant,"
and kept his head down. The Frenchman peered blearily
around the blanket edge. The Russian coughed again.

"Look. We can't just sit here and take this. We have to
do something."

"I told you before," said Ricard, "we can do nothing.
We must wait."

"Yeah. You told me. But you're wrong. We can do

something. And I'll tell you what it is if you'll quit playing dead.''

Eyes flashing, the French major levered himself onto one elbow. ''Perhaps you should watch your language, Lieutenant. It does not suit your rank.''

''Rank? Maybe you guys don't understand. These krauts are going to light off World War Three in about seven hours. Maybe less. What the hell use is rank, Major? What counts is action.''

Findlay sat up and faced him. His eyes were narrow but not in anger; the cold squeezed them. ''Steady on, Leftenant. Even POWs maintain the forms. As senior man—''

''You ought to be leading us. Well, with respect, Major, you're not, so I will. I have a plan.''

''For what? Some heat?'' The Russian captain, who'd seemed oblivious, wheezed it out in his thick accent. The word *heat* came out *kheet*.

''No. For stopping these people.''

''Of course. What shall we do? Send in the bloody cavalry?''

Moss shook his head. ''Hardly. They'll fire at the slightest sign of an assault. I believe that. Don't you?''

''Yes,'' said the Russian. He finally poked his head through the blanket. ''Yes. We must not underestimate them.'' He coughed again.

''What do you propose, Lieutenant?'' Ricard asked. He showed some interest by sitting upright.

''It's pretty obvious really. This whole shooting match depends on that black box as far as I can tell.''

''The CDS. Yes,'' said Kulikov.

''Without it those rockets are just so much useless junk.''

''So?'' Findlay's tone implied impatience.

''So if we liberated it, they'd be stuck. The whole plan would be out of whack.''

''What's to prevent the chaps in the West from launching their missiles?'' Obviously Findlay had assumed the role of opposition counsel. It might be because he felt he had to control the events as best he could because he was senior. Or it might be because of something less admirable. Max addressed his words to him.

"Nothing—except the German fanaticism for order. I don't think they'd just blackmail the West. There's no percentage in it, why launch if you can't win everything. This isn't a piecemeal operation. Either they win or they lose—everything. Without both his sites the German CO has lost it all."

Findlay grunted. The Frenchman leaned closer. His eyes glittered.

"Suppose we could do this. We will not discuss how, for the moment. But suppose we could. What would we do with the control box? Destroy it?"

"Sure, if we could. But all we need to do is remove it from the console. Doesn't matter, really. Right, Captain?"

"Correct. Without the CDS nothing happens. Computers will not accept commands. Rockets will not work." He shrugged elaborately. The blanket fell from his shoulders. He hurriedly pulled it up again.

"Unlike the major, while I think you may have a point, Leftenant, the whole affair boils down to that simple question. How?"

"First, we get out of here. Quietly. I don't think they have a guard on us. We would have heard something. Second, we sneak into the trailer and eliminate the men there. Disconnect and steal the box. Then split up and run like hell into the woods. Whichever way we go, we'll run into friendly people; Czech and MVA border police to the south and west, Red Army units to the north and east. Muth said he has 'enough' men. From what we saw, this battery is pretty well spread out, so his people have to be thin as hell on the ground. We ought to be able to penetrate the picket lines before he catches on. If we're lucky."

"A lot of little problems there, old man. Like how we get out of this thing."

"Don't ask me," said Moss, "ask the captain. How about it, Kulikov?"

The Russian looked expressionlessly at Moss. His glasses reflected the red bulb in the low ceiling. He turned to each of the others slowly. "I cannot," he mumbled.

"Why?" asked Ricard. "Is there no way besides the rear and fore hatches?"

"I—I cannot," he said.

Silence filled the chilly air again.

"I think the captain means he knows but is afraid to tell us," said Max. "Why, Captain? Worried about reprisal? You must realize we will be the first to go when the attack starts. And you know it will start, don't you?"

"Yes," the Russian muttered. "There is no question." He spoke at the floor, almost to himself. "First there will be gas. Then there will be helicopters. Many helicopters. With troops. Shock troops. They will not stop until they have won." His voice was a whisper. He coughed again, violently.

"Exactly," said Max. "So what have we to lose?"

Kulikov looked again at Max. His face seemed flushed despite the pinching cold. "So. Yes. You have right." He looked at the others. "There may be a way. In the floor is a small hatch. You see?" He pointed at the steel plates of the floor. They peered where he indicated and saw a hairline crack running around a square shape, about two feet by two feet. No handle was visible.

"How does it open?" asked Max.

"Electric. A switch."

"Here? In this compartment?"

"Yes."

"Where?" he asked, half-rising.

"There," said Kulikov, pointing to the upper right rear corner. In the gloom could be seen a rubber-covered switchbox, much like a light switch. Ricard cast off his blanket, fumbled for a moment with the rubber, and finally ripped it from the box.

"*Merde!*" He dropped the cover and sank down. "Nothing. They have removed the switch."

"Of course," said Kulikov. "I saw it at once."

"Can we move the hatch manually?"

"No. Too heavy. Springs, gaskets, electrohydraulics."

"So that's it, Leftenant," said Findlay. He sounded relieved. "Good try though. We'll see your superiors hear about it."

Max stared at him. "You don't get it, do you, Findlay? This isn't a damn exercise, man. There isn't going to be a happy ending unless we make it happen."

"Mind your tongue, Leftenant. I know what we're in for here. But there's no use pretending we can make any bloody difference. It's all up to the red-tab boys and the politicos now. Our bit's done. Right, Major?"

Ricard regarded him solemnly, and with obvious distaste. "No, Major. It is not right. The young lieutenant has reminded us of our duty. We must not stop." He turned to the Russian. "Now, Captain, is there no way to activate—"

"Hang on, Ricard! I'm in command here. If there's to be any action—"

"No! You are not in command. We are allies, not recruits, Major. Please remember that. The American has a good plan. The only plan. We must do something. I know my people. They will not let the Germans do this. They will try to save their pride the only way they know— the attack. And the result will be as the lieutenant says. We must act. So, Captain, is there no way to activate the switch for the hatch?"

Findlay's mouth closed. He looked like a fleshy bass swallowing water. Nobody noticed. Max and Ricard were waiting for the Russian to reply. He pushed his wire-rim glasses back up his nose.

"Perhaps," he said. "Perhaps. If we can get the switch cover off, perhaps I can guess the wiring. If I fail, we will lose our light. There may be an explosion in the battery. If I am correct, the hatch will open."

"Well, begin!" said Ricard. He slid over and urged the Russian into the corner. Kulikov got up and, hunched, went to the corner. He peered at it for a moment, then turned back. "No use. It is attached with hidden, ah—I don't know the English—"

"Countersunk?" said Max.

"Yes. Countersunk screws."

"That should be no problem," said Ricard. "We have bits of metal to use. Coins. Belt buckles. Even your glasses."

"No." Kulikov shook his head. "They are set too deep. There would be no leverage."

"There must be something," said Ricard. "Major Findlay. Do you—"

Findlay regarded him archly. "Hardly. I'm not a mechanic, you know. British officers don't carry toolbags about with them."

Unfazed, Ricard persisted. "No nail file? No penknife? Keys?"

"Sorry. Wallet, a few pfennig, credit cards." He sounded smug.

"Lieutenant Moss?"

Max had been thinking. What had he taken with him on this jaunt? He didn't carry a wallet. Instead, he used a steel clip for his credit cards and a money clip for his cash. The money clip! He pulled the stainless clip from his pocket, slipped out the bills, and handed it to Kulikov. The Russian held it and said, "No. Too big. The edge—"

"Press the end," Moss said. Kulikov fumbled with it

and pushed the round end of the clip. A thin blade slid out. He looked up at Max.

"Push it again," Max said. Another blade came out of the other side. This one ended in a curious sort of thick fishhook.

"It may work," said Kulikov slowly. Ricard beamed at Moss.

"American officers do carry toolkits, Major," Max said. "Goes with the territory, I guess." Findlay sniffed.

It was a present from the DIA. The two blades had been tested at incredible loads under wildly different conditions. It wasn't James Bond gimmickry; it was better. They could be simply fingernail cleaners or knife blades, but many agents had found them to be useful. Best of all, such a money clip was not suspicious at all. It was a standard Japanese export item, found in many department stores in America. Max made a mental note to thank the instructor who had directed them to ditch their wallets in favor of the clips.

Suddenly the metal switch cover clattered to the metal bench. The racket seemed deafening. Kulikov froze. "Sorry. Please. My hands—cold—"

"Quiet!" said Ricard hoarsely. They all held their breath, waiting for someone to come pounding on the hatch, to thrust an AKM inside. Ricard crouched and peered through the periscope. Ten seconds later he had completed a slow scan of the area. Nothing had happened. Max slowly began breathing again. Ricard motioned Kulikov to continue. Instead, the Russian eased himself down to the bench.

"What's wrong?" asked Max.

"My hands. I must warm my hands," he said. "And—the noise. The hatch will make noise if I succeed."

"Much noise?"

"Yes. Like a sewer cover on the road, being dragged. You know?"

"Yeah. I know." Max looked at Ricard. The Frenchman nodded.

"There will not be time for a conference after the hatch opens. We must plan now, and be ready to execute. Lieutenant? Is there more to your plan?"

Max licked his lips, which had gone dry again. In the cold they were chapped and painful. "No. I don't have a lot of experience at this sort of thing. But I figure there can't be more than three, four men inside. If we can surprise them—"

"Harder to do than you might think, Moss." Findlay seemed finally resolved to participate. His tone had hardened. "Remember the chap at the end of the trailer is the key man—and he'll have the most time to see what's happening. Hard to stop a man who wants to send a signal if his hand is on the key."

"Sure, Major. What else can we do?"

"Without gas, guns, or gelignite, not bloody much."

"You will not help, Major?" Ricard asked.

"Of course I'll help. What do you think I am?"

Ricard let the question hang in the air, then returned his gaze to Max.

"So. We get to the trailer. Get inside. Eliminate those inside, remove the control box, and scatter. Correct?"

"The way I saw it, Major."

"A good plan. But you should know, Lieutenant, that such plans usually fail. I speak from experience. I have been on the receiving end of ones like it. In Libya. Chad. Syria." He shrugged. "But who knows? Perhaps this one will work." He paused and rubbed his hands together vigorously. "There remains the details. Who goes first? Who takes the box? If we get weapons, do we use them? Do we run in predetermined directions? Who goes east? Who west?"

"I will take the box," said Kulikov. His voice had

changed. He sounded confident. "It is my responsibility. It is Soviet. I am Soviet. I will go north with the CDS."

"Wait a minute," said Findlay. "Given that we have to get in and be the bloody heroes, why not just deactivate the box? We could destroy it. Why take it anywhere?"

Kulikov waved his hand as if dismissing something. "We can't take the chance that our effort to destroy it wouldn't be entirely successful. The CDS is designed to take high stress. No. Only removing it entirely will ensure that they cannot use it."

Findlay grunted.

"Besides," Max said, "this way we tie them up. If we zap the box, who knows what they might do? But taking it leaves them the chance of finding it—and that means they might be a bit more reluctant to launch the Pershings."

"Might be, eh? Not very reassuring." Findlay snorted.

Nobody answered him. Finally, Ricard spoke, softly. "So," he said, "I will enter first. I have killed men with these before." Ricard held out his hands. "Has anyone else?"

Nobody answered.

"I go out of the hatch first. I go into the trailer first. Major Findlay, you come next, no? Then the captain. Finally the lieutenant. You cover us, if you can, with whatever weapon is at hand in the trailer. Then, after we have done it, we leave in opposite order: the lieutenant, the captain, Major Findlay, and me. I will go east. The captain goes north. South, Lieutenant?"

"Sure."

"And west, Major?"

Findlay grunted again.

Ricard rubbed his hands again. "Good. It is clear. We must stay free as long as possible, and stay apart, so they will not know which of us has it if we are caught. Agreed?"

"Sounds good," Max said. The voice seemed to belong to someone else. He had that pre-race gulf in his gut.

"Agreed," said Findlay at length. "Absurd. But agreed."

"Yes," said Kulikov.

"Then, my friends, let us do it. Comrade Captain, it is up to you." Ricard slid sideways on the bench and raised his hand to the dark corner, where the switchbox gaped down at them like the mouth of doom. In the red light the tangle of wires inside looked like so many writhing worms, all the same color.

Kulikov slowly got to his knees on the bench and peered inside. He took off his garrison cap, wrapped it around the steel money clip, and put his face as close to the box as he could. As a surgeon would probe a wound, he inserted the thin hooked blade slowly, carefully, deliberately. He fished for long seconds.

Max held his breath. He was suddenly thirsty beyond belief. His tongue seemed to stick to the roof of his mouth. What the hell had he started? Here he was again, stuck in a—

"I think," breathed Kulikov, "I think I have it—"

A huge blue-white spark arced through the switchbox. It seared the air, blinded them all, and knocked Kulikov down. Before anyone could react, deep in the guts of the BMP there was a distant thump, as if someone had thrown an immense dirt clod at the underside. Struggling upright, Kulikov shouted, "The battery—"

He was cut off by another noise. It was the screech of metal on metal, of a thousand fingernails scraping across a dry blackboard, the noise that reaches through bones to the roots of incisors and sets teeth vibrating like tuning forks. It was the sound of the hatch at Max's feet grinding slowly open.

TWENTY

Sleeping soldiers were kicked out of bed, to awaken amid howling sirens and confusion. Sailors were jerked from their swaying sleep to find themselves strapping on steel helmets and running for their battle stations. Airmen stumbled from their ready-rooms to their aircraft, engines whining in the darkness. Tanks by the thousand roared to life. Hidden rocket batteries ripped away their camouflage. From Cuba to the Chinese border the Red Army reacted to the order to assume war readiness without hesitation. More than a million men stood ready at their weapons within fifteen minutes of the Politburo's command. Their commanders, from ensigns to marshals, patiently awaited further direction. It had all been practiced so many times before.

Sensors scattered around the world detected the frenzied activity. Seabed listening stations heard the Soviet submarines leaving their ports in huge wolf packs. Satellites ceaselessly scanning the known military bases spotted surface transport movement. Spaceborne radars watched as aircraft rose into the sky all over the Soviet Union. The huge increase in signal traffic was monitored by land, sea, air, and space receiving and decoding stations. Twenty minutes after the Politburo had ordered war readiness, units of the National Reconnaissance Agency, Air Force Systems Command, and Naval Systems Command had funneled their data to the National Military Command Center in Washington.

Because the President and his staff were already in the Situation Room, because the chain of command was already functioning fully, response was swift. As soon as he had been briefed, the President gave two orders. The first activated the hot line. The second ordered a worldwide American military alert. He was committed to peace, and especially to a peaceful resolution to the German crisis. But he had not been informed by the Soviets of their intent to mobilize. And in the absence of such prior warning, he did not need a military type to tell him that the mobilization might be a Soviet attempt to use the crisis as a pretext for launching the long-feared assault on the West. Until he knew otherwise, he had to assume the worst. And so, thirty-one minutes after Ulanov raised the battle flag, the order flashed around the world for American soldiers, sailors, and airmen to lock and load their weapons.

Von Grabow heard it all.

Schoener watched the data shift on the screen. He had the setting placed on wide view, which meant he was watching most of Europe, including the United Kingdom and a good piece of Russia. Radar targets kept appearing. The computers kept identifying them as military. On the ground, traffic patterns suddenly altered all over the Soviet Union. He watched expressionlessly. But inside, his heart sank. He toggled the intercom.

"Herr Hart. What is the sigint situation?"

"Herr Oberst, very confusing. The huge increase in traffic continues. Now the English have joined."

"So we have the French at high traffic, the English, the Americans, and Russians?"

"Yes. Also, we have intercepted relay data that indicates the Chinese and Indians are starting."

"Thank you, Hart. Good work."

"Herr Oberst."

Schoener called von Grabow. The data blocks on the screen kept shifting. More targets kept appearing.

"Yes?"

"Herr General. The mobilization apparently continues. China and India have joined, Hart thinks."

"So. The fools. We were right. These men are almost insane. They will risk nuclear obliteration to save their pride." He sighed heavily.

Schoener noted the exhaustion in his voice. It wasn't because they had all been up so long. It was because of the strain. As far as he knew, von Grabow had had no sleep. Schoener felt a stab of shame for having taken an hour with the men off shift.

"What should we do, Herr General?"

"Nothing. There is nothing to be done. They will not listen to us. It is 1914, all over again. The plans have taken over. Unless something happens, they will begin the end almost by accident. No one will be responsible, they will say afterward. If there is an afterward."

"Konetsov is gone. Ganinov has taken over his place on the Politburo. But he may not have enough power to stop them."

"I know. So did your computers. The odds were never good."

"Should we threaten them again? Or even begin a launch sequence?"

"No. We gave them until the morning. They know the threat. Everything now depends on who lives in reality and who lives in dreams. It is out of our hands." He paused. "Helmut."

There it was again. The first name. "Herr General?"

"I am going to make the rounds with the men. Their spirits must be kept up. The hours before dawn are always bad for morale. They have done superbly. As have you."

Schoener flushed. "I—"

"Never mind, Herr Schoener. Think of the final victory. Not of defeat. I will go now."

"Herr General. Thank you—"

But von Grabow was off the line. Schoener watched helplessly as the targets continued to multiply on the dispassionate computer screen. The general was right, as usual. It was worst in the predawn hours. But the dawn was still far away.

————————TWENTY-ONE

They sat, immobile, as the hatch ground to a halt. The screech still echoed through their ears. Surely the Germans had heard it. Surely someone would run to investigate. They held their breath, frozen in position.

Ten seconds passed.

Twenty seconds.

Half a minute.

Ricard smiled. "Friction," he said quietly. "Friction."

"Certainly was," said Max. "It sounded like a boiler factory."

"No. I meant Clausewitz's friction." The others looked at the French major as if he'd lost his mind. "Friction is why the easy is usually so hard. Now it works for us instead of against us. Keeping us locked up was so easy for Muth, he ignored friction. No guards. No need for them, you see? So nobody comes to investigate the big noise." He smiled. "We go now, yes?"

He didn't wait for an affirmative. Instead, he threw off his blanket, went to his knees on the floor, studied the ground underneath for a moment, then wriggled through. Findlay followed, apparently no longer the reluctant warrior. Then Kulikov went through awkwardly. As his feet disappeared toward the front of the BMP, Max shrugged off his blanket and slipped through the hatch behind him.

The ground was wet, but mercifully warmer than the steel. There was plenty of room under the belly of the BMP to crawl, since the designers had given the vehicle a tall stance for obstacle clearance. Max joined the little group huddled under the front edge of the armored personnel carrier. Ricard and Findlay studied the command trailer, which lay about thirty yards across the parking lot. A half-dozen vehicles now stood in the muddy area. It would be easy to use them to get close to the door.

Light poured through the window of the door, the only one in the trailer. No movement showed. They listened for what seemed like an eternity for voices. The only noises seemed to be mechanical; generators nearby, generators more distant. Power for the rocket launchers and power for the trailer. It would be a useful racket.

Ricard looked at them all. He pointed to himself, then Findlay, then Kulikov, then Moss. He aimed his hand at the trailer and nodded. He weaved it from side to side, indicating how they should move from vehicle to vehicle. They all nodded. Kulikov, jammed against the wheels of the BMP's tracks beside Moss, shook palpably. Max admired his guts. To be so afraid, yet to go on with it. Life in the brutal Red Army must be tough for such a man, Max thought.

All at once Ricard was off, hunched low, scuttling like a beetle to the nearest vehicle. Max's breath started coming in short, hard bursts. He tried to slow it, but it was no use. The single, brilliant mercury-vapor light over the door of the trailer cast everything in deep shadow and glaring highlights. The world seemed to be black and white. Ricard made it to the next APC and leaned against the big rubber wheel. He looked around carefully. Still nobody showed. He waved for Findlay to come.

"Here goes nothing," muttered Findlay under his breath, and started off. He couldn't hunch as low as Ricard, not being as small or thin, but he made good time. He thudded to the ground next to the Frenchman.

Ricard waved again after listening. Kulikov looked at Max. Moss smiled. He hoped it looked like encouragement. The Russian pushed his glasses up his nose and clenched his teeth. He crawled a little way out from under the BMP, then stood. He began to half-walk, half-run. Midway to the APC his right foot went from under him. He threw out his arms, but it was too late. He fell to the mud with an enormous splat. Max held his breath. Kulikov lay, frozen, for two heartbeats. But still nobody came. He struggled to his feet and made his way to the APC on all fours. Ricard waved for Moss.

Finally under way, Max felt better with each step. He seemed to fly the last yards to the others. He slipped down behind Kulikov and watched Ricard.

The Frenchman peered around the tire, rose, and repeated his scuttle to the next vehicle. This time they all did the same without incident. In a few more minutes of run-and-wait, run-and-wait, they were at the last BTR before the door of the trailer. Ricard studied it for a long while. Max began to shiver. Finally Ricard held up his hand. When he dropped it, he stood and ran to the door. They all followed. It was too late for solo work. Max turned his back on the door and watched the menacing darkness for signs of attack. There were none. The bright light painted only the half-dozen vehicles, the front rank of the tall conifers, the slick, fat cables snaking through the mud to the launchers spread throughout the forest, and the barrels of the anti-arcraft guns in the nearby clearing. The generators clattered away. Nothing seemed to move.

Ricard grasped the metal rail of the stair and walked deliberately but quietly up. Findlay and Kulikov followed close behind. At the top Ricard put his face close to the window. He laid his ear against the door and listened some more. Then he glanced down at them solemnly and turned the door lever.

The hinges didn't squeak. He and Findlay were in within seconds. Kulikov hesitated, but Max nudged from behind. He almost fell through.

Blinking under the fluorescent lights, Max recalled the layout. Muth's apartment was to the right. The door was closed. He stood by it while Ricard and Findlay tried to use the shadows to get down to the command room. Through the partition Max could see two men. One, as before, sat at the radio, headset and tuning dial occupying his attention. The other, the skeletal one Max had noticed before, sat with his feet up on the launch console, rocking back and forth. An AKM lay on his lap. A pistol butt stuck out of his side holster. He seemed to be staring into the middle distance.

Back and forth.

Ricard, creeping along on his haunches, stopped at the partition. Findlay did likewise. Kulikov waited five paces behind.

Back and forth.

Ricard reached for the handle to the door. The air hummed with the electrical activity of the radios and computers. Max licked his lips. As cold as he had been, now he was roasting. He watched, mesmerized, as Ricard painstakingly turned the handle.

Back and forth.

The cam activated by the door handle suddenly went overcenter. The door clicked open. Everything seemed to happen at once.

The skeleton with the AKM stopped and looked lazily at the door. He expected to see an officer.

He did. But it was a Frenchman, not a German. Ricard leaped to his feet and charged the man with all his speed. But the skeleton was younger and tougher and had lived

too long on the ragged edge to be taken so easily. He had
his weapon up just as Ricard's muddy hands caught his
throat and Ricard's knee drove into his chest. The radioman was slower, and Findlay had his head in an arm vise
before the man had done more than half-stand, wide-eyed.

Ricard's hands were like talons. He stared into the skeletal
German's face and willed him to die. But the infantryman
wouldn't give up. He tried to squeeze the trigger of the
AKM, which now pointed uselessly at the ceiling. Without Kulikov he would have made it. But the Russian
simply jerked the weapon from his weakening hands. And
then a dreadful snap deep in the soldier's neck killed
him. Ricard dropped him as if he were so much sand,
and helped Findlay.

The radioman was already unconscious. Findlay let him
slip back into his chair. Ricard glanced at him and at
Findlay. Then he stepped over the radioman, stiffened his
forearm, and drove the heel of his hand hard against the
man's nose. With a sickening crunching noise his head
jerked backward and the nose simply disappeared into a
lump of flaccid flesh. The body jerked as the splinters of
bone drove into the brain, the eyes flew open, then stared
lifelessly at the light overhead. Findlay scowled at Ricard.
The Frenchman ignored him and waved Kulikov to the
black box.

While Kulikov carefully unplugged the leads into the
box and worked on unscrewing the cannon plug umbilical,
Ricard grabbed the AKM and pulled the pistol from the
dead guard's holster. He handed the pistol to Findlay and
went back to where Max stood guard on the closed door to
the commander's section. He motioned Max aside, cock-
ing the AKM and bringing it to the ready.

"Major!" Max whispered. "Look—we might be able to
do this without anybody knowing for a while. Why take a
chance?"

Ricard's eyes were suffused with blood. His skin was

stretched tight over his cheeks, his lips thin and bloodless. He looked from the door to Max. "Perhaps you're right," he whispered. He turned and stood at the door, looking outside.

Kulikov held up the box in triumph. Findlay shoved him forward and the two hurried up the aisle. In his haste Kulikov caught his sleeve on the door handle as he went through the door. He lurched sideways and the box flew out of his hands. It struck the floor and clanged against the metal base of some big apparatus. They all froze in place.

The door behind Max swung open. He turned in time to see Muth standing there, a pistol in hand, dressed only in his undershirt, boots, and trousers. His eyes flicked from Findlay to Kulikov to Ricard and he brought up the pistol.

"Don't—" he began.

Ricard, still wheeling from his door position, couldn't aim properly, so his burst caught Muth in the legs. The German was kicked backward as if by a huge fist. His pistol cracked off a single shot into the wall as he slammed back into his apartment.

"Let's go!" shouted Ricard. He kicked open the door and ran down the stairs.

Findlay hesitated a moment, then ran past Max, who stood staring at Muth's almost severed legs. He grabbed Max's arm. "Move it, Leftenant, move it!" He dragged Max to the door. Max pulled free.

"No! Gotta help Kulikov. Get going!"

Max turned back into the trailer. Findlay watched for a second, then ran down the stairs and turned for the trees. Max found Kulikov tugging at the umbilical for the black box, which had wedged itself under the metal cabinet into which it had slammed. Max joined him. Together they pulled and jerked. Finally it came free, shedding its soldered connections.

"Come on!" Max grated, and they half-ran, half-stumbled through the door. At the base of the stairs they heard shouts. Max looked around. Lights came from every side. Kulikov seemed bewildered. He held the box as if it were his life preserver.

"This way," Max said, and ran for the nearest BTR. Almost there, he halted and thought for a second. "No. Back to ours. Let's go."

In seconds he was at the BMP. He jerked open the driver's hatch and slid down into the leather seat. He pulled it closed. Next to him the other hatch came up, then Kulikov did likewise. He tossed Max the box and carefully lowered the hatch so that it did not make noise when it seated. They sat, breathing heavily while the lights and voices milled around. Soon enough, they were coherent.

"The hostages!"

"Oberst Muth has been hit—"

"What should we—"

"Men, listen to me! The Oberst is alive. He says the hostages have escaped, and taken our launch control unit with them. We must find them, and quickly! Kollsmann! Fuerster! Mueller! Take a detail each and look in the trees!"

"*Jawohl*, Herr Hauptmann!"

"You men—look through those cars."

"Should we check the hostages' vehicle, Herr Hauptmann?"

"They won't be there anymore, but you might as well look—quickly. God knows how they got out, and we don't have time to find out. We must find the control box. Get moving!"

Max scrunched down as low as he could in the driver's seat. The Russian did likewise. Lights flashed across the inside of the cab as the detail searched the compound. He used the occasional flashes to check out the instruments and controls.

The lock on the rear doors rattled as a soldier fumbled with the keys. Then the door squeaked open. "The escape hatch!'' somebody said. "Herr Hauptmann! They got out through the escape hatch!'' he called to the captain in the stairs.

"Yes, yes! There's no time for that, Hirsch! Get *moving*!'' the officer yelled back.

The door clanged shut and the soldier ran off. Away from them. The lights grew less frantic as the search spread out from the parking area.

Kulikov craned his neck to look at Max. He lifted an eyebrow. Max shook his head. "Not yet," he whispered.

Frankel watched as the medic finished the bandaging. He winced as the obvious pain forced Muth to bite his lip until blood flowed from it too. After the medic had tied the knot Muth struggled to sit up.

"No! Herr Oberst, you cannot—" the medic said while trying to push him down on the bed.

"Don't order me, Feldwebel. I must. Help me. Don't resist me, dammit!"

Frankel and the medic eased him to a sitting position. Muth gasped as Frankel nudged his leg inadvertently.

"Sorry, Herr Oberst, I—"

"Never mind, Frankel. Report. What is the situation?"

"The control unit, as you said, is gone. Steiner and Boeller are dead. We are searching the area."

"If they had any sense, they split up. You know, all they have to do is get to a friendly unit with the control, and we are finished. Only the box counts. None of them do." He fell back against the wall behind his little cot, panting. He closed his eyes momentarily.

"Herr Oberst. You must rest. There is—"

"Much to be done. We cannot rest, Herr Frankel. I must speak to Oberst Schoener. Quickly!"

"But Herr Oberst—you cannot move!" said the medic.

"You did not hear me, Feldwebel. Your job is to help, not to hinder. Get me to the radio. *Now!*"

They obeyed. The narrow corridor eliminated using any kind of litter, so Muth had to be supported by the two of them and dragged, his legs trailing, to the radio console. He bit his lip through in the first ten feet. By the time they were at the partition door he was moaning softly through clenched teeth, his eyes squeezed shut. Frankel and the medic tried to keep all weight and contact off his legs, but it couldn't be done. They gritted their teeth and hurried him to the console chair. When they eased him into it the bandages on his legs were seeping scarlet.

"Herr Oberst, you must listen to me. You will die within the hour if you persist—"

"Then it is on your head, Feldwebel. Your job is to keep me alive until we are done. No more than that. Do you understand?" He wiped the bloody froth off his perforated lip. "Get me Bismarck," he grated to Frankel.

The captain grabbed the headset and microphone. "Hello Bismarck. Hello Bismarck. Iron calling. Over."

Response was immediate.

"Iron from Bismarck, go ahead."

Frankel handed the headset and mike to Muth. "Oberst Muth here. Get me Oberst Schoener immediately."

"Stand by, Herr Oberst," said the voice from the E3G.

"Oskar. What's happening?"

"They've escaped, Helmut. Taken the control unit. We're searching now," Muth said. He winced with each word.

"Escaped? How?"

"Never mind. What shall we do, Helmut? You understand? *We cannot launch the rockets!*"

It finally sank into Schoener. He was silent a moment.

"All right, Oskar. I understand. How far have they gotten?"

"They're on foot. Not far. We are searching now."

"How long ago did they do it?"

Muth looked at Frankel. "Ten minutes, maybe twelve. No more."

"Good. You will have to throw every man into it, Oskar. There is no point guarding the camp if you don't have the control unit."

"I know. I have, Helmut. But the plan—"

"Never mind the plan, Oskar. General von Grabow will modify the plan as necessary. What were your casualties?"

"Two dead. And . . . and I took a few."

"A few? Where?"

"The legs. I cannot walk. But I am all right."

"You're certain?"

"Yes."

"Then put out maximum effort, Oskar. I will contact you if anything changes here. Good luck."

"And to you the same, Helmut. Out."

He tossed the mike on the console and dropped the headset. He closed his eyes and took deep breaths. "Feldwebel," he said, "I will need your strongest pain-killer. Never mind the dose." When he opened his eyes he pinned Frankel with a fever-bright look. "Herr Frankel, you must use everyone. Helmut was right. Use the vehicles to scout the roads. Stay in touch. Leave me a few men—one radio operator—and get going."

Frankel touched his cap in salute. "Certainly, Herr Oberst. But you must—"

"Don't tell me to rest, Herr Hauptmann. If they get away, we are all dead men anyway. You understand that, don't you? So move."

Frankel moved.

The starter of a BTR armored car whined. Max knew at once what was happening. They were going to use the six-wheeled armored cars to chase the escaped hostages. He sat up and leaned forward, fumbling with the controls. The sealed personnel area had a light, but the cockpit had none.

"What are you doing?" hissed Kulikov.

"They're going to use the cars. We might as well join them. Say—how do you start this thing?"

"But—this is a BMP. It is slow. How can we get away?"

"That's my problem. You can help by telling me the start sequence. I think I know how to drive the thing."

Kulikov sat up. "There," he said, "that switch. When it is up it energizes the starter."

"Ahhh," said Max as he toggled it. The dashboard's three dials lit up. Two idiot lights came on. One glowed amber, then went out. The turbocharged twelve-cylinder diesel engine had quick-start glow plugs to get it working quickly.

"And the starter?"

"There," said Kulikov. He looked cautiously out his viewport. Men milled around each BTR. A pair walked toward the BMP. "Quickly," he said. "They're coming."

Max pushed the fat button. The starter whined somewhere in back and the diesel clattered to life. He fed it some throttle and it roared. The twin turbos were well designed.

The two Germans stopped when the exhaust poured from the stacks on the rear deck of the wedgelike BMP. They looked at each other, then ran to it.

"Hey!" one called. "Who's in that? Juergen? Is that you?"

Max grinned as he recalled the gear pattern. He depressed the clutch—it took considerable muscle—and engaged hi-low. This tracked BMP had a steering wheel to activate the speeding up and slowing of the two tracks, but it also had a manual override for turns on a dime. He used it now. As the soldier came up to Kulikov's side and tried to peer through the viewport, Max kicked the BMP's throttle hard and slammed one track to the reverse position. The eleven-ton vehicle kicked at the soldier like a mule as it spun sideways away from him. He flew backward, arms akimbo, and flopped into the mud. His partner pulled his AKM off his shoulder and loosed a burst at the cloud of blue diesel smoke that marked the BMP's path. Three inches of armor sent the 9mm rounds zinging uselessly off.

"Hold on!" Max yelled over the roar of the engine.

He peered through the slit only inches from his face and clumsily engaged second range. The tracks slipped and clawed for traction in the gummy mud. Ahead, the BTRs on the search mission blocked the way, moving ten mph slower than he was. A face above the turret of the BTR ahead of him looked back as he snapped on the bright driving lights. A hand appeared by the face, waving vigorously backward. Then the eyes in the face grew round as dinner plates as their owner realized that Max wasn't going to stop.

The impact jarred them both, but the BMP was made for just such work. The lighter, eight-wheeled armored car slewed sideways and rolled onto its left side, spilling the man who'd waved. Max savagely jerked the track controls to clear the tumbling car. The next one in line crashed off into the trees as its driver realized his intent. The one ahead of him did likewise. The big BMP roared between them and Max found his lights illuminating an empty road. Adrenaline pumped through him, and the combination of the road and the chemical had its usual effect. He mashed the accelerator and shifted into high gear.

─────────TWENTY-TWO

Like the rest of the Germans, von Grabow had learned to ignore the unconscious Americans in the crew rest area. He cradled a plastic foam cup of hot tea and stared at the rear bulkhead while Schoener summarized Muth's report in a monotone. The two of them sat side by side in the rearward-facing airline seats. Schoener trailed off after describing the escape by the armored personnel carrier. Von Grabow brought the cup to his lips and sipped it as if he were an automaton. He winced as the tea scalded his tongue.

"They are in pursuit with the BTRs?" he asked finally.

"Yes. But the roads there are a maze. The tracks will be lost in the mud. It will not be easy to find him."

"Even when they do, it is not certain that the BMP is being driven by the one—or ones—with the control unit."

"No."

"If I were in command, I would have split up. Each man would have gone a different way. It would give the one with the unit a better chance. I imagine that when Muth's people finally catch up with the BMP, it will turn out the man driving it does not have the unit. It's too obvious."

"Yes. I agree. I told Muth to spare no one in the ground search."

"Wise."

"I hope so. But Herr General . . . what happens if the unit is actually lost? Or if the other side finds out it has been stolen?"

"If you mean, do we launch, no. If you mean, do we surrender, no. We keep going. We find the control unit."

"I understand. But you are determined not to launch? This could be counted as aggression, as defying our demands."

Von Grabow considered the top of his cup intently. "Certainly. But what use is it to wipe out nine Western cities without the threat of the same on the East? None. It must be both or none."

"Perhaps we could demand that they ship us another launch control unit. Threaten the West, use their influence with the Soviets to force them."

"Don't be naive. You forget your own masters. Confronted with a situation like that, the Russians would only laugh and flatten us. No. Everything depends now on Muth's retrieving the box. And we must not let either side know we've lost it."

Von Grabow swallowed more tea. It seared him as it went down. He welcomed the heat, because inside he was ice cold. Somehow he had known that something was badly wrong when Schoener had called for a conference. Nobody could have foreseen that the Allied officers would break out. The ones in the West were docile. He suppressed his emotions ruthlessly as he considered the ramifications. He must not lose control. The plan could still work, even if the unit were lost. As long as *they* didn't know it was lost. The rockets need never be launched as long as they reacted as the computers had predicted. They only needed until a little after dawn, and it would be all over.

His heart thumped irregularly. He closed his eyes and concentrated on calming himself. He knew now the curse of the field general. It was to plan, to begin, and then to watch helplessly as events beyond his reach took over with a life of their own. He recalled his brave speech to Schoener about commanding troops from a hill. Here he was on the highest hill in Europe, watching as a god would watch. And it availed him nothing. The teacup began to shake. He squeezed his eyes tighter together and concentrated on fine thoughts. On Monika. Herbert, in the old days. The day he rose through the black clouds in that beautiful F84, shooting straight up from the rain and misery into the cold, clean, clear, brain-smashing blue. He had laughed and sung into his rubber mask, and danced with the silver jet effortlessly, alone in the heaven. He couldn't recall the ecstasy of sex, or the flinch of pain, but he could recapture that moment when he was free at last of the Earth, one with God and air and plane, trained, skilled, young, immortal.

No more. Now he was a passenger, facing backward, a man who had plotted and schemed to make things better. A man who instead was watching things get worse. His heart would not slow down. He opened his eyes. He turned to the right seat to ask Schoener a question. But the colonel was gone. His gaze, as if by itself, rested on the slack features of the young black navigator, now supine on a sleeping berth. A faint trickle of saliva trailed down the man's face and onto the blue blanket. He studied it for a moment, then looked at each of the Americans, noting remotely the differing effects of the drug. They lay with limbs akimbo, like corpses.

His corpses. Unbidden, the death he had seen began flicking through his mind's eye in high-speed detail. The last scene was the classified footage stolen from the Russians. Film of the effects of nuclear bombs on humans. They had deliberately killed thousands with blast, heat, and radiation, using the uncounted unknowns from the Gulag. He remembered the woman who had screamed helplessly, chained to her chair near the disintegrating window, while the glass shredded her face, the blast peeled the skin from her, and finally the bones themselves ignited, then crumbled. It had been in black and white, and the intelligence man who'd shown them had been impressed with the quality of the pictures. A triumph for the Soviets, he'd said. Superb technology. Imagine, a camera that would film right through an atomic bomb. He had banished the woman from his dreams for years. Now she returned as he closed his eyes again. His heartbeat rose. He clenched his teeth while her flesh again peeled back from her skull. The teacup split in his hands. The hot tea poured down his legs. Finally the film flickered out. His heart slowed at last. He took a long, shuddering breath and opened his eyes again.

He was in control. It was as it should be. He was Friedrich von Grabow, of the Gutshof von Grabow, Schwerin. He was Prussian. And he was German. He was a Prussian general commanding the best Germans there were in the finest cause there was. He had done what had to be done. All else was irrelevant.

He stood confidently and wiped the traces of tea from his flight suit. The smile that came to his face would inspire anyone who saw it. He left the crew rest area and went forward. The splintered cup rolled under a seat. Brigadegeneral Friedrich von Grabow, Deutsche Luftwaffe, son of Oberleutnant Ritter Karl Maria von Grabow, Kaiserliche Hussar, grandson of Generalmajor Ritter Heinz von Grabow, "Sieger von Paris," and great-grandson of Feldmarschall Baron Ritter Ernst Christian von Grabow, "Held des Reiches," was not at the highest hill in Europe to pay attention to such things. He was there to serve destiny.

The BMP responded like an overloaded Mack truck. Sweat oozed down Max's spine as he fought to urge every ounce of speed from the personnel carrier. It had been designed to go fast, but only in combat-vehicle terms. He didn't have a speedo, so the part of his brain that had been trained for such things took note of the velocity with which the trees whipped past and calculated that they were doing no more than 45 mph. Tops. He glanced from the driving slit to the primitive dashboard. The fuel gauge looked good. The engine seemed healthy. All he needed was time.

The road—such as it was—came to an abrupt end again. He slewed the heavy beast to a halt. Another T-junction.

"Which way?" he yelled at Kulikov.

"*Ne znayu!*" the Russian shouted back.

Max swore under his breath. The guy was a technowizard, but he'd answered "don't know" every time they'd come to one of these dead ends. What the hell. He jammed the BMP into reverse and backed up. He looked both ways into the darkness. Nothing, either side. These border restricted areas were terra incognita to Recovery crews. Nobody really knew the road layout of any of them. And naturally the designers of the BMP hadn't thought to fit it with a compass. He shrugged and gunned it to the right, spewing reddish mud from one track.

Reddish mud. When they'd left the compound it had been black, Iowa-style. Now it was Alabama as hell. He tried to remember anything salient about the topography of the area. Nothing. So much for being an ace intelligence officer. On the other hand, who would have thought he'd need to know what the fuck kind of mud lay along the regions of the Czech-German border? Maybe Kemp would.

Kemp. He was being an idiot. Kemp was as close as the radio.

"Kulikov! You know how to work this thing's radio?"

"I—yes, I think so," the Russian replied. He held on with one hand while Max slid the BMP around a hairpin. The inner track spun crazily. The differentials screeched their complaint at such abuse. "Why?" he panted after the track settled down and they were headed straight.

"Does it have the American guard frequency?"

"Which?"

"UHF . . . 243 megahertz."

Kulikov warily released the hold he had on the grab rail and peered at the dark radio. He toggled a switch. Two things happened almost at once. The tuning dial backlight snapped on, the radio speaker grille between them on the rear bulkhead emitted a squeal, and then the lights died as the squeal ended in a loud pop.

"What happened?" called Max.

Kulikov squinted through his dirty glasses at the silent, dark radio. "Fuse. Must have been because of the hatch switch."

"Shit!" Max growled. "Can you fix it?"

"If I can find the fuses."

Max looked into the rearward-facing periscope, as he had periodically. Even through the optical distortion it was obvious. He swore under his breath.

"Well, you better hurry."

"Why?"

"Because our pals have found us."

Max savagely upshifted and kept his foot planted hard on the steel accelerator pedal. The big diesel wound up tighter. But his mental speedo didn't change much.

Kulikov turned his periscope around and peered into it. He opened his mouth to speak.

"I don't see—"

A huge fist pounded on the rear of the BMP. It began as

a concussion, then, as the sound waves traveled through the steel armor, the noises followed. Each striking round of the 37mm cannon mounted in the turret on the pursuing BTR drove shock waves through their spines. It felt as if someone were reaching up through their bellies into their thoraxes, grabbing their hearts, and squeezing just enough to knock the wind from them.

"See it now?" Max gritted out.

A short burst of 37mm arced past into the night ahead of his headlights. Green tracer identified it. The track left a glowing red afterimage in his retinas.

"We can't outrun that bastard. Hang on!" Kulikov grabbed the rail just in time. Max brought the gear lever through the range from hi-hi to low-low, stamped on the track stopper, and slammed the BMP left into the brush. He had no idea what lay ahead. All he knew was what lay behind.

"Herr Oberst."

Muth opened his eyes. The drugs made him weary beyond belief. But the pain was kept at bay. And he was conscious. "Yes, Frankel?"

"We have two of them."

Muth sat up straighter in the radio chair. He had forbidden them from trying to move him. The pain was one reason. The need to be able to speak with Helmut was another.

"Which ones? Do they have—?"

"No. I am sorry. The Frenchman and the Britisher."

Muth slumped. "Oh. Do they know who has it?"

"If they do, they will not say."

"Do they know who is in the APC?"

"Their answer is the same."

Muth looked down at his legs. The blood was not clotting well. The drugs were slowing the process. It was a race between the loss of blood and the loss of consciousness. The blood didn't count if the consciousness was lost.

"Herr Oberst?"

"Yes?" His voice was remote, even to him.

"What shall we do with them?"

"Will they talk, do you think?"

"I don't think so. The Frenchman killed two of my men before we got him. The Britisher was not so hard. But he fought well too."

Muth realized his tongue was lolling. He drew it into his mouth. At least he could still feel shame for appearing ridiculous. He forced himself to sit up and concentrate. He blinked and his vision seemed to clear. Frankel stood beside him, holding an AKM. He was filthy. And his arm dripped a little blood. Muth felt a pang of remorse. Or something. He was too weary to know.

"Kill them then."

"We will need them no more as hostages?"

Muth smiled. It felt good, just for a moment, to smile. "No. Don't worry, Frankel. We will not need them."

Frankel was gone before he realized it. Muth knew he was in need of something to counteract the drugs. More drugs.

"Medic! Damn it! *Medic!*"

The man appeared. He might as well have materialized, for all Muth knew where he came from. He summoned his tumbling thoughts.

"Need to think. Must think. Be able to. Speak. Too much painkiller. Now. *Now!*" He wanted to reach for the man and shake him to make him understand, but he could not. His arm would not move. He stared at it until everything simply faded into blackness.

"I have the activity, Herr Oberst."

"Remote it to me, Herr Fritz." Schoener blanked his screen and enabled the remote access mode. In a few seconds the scene Fritz was observing appeared line by line on his cathode ray tube. He studied it for a moment.

"I can't read the tags, Herr Major. What's happening?"

"You see the one tagged TV275? It's red, flashing slowly?"

"Yes."

"That one is a BMP-9. According to the databank anyway. Now, you see the two yellow blips, both tagged WV150/37?"

"To the right. Yes."

"Those are BTR-60-Ps with 37mm cannon. That's what the 37 is for. And the 150—"

"Means 150 horsepower. Yes. 'WV' for wheeled vehicle. I see. You think this is Oberst Muth's quarry?"

"It's in the right area. Everything matches. No other vehicles moving in the immediate zone, as we demanded."

Schoener chewed his cheek as he stared into the screen. The resolution was not good enough to show whether the yellow blips were gaining on the red one. It must be the escaped BMP. The zone of no movement they'd decreed was still devoid of military activity. The few civilian vehicles the computer had identified had proved nonthreatening.

"Can we call the BTRs?"

"No, sir. I checked already. They must have the new radios. Even this commset hasn't got the ability to talk to them. We know where they are in the spectrum, but the scramblers—"

"Sure, Fritz. I understand. All we can do is tell Oskar. Thanks. Leave the remote on my screen, will you?" Schoener switched to the comm operator and directed him to contact Iron. It took longer than it should have.

"Iron here," he finally heard. The voice was not Muth's.

"Bismarck here. Who is speaking?"

"Hauptmann Frankel. Oberst Muth's exec."

"Is the Oberst—?"

"Alive. Is this Oberst Schoener?"

"Yes. What is your situation, Hauptmann?"

"The Oberst is resting. We could not keep him awake, as he directed, so our medic allowed him to sleep. This also will give the blood a chance to clot, he says."

"Excellent. You have done correctly. What of the escapees?"

"We have found two of them. The French and British majors. They were shot at the Oberst's order."

"Ah. And the control unit?"

"Not with them."

"So. Then my information is critical, Captain. We are watching the attempt by your people to capture the stolen BMP. But we cannot communicate directly with them. Are you in contact?"

"They have checked in, yes. But so far all they have been able to tell us is that they had the BMP, then lost it in the forest."

"We can direct them through you. Stand by." He dialed up a compass rose on the screen and keyed it to remain centered on the red blip. "Have your people steer 277 degrees. The BMP is about four kilometers in that direction."

"Two hundred seventy-seven degrees. Yes. Thank you, Herr Oberst." The connection was good enough for Schoener to hear Frankel give someone the order to contact the BTRs. Then he came back on. "Herr Oberst? May I suggest we keep this line open? I can put a man on who will relay your directions."

"Excellent, Hauptmann Frankel. I will turn it over to Major Fritz. Before you go—how is Oberst Muth?"

The pause told him a lot. "He has lost too much blood, Herr Oberst. But the medic believes he will be conscious again within a few minutes. Shall I have him speak with you then?"

"No. Not necessary. Just—just keep him well, Hauptmann. Keep him well."

"We will do our best, Herr Oberst. Now I should transfer."

"Yes. Good luck, Herr Frankel. Tell your men they are doing well. Tell them Germany is proud, that General von Grabow is proud."

"I will, Herr Oberst. Transferring now."

Schoener switched to Fritz, told him what to do, and then toggled out of the intercom net. He watched the blips. They were still the same distance apart. But soon that would change.

────────────TWENTY-THREE

When the nose of the BMP pitched down and Max saw the water, he knew they might have a chance after all. Crashing through the last of the brush on the bank over the creek, some speeded-up part of his mind—the Recovery jock part—noted that a road led straight down to it on the other side. A road thoroughly churned and used-looking. So he slammed the APC into a slide and headed straight upstream, not across it. The heavy vehicle sank like a stone, and tracks spinning through the water, lurched and swayed until they clawed creekbed. The water level seemed to be just above the top of the tracks. No problem for the watertight, fully amphibious personnel carrier. He doused the lights and slowed to a crawl.

Kulikov sank against the seat like a man who'd been shot. "You are a crazy driver, Lieutenant," he stammered.

"Maybe. But we're still free. Now, do me a favor and see if you can get the damned radio working," Max said. It took almost all his concentration to steer between the darker masses of the creekbanks. The diesel barely growled now that he had slowed to a walking pace. Water rushed and gurgled past the armor plate, and the tracks, even turning slowly, turned the cockpit into a reasonable facsimile of a barrel going over Niagara Falls.

Kulikov laid the control unit, which he'd been holding with a death grip, on the floor. He bent and peered along the edge of the dashboard. "Perhaps a light—" he said.

"No!" barked Max. "No light. We can't outrun 'em. But we may be able to outcrawl 'em. The only way is if they can't see us." Driving upstream helped Max a little. He thought he remembered seeing this or another little stream on the topo chart; he also thought he remembered it running almost north-south. If so, he was headed out of the restricted area. If not, he was heading somewhere else. It didn't matter. He had to go somewhere.

Kulikov cursed softly in Russian while he felt for the kind of shape that would tell him he had found a fuse box. Max concentrated on driving.

It was all so familiar. Here he was again, running like hell from the bad guys. Correction. Driving like hell. Was he doomed to this kind of nonsense forever? Was he nothing but a getaway-car driver? He would have shrugged if he could have spared the muscular concentration to do it. Who knew? All he knew was that he kept stumbling into these situations. And he was good at it, more or less.

Or maybe not. Maybe he didn't stumble into them exactly. After all, he could have chosen to run from Kulikov as the others had. It had been the plan. Why had he stayed? Why had he chosen to hide in the BMP—in the *driver's* seat?

Easy. It was home.

The nose pitched down and the water splashed up and into the viewing slit. He ducked his head as the cold water poured through the slit. As he wondered about the slit closure, the nose pitched up again. So much for philosophy, he thought. Gets you nothing but wet. He squinted into the night.

"Anything?" he called to Kulikov.

"I . . . think . . . so," the Russian said. He seemed to be half-lying under the dash. "Ah!" he said. "Here. Yes. Circuit breakers. I can feel them. All I need to do is—"

There was a sharp snap from the dash. The dial backlights went out. The idiot light went out. And the engine died.

"What the hell—?"

"Sorry—sorry, here, it is—"

The lights came on again. Before the APC had entirely stopped in the water the engine coughed back to life.

"It must have been the fuel injection. Sorry," said Kulikov. Max grunted.

"Ah. Yes. Here," the Russian said confidently. Another snap echoed above the waterfall noise. And the radio lights came on. Kulikov straightened up.

"You see?" he said proudly. "It works."

"Right. Now, try 243 megahertz."

Kulikov twisted the five tuning knobs until he had the digits 2-4-3-0-0 centered. "Yes? Now?"

"Give me the mike," Max said.

Kulikov detached the microphone from its retaining clip and reached across the center console to hand it to Max. He did not finish the hand-off.

A blinding white light came from the right riverbank. Max ducked his head, tromped on the accelerator pedal, and slewed the BMP all at once. Kulikov stared stupidly into the brilliant light, blinking, wide-eyed. Max ground his teeth as the tracks clawed for traction. It seemed to take forever for the heavy machine to turn.

Before it had made ninety degrees the first 37mm round spanged off the side armor near Kulikov's ear. He recoiled, dropped the mike, and covered his eyes. Max hunched in his seat, willing the machine to speed up the slippery bank. He flipped on the lights. The next round took off the right set in a shower of sparks and a concussion that shook their bowels. And then they were at the bank, climbing, climbing so slowly.

"Come on, you bastard, come on—" Max chanted as he always chanted, the incantation of speed. It didn't work.

Still pinned in the brilliant glare, the BMP took the next three 37mm rounds squarely along the weld between the cockpit side plates and the top. The first round split the crude weld, the second slammed into the hot metal and peeled the top back a little, and the third—an armor-piercing, high-explosive round—detonated just aft of the second.

The explosion ripped the top off the cockpit and sent metal slivers echoing crazily through the confined space, as the round's designers had intended. Most of the splinters were from the armor next to Kulikov, which bellied out under impact of the shaped charge into a swollen, red-hot blister of steel, then flew apart like an exploding land mine.

Kulikov took the brunt of it. He was hunched forward, hands over head, but it did him no good. The blister burst only inches behind his spine, and sent three-inch splinters through him as if his body were so much butter. The largest chunk spun off the armor and sliced his neck cleanly through. The sightless head flopped forward onto the perforated trunk.

Max saw none of it. The rounds stunned him, but the big splinters missed him. A small one whined across his chest, ripping open his clothing, severing his tie neatly and leaving a jagged tear in his chest. He didn't notice. He was blinded, deafened, and clamped to the machine by sheer will.

The BMP rocked sideways under the triple hit, teetering at the very top of the riverside bank. Max's foot remained planted on the accelerator, so the tracks still spun. The left one dug in and catapulted the BMP over the top. But just before it cleared, another burst smashed into the exposed belly.

Max's vision cleared in time to see the ground in his remaining headlight. He knew he was over the bank. Then the burst exploded in the BMP's guts and the ground spun in front of him. He realized he was rolling. And then something smashed the back of his head and he stopped realizing anything.

The BTRs approached the smoking BMP cautiously. Both armored cars halted at the top of the riverbank and played their spotlights along it.

It rested on its left side, only a meter from the riverside road. Where the burst had entered the belly, fuel oil dribbled out. Lying on its side, filthy and spewing fluid, it looked like a gutted wild animal dying in the night. There was no movement around the cockpit.

The hatch of the leading car clanged open. The reinstated ex-lieutenant, Kollsmann, hoisted himself out. He unholstered his Makarov 9mm pistol and jumped off the car. His shadow danced crazily before him as his driver kept the spotlight on him while he approached the smoldering BMP.

He walked around the back and peered into the ripped-open top. The lights were on the side away from him, so he had to look carefully. But the reflected light was good enough.

He climbed up the snout and looked at the bodies tumbled into the left side—now the bottom—of the cockpit. Blood covered almost everything, and he quickly saw why. The one on top was headless. Kollsmann had seen much worse, so it affected him little. He shielded his eyes from the glare and looked harder. The one under the decapitated one—it must be Russian, from the brown leather boots—wore blue. The American lieutenant. All he could see of him was his right arm and some of his right side. The rest lay buried under the detritus of the explosion and the Russian body. The arm looked lifeless. The hand was limp. Kollsmann scanned the rest of the cockpit. And, in seconds, had found what he was looking for.

The control unit was wedged under the righthand seat cushion, jammed there no doubt by the force of the explosion. Kollsmann holstered his pistol and reached in for the box. It was wedged tightly. But not too tightly. It came free on the third heave. He tumbled back off the snout and fell on his side. It knocked the wind out of him momentarily, but he got up, still holding the CDS, and examined it in the lights.

It seemed all right. The wires dangled minus their plug, but they could fix that. He held it up for the others to see, and hurried back to his vehicle. Inside, he tossed it down to the driver and jerked the microphone off the clip.

"Iron, Iron, this is Kollsmann."

"Go ahead, Kollsmann."

"Tell the Oberst we have it! We have the box! We are returning now."

"Excellent, Kollsmann! The hostages?"

"Dead."

"You're sure?"

"Yes. Very dead."

"Then return at once. Good work, Kollsmann!"

The lieutenant jammed the mike back down and clapped his driver on the shoulder. "Let's go!" he shouted, and in a moment both BTRs were past the wrecked BMP and headed south on the river road.

Frankel shook Muth vigorously. "Herr Oberst! Wake up, please!"

Muth's eyes rolled down. "Wha-what?"

"They have the control unit! They're coming back!"

Slack-jawed, Muth tried to focus. Suddenly he understood. He smiled faintly. "Good. Good. *Good!* Tell Schoener." Then he passed out again.

Frankel waved the medic back to Muth. He watched for a moment, then told the radioman to get Schoener.

Something inside von Grabow uncoiled when Helmut told him. He remained outwardly the same, but it was as if he had not been breathing for the last half-hour. He had never felt so free. So alive.

"Superb, Schoener. Superb!"

"I thought so too. It was, after all, what this aircraft was built for. Air-to-ground coordination. We directed them; they fought the battle."

Von Grabow looked at the clock. "They should be back in operation within the hour then."

"At least. They say that the box seemed undamaged except for the torn-off plug. A simple matter to replace. If the wiring and components are not damaged."

"Hardly. It was designed to withstand much worse, was it not? At least, so its designer claims."

Schoener flushed. "I—I'm sure of it. I took every precaution."

Von Grabow allowed himself to clap his hands. "Superb. Yes, it's superb. Tell the men. We are still in command." He paused, eyes alight, beaming. "I suppose this proves it, eh?"

"What, Herr General?"

"You know. That God is on our side after all."

Schoener's smile widened. He allowed himself a chuckle. After all, it was fitting if his general could quip. "Yes," he said, "it would seem so."

"Seem so? Hardly, Herr Schoener. No, we have bested them now. Now nothing can stop us. The worst is over."

Schoener's smile faded. He wanted it to remain. But it would not. God was all very well. But there were still the odds.

TWENTY-FOUR

Consciousness arrived as pain, nausea, and vertigo. The result was a convulsive heave of his guts. It began deep inside and brought Max to life as the vomit spewed through his mouth. Some of the hot, stinking fluid recoiled back onto him, splashed off something near. He couldn't tell what it was. He seemed blind. But he couldn't tell that either, because he also seemed paralyzed. For a while he decided to deal with it by just breathing. It took all his strength.

He was alive. He knew that much. The stench of his own vomit reminded him, even if the pain from the several hot spots in his otherwise numb anatomy did not. For the hell of it he tried to identify each one. There was the searing fire in his chest. And the throbbing factory in the back of his skull. And his legs. Both seemed to be bent backward. Or forward. Whichever, with each thump of his heart they swelled with agony. A spectator in his own mind, he observed it all remotely.

Memory crept back like a beggar at the door. Ah, yes. He had been driving a BMP. With Kulikov. All very interesting, in a far-off sort of way. What had happened to old Kulikov? Was that memory of an explosion, of spurting blood and tumbling, crashing madness real?

The pain in his legs became more urgent. It drove out, beat by beat, all other thoughts. It became less remote. He had to do something, blind or not.

Talk? He tried. He wanted to say Hello, I'm hurt, can anyone help me? But all that came out was "Urghk." He forced the fluid out of his throat by a supreme effort. It dawned on him that it should not have been so hard. He must not be upright. Like a disoriented skindiver, he did not know which way was up.

He gathered his resources. He had almost no sense of where his limbs lay—less of whether they'd work—but he knew time was running out for him. He had to do something. He recalled the little Japanese who'd taught body warfare at the special course at Fort Leonard Wood. Killing other people wasn't really what he taught. He taught understanding of the human machine—how to motivate it, how to use it. All through assembling spiritual strength to focus in a single spot. Max focused. For ten, fifteen, twenty seconds he focused. And then he shouted and shoved outward with every ounce of energy he could summon.

Something moved. He collapsed after his effort like a sagging balloon. But whatever had begun to move kept moving. Far away, as if through a wall, he heard a thump. Then another. Pressure came off some of his body. He felt air on his face. He gulped it greedily. And gathered himself for another try.

This time he felt his own body move. And suddenly he was almost free of the pain in his legs. Feeling returned to his arms, which burned. He flexed his fingers and felt them send the welcome news that they were there. After a gasping moment he reached blindly out and felt cold metal. A wheel. The steering wheel. It was above and behind him. So, he was jammed down in the footwell, upside down, sideways, with a sack of cement lying on him. Having a diagram helped. He grabbed the wheel with his right hand and heaved. The sack moved, and he felt better still. He flung his left hand out, found something—the door handle, upside down?—and held on. He heaved again. The pain in his legs washed away. He groaned and kept heaving. At once he was completely free of the weight. He flopped back against what had to be the door and sucked air dizzily.

He brought his hand to his face. It touched slick skin. He felt all over. He was covered in fluid. He rubbed it between his fingers. Vomit? Some, certainly. But that smell wasn't just his own dinner. It was—

Blood. Lots and lots of blood. He remembered the blood after the explosions. It had been like a shower, like someone had flung a water balloon full of it into the cockpit. It must be Kulikov's.

A sensation of coldness on his neck made him run his hand near his ear. More fluid, more blood. He gently inserted his finger into the ear cavity. It was full of sticky stuff. He probed. It ran out, and he found he could hear—buzzing, ringing, but he could hear. His ears were full of blood. He cleaned them idly, as if he were disposing of unwanted ear wax. That Kulikov had held all this was of no real interest to him. At least not now. What interested him was that he could hear again.

"Hey," he said weakly. The sound was almost laughable. But it was a sound, and he heard it. He touched his eyes again. The stuff was drying fast. He rubbed hard, so hard that it hurt. Stars shot across his vision, bits of colored lights. His eye sockets, like his ears, were filled with blood and crusting fluid. His eyelids had been glued together. He rubbed and wiped and cautiously tried to open his eyes.

It worked. After the total blackness the faint light of the predawn cast the scene before him in cool grays. He did indeed stand upright, more or less, on what had been the lefthand door of the APC. He stood parallel to the dashboard. And the sack of cement was Kulikov's body, now flopped across the driveline tunnel by the force of his freeing himself. Max eyed the body with almost idle curiosity. It was headless. No wonder he had been drenched in blood. He looked slowly around the interior. He saw the gaping rent where the 37mm antitank rounds had peeled away the armor roof.

And he saw the radio lights glowing dimly. The mike cord hung straight down. Without thinking about it he shoved himself away from the supporting wall and reached across Kulikov for the mike. He pulled it up by the cord. The digits were still reading the guard frequency. He lifted the mike to his lips and keyed it. Something popped behind him. He tried to speak, but only a guttural croak emerged. He brought the phlegm and blood up, spit it out, and tried again. Things were getting hazy again. He keyed the mike again and brought it very close to his mouth.

"Recovery . . . Recovery. This is Moss. Recovery . . . this is Max Moss. Mayday. Mayday. Mayday." He paused. The effort taxed him almost to the limit. He panted for a moment, then tried again. "Say again. Mayday. Mayday. Help me. Please." He wanted to say more. He wanted to listen, maybe fiddle with the radio to see if it would receive, give somebody directions, be helpful in the hoped-for rescue. But somewhere inside, something decided it had had enough. He thought he was about to key the mike again. Instead, he dropped it and sagged back against the wall. He thought he felt the handle poke him in the back. And then the blackness came again.

Major Fritz frowned into his tube. He watched for a moment, adjusted the scale up one notch, and waited for the computer to tell him what the blip was. It painted the thing blue, but no number appeared next to it. He tapped the keyboard on his console with the command to identify and ran the cursor mouse over to the blue blip. He hit the execute key.

The computer flashed a message he had not seen before in this E3 or its predecessor.

CLASSIFIED, it said. VERIFY CATEGORY CLEARANCE.

What? He thought. The whole damned airplane was top secret. The computer didn't know he was German and not the American who usually sat here. What this meant was that some parts of the computer's memory were off limits even to the E3G operators. He toggled his intercom.

"Herr Oberst. I have something you should see."

"Herr Major, I am scanning the Oder line now. Is it vital?"

"Yes."

"Very well. Remote it."

Fritz sent the screen to Schoener's console. He waited while Schoener looked at it.

"You see the blue blip?"

"Yes. So?"

"It approaches—at high speed—the site of the encounter between the BMP and our BTRs."

"Oh. Yes. I see. What is it?"

"The computer will not tell me, Herr Oberst. Watch."

He keyed the ID sequence again. And again got the same message.

"This is absurd!" said Schoener. "Let me try." He initiated another ID directive. The computer told him the same thing.

Schoener was silent a moment. "This is important, Fritz. I don't like not knowing what's happening down there. It was only a few minutes ago that our people got the CDS back. Those are their blips, no?"

"Yes. The yellow ones."

"They're moving slowly enough."

"The roads are complicated down there. It's a maze."

"Yet this blue target moves almost twice as fast. Maybe more. You're certain it's a ground target?"

"Positive. IR signature indicates some kind of car or truck. It's doing at least a hundred kilometers per hour."

"Stand by, Herr Fritz. I am going to try to break into the databank without the code." Schoener clicked off. Fritz watched the blue blip. It was less than a kilometer from the BMP now. As he watched, the screen suddenly rolled once. The data shifted on each block. When it was done, the blue target carried an ID tag.

"Now," said Schoener before he could say anything, "you have it. MLM4WD/500. What does it mean?"

Fritz keyed the glossary. Then he whistled low. "Sir. It means, U.S. Military Liaison Mission four-wheel-drive. Five hundred horsepower."

"What? What can the idiots be thinking? How could they know about this? Why would they send a single vehicle into our zone? They must know we can see them."

Fritz had no answer. He simply watched as the blue target stopped at the site of the blown-up BMP. "Shall we tell their commanders about this? Demand that they leave the area?"

"No," Schoener said at length. He watched also. "We'll wait a little. It may be an accidental encounter. It may signify nothing. Monitor it though. Let me know if anything significant happens." He paused. "Not much should. The Americans won't find anything down there except bodies."

The face that slowly came into focus above him was faintly familiar to Max. He looked at it for what seemed like a long time. Then all at once he recognized it.

"Sandy." His croak wasn't much better.

The face smiled. A hand brushed the stubborn wave of short blond hair from the blue eyes.

"Damn, Moss. You're alive after all," she said. Her

voice made him smile reflexively. Maybe he'd just look at her for the rest of his life. Or the next two minutes. Whichever came first.

Somebody said something behind his head. She looked up and said, "No. Not yet. He's not ready."

"Ready for what?" Max asked. He tried to sit up. It didn't work. Koppel shoved him gently back down. He realized he was lying on a quick-inflating mattress. He glanced around. He was inside a vehicle. He recognized it with a start as the rear of a Cherokee. A Recovery vehicle.

"Jesus," he said. "You heard me."

"You bet. We weren't more than five klicks away. Just outside the PRZ, in fact. Nobody was on the gate."

He blinked, absorbing the information too slowly. Something nagged at him. He ought to remember something. Something big. Something important.

The control unit.

He lurched up. She tried to push him down again, her eyes widening. "No way, cowboy. Your day is—"

"No. Wrong. Listen, Sandy. They got the control unit."

"What?"

"The control unit." He realized she had no idea what he meant. "Look. We broke out. Stole the control unit that operates the whole damn launch site. Without it the krauts can't fire their rockets. Kulikov and I grabbed that BMP. He had the unit. I was about to call when—"

"Yeah. Something took you out like a can opener."

"Two BTRs. From the camp." He held his head, which pounded as if somebody inside were using a jackhammer to break out. "Okay. What time is it?"

She looked beyond Max and raised her eyebrows. "Max. Don't worry, kiddo. Doesn't matter what time it is. Just take it easy, will you? Mel and I had a rough time getting you out. Covered with blood and guts—"

"Listen, dammit! We may be able to stop those guys.

This PRZ is a maze. Roads everywhere, and none of them are marked. Now—what time is it?''

"Okay, okay. Just before dawn, I guess. Six-twenty. Why?''

He frowned. Had he noticed the time? Maybe . . .

"Look. We have to try it. If we can get that damned unit away from them again, they can't launch. The whole deal stops. And if we let everybody know we have it—''

"Sure. I get it. But Max, you're in awful shape—''

"I've been worse.'' He frowned at her suddenly. "Wait a minute. What the hell are you doing out here anyway? Since when are you a Recovery type?''

"Since I convinced Charlie Kemp that I'd shoot him if he didn't let me out of the damn Mission, that's when.''

"Who's driving?''

"Me, Lieutenant. Nichols.'' A man appeared behind Koppel. Like her, he wore fatigues. But he was Air Force. A tech sergeant. He grinned. "Good to see you alive. Sir.''

Max threw off the emergency Mylar blanket. He tired to wriggle down the air mattress to the open hatch where the others stood. Each movement hurt. His clothes were filthy with mud, blood, and vomit. He realized he smelled like a bum. But he kept trying to get out. Koppel reached in and held a hand against his chest.

"Okay. We'll go after those guys. But you're not doing the heroics. Mel here will ride shotgun. I'll drive.'' Nichols started slightly, his eyebrows raised. "You'll stay in back. Understood—*Lieutenant*?''

Max wriggled to the tailgate. He sat, breathing hard, stars in his eyes, turned, and popped the special medkit off the wall. He scrabbled inside the pill section until he found the little red capsules. He ripped them out of their protective pouch and shoved them into his mouth. They tasted like sour limes. But he chewed viciously to break them up quicker. When he swallowed he imagined the enhanced speed and painkiller was already at work. Things were looking clearer.

"Yes, sir, *Captain*. Whatever you say. But let's get the hell into gear."

They let him climb out. He stood, weaving a little, in the cold, one hand on the Jeep's tailgate for support. The drugs raced through him. Koppel and Nichols moved to the front. Max started along the flank of the big blue Cherokee, whose lights were aimed at the hulk of the BMP. Even from here he could see the drying blood splattered all over the cockpit. Some even had dribbled through the driving slits. He shut his mind to it and climbed into the backseat. There would be time enough to deal with all that later. If there was a later.

Koppel slammed her door and hit the starter. The 427 cubic inch turbocharged V-8 came alive with that distant thunder Max knew so well. Koppel adjusted her racing-style seat, snapped her harness on, and toggled the hatch switch. The hydraulics whined and the hatch closed behind Max, shutting off the cold. He fumbled with his own seat belt as Nichols pulled his on. The electronics on the dash and console came to life. As Sandy allowed the oil pressure to build, she called to Max, "Which way?"

He leaned forward to peer at the five-inch CRT between the front seats. "Switch to nav mode," he said. Nichols turned the Mode Select knob. The nav system on this unit was much like the one he'd had on his first Fairmont, except that in place of the slow-starting mechanical gyros, this one's inertial navigation system used instant-on laser gyros and a sophisticated memory unit that kept the location of the previous coordinates in memory so that it "booted" itself when the system was brought on line. It saved a lot of time.

"Okay," Max said. "Call up the topo overlay." Nichols did so. The CRT displayed them as a bright green X in the center of a realistic topographic map. Max oriented himself. The years of Recovery work paid off; he had been able to recall each twist and turn as he left the camp. He spotted the riverside road and realized that the BTRs would have taken it. He visualized their probable path. There was no guarantee they'd go that way, but he had a hunch they might. He reached forward and pointed at an intersection some klicks away, and only three klicks from the camp.

"Here," he said, "get us there as fast as possible. And I mean fast."

Koppel checked the map. "Okay, Max. Think we ought to call Charlie?" She snicked the big shifter into first.

"No," said Max. "Not yet. Too many emissions too soon and those guys'll have us nailed. Let's wait."

"Sounds good," she said. "Which way?"

"Left on this road—" began Nichols. The roar of the 500-hp V-8 drowned him out. Koppel spun the wheel hard left. The Jeep juddered and shook as it lurched over the BTR ruts. Max grabbed the well-worn grabrail in back. Koppel had the Jeep to sixty mph before they even hit the road itself. They might not make it in time. But it wouldn't be because she couldn't drive, thought Max.

"Herr Oberst."

"Go ahead, Herr Major."

"The MLM vehicle. It has left the site."

"Show me."

He remoted the scene. Both men watched the blue target gather speed.

"It is heading southeast."

"I can see that. Why?"

"Perhaps . . . perhaps they hope to intercept the BTRs."

Schoener studied the scene for a moment. "It hardly seems likely. They would have to know the roads, and they cannot. They would have to average well over—let's see—one fifty, one seventy kph even to catch up. How could they do both of these things?"

Fritz was uneasy. "They are moving very fast, now. Perhaps as much as one hundred eighty kph."

"Those roads are just dirt. Mud now. How can they go so fast?"

"The four-wheel-drive maybe. I don't know, Herr Oberst. But maybe we should alert Iron."

Schoener thought for a moment. Muth had his hands full. His exec was trying to save Oskar and the situation. He needed all the help he could get. They could do nothing about the blue vehicle anyway.

"No. Let's see what develops. If the target gets too close, we'll call them. Otherwise leave Muth and his people alone."

"Herr Oberst." The major's assent was doubtful. The targets seemed to wander more or less aimlessly across his screen, but each twist and turn of the blue target brought it a little closer to the yellow ones.

Hans slowed the BTR at the junction. The headlights painted the trees across the dead end in bleak grays. Kollsmann sighed.

"Well, Hans? Which way?"

"I don't recall, Herr Leutnant. Um, left, perhaps."

Kollsmann drummed his fingers on the rim of the turret. This was absurd. He decided suddenly what to do. He picked up the headset and flipped on the mike.

"Hello, Iron, this is Kollsmann."

"Go ahead. This is Iron."

"We're having trouble with the fastest route back. There are too many damned little roads in this area. Can you get Bismarck to direct us?"

"Certainly. Stand by the radio, Kollsmann." Frankel's voice betrayed his mood. He was edgy and nervous. Dawn wasn't far away. When he came back on the line more than a minute later, he was more than edgy.

"Kollsmann. This is Hauptmann Frankel. Listen to me.

Bismarck says there is some kind of vehicle moving fast in your area.''

"What? What kind of vehicle?''

"Some sort of American truck. They don't know much about it. They had been tracking it for some time.''

"Why didn't they tell us before?''

"I don't know. Anyway, Bismarck says to turn left. Stay in that direction as long as you can. They'll try to keep us aware of what the other vehicle is doing. Do you have any idea how far from camp you are?''

"No. Sorry. But the chase was too confusing. We just followed their directions. Look—maybe we should intercept this truck. We still have plenty of ammunition.''

"No. Get back here as fast as possible.''

"Understand, Iron. Kollsmann out.'' He slammed the headset down. Hans looked at him questioningly.

"Something is after us,'' the lieutenant said. "You were right, Hans. Go left.''

Von Grabow stood behind Wolf, leaning casually on the pilot's ejection seat. He chatted aimlessly about the airplane. Wolf, the co-pilot, and von Grabow shared that secret fraternity of pilots. Despite the difference in ranks, they joked with each other, using the talk of endless figure-eight flight paths and power settings to keep the purpose of the flight in the back of their minds. From up here, eleven thousand meters high, the sliver of light in the east painted the cockpit in pale golden light. Schoener felt like a heathen interrupting a religious service when he tapped the general on the shoulder.

Still smiling, von Grabow turned and finished his joke. The others laughed, and Wolf leaned forward to reset the heading bug on the flight director. Von Grabow followed Schoener's request to step off the flight deck. At the mission commander's area von Grabow perched on the console. He rested one foot on the ground and dangled the other. He folded his hands and looked at Schoener. He seemed calm, rested, and happy. He had shaved and seemed fit and every inch the general in command.

Schoener had shaved, too, but he felt worn out. He had come to von Grabow with many problems during the night. For some reason it bothered him much more to bring this one to him just as dawn was breaking in the sky.

"Well?" Von Grabow smiled the question.

"There is a problem on the ground."

"Blood?"

"No. Iron again."

Von Grabow's smile remained fixed. He waited.

"Some kind of vehicle is after our BTRs."

The smile disappeared. "But—it has been a long time. Surely the control unit is back in place by now?"

"No, Herr General. I'm afraid not. You see, the roads slowed them down. They got confused. We're helping them now, but—"

"How long?"

"Minutes only. Five, ten at the most."

Von Grabow glanced out the little window behind Schoener. The sky was almost blue.

"And this vehicle?"

"Belongs to the U.S. Liaison Mission. In Potsdam, we assume."

Von Grabow's smile disappeared. His eyes narrowed. "The MLM? Why didn't you tell me immediately?"

"But it is only a truck—"

"Herr Schoener. It is not only a truck. It belongs to an elite unit. Special drivers. Trained to recover aircrew. And objects." His hands clasped themselves tighter. "You couldn't know. You're not a pilot. But these people are not to be underestimated. They are very, very good. Quick. Tell me the status. Are they close to our men?"

"They're closing. They seem to know where we're heading them. Here. I'll show you." He reached behind von Grabow and selected the remote-seven toggle, which brought the number-seven screen to the master console. The blue target was running almost parallel to their BTRs. Von Grabow watched and balled his fists. The blue target was moving twice as fast as theirs. Maybe more.

"Damn!" Von Grabow ground his teeth. He slid off the console and paced to the little window across the fuselage. The airplane banked gently left as Wolf completed yet another leg of the figure-eights he had been flying for the whole night. Von Grabow turned to Schoener, scowling, arms crossed. "It's too late to call them off by calling Potsdam. Everything depends on our getting to the camp before they intercept us."

"But the BTRs are armed, Herr General. With 37mm. Is the Recovery vehicle armed?"

"Usually, no. But with the Potsdam people, you never know." The blips drew his eyes like magnets. The blue blip suddenly turned away from the yellow ones. Von Grabow's eyes narrowed. "You just never know," he muttered.

TWENTY-FIVE

Max liked being a passenger even less than he liked having the dope racing through his veins. Both were unavoidable now though. He gritted his teeth while Sandy threw the Jeep sideways through a ninety-degree turn. Five hundred horsepower drove all four wheels through the slippery muck. The Jeep rocked and shuddered, seemed to almost tip over to the outside, then, as she had planned, found traction and direction. It shot out of the turn as if rocket-boosted.

She was good. Damn good. Max had known that when she drove her Porsche. But keeping one of these monsters in line and moving fast was a real accomplishment. Someday he'd find out how she'd gotten so good. Now the trick was to make sure there was a someday.

"Sandy!"

"Yeah," she spat between shifts. "What, Max?"

"Two things. First, I think it's time to call Kemp. Tell him what we're up to. Second, what have you got on board we can use to stop the BTRs?"

Nichols broke in. "Left here, Captain. Then a hard right." Sandy dropped two gears and arced through the lefthander. The righthander appeared as a faint trace through the woods, barely big enough for the Jeep. She slowed to fifty mph to make it. The branches of the trees screeched along the metal flanks while she accelerated down the tiny lane. The previously black sky was slowly getting a grainy gray look.

"Don't you think it's time to call?" Max asked.

"Maybe. But Charlie's probably still got his hands full just now."

"What was going on when you left the Mission?"

She was silent a moment, flicking her eyes left and right down the trail. "Bad stuff. Mobilization. Everybody. Even us."

"Jesus. Just what I thought. Look. That means Kemp can slow them down a little. If he lets the brass know—"

"Yeah, I understand, Max. Just shut up a minute, will you?" He couldn't see her expression, but her deft hands on the wheel were eloquent enough. The task of going faster and faster down the tiny trail kept her fully occupied.

"Okay. Mel, get the colonel on the horn."

Nichols pulled the mike off the clip, selected the Mission frequency, and spoke briefly into it. Max couldn't hear his words over the din of the flying mud and roaring engine. The Jeep kicked high into the air over a bump. He held the rail tightly.

When the truck steadied again Mel said, "Got him, Captain. Do you want to talk to him?"

She shook her head. "Too busy. Summarize for me, Mel." Nichols squeezed the mike and spoke into it. Max fought nausea as the Jeep hammered at eighty mph over a series of whoop-de-dos.

"Holy shit!" Kemp looked dazed. He laid the mike gently back on the comm console.

"Problems, sir?" The comm man replaced the mike in its socket.

"No. No! Jesus, this is incredible." He scratched his jaw, still looking confounded. He swung around and looked at Williams, eyes wide.

"Did you *get* that, Jack?"

"Not all of it. Something about a control unit—"

"Moss goddamn well stole their control unit. Broke out, stole the fucker, and split-assed out into the trees. Jesus. Then the bastards got him—and it. Now he's after them." His expression soured. "With Koppel. I told that lady—"

"She's no lady, sir. She's infantry, all the way."

Kemp raised his eyebrows at the major. Williams wore a placid expression.

"We'll discuss that one later. Anyway, now he's got Koppel and Nichols chasing off to try to get the damn thing back, for chrissake."

"What are their chances?"

"Who knows? With Moss anything's possible. Point is, he's given us a break. Our pals still fully mobilized?"

Williams nodded soberly. "The whole shooting match. Ready and waiting."

"Brits, Frogs, krauts, wops?"

"Everybody in Europe. The word got out, somehow, that something big was up, so everybody's getting set. Civilians don't know yet though."

Kemp looked grim. "If I know our Red friends, they'll roll the tanks on the slightest excuse. This could stop the whole thing, or at least slow it down." He frowned, thinking hard. "Okay. Here's what we're going to do. Sparky, get me Fort Meyers, Brussels, and Berlin Command, in that order. Secure voice, flash priority. Jack, open a line to Zossen. I want those guys to know what's happened, fast, and I don't want to wait while it percolates through our command. Also, let the Brits and Frogs know after you tell the Russians."

"Got it. What about the Germans?"

"Fuck 'em. They're not serious players in this sweetheart anyway. The only Germans who need to know already do.''

Williams looked puzzled. "Who's that?"

"The dudes in the E3 and the guys Moss foxed. *They* know what this means. Believe me.''

The signal processors aboard the E3G had done their jobs perfectly. They had detected not only Max's mayday but also the Jeep's powerful scrambled transmission to Potsdam. As they were programmed to do, they recorded the messages and then signaled that they had done so on the data processor's number-two CRT. The system was designed so that swift capture, analysis, and decoding was possible. But it depended on human direction. Because so much electronic activity was going on at any one time, a human had to tell the system which sources of activity he wanted to work with. And the human who was responsible was not at his console while this was occurring. He was relieving himself in the aft lavatory. That there was no backup for him was the result of having too small a crew. But von Grabow could do nothing about that.

Software existed within the system to display on Major Fritz's screen the information that the target he was tracking had transmitted something. But only two Germans on board knew how to bring that software into play; Schoener was one, and he was exhausted, his mind numbed by too many hours of strain. The other was the data-console operator. And nobody had told him that merging the software with Fritz's would be necessary. So minutes ticked in which Schoener was ignorant of the transmissions. And with each minute Sandy Koppel gunned the Jeep closer to the intersection Max had pinpointed.

"Now—what have you got in back?" The road was so rough Max had to yell to be heard over the thumps and bangs. They all swayed and lurched like sailors in a dinghy during a hurricane.

"Grenade launcher and M16s. That's it, I'm afraid," said Nichols. "Sorry, Lieutenant. I didn't know we were gonna take on the tanks."

Sandy kicked the accelerator hard. The Jeep launched itself skyward over a huge bump. It landed level and the tires howled against rocks under mud. The gray light now allowed shapes to be discerned.

"Did you say they were BTRs?" Sandy called.

"Yeah, I think so," Max yelled. "Dash 60s, I think. Thirty-seven mm turrets."

"No sweat," she yelled back.

"No sweat? What do you mean?"

"The M203'll knock the wheels off a BTR-60. Stop one dead." She pointed to the wall of trees approaching. "Another T-junction, Mel. Which way?"

"Left and then about four hundred yards, Captain, and that's it. That's the place."

"Okay," she said, and pushed harder on the accelerator. Max held on and tried to figure out what to do at the site he'd picked to ambush the BTRs. His mind seemed sharp and clear, but nothing came to him. Sandy slewed the Jeep through the turn and slowed down immediately. She peered off into the bush on both sides, then stopped.

The relative silence seemed unnatural. Max's ears rang, his body vibrated, and the dope made him nervous.

"What's wrong?" he asked. His voice seemed loud.

"We've got four assets in this action," she snapped briskly. "You, me, Mel, and this truck. We can't put 'em all in one spot. A lucky shot by those Reds and the game's over. Here's what I think we ought to do." She pointed down the road, which was getting easier to see every second. The headlights seemed to fade even as they followed her finger.

"Max, you and Mel dig in at the crossroads. One on

each side. Mel, you take the M203. You're stronger. Max, grab an M16. I'll take the Jeep down the road toward the camp and stick it in the bushes at the side, but in a place where I can see what happens. When they show, Mel, you get the leading tires of the BTRs. Max, you wait for troops to appear, then pick 'em off. If you have any trouble, I'll come in. If it works right, I'll get there anyway, and we'll haul out of here. Comments.''

Nichols shook his head. "Been a long time since I used a grenade launcher, Captain.''

"Good. You'll enjoy it all over again. Max?''

For some reason Max felt humiliated. He was flushing, and glad she couldn't see it. Must be the dope, he thought. "Okay. No problem. Sure. Let's go,'' he said. Something in his voice made them both turn and look at him. Sandy studied him carefully. Even clinically.

She reached out toward him and said, "Let me see your eyes. Look right. Now left.'' She watched as he rolled his eyes. "Yeah. Lieutenant Moss, you're under the influence of dangerous drugs. Can you handle it?''

"Sure. Why not? Let's go. Let's go!'' He grinned. It threatened to split his face. She did not grin back. Slowly she dropped her arm.

"Okay. Mel, when I stop up here, check to see if anything's been by in the last hour or so. If so, then the game's probably up, and we'll wait here until doomsday. Otherwise, if Max's guess is right, we'll see some action soon.''

Max's pulse raced. He touched his face. It was dry and hot, like heated parchment. It was all he could do to sit still as Sandy crept the Jeep toward the intersection.

"Iron, Iron, come in.''

"Iron here, Bismarck. What do you see?''

"The vehicle has stopped. About a thousand meters from your perimeter.''

"How far are our cars?"

"Not far. But they seem to be heading south. The vehicle is east. Perhaps something has happened to it. It halted once before, minutes ago, then went slowly forward."

"But our vehicles are not in danger of contact?"

"No. Not at present."

"Good. I will tell them. Iron, out."

"Bismarck, out."

"Leutnant Kollsmann."

Kollsmann squeezed the key on the microphone. "Go ahead, Guenther."

"We seem to have trouble. George thinks it is the fuel."

"What?" Kollsmann climbed back into the turret as he spoke. He spun the turret to face rearward. The other BTR's lights were getting smaller.

"Hans!" he called to his driver. "Stop." The BTR halted.

"The engine cuts out," said Guenther. "I can't—keep it running." As he watched, the BTR slowed, then stopped. Kollsmann swore under his breath.

"Guenther! Does Georg think he can repair it?"

"He thinks so, Herr Leutnant. He says—what?—he says it is the fuel filter. The river water may have—"

"Never mind, Guenther." He drummed his fingers on the turret housing and chewed his lip. "Guenther," he said into the mike at length, "we must continue. Do you remember the way from here?"

"Oh, yes, Leutnant. Left at the junction, then straight, then right and—"

"Yes, yes, you have it. Do your repairs, but quickly, and return at once."

"Herr Leutnant—the vehicle shadowing us—"

"They say it has stopped about a thousand meters from

us. Don't worry, Guenther. Just get that damned thing going and meet us back at the camp. Out.''

Kollsmann cranked the turret back around and clambered back down to the commander's position. Hans looked across to him.

He waved his arm irritably forward. Hans ground the gears getting into first. Kollsmann looked again at the control unit. A lot of trouble it's caused, he thought. It had better be worth it.

Max slithered down the slimy mud to lie with his head below the level of the road. The ditch was only a few feet from the road, but it would do. He raised his head and saw Nichols, down toward the intersection twenty yards, awkwardly manhandle the M16 and grenade launcher as he slipped down into the other ditch. The light was weak and murky. The cold should have driven nails into his bones, especially since he still wore only his filthy, mud-, blood- and vomit-streaked blues under the fatigue jacket he had liberated from the back of the Jeep.

He couldn't even hear it now. Sandy had waved as she'd driven carefully around the turn and headed for her chosen hiding place. Max found it impossible to concentrate on anything for more than a few seconds. His eyes seemed to flick from object to object by themselves. His body twitched. He felt almost nothing, although he tasted and smelled everything with unnatural clarity. He had to keep reminding himself that it was unnatural. He checked the thirty-round clip for the tenth time and patted the other two clips in his jacket pockets. Still there. Where were they, dammit?

They'd better show. He'd shoot something even if they didn't.

He pulled a piece of sodden grass from the mud and chewed it nervously. He poked his head up and looked around the road. Nichols waved him down vigorously. He ducked down and pulled out another blade of miserable grass. It tasted like—

A noise. He heard a noise. He stuck his head up again. He cocked an ear. Yes. From the left. A big diesel. He waved his weapon at Nichols, who waved back, again admonishing him to get down. Nagging dummy. He knew what the hell he was doing. As the rattling roar approached, Max slipped the safety off his M16. He coiled like a snake against the side of the muddy ditch. It occurred to him he ought to be scared. Or something. But he was just nervous.

The distant roar became a close drumroll, the sound of a big V-8. Other noises overlaid it. The hissing and pounding of giant tires. The squeal of metal on metal, badly lubed bearings. The clank of steel plates. A cacophony. Max bared his teeth, trying to guess when it would pass. There ought to be two. But he couldn't hear the other one. He thought about the riverbank and what these bastards had done to him. Time to square things, he thought. Time for a little showdown at the O. K. Corral.

All at once the BTR passed by, doing about thirty mph. A shower of muddy water and debris splashed down on him. The driver was closest to his edge of the road. He closed his eyes and waited for it to pass. He strained to hear the other one. Nothing.

Panic gripped Max. What if they'd split up? What if the one with the box went some other way back to the camp? What if he'd screwed up and misremembered the twists and turns? What if there was one more intersection between them and the rockets? What if Nichols realized there was only one and didn't shoot?

He began to shake uncontrollably. What if he *died* here for nothing? He clutched the M16 to himself and tried to roll into the fetal position. What if—

The rumble and thrash of the BTR was suddenly accompanied by another noise. A clang and thump, as distinct in the foggy morning air as a bell tolling. Max blinked. One second, two—

An explosion that walked through his stomach like a steel-shod belch shook the earth. The BTR noises stopped. For a second there was only a sort of chuffing, the sound of an engine dying. Then there was a series of clangs, thumps, and hisses. Something big and metallic grated on something else big and metallic. Max realized he had to stand up.

He tried, but his legs didn't work right. He looked down and realized something warm was spreading out along his inner thighs. He'd pissed in his pants.

Another clang-thump sounded. This time the explosion sounded different. There was no metallic overtone in it. And it was followed by the hateful bark he'd last heard at the riverbank. The BTR's 37mm cannon was firing. At Nichols.

He had to get up. Shaking like an old man, he levered himself to his feet and peered over the edge of the ditch.

TWENTY-SIX

At eleven thousand meters the sky was clear and blue, the sun already beginning to clear the eastern horizon. The world below was remote, a remembered rather than realized reality for the men who flew in Yellow Rose 5. The endless fascinations of flight occupied the pilots, who thought about the goals of the mission only between the little, precise chores of flight. For most of the others the work was so familiar that it was all almost routine. They knew the stakes. They knew what was happening down there, knew about the subs and missiles and bombers and divisions of men getting ready for Armageddon. But it was all so remote from the whispering turbofans, the silver wings, the cloudless sky. Any airplane in flight defines its own world, and Yellow Rose 5 was especially beguiling. The U.S. Air Force had known this phenomenon for a long time, which is why it staffed such long-duration airborne sentries with big crews. A man needed a break from the airplane's reality if he was to stay sharp, alert, and effective at his job when it was critical.

But von Grabow did not have two crews. He had barely enough for one. And so because he had been on-station for far too long, Major Juergen Fritz saw what was happening on the ground near Camp Iron and didn't immediately understand it. His eyes received the visual data, but it didn't mean anything. He saw the two BTRs separate. He saw the leading one continue. He saw it stop suddenly, and watched its infrared signature blossom fourfold. But it didn't register.

He knew he should do something, but he couldn't figure out what. Was this an emergency? What was happening? He rocked back in his swivel chair and rubbed his eyes as he had done a hundred times that long, long night. When he rocked forward again the scene had not changed. He scowled in thought and realized Schoener had to know.

The colonel didn't answer his intercom. Fritz frowned again. He tried the general. Was the colonel there? No? Where then? Fritz pushed back from his console and peeled off his headset. He stood and looked down the aisle. Schoener wasn't at his station. He glanced at the screen again and hurried down the aisle.

The lavatory. Of course. The little Occupied sign was lit. He knocked hard. Schoener answered. Fritz told him what was happening. Schoener told him to wait a moment. Of course, he said, and Fritz stepped back from the door.

That moment was the wrong one for Helmut Schoener to wait. It was the moment Max Moss climbed over the edge of the ditch.

The BTR was leaning drunkenly on its left side. The front wheel lay a few feet away from it, the rubber burning furiously. The turret was aimed right at where Mel lay. Some gray smoke eddied up from the engine cover of the BTR, but otherwise it seemed unharmed. A small crater lay just behind it, where the other grenade launched by Mel had landed.

Max stumbled a bit, then hunched and went forward. It seemed to be the hardest thing he had ever done. He had to clamp his teeth together to keep them from chattering. He inched closer to the BTR, waiting for Mel's M16 to answer the burp-burp of the 37mm. He was approaching from the right rear of the armored car and couldn't see where the shells went. But he could hear them. And there was no sharp crack-crack-crack to show that Mel was still there. Or still alive.

When he was twenty feet from the BTR the 37mm stopped. Max froze. The only sounds were the crackling and hissing of the rubber tire blazing and his own pounding heart. He stooped, knelt on the ground, and took aim at the turret.

The turret began to swing in his direction. The operator was obviously scanning for more targets. It was too late to run back to the ditch. Just before the ugly little barrel came to him Max brought the M16's sights up to the small opening beside the gun barrel. Unlike a tank, the BTR was not wholly armored. It was a scout car, really, lightly armored, and there was an opening in the turret about a foot square through which the barrel poked. As the turret grated around, Max held his breath, squeezed off the safety, and fired.

The weapon was set on full-auto. The thirty rounds burst from it before he realized it. They cracked and whanged and sparked off the inch-thick armor plate. He released the trigger and blinked. The turret had stopped. A remote clicking sounded inside the BTR as if something were broken. Max jerked the clip out of the M16 and fished in his side pocket for another.

The top hatch of the BTR flew open. Max dropped his clip into the mud. He cradled the M16 and desperately fumbled for it in the muck.

A man appeared. A German. He leaped from the turret holding a pistol. For a moment he stood on the side of the BTR, looking at Max. Max found the clip and jammed it in. The brown-uniformed soldier lifted his pistol. The moment seemed frozen. Max seemed to move in molasses as he tried to get his weapon to his shoulder. He noted, almost casually, that the soldier held the control box.

They fired simultaneously.

Max got off three rounds before the mud stopped the M16's action. One of them went wild. One of them knocked off the soldier's cap, in the process digging a bloody furrow across his scalp. The last one caught the hand holding the 9mm pistol right behind the grip. The grip itself deflected some of the force of the high-speed bullet. But not enough. The pistol was ripped from his hand along with his thumb.

The Makarov had spat at Max only once. The heavy slug dug into the mud at his feet.

The man staggered but did not fall. He stared at Max while Max squeezed the trigger mechanically, and nothing happened. Max blinked and realized the gun was worthless. He let it fall to the ground. He knew he should get up. Do something. But he was still semi-paralyzed.

The German half-fell, half-jumped from the BTR. Max observed him as if he were in a movie theater watching something happen on the screen. The man appeared from behind the BTR. He looked at Max once again. A trickle of blood ran down his scalp. More oozed from his hand, which dangled at his side like inanimate meat.

They stared again at each other.

Then the soldier began to lurch up the road in the direction his car had come. Max watched. The man passed only fifteen feet away. Max watched, squatting in the mud on both knees, his arms at his sides.

Suddenly the man began to run.

Something snapped inside Max. When the German had run in his crazy stumble a few dozen yards, he started shaking his head.

"No. No. *No!*" He yelled hoarsely. The German ignored him. Max lurched to his feet. The mud sucked at his clothes as if reluctant to let him go. He started after the German.

It was a race, something he understood. The man in front had to be caught. He had to be. Caught. Max lifted his sodden feet and tried to run.

The drugs and the exhaustion turned his legs to lead, his feet to stones. But slowly, slowly he caught up with the man.

The cold wet air rasped in his lungs as if he were breathing fire. He sobbed with every lurching step. His vision came in crazy flashes. He saw the German look back once, and fear was on his face. He saw the blood spurt from the man's pulped hand. He saw the box. The box.

His own hand seemed to detach itself from him. It reached forward, a talon, to claw at the German's back. The two of them stumbled along, a race between cripples, and Max's hand clenched at air. Run. Gasp. Run. Grab. Run. Gasp. The pounding rhythm drove through his brain until he felt nothing.

Until his outstretched hand connected. Suddenly he clenched not air but rough wool. His hand locked by itself. The German jerked. Max almost tumbled down. His feet danced to keep him upright. Croaking, gasping, choking for more air, Max flung his other arm around the German's neck.

Together they fell to the mud. The fall stunned them both. The race now was a chemical one. He who reacted first to the gush of adrenaline would win.

Max won. A split-second before the German tried to bash him with the box he got both hands on the man's windpipe. The German thrashed violently under Max, trying to throw him off. He flailed with the box at Max's back. Max never felt it. He bared his teeth and glared down into the German's face. He got his knees on the man's upper arms in that hated schoolyard-fight position from which there is no escape but the cry of uncle.

Leutnant Karl Kollsmann did not cry uncle. He fought as he had been trained to fight. He used every sinew, every nerve, every ounce of his swiftly ebbing strength to remove Max from his chest, his arms, his throat.

Too much blood had been lost through his hand. Too much effort had been expended already. As Max pushed his thumbs deeper and deeper into Kollsmann's throat, the control unit slipped from the German's left hand and fell into the mud. A second later he died.

TWENTY-SEVEN

The E3G's data-sharing system had been designed specifically to provide every console with the potential of simultaneously displaying any other console's data. The designers considered this imperative, so that the various operators and commanders could ponder events on the screens without crowding around a single tube. Yet at the moment von Grabow, Schoener, and Fritz huddled around a single CRT. None of them knew why. None even thought about it. It simply seemed natural under the circumstances.

They studied the puzzling display in silence. Around them the other operators continued their duties. Their little sounds—clicking relays, squeaking chairs, stifled coughs—were as fully a part of the background noise now as the engines, which continued to gulp their kerosene at four thousand pounds per hour each.

"Perhaps we should call Muth," said von Grabow.

"Yes. But what do we tell him?" asked Schoener. "That something is happening? That we don't know what it is?"

"His lead BTR has stopped," von Grabow said. "That's something he'll need to know."

"But the other is coming up fast." Schoener pointed to the screen, where the second yellow blip moved rapidly along an unseen road. "These BTRs are sometimes unreliable. Perhaps the first one suffered a failure."

"But then, Herr Oberst, why the sudden IR flareup?" Fritz scowled. His mind seemed to be working through a layer of gauze.

"Who knows? But the blue target has not moved. That's something."

Nobody said anything. They watched the yellow blip. Von Grabow straightened up.

"So. Herr Schoener, call Herr Muth. Let him know—"

"Herr General." Von Grabow turned to see who'd touched his sleeve. It was the radioman. He raised his eyebrows.

"Sorry, Herr General. But it's the emergency channel. From Brussels. The American general."

"Morse?"

"Yes. He says it's urgent."

Von Grabow grinned at the others. "You see? I told you. With the dawn they have realized they can't outlast us. They have run their checks. They know it can be done. And they will do it."

Schoener tried to respond to his winning smile with one of his own. He couldn't do it. His eyes were drawn by the yellow and blue blips. "I hope so," he said.

"Tell General Morse I'll be right there," von Grabow said to the radioman. "Schoener. Keep me informed."

"Of course, sir. And Oskar—?"

"Not yet. Let's see what Wade Morse wants. If it's what I think, Oberst Muth can relax for a while."

Somehow Helmut Schoener knew that what Wade Morse wanted to say wouldn't make any of them relax. But he didn't share that with the others. He might be wrong. As von Grabow went back to the commander's station, Schoener joined Fritz in staring at the screen.

*   *   *

Max had never killed with his bare hands before. He didn't
know that the man whose neck he squeezed was dead. He
panted and grunted like a wild beast, glaring sightlessly
into the bulging eyes and lolling tongue of the German
under him. Slowly it penetrated his killing haze that the
man was finished.

His hands ached suddenly. He groaned and rocked back
on his calves, freeing them as if pulling them from bond-
age. He threw back his head and gulped in huge amounts
of air, eyes closed, hands and arms throbbing limply at his
sides. When he began to sway he leaned forward, planted
his hands in the cold mud, and tried to stand up.

It was almost as hard as running. Weird flashes of light
spiked across his vision. Hot and cold shot through him,
bringing gooseflesh, making him shiver uncontrollably. He
had to remember something. He hugged himself in the
grim gray dawn and struggled to remember what it was.

The control box. He had to get it. He jerked his head
down and forced open his eyes. There it was. Lying in the
muck next to the outflung hand of the dead German. All
he had to do was pick it up.

Stooping was a controlled fall. He thumped to one
shaking knee and pulled the box free of the mud. It came
out with a sucking noise. He jammed it into the big pouch
pocket of his fatigue jacket.

Sandy. She waited around the corner. He started sham-
bling toward the intersection. The flashes of light came
with each jarring step. His ears buzzed and hummed with
each heartbeat. He wanted to throw up and lie down. But
he kept moving. The air seared his lungs.

Something hit his foot. He halted sluggishly. He looked
down. The box had fallen out. He stared stupidly at it for a
long moment, then clawed it up again. He held it close to
his chest with both hands and started off again.

The buzzing got louder. He stopped and shook his head.

What was wrong with him? He closed his eyes and swayed in the middle of the road, ankle-deep in mud, trying to get his body under control.

And then the buzzing became a roar. The noise connected somewhere in his head. It wasn't just a noise. It meant something. It was a familiar noise. An . . . engine. Yes. Sandy?

No. He frowned. A diesel. Big diesel. Behind him somewhere. Coming fast and hard.

Fast. And hard.

The other BTR. The sudden connection shot a jolt of adrenaline through him. He jerked and jinked around, almost tumbling to the ground. Wide-eyed, he watched the ugly green armored car turn the bend a hundred yards away slowly, and then gather speed. Right at him.

He looked around like a deer caught in headlights. He was too far from the disabled BTR. He'd never make it there to hide. The roadside ditches were his only chance. They were only ten feet away. He had to run.

Nothing happened. He seemed rooted to the spot, hunched over, clutching the box to his chest. He gasped and groaned and willed his legs to work. Instead, he simply fell down.

There was no pain. There was nothing. He lay, almost full-length in the slimy, chilly mud, the box under him, and sobbed for breath. The adrenaline had not been enough. His body had given up. It had no more strength to give him.

The BTR slowed fifty yards away. Its driver was undoubtedly suspicious. Max should easily have been able to get to the roadside. Yet he lay in front of the advancing car like a drunk. Max heard the driver gear down and creep forward.

No, not this way, no, *no!* he cried to himself. "Come on, you bastard, move. Move. Move!" His voice was a hoarse, cracked shadow. "Okay. Okay. If you won't walk. Crawl. Come on, asshole. Crawl. Crawl. Crawl." He found himself on his elbows. His hands still clamped the box. He looked straight ahead. The roadside weeds, miserable, gray-green, dense, looked like heaven. He could make it. He had to make it.

He began to inch forward, half-dragging his useless legs. A foot. Then another foot. The mud slid under and around him like congealing cement. It dragged at him. The BTR was twenty yards away.

A crack split his ears' buzzing. He flinched as the 37mm round blew his weeds into the air. They were trying to halt him. They knew he had the box. They didn't want to chance hitting it as well as him. He ducked his head and kept crawling.

Another *crack!*, and another explosion of weeds and mud. He squeezed his eyes and lowered his head. The concussion swept over him like a tidal wave. Debris stung him. But he wasn't even in his own body anymore. The world had become the roadside ditch and the need to crawl. He spat dirt from his mouth and moved one elbow. Then the other.

A hatch clanged open on the BTR. Max heard it, knew what it meant, and kept moving his elbows. They made little troughs next to his body. His progress was down to inches at a time. But he kept going. Left elbow. Right elbow. Left elbow. Boots rang on metal. He ignored them.

Von Grabow placed his hands on the edge of the plastic console. The severed connection hissed in his earphones. He spread his fingers. Strong, manicured, well-formed. And white. Deathly white. The blood was somewhere else. They trembled like an old man's. He made one snap the intercom toggle for Fritz.

"Major Fritz."

"Herr General."

"Please ask Oberst Schoener to see me immediately."

"Of course, Herr General."

The sun wheeled around the airplane, or seemingly so, as Wolf banked again at the loop of his figure-eight. Von Grabow watched the dazzling slice of light thrown through the window on the fuselage shift around and finally disappear.

"Herr General?" Schoener stood behind him. Von Grabow slipped off his headset, swiveled his chair, and looked up at the colonel. Schoener was pale as death.

"They know," von Grabow said. "Somehow they found out."

"Ah," said Schoener.

"Morse demands our surrender. He says he speaks for the British, French, and Soviets."

"Ah," repeated Schoener.

"Should we surrender?"

"No," said Schoener without hesitation. Nothing underlay his voice. No tone at all. He stood, arms at his sides, every line of his face and body expressive of exhaustion. "No."

"Is there still a chance?"

"Something is happening down there. We don't know what. I told Fritz to call Oskar. Get more people out there. I hope we didn't wait too long."

"It was a mistake then? Not to call earlier?"

"It was, Herr General."

"How did they find out do you suppose?"

Schoener shrugged.

Von Grabow looked past him to the small fuselage window. A patch of intense, brilliant morning blue shone through it. "What shall we do now?"

"We'll think of something," Schoener said. "We'll have to."

The boots clanked off the metal skin of the BTR. They squished in mud. Toward him. He kept his elbows moving.

"Hey, American," a voice called. "Stop. Now."

He kept moving. He stared at the weeds. Only a few yards now.

A pistol shot split the air. The slug kicked mud a foot from his face. He kept moving.

"Stop, American. Now." The boots stopped, still ten yards from him. One part of Max wondered why. The other part kept his elbows moving. There was no room for any other part.

"I said—" The voice stopped suddenly. A new noise burst through to Max. An even more familiar noise. He kept his elbows moving. But now he realized that they were just jerking back and forth uselessly, digging mud. He began to sob. But he kept them moving.

The noise grew louder fast. Connections were made in his brain at last.

The Jeep. Sandy. She was coming. He rolled over on his back.

Fifteen yards up the road stood the BTR, turret pointed at him. Ten yards from him stood the man with the pistol, an East German sergeant. He stared open-mouthed toward the intersection, beyond the still-burning, crippled BTR. All at once the object of his stare burst through the black smoke that poured from the burning tires.

Things moved in slow motion. He watched the Jeep slide, all four wheels throwing mud around the burning BTR. He watched the sergeant slowly, slowly bring up his pistol, his mouth still agape. It seemed at first as though the thirty yards between the Jeep and the standing man were a mile. The Jeep rocked and swayed and spewed mud but didn't grow any bigger.

Then the pistol cracked. The report seemed faint, distant. Three, five, seven times. A Makarov on full auto. Nothing happened to the Jeep. The sergeant fumbled with the pistol, still in slow motion. The BTR didn't move.

Suddenly the Jeep was on him. Sandy smashed into the sergeant with the Jeep's left fender, hooking him neatly as she swung the snout to the right. The slow motion stopped. One blink, the sergeant was doubled over, his arms outflung. The next blink, he was tossed aside like an old rag doll, up, out, into the mud. Then everything happened at once.

The BTR driver woke up. He tried to get all four of his eight driving wheels going. They spun uselessly in the mud. He cranked the front four steering wheels left as Sandy slid the Jeep around past his left side. The big green armored car finally began to move. Exhaust smoke poured from its twin stacks.

The Jeep seemed to change directions without stopping, swapping ends. It had passed the BTR and now aimed at its right rear corner. It paused, then the four big high-flotation mud-and-snow tires flung mud in all directions as Sandy took aim.

The BTR, like some prehistoric beast, moved sluggishly, jerking up and down as its driver tried to turn its snout toward the smaller Jeep, now out of sight behind its left flank.

The huge steel winch-and-pusher bumper Nubs Pierce had installed on all the Recovery Cherokees contacted the upper splash guard of the BTR's leftside wheels. The BTR weighed close to seven tons, the Jeep only half that. But Koppel had picked her spot well. The big steel guard on the American truck smashed into the rail. Both vehicles halted momentarily. Koppel kept the power to her wheels. They groaned and spun. So did the BTR's. The Jeep had more power but less tire area to deliver it. The two big vehicles were locked together like dinosaurs.

Koppel relentlessly mashed the throttle. The turbocharged Chevy V-8 howled out its power as the tires slipped and the engine revved to its redline. Smoke poured from the mud, from the exhausts, from everything. But slowly, as the BTR tried to turn, it moved sideways. Sandy had found the leverage point.

The four wheels on the Jeep side of the BTR began to

lift. As soon as the driving wheels were clear of the mud the limited slip differentials clacked into operation. The BTR was well made, rugged, reliable. But it was not powerful. And shortcuts had been taken in its manufacture, shortcuts necessary to produce many machines quickly. None such had been taken in hand-crafting the snarling Jeep Sandy drove. One differential broke in the BTR's drive train. Then, overloaded, the next broke. Finally only two remained. Dense gray smoke gushed from the BTR's innards. And now it moved sideways in three-foot slides as the five hundred horsepower of the Cherokee overcame resistance and produced its own inertia.

In an eye blink it was over. The Jeep's V-8 howled through its turbocharger, spinning at sixty thousand rpm, and the Russian armored car suddenly was at the edge of the road. One minute it was jerking sideways, left side up. Then it was slipping over the edge of the steep ditch.

It tipped, rolled, and kept rolling. It crashed through the underbrush and lay, wheels rotating skyward like the legs of a dead beetle, until a huge gout of flame spurted from its fuel tank.

Max watched, immobile, lying full-length in the mud. He saw the Jeep slew around as Sandy looked for him. Then at once she had pulled up next to him. Her door popped open and she jumped into the mud.

Her face was drawn and tight. She dropped to one knee and lifted Max's head.

"Jesus," she whispered. "Jesus, Max. Are you okay?"

He thrust the box at her, unable to speak. She grabbed it and pulled at his jacket. "Come on. You have to get up, Max. We have to get out. Mel's dead. They're coming, They're coming."

The German mud tried to hold him. It pulled almost as hard as she did. But not quite. First his head came free, then his shoulders. He felt strength of a kind returning to his body. He fought to get up. Together they got him to his feet. He leaned on her little shoulders, which stiffened under his weight. She guided him to the passenger door of the Jeep in a series of stumbling, dragging lurches. She jerked open the door and almost threw him in.

Max sat in the sculpted racing seat like a dummy. Heat poured from vents near his feet. Something stank. It was him.

Koppel jumped in, jammed the Jeep into reverse, and it whined backward. Where they had been a geyser of mud sprouted. A rattling crash followed a half second later.

"Holy shit! Here they come," cried Koppel. Beyond the burning BTR three BMPs clanked. All armed with 37mm cannon. And heat-seeking antitank rockets. Max noted it all idly.

"Hold on, Max!" Sandy yelled. "We're going home!"

Max reached slowly for the steel grab rail Nubs had welded onto the dash. There was a spot where the gray paint had been worn right through by countless hands holding on for dear life. He clamped his around it on the shiny spot. It felt warm. Alive.

The engine snarled, tires spun gain, and Max was thrown back against the headrest. Koppel jinked the big blue truck from side to side and didn't back off the accelerator, powershifting through three gears. In a couple of heartbeats the Jeep had slid around the corner. If Max had looked, he would have seen the antitank rocket fail to make the turn and slam into the trees, launching thirty cubic yards of forest into the air when it exploded. But he didn't look. He couldn't. His right hand still locked on the grab bar, he had fallen unconscious.

Sandy saw him slump, but couldn't do anything about it. "Max!" she yelled. "Goddamnit, Moss, wake up!" She spared a glance at him. His hand slipped from the grab bar. He hung limply in his harness as she powered the Cherokee through the ruts and humps of the muddy road. "*Max!* For God's sake, you bastard! Stay alive! Do you hear me? Stay *alive!*'' Her voice cracked. She had to get out. She had to keep going. The din in the cockpit was deafening. But her swearing was not quite buried by it. ''You can't die on me, you son of a bitch. You can't die. *Hey!*''

She hammered the Jeep around a turn and Max flopped sideways onto the center nav console. His head cracked hard. A little blood spit out from his scalp. She shook her head. ''No. I won't let the bastard die.'' She slammed the brakes on and the Jeep slid sideways in the muck for a hundred feet, sloughing off speed agonizingly slowly in the slippery mud. As soon as it had stopped she jumped out and ran around to his door.

She jerked him upright by his filthy jacket. She ripped his stained shirt off and listened to his chest. His heart still beat. But too fast. Like a little bird's. She shoved him back into the seat and snapped the four-point harness on him. Then she ran to the tail, pulled open the gate, and dug frantically through the medkit. She found the syringe, then the bottle. She forced her fingers to slow down. She filled the syringe and ran back to Moss.

She pulled his jacket and shirt down until the fleshy part of his right arm was exposed. His head hung limply to one side, resting open-mouthed against the headrest. She swabbed the area over the vein and pinched below it to bunch it up. It swelled enough for her to slip the needle in. She slowly forced the clear liquid into his vein. Then she jerked it out, slammed his door, closed the tailgate, and climbed back in her side.

Her hand shook as she pulled the mike off the clip. The radio was still set on the day's operations frequency. She keyed the mike viciously.

''Pigpen, Pigpen, come in. This is Koppel. Goddamnit, come in!''

''Koppel, Pigpen. What's—''

She keyed the mike again. The radio squealed. ''Shut

up. Listen to me. We have the box. Do you copy? We have it! I'm on the PRZ access road. Moss is hurt bad. Nichols is dead. I need help. You copy that, Pigpen? I need some help!"

"Roger, Koppel, understand. Good work—"

"Can it! Get me some help!" She almost screamed into the mike.

"Okay, Captain. Will do. We have your location now. Maybe—"

Another fountain of earth and an ear-shattering explosion interrupted the radio operator at the Mission.

"No time!" She yelled and dropped the mike. She revved the engine, dropped the clutch, and the Jeep roared back up the road.

The next bend was only fifty yards away. She hunched her back and gritted her teeth as another cannon round shattered the glass in the rear window. The tail lifted slightly, then settled back down. She jammed the gear lever into third. Only a few more yards and she'd be out of range again.

The rocket wasn't very big and was designed to penetrate the thick armor of enemy tanks. So when it was deflected at the last minute by a faulty guidance chip in its circuit, its explosion in the mud wasn't as effective as it would have been had it knifed through the Cherokee's tailgate and burst inside. Instead, it entered the mud behind and to the right of the Jeep. Its high-explosive warhead spent most of its energy in digging a hole forward into the dirt, not to the side. But the explosion it did produce was enough.

The Cherokee was flung into the air in a tumbling nosedive. It stood on its left front wheel and skated along a few dozen feet until it tipped and slammed down on its left flank. Sandy had not cinched her seat belt. She was thrown forward, smashed scalp-first into the windshield, then back against the seat, and finally bounced between the steering wheel and the door pillar. When the Cherokee slid to a halt she was wedged between the seat frame, which had broken, and the door.

The auto-fuel shutoff cut the fuel flow, and there was no fire. The air was foul with smoke. Sandy came to with a convulsive gasp. Something fell on the dashboard. It was the control unit. Far away she could hear the rattle of a diesel. And the whirring clank of tank tracks. She was pinned. She craned her neck to see Max. He hung in his straps. His eyes were half open. They seemed sightless.

Pain stabbed through her gut. She sobbed. It worsened.

TWENTY-EIGHT

NATO called the Tu-201 the "Frogback." To Western intelligence it was a shadowy aircraft, seen rarely even by the most sophisticated spy equipment and used, some unverified reports said, with devastating effectiveness against the guerrilla ground forces in Afghanistan. They knew in the West that it had extraordinary ground-attack capabilities. They knew it was built on lessons learned from the American A-10 attack fighter. They knew it was powered by two quiet, hard-to-spot turbofans. But they didn't know about its cloak.

To the Soviets the Frogback was the "Silent Killer." It was the most secret airplane they owned, even more so than the big bombers. Its actual capabilities were the most closely guarded secrets in the country. It was always based far from prying Western eyes. The Politburo intended to follow hallowed Soviet tradition with it, and keep it as secret as the MiG-15 had been, and as the T-34 tank had been, for the same reasons.

Its flight systems were simple to the point of crudeness. No fancy electronics relayed the pilot's wishes to the flight controls. The planners decided to use only the best pilots in the nation to fly it, and reasoned that a superb pilot was better than a smart but unreliable airplane. So they lavished their electronics wizardry on another area. They made it invisible.

It was small, and there were no hard angles on it. It was hard to say what color it was. Gray, maybe. Or blue. Or even green. It depended on the terrain. The Afghans who had died under its guns and rockets almost never saw it in time to decide. But its paint wasn't its secret. Its array of radar-beating electronics was. The big computer that took up the room between the armored pilot's seat and the fuselage fuel tank was more advanced than most of the West's. Sensors all over the airplane told it what kind of energy was painting it at any time, and it swiftly calculated which countermeasures to deploy to defeat the probes. When it did it was effectively cloaked. It was invisible to radar, even to infrared, due to the effort spent to cool the engine's efflux. The Tu-201 was the "stealth" aircraft the West kept talking about building. Only it actually flew and fought while the West's versions were mired in politics.

There had never been any doubt in Room 33 that the Silent Killers—*Bezmol' veniye Ubitsi*—would be dispatched to the captured rocket battery. The Politburo was almost certain that the E3G couldn't see the airplanes. Nothing extant could see them. They were assured of that by the experts. And the spies.

Kemp's message got to the operational commander of the Tupolev flight as he and his flight orbited low over a road intersection fifteen kilometers from the battery. The flight leader awaited only daylight to attack. He had been given his orders hours before. He and his flight had refueled three times en route from deep in the Soviet Union. His controller gave him his new targets and he smiled in his rubber mask. This was the sort of work he loved. As required, he did not acknowledge his new orders. Nobody could make a radio transmission undetectable. He toggled his fin-mounted lights. His flight formed up closer. He lifted his hand until they all could see it, then he signaled in their special sign language. They each nodded understanding and fell into trail formation behind him.

"Herr General! Hauptmann Frankel reports his BMPs have knocked out the American truck! They will be on it in minutes!" The operator could barely restrain his obvious joy. "They will have the control unit in no more than five minutes. Twenty, and it will be back in operation."

"Good. Tell them good for me. They are remarkable men. Tell them."

"I will, Herr General."

"And get me General Morse. Quickly. The game is not over yet."

"*Jawohl*, Herr General!"

The flight leader came in low over the trees, fifty feet above the road, at 250 knots. As he popped his airplane up over the treetops and scanned the scene, he understood it immediately. The three BMPs were driving straight for the blue truck that lay on its side. He smiled again. He loved his work. And because of endless practice and thousands of hours of combat against Afghans, Cambodians, Iranians, and Chinese, he was very good at it. So were his wingmen.

The little green pipper on his heads-up display centered easily on the leading BMP. The Russian pilot slowed a bit, held his breath, then expelled it and squeezed the trigger.

The rocket left its ramp and, locked on the vehicle's hot exhaust, accelerated to Mach 5 within a hundred feet as its solid-rocket motor burned furiously. The leader's pipper was already on the last BMP when his first rocket blew the first BMP into shrieking metal fragments. The third BMP brewed up as swiftly, then he was past them all and cranked hard into the nine-gee turn he always used to get back on target. He looked over his shoulder while he grunted to breathe under the gee-loading. His number two took out the second BMP perfectly. And number three hosed down the road beyond the blue truck so that nothing escaped. The heavy 30mm cannon tore through the remaining metal chunks and brought the mud to froth before number three began his climbing turn.

The leader eased off the turn and leveled out. His men formed on him. He nodded, then waved to the east.

It was time for the main action. He stood on his left wing, dove at the ground, and pictured the layout of the battery in his mind one more time. He toggled the rocker switches that armed his bombs. He still had plenty of ordnance. And now he and his men were warmed up.

The exploding BMPs made Sandy cry out. Whatever was poking in her stomach drove harder in with every detonation. She screamed in agony, but also to equalize the pressure in her body as the concussions ripped through the Jeep. The airplanes whistled over too fast to be seen. The BMPs blew like canisters of napalm. The heavy cannon slugs shook the ground when they struck. And suddenly there was nothing but a far-off whine and the hissing crackle of flames. She gasped and choked as her stomach tried to rebel.

She concentrated on pushing the seat frame back and away. But she couldn't do it. She was too weak. She bit her lip and panted.

"Hey?"

She jerked her head up. It was a thin, faint word, but it made her pain disappear for the moment.

Max, hanging from his straps, looked ridiculous. He blinked and tried to smile at her. "Hey?" he repeated.

"Hey," she croaked.

Max's eyes darted around. "You look silly," he said.

"You don't look too great yourself." She tried to grin,

but her stomach contracted again. She jerked forward as far as she could. She retched dryly.

"Hey. Don't move," Max said. He struggled to hoist himself back to relieve the pressure on his seat harness. He fumbled with the emergency release. And found it. He dropped suddenly half across the console and half across her. She gasped in pain.

"Sorry," he muttered. "I'm not too good at this when I'm doped up."

She shook her head. Tears of pain rolled down her filthy cheeks. "S'okay," she panted. "It's my goddamn gut."

"Oh," he said. He levered himself away from her, trying to take his weight from the seat frame. He perched more or less on the console and studied her. She returned his look.

"You up to being a hero rescuer?" she asked. "A few minutes ago—"

"Yeah. I know. Sorry about that. A little tired, I guess. Feel better now."

"Because I shot you with ten cc's of dope. When it wears off—"

"Yeah. Crash city. Got it. Meanwhile, let's get you out."

He put a foot gingerly on the twisted windshield frame. Then he planted the other on the seat back that pinned her. He fished for a place to hold on. He grabbed the shift lever and his own seat back. "Okay. This may work. May not. But it might hurt a little."

He pushed. She screamed. He pushed harder. She screamed again, a helpless, gurgling croak. Something snapped in the seat frame, and it pulled away from her. A jagged piece of metal oozed out of her side. A little blood followed it.

She gasped and fell against the door. Max's legs shook. He fought to clear his mind of the cobwebs that kept coming back. "You okay?"

She put a hand to her side. "Yeah," she panted. "Thanks."

Somehow he managed to kick out the remains of the bulletproof glass in the windshield. Somehow she crawled out with him. Somehow he managed to stumble to the back through the sideways cab and find the medkit in the pile in back. And then apply a crude field dressing. They lay together on the ground afterward, simply trying to live. After a few moments Max pulled the emergency Mylar blanket tighter around her. She shivered almost as badly as he did. Her eyes seemed dull, hooded.

Max put his hand on her shoulder. "Want to know something?" he asked.

"Sure," she mumbled.

"You're one hell of a driver."

She flashed a weak smile. "Thanks. I needed that."

"I mean it."

She began to smile again, making an effort to look up at him. But a huge explosion far away cut her short. It was followed by another. And another. For a few moments the air shook and the ground trembled to the distant thunder. Then the cold gray silence returned. It seemed they could hear a faint whine in the sky.

"Who won, do you suppose?" she whispered finally.

"We did," he said, looking at the sky.

"How do you know?"

"Easy," he said, slipping down to the ground next to her. He lifted her head gently and cradled it under his arm. "We're still alive, aren't we?"

TWENTY-NINE

"What happened?"

Schoener did not answer. Von Grabow hit the intercom switch again. "Schoener! What happened?"

"They're . . . gone. All of them. Everything." Schoener's voice was husky.

"But—how?"

"Frankel got off only a short transmission. He said something about aircraft. Russian aircraft."

"We saw nothing—"

"No. And we still see nothing. I heard rumors of such an airplane. But it was too secret. I thought it was a hoax. It was not."

"The whole battery?"

"Gone. Blasted to ruin. We watched the explosions. Nothing could have survived. We heard the command trailer go up. Someone held the microphone open."

The tone sounded in his intercom, telling von Grabow that the communications officer wanted him. He switched to his line.

"Yes?"

"Herr General. General Morse wishes to speak with you again."

He should have felt something. Anything. Yet he was completely calm. His heart thumped out its rhythm slowly and dutifully. Everything was in order. Except that Iron was obliterated. He said, "Yes. Fine. Put him on my line," and wondered why he felt nothing at all.

"Von Grabow?" The American general's voice was hard. The voice of a man who knows he has won.

"Yes, General Morse."

"Your boys in the East ate it. Did you watch?"

"We watched, General."

"It's over, you know."

"Yes. It is."

"Will you tell your people in Hohenfels to release our men and surrender?"

"Certainly, General."

"And you? You'll land, give yourself up?"

"That may be a bit too much."

"What about those men up there with you?"

"We'll see. I'll call you back."

"Freddy. For God's sake. Don't make this insanity any worse."

"Thanks for the advice. I'll call you back." He flipped the toggle and the line died. He took off his headset. He still felt nothing. His body was alive. But he must be dead. Is this what it's like? he thought. He stood and walked to Schoener's station. All the men watched him as he passed. He couldn't return their glances.

"Oberst Schoener. Please assemble the men in the rest area."

Schoener nodded. He was gaunt, haggard, and worn. Von Grabow went to the lavatory in the rear of the airplane. He closed the door and looked at himself while the fluorescent lights flickered to life. He studied his image in the mirror. He washed his hands and combed his hair, all the while noting every detail of his features. He dried his hands and opened the door.

All the men, including the pilots, sat in the rest area. Helmut stood at the curtained entryway. He walked past and stood in front of the bulkhead, facing all the seats. He looked at each man in turn. They returned his look with emotions clearly stamped on their features. He read hopelessness. Fear. Remorse. Anger. Even determination. On the pilots' faces something like his impassivity was legible. He cleared his throat.

"You know the situation. Camp Iron has been lost. We have been asked by the Allied commander to surrender Camp Blood and ourselves." He paused. "I will not do that. Oberst Helling and the men at Blood will not be sacrificed. They will be told to surrender. But I will not suffer the travesty of justice that will occur if I give myself to them. The choice then for you is as follows.

"You can leave, every one of you. All I ask is that each man who decides to bail out take an American with him. There is no further need for death. Not today anyway. I shall stay. I intend to fly this airplane toward the Baltic until the fuel runs out. My action should not be understood as suicide out of fear or humiliation. I wish simply to end this correctly. Any man who wishes to join me may. But you must all understand that I consider it the more patriotic act to return to Germany, face the consequences, and continue the fight. None of you planned this. Your service careers will be over. Perhaps you will face a prison term. But you can live and continue the struggle. I cannot be effective in it." He stopped and waited for a reaction. There was none. "What we have done cannot be kept secret. You can ensure that your fellow Germans understand what we did and why. That is all."

They looked at one another. They looked at him. None would speak.

"Very well. I think I understand. I order all of you to bail out. Questions?"

Wolf raised his hand. "Herr General. We don't wish to be cowards."

"This is not the field of honor, Herr Wolf. This battle is over. But the next has yet to be fought. And the war is far from lost. You must carry it on. Unless any of you can produce a convincing reason why you should remain on board, you are to leave as soon as we can reach lower altitudes."

Nobody could speak. Von Grabow knew that emotions raged through them—the traces were obvious—but he couldn't bring himself to care. "Good. It is settled. You men have been superb. You have done more than your duty. No matter what happens below, you should remember that. Germany will someday honor you. I honor you now."

Someone choked back a sob. Schoener sensed his cue. He snapped to attention as von Grabow began to move from the bulkhead.

"Gentlemen, attention. The commander!"

They leaped to their feet and stood at a brace while he walked past them, staring straight ahead. He signaled to Schoener to follow him. In the aisle he turned to the colonel.

"Now. I must speak to Helling."

Schoener followed him to the duty officer's console. He dialed the radio frequency, contacted the commander, and held the headset to von Grabow. In a few short phrases the general summarized the situation, told Helling to surrender, and told him he was proud of him and his men. It took less than two minutes. Helling did not argue. He obeyed. Von Grabow handed the headset wordlessly back to Schoener and went forward.

The flight deck was bathed in golden light. The autopilot kept the E3G on the eastbound leg. Von Grabow slipped into the pilot's seat and automatically fastened the harness. He checked the panel and adjusted the seat. Like the E3G, his mind was on automatic. He pulled on the small pilot's headset.

The feel of the plastic yoke was like coming home. He disengaged the autopilot and turned the wheel, simultaneously feeding in a little rudder to counter the inertia of the big rotating dish above the fuselage. His eyes flicked across the flight and navigation gauges replicated on the central cathode ray tube in front of him. All nominal. He triggered the mike by squeezing the button on the lefthand arm of the yoke.

"Yellow Rose Five from Rhein-Main," he said.

"Yellow Rose Five, go ahead."

"We're departing from flight plan, Rhein-Main. We're heading north, along the buffer zone. In about five minutes we'll level out at six thousand feet. I've got a load to drop then. Parachutes. We ought to be over the potato fields near Uenterheim, so please alert the British to have medical help standing by. After that we'll continue up along the buffer zone to the Kiel Bight, then into the Baltic."

"Ah, roger, Yellow Rose Five. Copy. What are your intentions from the Baltic?"

"Rhein-Main, we'll let you know then. Yellow Rose Five, out."

He bled off power and trimmed the big silver AWACS for a steady descent. He flipped open the enroute charts in the flight bag beside the seat and selected one with low-altitude information. He busied himself dialing in waypoints and frequencies for the navaids. He didn't notice Schoener until he had slipped into the copilot's seat. He glanced at him.

"Ah. Herr Schoener. Why aren't you strapping into your chute?"

"Herr General. Surely you don't think I would abandon you."

"No. But I thought I made certain everyone understood that bailing out was an order. You did not understand?"

"I understood. But I also understand my fate if I return. I am a spy. If the West does not shoot me, the East will someday. Why make it easy for them? Why make it hard for me?"

Von Grabow looked at him. "Fine. Here, would you find the Durflinger TACAN for me?" He handed the chart to Schoener.

The altitude alert bell sounded just before he reached six thousand feet. This part of the country lay under a thin, high overcast. The ground was clearly visible below.

"Herr Schoener. Please go back and tell the men to begin anytime. They can release the hatch themselves. Let me know when they are all gone."

Schoener unstrapped and clambered through the flight deck. Soon after, a master caution light blinked on. The CRT told him the door was open. He pulled the throttles back farther. He held the E3 at just above 170 knots, flaps and gear down. It wallowed a bit. But such a speed was better for jumping.

After about three minutes the door-open light went out. Then Schoener tapped him on the shoulder. He eased the throttles forward and pulled up the gear and flaps. "All gone?"

"All gone," Schoener said. "Americans too." He strapped in again.

"Good," said von Grabow. He kept the E3G flying north, at 250 knots indicated. Neither man spoke. The airplane clicked and whined and muttered to itself, working perfectly, all systems functional. In the empty fuselage the displays flashed their messages at vacant seats. The radome rotated above them, feeding signals to the computer, which processed them for nobody.

After ten minutes the coastline appeared ahead in the

hazy sunshine. The air rushing past the cockpit was the only sound.

"Helmut, have you ever flown along a beach a few feet off the deck?"

Schoener glanced at him. The Christian name again. "No."

"Of course not. I forgot. You're not a flyer." Von Grabow smiled. "Well, you'll like it. I promise you. It is the essence of flying." He pushed the yoke gently forward and the airplane accelerated toward the strip of sand separating the green fields from the slate-blue water. Von Grabow's smile widened as they lost altitude. He leveled the airplane off at fifty feet.

The sand blurred by on the left, the water on the right. A little village flashed into sight, then disappeared under the Boeing's nose. Helmut looked out toward the Baltic.

"We have company," he said.

Von Grabow bent down and looked out Schoener's window. Two Luftwaffe Tornados flew just off his wing.

"Ah!" Von Grabow said. "Jagdgeschwaeder 35. My old outfit. We used to dance through these little islands, Helmut, in our F84s. We told the CO we were looking for Russians"—he grinned at Schoener—"but we weren't. We were just flying." He studied the terrain rushing under the nose.

"Better go out to sea a bit. It would be messy here."

Schoener let his hands lie in his lap. The yoke moved on his side as von Grabow banked the big airplane gently toward the sea. The Tornados stayed on his wing until he completed the turn. Then one accelerated and rolled over the E3G until it was on von Grabow's side. The pilot tucked the fighter in close. He flipped up the tinted sun visor of his helmet. Little was visible of his features except his eyes. Above the green oxygen mask they looked steadily at the general. Von Grabow brought his hand up to his brow in a salute.

The fighter pilot did not react at first. Then he returned the salute. He held it for a moment, then reached up and flipped his visor down. He shoved his throttles into afterburner and pulled the Tornado's needle nose up. His camouflaged fighter disappeared in a wide, arcing turn to the left.

Von Grabow watched the turn, then smiled at Schoener.

"Would you like to fly for a while, Helmut?"

"I've never done it before, Herr General."

"There's a first time for everything. Try it."

Schoener put his hands on the yoke. As he felt the other man take the controls, von Grabow released them. He sank back against the soft leather of his seat and closed his eyes, still smiling.

"You see, Helmut? There's nothing to be afraid of. Nothing at all."

Schoener held the yoke steady, and the four Sidewinder heat-seeking missiles fired by the two Tornados ripped into all four of the E3G's engines. The explosions severed the wings. Without their stability the fuselage skewed into a half turn and began disintegrating even before it struck the cold dark water of the Baltic Sea.